A HUNDRED THOUSAND DRAGONS

Dolores Gordon-Smith

severn
House

This first world edition published 2010
in Great Britain and in the USA by
SEVERN HOUSE PUBLISHERS LTD of
9–15 High Street, Sutton, Surrey, England, SM1 1DF.
Trade paperback edition published
in Great Britain and the USA 2010 by
SEVERN HOUSE PUBLISHERS LTD

British Library Cataloguing in Publication Data

Gordon-Smith, Dolores.
  A Hundred Thousand Dragons.
  1. Haldean, Jack (Fictitious character) – Fiction.
  2. Novelists, English – Fiction. 3. World War, 1914–1918 –
  Veterans – Fiction. 4. Detective and mystery stories.
  I. Title
  823.9'2-dc22

ISBN-13: 978-0-7278-6910-4   (cased)
ISBN-13: 978-1-84751-253-6   (trade paper)

All Severn House titles are printed on acid-free paper.

Severn House Publishers support The Forest Stewardship Council [FSC], the
leading international forest certification organisation. All our titles that are
printed on Greenpeace-approved FSC-certified paper carry the FSC logo.

Mixed Sources
Product group from well-managed
forests and other controlled sources
www.fsc.org Cert no. SA-COC-1565
© 1996 Forest Stewardship Council

Typeset by Palimpsest Book Production Ltd.,
Grangemouth, Stirlingshire, Scotland.
Printed and bound in Great Britain by
MPG Books Ltd., Bodmin, Cornwall.

To Helen, with love

ACKNOWLEDGEMENTS

I would like to thank Major Gordon Corrigan (author of an outstanding book about the First World War: *Mud, Blood and Poppycock*, plus many others); Professor D.B.G. (Beatrice) Heuser; and Mrs Maria Cochrane for their generously given technical advice. I am very grateful to you all.

OZYMANDIAS

I met a traveller from an antique land
Who said: Two vast and trunkless legs of stone
Stand in the desert . . . Near them, on the sand,
Half sunk, a shattered visage lies, whose frown
Tell that its sculptor well those passions read
Which yet survive, stamped on these lifeless things,
The hand that mocked them, and the heart that fed:
And on the pedestal these words appear:
'My name is Ozymandias, king of kings:
Look on my works, ye Mighty, and despair!'
Nothing beside remains. Round the decay
Of that colossal wreck, boundless and bare
The lone and level sands stretch far away.

Percy Bysshe Shelley

ONE

In the lounge of Claridge's Hotel, Jack Haldean met his cousin Isabelle's irate glare. 'I am not,' he said firmly, 'appearing at the Stuckleys' fancy-dress ball in what is virtually a state of nudity, Isabelle. Absolutely, definitely not.'

'But I don't see *why*, Jack. You'll look wonderful.' Isabelle turned to her fiancé, Arthur Stanton, for support. 'Won't he?'

'Altogether now,' murmured Jack. 'Or should that be, *in* the altogether now?'

Arthur Stanton gave a snort of laughter, which he tactfully cut short at the sight of Isabelle's outraged expression. 'I think it'd be very striking,' he said diplomatically.

Isabelle looked triumphantly at her cousin. 'You see, Jack! Arthur agrees.'

'Well . . .' temporized Arthur.

Isabelle pushed her chair back and stood up. 'Maybe you can talk some sense into him,' she said in exasperation. 'I've never known anyone so *stubborn*.' She picked up her handbag. 'I'm going to freshen up. I hope you're in a more reasonable frame of mind when I return.'

'Fat chance,' said Jack, politely getting to his feet with a charming, if insincere, smile.

Isabelle gave an irritated toss of her head, put her handbag under her arm and marched off, her shoulders rigid with annoyance.

Arthur raised his eyebrows ruefully. 'You've upset her. She had her heart set on it, Jack.'

'Tough,' said Jack.

Arthur Stanton sighed. In less than a month he and Isabelle would be married. Isabelle, he thought, was the tops, but there was no denying that she liked her own way. It was probably his imagination, but Isabelle's hair seemed to turn a deeper shade of red as she realized that Jack was flatly refusing to cooperate.

'I'm not,' said Jack, 'fancy-dress ball or no fancy-dress ball, making an idiot of myself. Good God, Arthur, you'd agree if you weren't goofy about the girl.'

Arthur gave a sheepish smile. 'Well, if you want the truth, I do, but I thought it'd be better coming from you.'

Jack looked at him with dawning comprehension. 'You sly devil. You knew perfectly well that I'd put my foot down.'

'Shall we order another cocktail?' asked Stanton innocently.

Jack grinned. 'All right. You'd better get another Mother's Ruin for Belle, too. With any luck it'll put her in a better mood. I'd rather talk to her about your wedding than the fancy-dress ball, and that's saying something.'

For the last month, his cousin Isabelle had been a voice at the end of a telephone. Her wedding plans were going well; rapture. Her wedding plans had hit a snag; deep gloom. Did he think that St George's, Hanover Square was suitable? Well, yes of course he did. *What?* With Clarice Matherson and that dreadful mother of hers making it a byword for showy ostentation? Could he be *serious?* Did he expect her to *compete?* Wouldn't it be better, more dignified, more in keeping with the solemnity of the occasion, to be married at the village church which she had attended all her life? Wouldn't that mean *more?* Well, he supposed it might. Did he *care?* She was glad of that, anyway.

And, by the way, added the Champion of Solemnity, he was coming, wasn't he, to the Stuckleys' fancy-dress ball?

What did he mean, 'Oh God?'. . . He wasn't talking about the wedding, was he? Oh, the *party* . . . So what if Marjorie Stuckley was going to be there? If Marjorie Stuckley chose to think he was the bee's knees, that was her lookout. Besides, Marjorie made sheep's eyes at everyone. Don't mention it.

It was Marjorie Stuckley who suggested to Isabelle that Jack would look very dashing as a sheikh. ('He's got those black eyes, Isabelle, and that dark hair. He could look so exotic. So *foreign.*')

Which was, as Isabelle said to Arthur, very true, but in her opinion, sheikhs, since Hollywood and Rudolph Valentino had taken the world by storm, had been done to death. She wanted something more unusual, something outstanding, something memorable.

Jack, sitting across from her in Claridge's Hotel, listened

to her ideas for their fancy-dress costumes, his eyes wide and his jaw open. It would be memorable, all right, he said. Good God, neither he nor Arthur would ever be allowed to live it down.

For Isabelle, entranced by an article in *Vogue* about classical influences in fashion, had decided to be Diana, goddess of the hunt. She could have a golden bow, her hair would look wonderful, and the dress, a diaphanous, floating affair, was nothing short of dreamy. So far so good, and Arthur Stanton had agreed wholeheartedly with Isabelle's estimation of how she would look. What he didn't agree with – what, in fact, he was privately horrified about – was her announcement that, as she was going to be Diana, he would, of course, be Apollo. Tactfully, he hadn't disagreed but suggested that, as Jack was coming as well, the three of them should all be Greek gods. Jack, he said, having a fairly accurate idea of how his friend would react, could be Cupid. They would, he added, discuss it over lunch.

'*Cupid?*' said Jack when the idea was broached. '*Cupid?*' he repeated in a dazed voice. 'Like the statue in Piccadilly Circus, you mean?'

Isabelle's knowledge of the Classical pantheon was more or less limited to *Vogue*. 'Isn't that Eros?' she asked, her nose wrinkling.

'It's the same thing.'

'Is it? I don't know why all these gods have so many different names, but whatever you want to call yourself, I'm sure you'll look really *different*.'

Jack gave a laugh which Isabelle described as coarse. 'Absolutely I'd look different. Are you seriously suggesting I should turn up at the Stuckleys' in bare chest, gold skirt and sandals, proclaiming I'm the God of Love?'

'Well, perhaps not that then, but there's lots of gods. Mercury, for instance.'

'That's gold skirts, too! And,' said Jack, turning on Arthur, 'I don't know why you're laughing. What the devil d'you think you'll look like, rigged out as Apollo?'

'Go on, Jack,' pleaded Isabelle.

Politely, firmly and, as Isabelle had remarked, stubbornly, he said he would go to Ronald and Scott's, the outfitters,

and choose a costume which, although it might be less spec-
tacular, would at least mean he was fully clad. A Greek god?
'Nothing,' said Jack firmly, 'doing.'

'So you're not playing ball?' said Arthur.

'Too right. If she's that desperate to see my chest, I'll
arrange a private viewing. What on earth put it into her head?'

'It was some article in a magazine. After reading it she
was torn between Greek gods and ancient history. It's
nobody's business what they wore then, Jack. She talked
about Tutankhamen –' Jack hid his head in his hands – 'but
she went off that idea.'

'Assyrians,' said Jack from behind his fingers. 'What about
Assyrians? Purple and gold. They came down like the wolf
on the fold, if you remember, according to the poem, with
all of their cohorts in purple and gold. That's long robes.
They'd be all right.'

'It'd mean beards,' said Arthur doubtfully. 'Great big curly
things. Isabelle dragged me round the British Museum the
other week and I saw the Assyrian Bulls. The legs would be
awfully hard to do and they had bare chests, too, and beards.
I can't say I'm too keen on the legs. I don't see how we'd
bring it off, even if we wanted to.'

'I wasn't thinking of being an Assyrian Bull, just an
Assyrian,' said Jack.

'It still means beards,' said Arthur. 'You've got to be careful
with beards. Food and so on gets stuck in the hair.'

He turned to summon a waiter and nodded his head to
where a sturdy, aggressively bearded, middle-aged man was
standing in the entrance to the lounge. 'That chap over there
is a bit of an Assyrian Bull himself, isn't he?'

The man by the entrance had evidently just come in and
was gazing impatiently round the room. He looked, thought
Arthur, out of place in Claridge's. He was conventionally
dressed in a suit and tie, but looked as if belonged on the
quarterdeck of a ship, traversing the Arctic or scaling some
mountain peak. Even without his brindled beard he would
have been a striking man. An Assyrian Bull wasn't a bad
description of him. He was strongly built, with large hands,
massive shoulders and his skin was as deeply tanned as if
he'd been carved out of some dark, solid wood.

Jack glanced round, then froze. The smile petrified on his lips and the colour slowly drained from his face.

'Jack?' asked Arthur, shocked. 'What's wrong?' Jack was staring at the man as if he'd seen a ghost.

Jack dragged his gaze from across the room. He bowed his head, shielding his face with his hand. 'It's Craig,' he said quietly. 'Durant Craig.'

'Who . . .'

'Tell me what he's doing,' interrupted Jack, stammering in his urgency. 'Craig, I mean. The Assyrian Bull. What's he doing?'

'Another chap's seen him,' said Arthur in a low voice. 'They're shaking hands. Hang on, Jack, I think I know him. The second chap, I mean. It's Mr Vaughan. He knew my parents years ago.'

Jack kept his head turned away. 'What are they doing now?'

'They're coming into the room. I think Vaughan's asking the other bloke if he wants to go in to lunch or have a drink first.' He sat back in apparent unconcern. 'I think we're in luck. It looks as if they're going into the dining room.'

Jack's shoulders drooped and he let out a ragged gasp of breath.

Arthur sat upright. 'Oh no, Vaughan's seen me.' He raised his hand in reluctant greeting and got to his feet. 'Bad luck, Jack,' he said quietly. 'Vaughan's coming over.' He glanced down at his friend. 'We can't get out of it.'

Jack took a deep breath, stood up, squared his shoulders, and turned round.

Vaughan smiled in recognition as he walked towards them. 'Captain Stanton? I thought it was you.' Although he was much the same age as the man they had labelled the Assyrian Bull, he was a very different type, tall and spare with a wiry strength. He had an intelligent, decisive expression and the fresh look of someone who spent a lot of time outside.

Stanton summoned up a smile. 'Hello, sir,' he said, then, following Vaughan's enquiring gaze, was forced to add, 'this is my friend, Major Haldean.'

Jack nodded stiffly.

'Major Haldean?' said Vaughan with interest. 'I believe I

know the name. Now why is that? Something to do with Sir Philip Rivers I think . . .' He snapped his fingers in triumph. 'I've got it. Are you Sir Philip's nephew?'

Once again, Jack nodded.

'Of course. Stanton, you're engaged to Sir Philip's daughter, aren't you? I saw the announcement in the *Morning Post*. Congratulations.'

'Thank you, sir,' said Arthur. Jack, who still hadn't spoken, was standing rigidly beside him. What the devil was the matter with him?

'Major Haldean . . .' Vaughan frowned. 'There was something in the papers . . .' His face cleared. 'Of course, Major, you're the man who was involved in the Lyvenden case.'

Again, Jack didn't speak.

Vaughan turned his head away. 'Craig!' he called. 'Just a minute. There's someone I want to introduce.' He turned back to Arthur and Jack. 'I'm lunching here with Durant Craig. He's a well-known man.' He looked at them with modest pride, obviously pleased to be seen in Craig's company. 'Ah, Mr Craig,' he began, as Craig reached him. 'This is Captain Stanton, whose parents were neighbours of mine, and this is Major Haldean, Sir Philip Rivers' nephew.'

Craig looked at the two men with casual interest, then his eyes narrowed in recognition. 'Haldean?' He thrust his shoulders forward, his jaw clenched and his face darkened in an angry flush. 'I know damn well who this is,' he ground out. '*Major* Haldean, you say?' He stood back with a contemptuous bark of laughter. 'So you got away with it, you little runt?'

Arthur drew his breath in with a gasp. Jack put his hands behind his back and stood rigidly to attention, his chin raised and his eyes fixed forward.

His posture, the posture, as Arthur recognized, of a solider on parade, seemed to infuriate Craig. 'Haven't you got anything to say?'

Jack didn't move. Only the tightening of his throat muscles betrayed that he had heard Craig's question.

Craig's face contorted in fury. 'You filthy little dago.' He dripped the words out one by one. 'I swore if I ever cast eyes on you again you'd be sorry!'

There was a stunned silence which knifed into the low hum of conversation around them.

Vaughan, staring at Craig in disbelief, dropped an agonized hand on his shoulder. 'Craig! For God's sake, man! You'll cause a scene. People are looking.'

Craig shook off the hand. 'Let them look,' he grated. 'I've got a score to settle with this lousy little wop that's been waiting a long time.'

Arthur Stanton listened in shocked amazement. Jack, his face set in a blank mask, was simply standing there, eyes fixed on a point above Craig's head.

'Well, *Major* Haldean?' demanded Craig. He crossed his arms over his chest. 'Haven't you got anything to say?'

For the first time, Jack met Craig's eyes. He flinched, looked away and shook his head slowly. 'No,' he whispered.

'Wait a minute,' put in Arthur vigorously 'I've got something to say.' He started forward but Jack gripped his arm tightly.

'Arthur, don't. I . . . I deserve it.'

Craig gave a short laugh and, reaching out, pushed Jack so he staggered and almost fell back into his chair. 'Coward! I knew it. Come on, Vaughan. I'm not staying near this scum. The air seems foul. We'll eat somewhere else.' He strode off.

Vaughan wrung his hands together, his face working with emotion. 'I must apologize, gentlemen. I had no idea anything of this sort would happen.'

'Vaughan!' came a voice from the doorway.

Vaughan leaned forward urgently. 'I can't apologize enough.'

'I know that, sir,' said Arthur, torn between an anxiety to get rid of him and genuine sympathy for his position. Once again, Jack said nothing.

With a final, apologetic look, Vaughan turned away to join Craig.

The conversation around them began to swell once more and two waiters, who had been hovering in a meaningful way, faded into the background.

Arthur dropped into his chair beside Jack. 'What the devil was all that about? Are you all right?'

Jack fumbled for a cigarette. 'Yes. Yes, I'm all right.

I'm sorry you were here, old man. Thank God Belle wasn't around. Don't say anything to her, will you?'

'Of course I won't. Who on earth was he, Jack? He was an absolute oaf.'

Jack lit his cigarette with unsteady fingers. 'He's not an oaf. His name's Durant Craig. You must have heard of him.' Arthur looked blank. 'The explorer, you know?'

'Hang on.' He had a vague memory of a story in the newspapers some time ago. 'Did he walk across a desert or something?'

Jack sucked in a mouthful of smoke. 'That's the one. He's . . .' He stopped and swallowed. 'He's a great man in his way.' Arthur felt sure that wasn't what Jack had been going to say. 'He's one of the few Englishmen to have been through the Yemen. He's more at home in the desert than most Arabs.'

Arthur raised his eyebrows. 'Is that who he was? What on earth has he got against you?'

'I let him down rather badly once. I deserved everything he said.'

'You can't have done.'

Jack's mouth twisted. 'You think so? I'm sorry, Arthur.' He hesitated. 'I can't explain.'

'But you . . .' began Arthur when Jack raised his hand warningly.

'Here's Isabelle,' he said. 'Please don't tell her.' He crushed out his cigarette, stood up and gave a shaky smile. 'Isabelle! You look even more radiant than you did ten minutes ago. Shall we go in?' And standing behind his friend and cousin, he shepherded them firmly into the restaurant.

TWO

Holding two glasses of champagne, Jack skirted his way round the side of the ballroom. Old Lady Stuckley, Mark Stuckley's grandmother, had nabbed him as he arrived and sent him off to get drinks.

He was glad he had come to the Stuckleys' party. After his bruising encounter with Durant Craig, his first thought was to make some excuse and to skip the ball, but that would mean questions to face and explanations he didn't want to make.

And really, what had changed? Nothing. So what if Vaughan did know what Craig thought of him? He'd never met the man before and probably wouldn't meet him again. Even if he did, Vaughan had clearly disliked Craig's attitude and, with any luck, Craig, an imperious beggar, wouldn't stoop to explain. Arthur had seen far more than Jack was comfortable with, but Arthur was a friend.

He had been grateful to Arthur during lunch at Claridge's. Arthur, anxious to keep Isabelle from guessing anything more untoward than a second cocktail had occurred during her absence, went on the attack immediately. His battery of conversational weapons included the wedding, the guests, the presents, the honeymoon (they were sailing to Egypt the day after the wedding) and, as a remarkably effective smoke-screen, deciding exactly what they were wearing for the fancy-dress ball.

There were intervals during lunch when Jack found himself so engaged that he could almost forget that any such person as Durant Craig existed; almost but not quite. There were gaps – awkward gaps – when he should have responded but didn't, gaps when Isabelle looked at him with puzzled, intelligent eyes. Then Arthur would come to the rescue once more and the situation was saved, but it was a real relief to say goodbye and get back to the privacy of his own rooms.

But, thought Jack, he couldn't stay hidden away. Life, as he had observed before, went on, no matter how chewed-up

he was feeling, and he still had a living to earn, especially
if he wanted some time off. There was a story to complete
for *On The Town,* another two to edit, three long stints at
the sub-editor's desk, an article entitled *Jazzing up Murder*
for *Modern Music* to write and a visit to Ronald and Scott's
to hire a costume. By the time the weekend came he felt
he'd earned his trip to Sussex. He parked the Spyker in the
old stable block at Hesperus on Saturday afternoon and, for
the first time in four days, relaxed.

He felt the tension ebb out of him as he sat, listening as
the little ticking noises made by the hot metal of the engine
cooling were gradually replaced by the sounds of distant
cattle, horses and birdsong. Even so, he was on edge as he
went into the house. Had Arthur said anything? Had Isabelle
guessed? The answer, judging from Aunt Alice and Uncle
Phil's reception, was no, and Jack breathed a sigh of relief.

And it was, he thought, taking a sip of champagne as he
waited for the dancers to let him through, a very good party.
With a shriek of glee, Marjorie and Phyllis Stuckley
descended upon him.

'Jack! There you are!' said Phyllis. 'You look absolutely
spiffing! Dance with me, darling, won't you? We really have
to dance.' The band started an energetic version of *Walking
My Baby With The Pink Pom-Pom.* 'Come on, Jack. This is
a ripping tune.' She looked at the two glasses he was holding
and her face fell. 'Don't say you're taken already.'

'Only by your grandmother,' said Jack, laughing.

'Grandma's an absolute menace,' said Marjorie petulantly.
'She always collars all the best men.' She looked at his
costume. 'I wanted you to come as a sheikh,' she said with
a pout. 'You'd look just like Rudolph Valentino.'

'Is that meant to be a compliment?' asked Jack with a grin.

'Oh, *yes*,' said Marjorie fervently. 'He's scrummy. What
are you, anyway? Isabelle said something about Greek gods,
but you don't look very Greek to me.'

'I'm a Corsican bandit,' said Jack. 'I refused to be any sort
of god.' He was wearing a scarlet shirt, a scarlet scarf, baggy
trousers, one gold earring and what seemed to be an arsenal
of weapons. 'Now I'm here, I feel quite soberly dressed.'

'The costumes are marvellous, aren't they?' said Phyllis,

looking around at the knights, fairies, Vikings, princesses, cowboys, harlequins, columbines, sheikhs, geisha girls and various unidentifiables who thronged the dance floor. 'I bet you can't guess what we are.'

'The most beautiful girls in the room?'

Marjorie and Phyllis giggled in delight. 'That's right, of course,' said Marjorie, 'but what else?'

The two sisters were wearing long silky dresses of midnight blue picked out with stars. 'I give up,' said Jack after a few moments' frowning consideration.

'Go on, guess!' pleaded Marjorie.

Jack glanced at the seats at the side of dance floor where old Lady Stuckley, dressed as The White Queen, was waiting. She caught his eye and beckoned him over. 'Can I catch up with you later? I really should talk to your grandmother. Besides that,' he added, looking across the room, 'I think that monk chap is waiting for you.'

'Rasputin?' Marjorie's face fell.

'You promised, Marjorie,' said Phyllis.

'All right, but he's so *old*. Afterwards, Jack?'

'I'll count the minutes.'

He carried on threading his way through the crowd. Blackbeard the pirate put a hand on his arm. 'Avast, me hearties,' he growled, adding, in a normal voice, 'D'you fancy a smoke on the terrace, Jack? It's ages since we caught up with each other and I can't hear myself think in here.'

Jack grinned. Under an exuberant beard and eye patch, topped off by a bandanna and three-cornered hat bearing the skull and crossbones, was his old friend, Mark Stuckley. 'I didn't recognize you under the shrubbery.'

'The beard, you mean? Yo ho ho and a bottle of rum.' Mark raised his voice to carry over a saxophone solo. 'Are you coming outside?'

'I promised your grandmother I'd get her a drink,' said Jack regretfully. 'I'll join you later.'

'Okey-doke,' said Mark. 'Have my sisters seen you?'

'Yes,' said Jack, nodding to where Marjorie Stuckley was being steered round the floor by Rasputin. 'Marjorie's nabbed me for a dance after the Mad Monk. Who is he? I can't make out who's who under all these beards people have sprouted.'

'Rasputin, you mean? That's a bloke called Vaughan. You know him, don't you? He said he'd met you.'

Jack felt as if someone had thrown a bucket of cold water over him. He didn't know how, but he managed to keep his smile fixed in place. 'Vaughan?' he repeated in as casual a voice as he could manage. 'Yes, I've met him.'

'I find him uphill work,' said Stuckley. 'Goodness knows how Marjorie's coping. I'll see you later.' He strode off to the terrace.

Jack forced himself to look away from Rasputin and walk towards Lady Stuckley.

'Goodness, Jack, what a time you took,' said Lady Stuckley as he put the drinks on the table. 'I saw those silly girls of mine stop you and my heart sank.'

'I pleaded a prior engagement.' He smiled. 'After all, it was a royal command.'

'Quite right too,' said old Lady Stuckley with a delighted smile.

He stood back and gave an elaborate bow, which made Lady Stuckley giggle like a schoolgirl. 'My respects to Your Highness.' Adjusting his inconvenient array of weaponry, he lowered himself gingerly on to the seat. 'Daggers and things are all very well,' he complained, 'but you never know where they're going. If I can refrain from stabbing you, you will dance with me, won't you?'

Lady Stuckley chuckled in great satisfaction. 'Once I sat down in this outfit, young man, I thought it might be as well if I stayed sitting for the rest of the ball.'

'You can't possibly do that.'

'Perhaps I could manage a waltz before the end of the evening.'

'My life will be a blank until the moment comes.'

She smiled. 'If I were forty years younger . . .'

Jack sighed. 'What an opportunity I lost, by being born too late. We would have taken London by storm.'

'I did take London by storm,' said Lady Stuckley complacently, which was nothing but the truth. 'Do you know I was nearly your grandmother? Your grandfather proposed to me.'

Jack did know, for Lady Stuckley mentioned it virtually every time he met her, but he expressed suitable surprise. 'Did he? I'm sure I would've been much improved.'

'Well, your father certainly would have been,' she said dryly. 'You haven't turned out at all badly, all things considered.' Lady Stuckley looked at him perceptively. 'What's the matter?' she asked. 'Something's upset you.' She paused for Jack to answer. When he didn't, she shrugged her shoulders. 'Ah well, it's none of my business and I'm a nosy old woman, only you're too polite to tell me so.'

'It's nothing,' said Jack, chilled by Lady Stuckley's unexpected insight. He glanced up and saw Isabelle dancing with Arthur. He had to think of something to tell the acute old lady. 'Isabelle wanted me to wear a different costume. She was a bit shirty when I refused.'

Lady Stuckley pursed her lips in disbelief, but, thank goodness, didn't contradict him. 'They make a very handsome couple,' she said, following his gaze to Isabelle and Arthur. 'Young Stanton has more nerves than are good for him but he's sound enough, like all his family, even if he is too inclined to think. Thinking's no good for a man. They brood too easily. Still, he should get on well enough with Isabelle Rivers. She's a clever girl. I wondered if she was too clever. Clever girls can see a man's faults and men don't like it.'

'A really clever girl wouldn't point them out,' said Jack. 'Or perhaps the man hasn't got any faults.'

Lady Stuckley gave a crack of laughter. 'I've never met a man yet who didn't.' She looked at Isabelle once more. 'Being clever's all very well but since she took up with Arthur Stanton I've had a far greater opinion of her sense. She suits that mediaeval dress. Marjorie and Phyllis told me she was going to come as some sort of Greek goddess. She doesn't look very Greek.'

'No, that notion went by the board. She went for Camelot in the end. He's Lancelot and she's Guinevere.'

'And very pretty she looks, too. I can't think the chain mail young Stanton's wearing is particularly suitable for dancing in, though.'

'No, I don't suppose they had jazz at the court of King Arthur.'

'Good for them. All these modern dances are far too energetic.' Lady Stuckley raised her lorgnettes and peered across the ballroom with aged but sharp eyes. 'Goodness knows why young Vaughan chose to dress up as Rasputin. He cannot be comfortable, smothered by that beard.'

Jack felt his knuckles tighten. 'Young Vaughan?' he repeated.

She glanced at him. 'Do you know him?'

'I met him the other day,' said Jack in what he hoped was a casual manner.

'Young Vaughan,' she said reflectively. 'He was in the Diplomatic Service for a time. He never sits still. He's always rowing round something or shooting animals or climbing up a mountain somewhere.'

It was obviously expected of him to make some sort of comment. 'Isn't he a bit old for that sort of thing? He must be at least fifty.'

Lady Stuckley laughed. 'At my age, that's not old. Since his wife died he's only had himself to please, not that that ever mattered. He's always done exactly as he liked. I suppose everyone's got to have their amusements, but I find some of the things he does very odd.'

'There's nothing odd about climbing mountains, is there?

Lady Stuckley sniffed. 'When he was up at Cambridge, he started digging up dead people.'

'Digging up dead people?' repeated Jack in surprise. It seemed a peculiar sort of pastime, even for the most wayward student.

'Dead people and pots,' said Lady Stuckley with a sniff. 'Treasure hunting, you know? He calls it archaeology but it boils down to dead people and pots. I believe his house is full of things he's dug up. I asked him once if he'd found any treasure and he told me he'd found a gold pin from a brooch. It'd be much easier to go and buy a gold pin, surely – and a brooch as well, if he wanted one – than try and dig them up. It seems a very haphazard way of obtaining jewellery.'

Despite his tension, Jack couldn't help laughing. He could quite see that the practical Lady Stuckley would find little point in merely academic pursuits. He finished his champagne and stood up. She stretched her hand out to him in a queenly gesture that went well with her costume and, much to her pleasure, he bowed gallantly and kissed her hand. 'Your Majesty,' he murmured.

'Don't forget you promised me a waltz,' said Lady Stuckley, highly gratified. 'I don't know what the matter is but your manners haven't suffered.'

After that rather wearing session, all he really wanted to do was join Mark Stuckley on the terrace for a breather, but he was stopped by Isabelle. 'There you are, Jack. I saw Lady Stuckley had nabbed you. She's a holy terror, isn't she?'

'She thinks you're clever,' he said. 'And she's got a good opinion of your sense.'

'Has she?' Isabelle looked remarkably pleased. 'That's quite something coming from her.' She took his arm. 'Have this next dance with me, Jack. Arthur says he won't move another step.'

'Have you ever tried to dance wearing armour?' demanded her glowing fiancé. 'If I don't get a drink soon I'll boil.'

'Perhaps your next dance should be the Lobster Quadrille,' said Jack with a grin.

'Ouch!' said Arthur, smiling. 'I'm going to find some fresh air.'

Jack held out his arm to Isabelle. 'I'm all yours, Belle.'

They started round the room, expertly weaving in and out of the crush of dancers. Isabelle rested her head on his shoulder and looked at him with serious green eyes. 'Jack,' she said quietly. 'You do know Mr Vaughan's here, don't you?'

Unconsciously his arms tightened around her. 'Yes. Why are you telling me, Isabelle?'

'Because of the other day at Claridge's. I know what happened.'

They danced a few more steps. 'Arthur promised he wouldn't say anything,' he said quietly.

She drew back slightly. 'Don't look so grim, Jack. I knew there was something wrong. You were far too bright and brittle.' She looked at him thoughtfully. 'You're a bit like that now. You mustn't blame Arthur. I asked him outright what the matter was.'

They danced a few more steps in silence. 'I thought I hid it rather well,' said Jack eventually.

'Too well, Jack. I know you.'

He sighed and kissed her forehead gently.

'So what was it about, Jack? Who was that horrible man?'

It was some time before he spoke. To an outsider it would have looked as if they were concentrating on nothing more than the steps of the dance, but Isabelle could feel the tension flowing through him. 'You know who it was, Belle,' he said eventually. 'If Arthur told you what happened, he must have told you who it was.'

'It was a man called Craig, wasn't it?' She felt his hands tighten.

'That's right.' He took a deep breath and repeated the name in a whisper. 'Craig.'

She looked at him blankly.

'For God's sake, Belle, you can't have forgotten,' said Jack, suddenly impatient with her lack of understanding. 'Durant Craig. Don't you remember what I did?'

'Craig? I don't . . .' She stopped and held him closer. 'Oh, Jack. I understand now.'

A sudden, vivid picture formed in her mind of an autumn day at home, a cold clammy day with mist shrouding the trees in the park. She had forgotten it. It was in the war and seemed so long ago.

She had been coming down to breakfast when the door-bell rang. Egerton, the butler, walked down the hall to answer it and she'd paused at the foot of the stairs to see who it was. In those days they were used to all sorts of men turning up. Hesperus, like many other big houses, had been turned into a convalescent home for wounded soldiers, but the house was full and they weren't expecting any new arrivals.

Outside stood a thin, nervous-looking man, hardly more than a boy, twisting his cap round and round in his hands. He wore a Flying Corps jacket over dirty khaki and he had a few days' growth of stubble on his chin. In a barely audible voice he asked if Lady Rivers was at home. Egerton hesitated and the boy made a noise that was a cross between a laugh and a sob.

'Don't you recognize me, Egerton?'

And then she had flown across the hall to him. 'Jack! Jack, what's happened to you?' She tried to kiss him but he fended her off.

'Don't come too close. I was on a troop ship. I'm crawling.' He spoke in little jerky sentences. 'Vermin, you know.'

She laughed, happy to see him again after his long and silent absence. 'Is that all? Don't worry, we're used to it.' She heard her mother come out of the morning-room and turned. 'Oh, mother, it's Jack! He's got a creepy-crawly problem but we can deal with that, can't we?'

Her mother reached out and, regardless of his mumbled protests, put a gentle hand under his arm. 'We'll soon have you cleaned up, Jack, and find some decent clothes for you. But that's not all that's wrong, is it?'

He half-stumbled against her. 'No, Aunt Alice. I wish it were.'

He'd been given two weeks leave, a long time when leave was usually measured in hours and days. At the end of that time he talked longingly of flying once more and his hand was steady enough to hold his own razor. He even made the occasional joke. But he still had nightmares and once, when a log had cracked on the fire, Isabelle thought he was going to scream.

She came back to the present to find his black eyes fixed on her. 'I'm sorry, Jack. It was all so long ago. Surely it can't still matter?'

He gave an ironic lift of his eyebrows. 'It mattered to him. And to me,' he added in an undertone.

'But he can't make trouble for you, can he?'

'He very well might. He's not a very forgiving sort of man.'

'Well, I think he's horrible,' said Isabelle robustly. 'Forget him, Jack. He's not worth thinking about.'

He held her tightly once more, but this time in a hug of gratitude. He knew she wanted him to say something ordinary and everyday, to show that they were just two people at a dance amongst friends, enjoying the here and now.

For some reason a poem, one of Browning's, came to mind. It was set to the rhythm of a toccata, played while the people of Venice danced. Masked by their brilliant, increasingly artificial fervour, death (the plague?) drew closer and took them one by one. *Dust and ashes, dead and done with, Venice spent what Venice earned. The soul, doubtless, is immortal, where a soul can be discerned. Here on earth they bore their fruitage, mirth and folly were the crop. What of soul was left, I wonder, when the kissing had to stop?*

He shuddered. That wasn't everyday, for heaven's sake,

however relevant it might seem. He forced himself to smile
and, even though he felt it was a bit of a death's head grin,
Isabelle squeezed his arm, to show she appreciated it. 'Damn
the past. Let's tie a can to it.' They danced a few more steps
then applauded as the music stopped.

'Let's join the others, shall we?' said Isabelle, taking his arm.

Arthur was standing by an open window with Marjorie
and Phyllis Stuckley. Jack felt a sudden warm affection for
all of them. These were his friends. They were ordinary, they
were everyday, they were happy and they were all good sorts.
Even, he added to himself, if Marjorie did make him feel
slightly hunted on occasion.

'What about our dance, Jack?' asked Marjorie.

'Let me have a drink first,' he pleaded. 'And I did promise
your brother I'd join him on the terrace for a breather. Can
we have the first dance after supper?'

She was disappointed, he could tell, but she smiled at him.
'Promise?'

'Promise. Shall I,' he added, wanting to see a real smile,
not an assumed one, 'behave like all well brought-up Corsican
bandits and fling you across my saddle-bow and gallop off
into the night?'

Marjorie giggled delightedly. Phyllis wrinkled her nose.
'I wouldn't have thought they had anything but pack-ponies
in Corsica. Would they have saddle-bows?'

'It was a bow at a venture.'

'That was an awful joke,' said Phyllis amongst the laughter.
She gave a little pirouette. 'You still haven't guessed what
our costumes are. Go on, Jack, see if you can work it out.
There's a kiss for the winner. Arthur didn't get it.'

'That was very tactful of you, Arthur,' said Isabelle. Jack
stepped back and looked at both girls with an air of deep
concentration. Marjorie's hair was dressed with shimmering
spangles and she wore a dark blue dress covered in stars
with a flying arrow embroidered on the front. Phyllis was
also in midnight blue with stars but her dress had an upturned
urn on the front, flowing with water.

'You're stars,' he said thoughtfully. 'I can't think of any
star names.' The girls gave rather smug smiles and he hesitated for a moment. 'Hang on a mo! It's the signs of the

Zodiac, isn't it? Now who has arrows? Sagittarius, that's it. Marjorie, you're Sagittarius. That's half a kiss you owe me. Phyllis, you're whoever it is that carries water. Aquarius, that's it.'

'Well done, Jack.' Phyllis tilted up her chin and he kissed her. He smiled apologetically at Marjorie. 'Do you want to join the harem?'

She did. He kissed her and she broke away giggling. 'Go and have your breather on the terrace. It'll be supper-time soon.'

Once on the terrace he drew a deep breath and leaned against the wall. The light and the music from the ballroom streamed past him, on to the stone flags. He stood in the shadows, glad of a chance to relax. Isabelle had accused him of being too bright and brittle, and she was right. There was no sign of Mark. He was relieved, in a way. It was good to be alone, to stop pretending there was nothing wrong. He shook himself. Surely Isabelle was right. It was all so long ago that perhaps it really didn't matter any more.

It was March and, although it was fine, the terrace was icy after the sweltering ballroom. There would be a frost tonight. Jack shivered as the wind sliced through his thin shirt. He walked across the terrace and looked over the stone balustrade. It was a dramatic view. The Stuckleys' house, Hammerholt, was built into the side of a hill and the terrace, supported on pillars, stretched out from the side of the house.

Below him, the steep grassy slope tumbled away a hundred feet or so to the dark mass of rustling trees at the bottom of the valley. The name of the house, he knew, came from the little river Hammer – it was scarcely more than a stream – a tributary of the Breeden. From far below he could just make out the noise of the busy, shallow river as it chattered on its way. Overhead the moon scudded behind patchy clouds and the stars had the hard brilliance of a thousand spear tips. They were nearly as bright as the stars in the desert . . . He shook himself. He wasn't going to think of it any more. *It didn't matter.*

He lit a cigarette, seeing the tip glow red in the darkness, and looked round at the sound of a footstep. Vaughan was on the terrace. Jack felt his stomach give a little twist, and at the same time he was surprised. He hadn't heard Vaughan come out and yet there he was.

He wasn't going to say anything but Vaughan paused. 'Who's there?'

'Jack Haldean, sir.'

'Major Haldean?' Vaughan cleared his throat. 'Look, about the other day. I'd like you to know I was not responsible for that disgraceful . . .'

He didn't finish the sentence. A huge roar, like that of a gigantic tormented lion, broke into Vaughan's words. Simultaneously, a sheet of flame leapt into the air from the valley below. Vaughan spun round to see what was happening, his body black against the fire.

Jack, completely taken aback, dropped his cigarette over the balustrade, then ran to the opposite side of the terrace, craning to see. There was a ball of fire in the valley below and the air was full of the angry, ragged crackling of flames.

People spilled out on to the terrace from the French windows, chattering in anxious excitement. Marjorie Stuckley struggled her way through the crowd to him. 'What is it?' she said over and over again. 'What is it?'

Jack leaned over the balustrade. Below him, the trees, their leaves burnt away, laid black skeletal fingers over a mass of flame. He could pick out the shape of a car at the bottom of the valley, dark against the dancing red. 'Some poor beggar's had it,' he said quietly. Marjorie started to cry. He spared a glance sideways and saw Arthur holding Isabelle, their faces reflecting the quivering fire.

'It's that track down to the valley,' Arthur said dully. 'Some poor devil's taken the wrong turning and crashed into a tree. I nearly took that path myself earlier on.' Isabelle gripped him tighter.

Burnt pieces of leaves and twigs fluttered past, bringing a stinging, acrid smell. A fragment of what had been the fabric of the hood floated upward, borne by the terrible wildness of the ripping, crackling fire. There was a savage explosion and the flames vaulted to the level of the balcony. Thick black smoke, rank with burning oil and rubber, set them all coughing.

'Get back!' yelled Jack as another whumph of flame leapt past the stone banister. He saw Mark Stuckley, his face with its pirate's beard lit up like a pantomime devil in the flames.

'Mark, we've got to do something! If those trees catch hold, the house could go up. We need water.'

Stuckley, caught by a paroxysm of coughing, waved his arm in agreement. With his father's help, he organized a line of men and women to pass buckets of water from the stables through the ballroom and on to the terrace. The tops of the highest trees were at least thirty feet below the house, but burning twigs and leaves, floating high in the air, put the house in real danger of being set alight. It seemed a very long time – it was actually forty minutes or so later – before they heard the jangling of a fire bell.

'It's the fire engine from Market Breeden,' said Stuckley, peering down into the woods. His face was grimed with soot and his eyes were red. 'I told them they had to come across the river Hammer. They can't get into the valley from this end.'

The car had long since burnt out, a dull mass visible under a glowing tracery of branches. Shouts came up from the valley as the pump was brought into action. The water hit the trees with a noise as if a thousand furious snakes were hissing defiance. Then a black hole appeared in the carpet of fire, followed by another and another, then two of the holes joined together, widened and grew.

It was well over an hour afterwards before Jack, Arthur, Mark, and some of the other men were able to go down the steps of the terrace to the valley floor.

The burnt-out wreck of the car was still too hot to approach but Jack could see what had been the driver stretched out over what had been the front seat. He had seen men die by fire before but nothing could take away the horror of that charred, grotesquely human shape.

He retreated to the steps and slumped against the grassy bank, watching Mark Stuckley and his father talk to the firemen.

The darkened woods dripped with water. His eyes smarted and the dank smell of wet ash stung his throat. Arthur, in his smoke-blackened chain mail, sat wearily beside him.

'That was a close-run thing,' said Jack.

Arthur rested his head in his hands. 'We did it, though. We saved the house.' He rubbed his sore eyes. 'The poor bloke in the car didn't have a chance,' he said after a pause. 'I hate seeing men burnt. It's a horrible sight.'

'It's like a private room in hell,' agreed Jack quietly.

Arthur nodded and said nothing for a few moments. 'D'you think he was kettled?' he said eventually. 'He must have been going at a devil of a lick.' He felt in his pockets for his cigarette case. It was empty. 'Let me have a cigarette, Jack. I could do with one.'

Jack paused in the act of reaching for his case. 'A devil of a lick?' he repeated in an odd voice. 'Say that again.'

Arthur gave him a puzzled look. 'He was going at a devil of a lick.'

Jack stared at him. 'My God, Arthur, that's just what he *wasn't* doing.'

'What?' Arthur looked at him uncomprehendingly.

Jack lowered his voice. 'You'd expect the bloke to be going hell for leather, wouldn't you?' Arthur nodded. 'But that's just it. I was standing on the terrace talking to Vaughan when there was a tremendous bang and a sheet of flame leapt up.'

'So?'

'So there was nothing beforehand. Nothing. There wasn't any sound at all. No noise of an engine, no shouting, no sound of a car revving, no sound of a crash. Nothing.'

Arthur gaped at him. 'But there must have been.'

Jack lit his cigarette. 'I was there. It was as quiet as the grave.'

'But Jack, that means . . .' He trailed off.

'That means someone set it up,' said Jack grimly. 'It wasn't an accident, Arthur. That car didn't crash. It was deliberately set on fire.'

Arthur Stanton's gaze slid to the twisted, blackened figure in the car. 'But there's a man in the car. If someone deliberately set the car on fire, they must have known he was there. That means they killed him. It means . . . It means . . .' Arthur hesitated and swallowed.

Jack quietly finished the sentence for him. 'It means murder.'

THREE

At nine o'clock the next morning Jack drew the Spyker to a halt on the corner of the road that ran down to the Hammer Valley. The grass was rimmed with frost and he was glad of his woollen scarf, thick gloves and warm coat. Looking up the hill, he could see a few wisps of smoke from the chimneys of Hammerholt above the trees and wondered if the Stuckleys were up and about yet. Considering it was only five hours or so since the last of their guests had departed, probably not.

It was gone two in the morning when he telephoned Superintendent Ashley at his home in Lewes. He picked his words carefully, knowing there was a fair chance that anything he said would be listened to with breathless enthusiasm by the Market Breeden telephone exchange. Ashley, once he had snapped into full wakefulness, had, thank God, got the point if not the details.

He climbed out of the car as the chugging of an engine sounded on the main road. A Trojan four-seater rounded the corner and pulled in beside the Spyker. Ashley, carrying a briefcase, got out of the car, followed by two men, one of whom Jack recognized as Doctor Wilcott from Breedenbrook. The other, judging from the tripod and case he carried, was the photographer.

Jack waved a cheerful greeting. He had a great regard for Superintendent Ashley, a solid, kindly man in his early forties with a matter-of-fact manner and an unexpected sense of humour.

'Morning, Haldean,' said Ashley. 'It's good to see you again, even if you did disturb my night's rest. You remember Dr Wilcott, don't you? He gave me a lift over here, together with Mr Tarleton, who's come to give us a hand with the photographs.'

'You seem to have a habit of getting mixed up in police cases,' said Dr Wilcott with a grin. 'I understand you actually saw the car go up in flames.' He glanced in the direction of Hammerholt. 'We've been up to the house already. Mr Stuckley was still in his dressing gown, which didn't surprise me. It sounds as if you had an absolute night of it.'

'I did wonder if Mr Stuckley wanted to accompany us,' said Ashley, 'as this is his property, but he was happy to let us poke around by ourselves. Apparently there's a right of way down to the river so they're used to people coming and going. With any luck, though, everything should be as you left it last night. It'll be a blessed sight easier to work out what happened if nothing's been disturbed. It's a bit early for sightseers but I sent two men ahead from Market Breeden to guard the scene of the crash, just in case.'

He looked round the tree-lined road. 'I can see how someone would mistake this for the turning up to Market Breeden,' he said. 'Especially in the dark. I got the impression from your call that it wasn't much more than a path.'

'Yes, it would be an understandable mistake,' agreed Jack as they set off. He dropped back so Dr Wilcott and Mr Tarleton were a few paces in front. 'If I'm right, that's what we're meant to think,' he said quietly. 'As you say, the road's very wide here, considering it's really just a path through the woods. I asked Mark Stuckley about it. A few hundred years ago this was all dug out for iron, which is why the road's here at all. It narrows further on and falls away very steeply before it drops down to the glade beneath Hammerholt. That's where the crash was. The glade itself is like a huge bowl in the earth. That's where the old iron-workings were, although they're all overgrown now. It's overlooked by the terrace of Hammerholt. I was there last night. It was like having a seat in the gallery at a theatre.'

'And you're sure you didn't hear anything before the crash?'

'Not a thing. As I said, I was standing on the terrace, talking to a Mr Vaughan when whumph! There was a sheet of flame and all hell was let loose.'

'Mr Vaughan?' said Ashley. 'I didn't know there was another witness. I'll have to talk to him. Do you know him well?'

'No.' Jack shook his head. 'I've only met him once before.

Arthur Stanton knows him, though, and so do the Stuckleys, of course.'

'That's good,' said Ashley, shrugging himself deeper into his overcoat. 'They'll be able to give me his address. By jingo, it's sharp this morning.'

They walked on between the great soaring columns of beeches to where the road opened out into a grassy clearing. It was wide enough to turn a car and, judging by the tyre tracks, had been used for that purpose by more than one hapless motorist.

'Hello,' said Jack, stopping. 'What's this?' He knelt down at the side of the road, seeing where car tyres had dug into the banks of the path, ploughing up the reddish-brown earth in a raw slash of frost-rimmed colour. 'These are fresh, Ashley. The tracks are still sharp and the earth would have crumbled if they'd been here for any time.' A doleful line of crushed grass, cow parsley and nettles marked the trail. 'It looks as if he was trying to turn the car.' He stood up and retraced his steps back up the road.

Ashley followed him. 'That's him, isn't it?' he asked, pointing to where a diamond-patterned tyre had left its imprint against the sloped earth of the bank. He crossed the road and looked carefully at the mud at the side of the road. 'There's another imprint of those diamond-patterned tyres here, too. There are more tyre tracks, too, a wire-cord pattern. They've come from another car.'

Jack looked at the patch of earth. 'It definitely is a different car, not just a mixed set of tyres on the same car. You can tell that from the way the tracks are overlaid.'

'We've got a trail going down to the clearing,' said Ashley, following the tracks, 'and the same trail coming back up. The diamond pattern's driven away, so that's not the car which caught fire.'

'Hold on a minute,' said Jack. He walked across the clearing and went a little way down the path to the glade. He stooped and examined the ground, stood up and slowly walked back, his face puzzled. 'This is a bit odd, Ashley. The wire-cord car which is, I presume, the one which crashed, was here first and the diamond-patterned one came afterwards.' He shrugged. 'I suppose it could be someone who lost their way or realized there was a kerfuffle in the valley and stopped to take a look.'

They walked back to Dr Wilcott and Mr Tarleton, Jack idly following the trail of the diamond-patterned tyres. 'Hang on a minute,' he said, stooping. 'What's this?'

There was a rainbow-coloured liquid pooled into the depression made by the tyre tracks. He dipped his fingers in, rubbed them together and sniffed. 'Oil. The car's dropped oil. That usually means it's standing still.'

'There's something else, Haldean,' called Ashley. He pointed to a broad mark beside a slender footprint with a clearly marked heel. 'Footprints,' said Ashley. 'A man and a woman.'

Jack scratched his ear. 'That means that sometime after the crash, this couple in the car with the diamond-patterned tyres drove down here, got as far as this clearing, stopped the car, got out, then got back in the car and drove away.'

'Don't get too excited,' warned Ashley. 'They might not have anything to do with the accident.'

'Accident?' queried Jack.

Ashley smiled. 'I'll call it an accident for the time being, if you don't mind. It saves unnecessary explanations.' They walked across the clearing to where Dr Wilcott and Mr Tarleton were waiting for them. 'We were looking at car tracks,' said Ashley.

'You can see where the car's been,' said Dr Wilcott, starting down the path. 'The tracks are clear, to say nothing of the way the grass and vegetation have been crushed. I wondered, when I heard where the accident was, if it was some sort of farm vehicle that had got off the beaten track and come across the Hammer.'

'The fire engine came across the Hammer last night,' said Jack. 'The firemen took their water from the river, too, of course.'

'I suppose a motorist could think driving into the valley and fording the river was a short cut,' said Dr Wilcott with a frown. 'Goodness knows where it's a short cut to, mind. The man must have been an idiot. I don't want to speak ill of the dead, but I wouldn't be at all surprised if he'd had a bit too much to drink.'

'That's what my pal, Arthur Stanton, said last night,' remarked Jack. 'Hello, Ashley, what have you found?'

Ashley had stopped and crouched down once more. 'More tyre tracks,' he said in an abstracted voice. 'These are from the first car, the wire-cord pattern, but look, Haldean. What d'you think of that?'

He was staring at a woman's footprint, a footprint evidently made by the same shoe as had left the print in the clearing.

Jack whistled. 'What the dickens was she doing here?' He walked on a few steps further, then stopped and brushed away a clump of overhanging grass, looking at the ground intently. 'She's here again, Ashley,' he called. 'The man too.' He stood up. 'As I see it, there were two cars here last night. Car number one, the wire-cord, went on to crash in the valley. Car number two, with the diamond-pattern tyres, stood in the clearing for a time, long enough to drop some oil, while the couple in the car walked down the path.'

'There's a couple more footprints further on, as well,' said Ashley after a brief examination. He turned to Mr Tarleton. 'I think we'd better get a photograph of this.' He shook his head in a puzzled way as Mr Tarleton set up his tripod. 'I can't imagine what these people were doing here. It's one thing to stop and take a look from the clearing, it's quite another to plunge down this path, especially in the pitch dark and wearing heeled shoes. I wouldn't mind taking a plaster cast of both the tyre tracks and the footprints. I'll do that on the way back. I'd better advertise for this couple to come forward, too. They could be witnesses and if they were innocent sightseers, there's no reason why they shouldn't get in touch with us.'

Dr Wilcott frowned. 'What other kind of sightseer could they be?'

Ashley cleared his throat. 'We think the crash might not be as straightforward as it appears at first sight, Doctor. I'd be obliged if you'd keep that to yourself, though.'

The doctor raised his eyebrows. 'Fair enough. I'll keep it under my hat. But d'you know, I wouldn't be surprised if it wasn't straightforward. It seems so odd that anyone would drive down here by mistake.'

'As I say, keep it to yourself, Doctor. Let's get on, shall

we?' He raised his voice to call to the photographer. 'Mr Tarleton, can you follow us down when you're finished?'

They set off again, scrambling down the path into the valley. 'I wouldn't like to come down here at any speed,' said Dr Wilcott. 'It'd be a tight squeeze for most cars, to say nothing of the damage to the suspension. I've never been down this path, although I know the Hammer fairly well. It's shallow enough to wade through for most of its length, although there are a couple of interesting pools. It's very picturesque but not much good for fishing and useless for bathing or boating. I'm a bit of a fisherman in my spare time and I'm fairly well up on most of the rivers in this area. All the really interesting bits of river come further downstream, where it joins the Breeden. There's some nice picnic spots, though, I believe,' he added. 'And people paint and so on, too.'

'Mark Stuckley said the glade is a favourite spot for picnics,' agreed Jack. 'The glade is where it happened, of course,' he added, his nose wrinkling as the dismal, damp, decayed smell of burnt wet wood wafted up to them. 'I don't think anyone will fancy picnicking here for while.'

The path opened out into what should have been, on this crisp spring morning, a delightful place. Great gusty masses of white cloud scurried overhead, blown by a stiff breeze that shook the trees and the bracken, but the grass was scarred and blackened and the trees were reduced to sooty skeletons.

Ashley drew his breath in as he took in the scene. The twisted metal of the car lay smashed against a beech tree and forlorn, burnt fragments scattered the glade.

In the car, sprawled over what had been the front seats, was a lumpy black shape, still identifiable as human. 'Yours, Dr Wilcott, I believe,' Ashley said quietly. He had turned pale and was obviously making a huge effort to act as unemotionally as possible. 'After Mr Tarleton has taken his photographs, of course.'

'Lucky me,' said Wilcott grimly. 'I'm not going to do anything much here. We'll need a stretcher to take the remains back up to the clearing.'

Two uniformed policemen were standing by the car.

Ashley went to talk to them. Jack, overcoming his reluctance, followed him. It wasn't the first time he had seen a victim of fire. The war had hardened him to many things but the sight and the smell of a pilot in a burnt-out plane or the scorched remains of men once the Germans had turned their *Flammenwerfers* loose in a trench was always ghastly, no matter how many times he had to look at it. He glanced at Ashley and felt oddly protective of the older man. Ashley hadn't had his experience and was obviously finding this very hard.

'My God, that's nasty,' said Ashley with feeling. 'Anyway,' he said with a shudder, 'the men report there've been no sightseers, male or female. And you've been here since what time?' he asked, turning back to the men.

'Since first light, sir,' said one of the policemen. 'We haven't heard a peep from anyone.'

Jack looked at the wreck. It had been, as he'd seen last night, a very substantial car. 'It's a Rolls-Royce,' he said in surprise. 'Look, Ashley, even all twisted up like this, the grill's very distinctive and although the mascot's damaged, it's identifiable.'

Ashley looked at the broken flying lady on what had been the bonnet. 'A Rolls? Well, that shouldn't be too hard to place. They're not that common.'

Dr Wilcott crouched down beside the car, looking at the body. 'I can't tell you if it's a man or a woman yet,' he said. 'However . . .' With a professional calm that Jack could only admire, he reached out and touched the corpse's temple. 'I thought as much,' he said after a moment. 'He – I'll say 'he' for convenience – he's got a nasty head injury.' He rocked back on his heels. 'He could have cracked himself on the dashboard, I suppose, but I can't see anything that would cause the injury. It's a pretty severe blow. I'll be able to say for certain after the post-mortem, but I wouldn't be surprised if he was dead before the fire started.'

Ashley glanced at Jack. 'That would support your idea.' He broke off as Mr Tarleton arrived. With considerable reluctance the photographer set up his camera and, under Ashley's direction, got to work.

Leaving him to it, Jack walked away from the car up the

slope to Hammerholt. In the daylight it was easy to see how vital their efforts had been. The grass was blackened and scorch marks ran all the way up to the balcony above. Something grey caught his eye. It was the remains of a man's hat, a grey homburg, which, although damaged by fire, looked as if it had been new. He showed it to Ashley, who examined it in satisfaction, turning it over in his hands.

'It's a pity it's burnt,' said Ashley, looking inside the brim. 'I can't make out the maker's name but we might be able to see what it is back at the station.' He glanced round the glade. 'I wonder if anything else was thrown out of the car?'

They quartered the glade, but the hat was the only thing they found. Leaving Ashley by the car, Jack followed the path between the hawthorn bushes down to the river. He hoped he might find more footprints from the mysterious couple but, although there were plenty of footprints in the churned-up mud of the glade, they seemed to be all of firemen's boots. On the opposite side of the river, the grass showed clear marks where the fire engine had come across the fields, and the little pebbly beach was deeply rutted by its wheels. Apart from that, there was no damage, and no footprints either. The sun-flecked water chattered over the stones, a blackbird sang and a wood pigeon cooed somewhere out of sight. It was a pleasant spot, with grassy banks sloping down to either side of the water. Jack found it a relief to see something that wasn't scarred by fire.

He turned back at the sound of his name. 'Come and see what you make of this,' called Ashley. He crouched down at the back of the car. 'I'm trying to read the registration plate,' he said. 'The front plate's a goner, of course, but the back one's not too bad.'

Jack sacrificed his handkerchief to wipe the plate. 'I think it says A and that's a P followed by 61 something but I can't make out the next bit very clearly. There's an eight, I think, but I can't be sure.' He looked up. 'AP? That's a Sussex plate, of course.'

Ashley clicked his tongue. 'AP? I wonder if the driver was a local man.' He turned to the two policemen who were standing placidly by. 'Do you know who has a Rolls-Royce in this area?'

Constable Marsh and Constable Hulme looked at each other. 'Well, there's not a lot of them about, sir,' said Constable Marsh. 'I can't say I know them all, like, but there's Mr Wintergreen over at Lower Haverly. He has one, that I do know. Major Warren of Handcross has one and there's Sir Philip Rivers of Stanmore Parry, if you'd call that local.'

'It's not Uncle Philip's,' put in Jack.

'And then there's Mr Vaughan of Chavermere, not that that's so very close by. Those are the only ones I can think of off the top of my head, like.'

'It's not Mr Vaughan's,' said Jack. 'He was talking to me last night when the crash happened. His chauffeur could have been driving the car, I suppose. Not that I know he has a chauffeur, of course, but surely Mr Vaughan would have reported it if his car had gone missing.'

The two policemen looked at each other. 'But Mr Vaughan's car has gone missing, sir,' said Constable Hulme slowly. 'That was before this car crash, of course. About eight o'clock in the evening, it was. We had a report that Mr Vaughan's Rolls-Royce had been stolen.'

Ashley stared at him. 'And you haven't thought fit to mention it until now, man?'

'Well,' said Constable Hulme, aggrieved, 'we weren't investigating the theft this morning, sir, we were investigating this here car crash. No one said anything about investigating the theft.'

Constable Marsh coughed. 'Excuse me, sir, I don't know if it's anything to do with the theft, but I stopped a Rolls-Royce yesterday evening.'

'What happened?' asked Ashley.

Constable Marsh took out his notebook and thumbed through it. 'I've got a note of it here, sir. It was only a minor infringement of the regulations, though. Nothing to make a fuss about. I didn't know about the theft, then, of course.'

'Could this have been the car you stopped?'

Constable Marsh stared at the car doubtfully. 'It could have been, I suppose, but it's hard to say with it being in such a state.' He found the place in his notebook. 'Here's my record of the incident, sir. It was quarter to six p.m. on the 27th instant—'

'Yesterday,' put in Ashley.

'Yes, sir, yesterday. As I say, on the 27th instant, I stopped a motorist in a Rolls-Royce on the Haverly Road. Just coming out of Lower Haverly, he was. I apprised him that his front nearside headlight wasn't working. It looked like he'd banged it on something. Just coming on for dusk, it were. He thanked me and said that he'd have it seen to at the nearest garage. I told him where that was and he drove on. The registration of the vehicle was –' he glanced at his book again – 'AP 6168, sir.'

'Was it, by jingo? It sounds as if we might be on to something. Constable Hulme, what's the registration number of Mr Vaughan's car?'

'I don't rightly know, sir,' said Constable Hulme stiffly. 'Being as how I wasn't asked to investigate the theft. There's a note of it at the station.'

'Could it have been Mr Vaughan you saw in the car?' Ashley asked Marsh in a restrained way.

Constable Marsh shook his head. 'No, sir. I'd have recognized Mr Vaughan.'

'Can you describe the man you saw? Was he, for instance,' said Ashley glancing at the homburg in his hand, 'wearing a grey hat?'

Constable Marsh thought for a moment. 'I don't rightly know, sir. He was certainly wearing a hat but I couldn't swear to what colour it was. As I say, it was coming on for dusk. It was one of those hats with flaps that tie under your chin.'

'What, a sort of Sherlock Holmes affair, you mean?' asked Jack. 'A deerstalker?'

'If that's what they're called, yes.'

'Can you tell me anything else about the man in the car?' said Ashley.

Constable Marsh brightened. 'Oh yes, sir. He was a gentleman, if you know what I mean, and had a very pleasant way with him. I don't know about him being a thief. We had a bit of a joke together and I can't see a thief doing that.'

'What did you joke about?' asked Jack.

The constable smiled. 'He had a sort of rug or big tent rolled up on the back seat and I said it was a bit cold for camping. He laughed and said you wouldn't find him trying it at this time of year, so I reckon it must have been a rug, after all.'

Jack's eyes slid to the blackened body in the car. 'Was the rug large enough to cover a man?'

Ashley drew his breath in sharply. 'Well? Was it?'

Constable Marsh looked bewildered. 'But why should a man cover himself up with a rug, sir? If he had done, he must have been completely inside it. I couldn't see him. Why should anyone do such a thing, sir? It'd be all dusty and very uncomfortable. It doesn't make any sense.'

'Just answer me, will you?' said Ashley patiently.

Constable Marsh sucked in his cheeks in an effort of memory.

'Well?' prompted Ashley impatiently. 'Was it large enough to cover a man?'

'It might have been, I suppose, sir.'

Ashley glanced at Jack. 'Well done,' he murmured. He looked at Marsh once more. 'Describe the man driving the car, will you? What did he look like?'

Constable Marsh ran his finger under the strap of his helmet. 'I don't really know, sir. I couldn't tell you his height or colour of his eyes or anything like that. I wasn't looking at him with a view to describing afterwards, you see. All I can really tell you was that he had a big brown beard. A great bushy thing, it was.'

Jack's stomach twisted. 'A beard?' he repeated.

'What is it, Haldean?' asked Ashley.

'It's . . .' He stopped, then looked up and met Ashley's eyes. 'When I met Vaughan, he was in Claridge's,' he said hesitantly. 'It was last Tuesday. He was with a man called Craig. Durant Craig, the explorer. You might have heard of him. Anyway, he's got a very bushy beard. I wondered if it was the same man.'

'It could be, I suppose,' said Ashley.

And so it could; but there might be another explanation, as well, Jack thought, with a sudden lifting of his spirits. He didn't want it to be Craig in the car. He didn't want to have anything to do with Craig ever again. The last time he had seen Vaughan, Vaughan had been dressed up as Rasputin with a very realistic beard. Come to that, Mark Stuckley had been wearing a beard and so had a good few other people at the party last night. Jack looked at Constable Marsh. 'How well do you know Mr Vaughan? Would you recognize him if he was wearing a false beard, say?'

'Wearing a beard?' Constable Marsh grinned broadly. 'What, dressed up, you mean? Why should Mr Vaughan do that, sir?'

'He had a beard at the fancy-dress party last night,' Jack explained.

Ashley nodded in understanding and waited for Marsh's answer. 'Well?'

'Well, I couldn't say, sir,' said Marsh. 'I've never seen Mr Vaughan wearing a beard. I don't know what he'd look like.'

'Would you recognize his voice?' asked Ashley.

Constable Marsh shook his head. 'I'm sorry, sir, I don't know as I would. He speaks like a gentleman and, as I say, this man did too, but it never occurred to me it might be Mr Vaughan. It can't have been him, though. Why, if it had been Mr Vaughan, he'd be bound to say something, not make a fool out of me by pretending he didn't know who I was.'

'You'd have thought so,' said Jack with a smile, trying to smooth Constable Marsh's ruffled feathers. 'He could have been having a joke, though.'

Constable Marsh relaxed. 'I suppose that could be it, sir. It seems a pretty poor sort of joke,' he added doubtfully.

'Absolutely,' agreed Ashley dryly. 'I need to follow this up, Haldean. Rolls-Royces aren't so thick on the ground and tracing the car is a good place to start. Obviously the person I need to speak to is this Mr Vaughan.'

'The Stuckleys will have his address,' said Jack. 'I'm sure you can telephone him from the house.'

'I'll do that,' said Ashley. He looked at the policemen. 'You two had better stay here until Dr Wilcott has made arrangements to move the body.' He turned to the doctor. 'Will that take long?'

'If the Stuckleys let me use their telephone as well, I can start the ball rolling right away,' said Dr Wilcott.

'Good. In that case, as Mr Tarleton has finished, we can be off.' He looked at the two policemen again. 'As soon as the body's removed, you can go.'

They walked back up the path for the sole purpose, Jack thought, of getting out of earshot of the two policemen.

He was proved right when Ashley gave vent to his feelings in a sigh of irritation. 'Can you credit those two? I thought the Keystone Kops were only found at the pictures. It was obvious the crashed car was a Rolls-Royce and yet they didn't think to link it up with the fact that Mr Vaughan's car had been stolen.' He glanced at Jack. 'Can you give me a lift to Vaughan's? I don't know about any shenanigans with false beards and so on, but it's worth bearing in mind.' He jerked his thumb backwards towards the glade. 'I'm assuming the car is his missing Rolls, of course. It might be a coincidence, but if the registration of Vaughan's car is AP 61 anything, then I'll have to see him. I have to see him in any case, as he's a witness.'

'You can have a lift and welcome, Ashley,' replied Jack. He hesitated awkwardly. 'You know I mentioned a bloke called Durant Craig?'

'Yes. What about him?'

'Well, he's not one of my most fervent admirers. I don't blame him, but he's not. If, by any chance, he's staying with Vaughan, I'd better not come into the house.'

Ashley glanced at him appraisingly. 'I thought you seemed a bit rattled when Marsh started talking about men with beards.'

'It struck me how many men wore beards last night,' said Jack. It was the truth but not all of the truth. 'There must have been at least a dozen, if not more.'

Ashley looked at him for a few moments in silence. 'If you say so,' he said quietly.

The Stuckleys were happy to allow both Dr Wilcott and Superintendent Ashley to use their telephone. 'Anything,' as Mark Stuckley said, 'that'll get things back to normal as soon as possible. After all,' he added, taking Jack into the morning room for a cup of coffee while his father showed Ashley and Dr Wilcott to the telephone, 'it's pretty mouldy to think that part of our land is marked with an X. Marjorie and Phyllis wanted to go and have a look but Dad wouldn't let them.'

'Too right,' said Jack, picking up his coffee. 'It's not nice. Ashley looked pretty green, poor beggar. I think it's the first time he's ever seen anything like that. Dr Wilcott coped very well. Was he in the war?'

'He was in the R.A.M.C.'

Jack nodded. 'I thought he must have had some experience.'

Mark Stuckley shuddered. 'It was the smell that always got to me. It always reminded me of Sunday roasts and so on, and it was ghastly to think of things like that and know why you were thinking it.'

'Don't,' pleaded Jack. 'Mark,' he added, 'tell me about Mr Vaughan.'

'Why d'you want to know about Vaughan?'

'His Rolls-Royce has been stolen and there's a fair chance the one which crashed last night is it. Keep that to yourself, though, as it's not certain. Anyway, Ashley wants to interview him and I've offered to give him a lift to Vaughan's house.'

'Poor beggar,' said Mark. 'Vaughan, I mean. I didn't know his Rolls had been swiped. It was a lovely car. Have you any idea who stole it?'

'No. That's one of the reasons Ashley wants to see Vaughan. So what's he like? As a person, I mean.'

Mark shrugged. 'So so. I'll say this for him, he's as tough as old boots. He's done a lot of hunting and mountaineering, which is usually the sort of thing I'd like, but he's . . . well, I always feel he'd look after Number One.' He searched for the right words. 'You know in the war, how you could always tell who you could trust and who you couldn't? I wouldn't like to rely on him if I was up against it. He's a good oarsman, though,' added Mark in a warmer tone. 'He got his Blue at Cambridge and won a cup at Henley years ago. He's done some fascinating trips. I really envy him that.'

Jack grinned. Mark Stuckley had a passion for boats. A hazard of knowing Mark was being persuaded to crew for him on various boats where comfort was a very optional extra. Jack had been talked into it twice, and, rather to his surprise, had ended up enjoying himself very much.

'I tell you what else I envy, too,' said Mark enthusiastically. 'He lives a little way out of Chavermere, by Stour

Creek, and he's got a first-rate boathouse. I'd love to have a really good bit of navigable river close to hand. We can't do anything with the Hammer. It's far too shallow for any sort of boat. I'd . . .'

Jack stepped in before Mark got carried away. 'Your grandmother said he was an archaeologist.'

Mark snorted with laughter. 'I bet she didn't put it as politely as that. I glaze over when he starts holding forth. The last time he came to dinner I nearly died of boredom before I could get him back on to boats. I know Tutankhamen and so on sounds exciting when you read it in the papers, but Vaughan's never done anything like that. It's all old pots and he doesn't half *go on*. Grandmama cuts him down to size, though. She talks about treasure-hunting and it irritates the life out of him.' He grinned. 'She likes you.'

'She's got superb taste,' said Jack. He looked up as Ashley came into the room. 'Any luck?'

Ashley nodded. 'I spoke to Mr Vaughan and he's agreed to see us. I've got the address. It's a place called Two Bridges on Stour Creek Road. Incidentally, Haldean,' he added, 'I told Mr Vaughan you were with me.' He cleared his throat. 'He's alone,' he added. 'No guests.'

Jack relaxed. 'That's probably just as well.'

'Anyway, the registration of his Rolls is AP 6168.' He looked at Mark. 'Did Haldean tell you Mr Vaughan's car was stolen? We think it was the car which crashed last night, but I didn't say as much to Mr Vaughan. I told your father, though. He's been very helpful and it was on your land, after all. I want to get the story of this theft. Mr Vaughan made it sound very mysterious. So, Haldean, if your offer of a lift is still on, we'll go now, if that's all right with you.'

'Mysterious, eh'? Jack finished his coffee. 'That sounds fun. Let's go and hear all about it.'

FOUR

Vaughan's house, Two Bridges, was flanked by two ancient humpback bridges which gave the house its name. It lay snuggled down in a roughly triangular piece of land between the Breeden and Stour Creek: a modern, white-walled building with large windows, a green tiled roof and ruler-straight lines, softened by the surrounding trees. A wrought-iron gate in the low wall, separating the grounds from the road, opened on to the driveway. On the right-hand side was a large garage and, on the other, a white wall with an arched gateway ran all the way down to the tree-fringed, sunlit creek.

Jack drew to a halt on the road and Ashley climbed out to open the gate.

He paused, a hand on the latch, looking at the grass verge. 'Haldean,' he called. 'Come and see this.'

Jack switched off the engine and joined him. In the muddy fringe separating the grass verge and the driveway was a clearly marked tyre-track.

'It's a diamond-pattern,' said Jack in astonishment. 'It's just like the one in the Hammer Valley. What the dickens is it doing here?' He stopped, suddenly cautious. 'I suppose it is the same, is it? After all, there must be lots of cars with those tyres.'

'I can check that easily enough,' said Ashley. He went back to the Spyker and, bringing the plaster cast he had made in the Hammer Valley, placed it in the tread-mark. It fitted perfectly.

The two men looked at each other. 'I don't understand this,' said Ashley. 'That's the car which was in the Hammer Valley, right enough. I wouldn't be surprised to find a tyre track from Mr Vaughan's Roll-Royce, but that's not the Rolls, it's the other car, the car which dropped oil.'

'And the car with the man and woman in it,' said Jack quietly.

Ashley pushed his hat back. 'So they weren't casual sight-seers, after all. This can't be a coincidence.' He straightened up and looked at the white-walled house. 'I wonder what Mr Vaughan knows about them?'

'I wonder if Mr Vaughan will be willing to tell us,' said Jack. 'Hang on a minute. Let's see if the car came into the driveway, shall we?'

He opened the gate and, hoping they wouldn't be seen by anyone in the house, walked down the drive, examining the ground. 'There don't seem to be any tracks,' said Jack in a low voice. He stopped and looked at the front of the house. If the car wasn't going into the garage, the obvious place to park was the space between the trees and the wall of the outbuilding. It was where he had intended to leave the Spyker. The gravel was disturbed but there were no clear tracks. They retraced their footsteps to the gate.

Jack paused with his hand on the car door. 'Let's scout around,' he said. 'If that car didn't drive up to the house, I wonder where it did go?' They walked back up the road, their eyes fixed on the ground.

'Here it is!' said Ashley in excitement. There was a muddy tree-sheltered verge with ample space for a car to park away from the road. There, clearly imprinted in the mud, were tracks from a set of diamond-patterned tyres.

Jack crouched down and touched a rainbow smudge on the ground. 'Oil,' he said, raising his eyebrows. 'I've struck oil.'

'And I've found the woman,' said Ashley, pointing to a slender, heeled footprint. He gave a low whistle. 'By jingo, this needs some explaining. I need to take a cast of these prints.'

While the plaster of Paris was setting, they walked back up to the Spyker and sat in the car. Jack took out his cigar-ette case and offered it to Ashley. 'Let's see what we know before we go into the house,' he said, striking a match. 'In the first place, I'm convinced that the accident wasn't genuine.'

'Because you didn't hear a car before the explosion,' agreed Ashley.

Jack nodded. 'Yes, that's it. I was speaking to Vaughan

and – bang! There was a terrific explosion and a sheet of flame. So far, so good. Now, earlier in the evening, Vaughan reported his Rolls had been stolen.'

'And at quarter to six Constable Marsh stopped a Rolls – I'll eat my hat if it's not Vaughan's Rolls with the number plates being so similar – on the Haverly Road. All Marsh could really tell us was that the nearside headlight was damaged and that the motorist had a cheerful manner, a full brown beard and a rug on the back seat.'

'That's part one, so to speak,' said Jack, drawing on his cigarette. 'Those are all observed or reported events. What we're meant to think is that some poor beggar swiped Vaughan's Rolls-Royce, piled it into a tree in the Hammer Valley and died in the fire.'

'And what do you think actually happened?' asked Ashley.

Jack paused to arrange his thoughts. 'I think there was a murder,' he said eventually. 'I think the murderer concealed the body under a rug and drove to the Hammer Valley. I think the murderer positioned the car against a tree and subsequently set fire to it.'

'And do you,' said Ashley, with a deep breath, 'think Vaughan was the murderer?'

'You're getting very daring in your assumptions in your old age,' said Jack appreciatively. 'Let's say it is Vaughan. The fact that Constable Marsh didn't recognize him is neither here or there.'

'Too right,' agreed Ashley.

'It could be Vaughan. A cheerful manner, even with a corpse cluttering up the car, is easy enough to assume, and I know Vaughan has a false beard in his possession. You should have seen him at the party last night, Ashley. His chin was like an exploding mattress.' Despite himself, Ashley smiled. 'And, if you have used your car to transport illicitly acquired mortal remains, it's only common sense to report it as stolen. Let's say that's what happened. After his encounter with Constable Marsh, Vaughan arranges the corpse and the car neatly against a convenient tree and tootles back home.'

Ashley choked on his cigarette. 'That's where the other car comes in! The diamond-tyred car, I mean. Vaughan abandons the Rolls and gets driven back here by the diamond car.'

Jack's eyes narrowed thoughtfully. 'I wonder if you're right.'

Ashley clicked his tongue in irritation. 'Hang on, it won't work. Vaughan was talking to you when the damn Rolls blew up.'

Jack grinned. 'It'd work well enough if he had a fuse of some sort. Let me take you back to last night. I was on the terrace, as I said, and I seemed to be completely alone. Then Vaughan popped up like the demon king. Naturally, I assumed that he'd come on to the terrace through the French windows, but he could have come up the steps from the valley just as easily. We had about ten seconds' worth of conversation and then the car blew up.'

'A fuse?' queried Ashley doubtfully. 'Where would he get his hands on a fuse?'

Jack shook his head. 'Don't be so literal. A fuse merely conveys a spark from one place to another. A line of petrol would do it. You'd have to set fire to it right away, otherwise it'd evaporate, but there'd be nothing to stop Vaughan going down to the Rolls from the terrace, taking a can of petrol from the car and laying a trail back to the house. Then, standing on the steps and sheltered by the overhang of the terrace, he simply strikes a match, nips back up top, has a word with any passing guests he happens to see —'

'Such as your good self.'

'— such as my good self, and is there to evince surprise, alarm and horror when the sky falls in.' Jack tapped the ash off his cigarette. 'So yes, Ashley, it looks as if Vaughan could very well have done it.'

'We're going too fast,' said Ashley, suddenly doubtful. 'Mr Vaughan didn't say much on the phone when I rang him but he did say that the theft wasn't straightforward. He hummed and hawed a bit and said he'd explain it fully when I arrived. There could be a whole raft of things we don't know.' He glanced at his watch. 'That plaster should have set by now. I'll lift the casts and open the gate for you.'

'Right-oh,' agreed Jack. He started the engine as Ashley climbed out. 'By the way, don't be surprised if I have a sudden lapse of memory about last night. You see, if he says positively he did hear a car engine, I know he's telling bouncers.'

He parked the Spyker in the space in front of the outbuildings and, after stowing the plaster casts in the car, rang the bell.

The door was opened by the butler, a burly, middle-aged man. 'Mr Vaughan, gentlemen? I'll tell him you've arrived. He asked me to show you into the study. He'll be with you shortly.'

The butler led the way through a hall adorned with various heads of animals mounted on wooden plaques. He paused and coughed deprecatingly before he opened the door, looking at Ashley. 'Excuse me, sir, I hope you don't mind me mentioning it, but my son's in the force.' Ashley looked at the butler with interest. 'His name's Oxley, sir. Sergeant Robert Oxley.'

'Robert Oxley?' said Ashley warmly. 'He's in London now, isn't he? He's a very able officer. You can be proud of him.'

'We're very proud of him, both me and my wife,' said the butler, obviously gratified by Ashley's response. 'My wife's Mr Vaughan's housekeeper. Robert's mentioned you a few times, sir.' He opened the door to the study and showed them in. 'I'll just tell Mr Vaughan you're here, gentlemen.'

'That could be useful,' said Ashley, as the door closed behind the butler. 'That he's Bob Oxley's father, I mean. It can be an uphill struggle at times, getting information out of the servants, but I won't have any trouble.' He looked round the study in appreciation. 'There are some interesting things in here.'

The study was a spacious and comfortably cluttered room lit by French windows looking out on to the gardens. There were buttoned-down leather chairs, a desk, a large bookcase, shelves of pottery, various silver cups and, in a corner of the room, a substantial safe. An oar, bearing names and the date 1889, was hung on the wall over a framed photograph of a group of fresh-faced young men in boating costume. Photographs of some of the remote and high places of the world bore testament to Vaughan's love of the outdoor life. The tiger-skin rug which lay, its teeth bared, in front of the fireplace, was presumably the same animal that appeared in a large photograph on the back wall. Vaughan stood with one foot negligently on the tiger's shoulder, rifle in his hand.

'He gets out and about, this chap, doesn't he?' said Ashley, gazing at the photographs with respect. He looked at the far wall, which was completely filled with books. 'Is he a scholar as well, I wonder?'

'According to old Lady Stuckley, he digs up dead bodies.' Jack grinned at Ashley's bewildered expression. 'She said as much last night. Apparently Vaughan's an archaeologist.'

Ashley's face cleared. 'I see. Tutankhamen, and so on.' He looked at the pottery with interest, picking up a small terracotta dish. 'It's like a museum in here. Is this a lamp?'

'It looks like a Roman lamp. It's probably about two thousand years old, maybe more.'

Ashley hastily replaced it on the shelf and continued to look round the room, pausing before the fireplace. A striking coloured print of an ancient temple carved out of red stone bathed in brilliant sunlight hung over the mantelpiece. '*Petra – The Treasury by David Roberts,*' he read. 'Is that the place in the poem? You know, *The rose-red city of Petra, half as old as time?* I like the way the sun brings out the colours in the rock.' Jack seemed oddly reluctant to comment. 'Haldean?'

'It's not bad,' he said eventually.

Ashley looked at him in mild surprise. In his experience, Haldean could usually talk the hind leg off a donkey about art. 'What's the matter?'

Jack made an obvious effort. 'Nothing.' He took a deep breath. 'It's a good picture but it's not the most dramatic angle. If I was painting it, I'd show how it looks when you first see it. There's a narrow passage through a cleft in the rocks that must run for a mile or more before opening out in front of the building in the picture. It's a stunning sight.'

Ashley's surprise increased. 'Have you been there?'

'I was there in the war,' said Jack. 'I was stationed at Ismailia on the Suez Canal. Most people know the poem about the rose-red city,' he said, turning away and idly flicking his finger along the spines of the books, 'but there's just about every shade of red except rose. Rose makes it sound pretty. It's not. It's a harsh, twisted sort of landscape.'

Ashley could virtually hear the full stop at the end of the sentence.

'D'you know,' continued Jack, 'Vaughan must have damn nearly everything ever written about the archaeology of Arabia.' He took a book from the shelf. 'Vaughan wrote this. *An account of the excavations in Petra in 1897-98, with some notes on the origins of the Nabateans.* Published by Wheeler and Street, 1900. I think Mr Vaughan might be a better archaeologist than Lady Stuckley gave him credit for.'

'Perhaps,' said Ashley. 'I'm surprised you've never mentioned you've been there.'

'It was a very brief visit.' Jack replaced the book back on the shelf.

Ashley waited for a moment, shrugged and wandered round the room once more, stopping in front of an unframed, mounted watercolour propped up on a raised reading-stand. It showed an ancient temple, its white stone dazzling in the sun, set against a background of towering red cliffs. On either side of the temple, stretching out in two curved arms, more buildings were carved out of the rock. 'Is this Petra?'

Jack picked up the picture and frowned. 'I don't think so,' he said after a little while. 'I don't recognize it.'

'It's an original,' said Ashley. 'Who painted it?'

Jack read the signature on the bottom. 'Someone signing themselves I.E. Simes, R.A. R.A. means Royal Academy, I suppose.'

The door opened and Vaughan came into the room. He stopped as he saw the painting in Jack's hands. 'Good morning, gentlemen.'

'Good morning, sir,' replied Jack. He replaced the picture on the stand. 'We were trying to place the temple in this picture.'

Vaughan gave a short laugh. 'I'd like to know, too. I hope to find out shortly. I'm sorry to keep you waiting but I was down at the boathouse. Now that spring's well and truly here, I wanted to get a couple of the boats caulked and varnished, but it's a messy job. I had to change before I came into the house. Do take a seat, gentlemen.'

'Thank you, sir,' said Ashley, sitting down.

Vaughan took a silver cigarette box from the mantelpiece,

opening and shutting the box with nervous fingers. 'Major Haldean, the Superintendent told me you'd be with him.' He glanced at Ashley. 'I know you want to ask me about my car, Superintendent, but first of all I'd like a brief word with the Major.'

'You carry on, sir,' said Ashley. 'It's your house.'

Vaughan sat down. He lit a cigarette, offering the box to Jack and Ashley. 'I want to apologize, Major, for that disgraceful scene in Claridge's last week. Durant Craig is a man whose abilities I admire, but his temper can be very difficult. Very difficult, indeed. Perhaps it's because he's lived so long abroad, but he's not a conventional man. He didn't tell me why he acted as he did but any fancied slight or minor mishap – the sort of thing an ordinary person would laugh off – becomes blown up out of all proportion.'

Jack, aware of Ashley's curious eyes, shook his head dismissively. 'It certainly wasn't your fault, sir.' He sucked deeply on his cigarette. 'Let's forget about it.'

Vaughan looked relieved. 'It's very good of you to take it like that, Major.' He looked at Ashley. 'Now, Superintendent, I gather you want to talk to me about my car. Have you found it?'

'In a manner of speaking, sir, but before I ask you for the details, there's something I'd like to clear up first.' He cleared his throat. 'I understand from Major Haldean you were with him at Hammerholt when a car caught fire last night. As you can imagine, sir, we're trying to piece together the events that led up to the fire. How fast would you say the car was going before the crash?'

Vaughan looked puzzled. 'I couldn't possibly guess. I don't know how the accident happened, if that's what you mean. I didn't see the car.'

'I didn't mean so much what you saw as what you heard,' explained Ashley.

Vaughan shot a glance at Jack. 'What I heard?' He hesitated. 'I heard an explosion, of course.'

'Before the crash, sir,' Ashley said.

'Before the crash?' Vaughan paused. 'I . . . I don't think I can help you, Superintendent. I'd only just come on to the terrace when the accident happened.' He picked at the buttoned arm of his chair. 'You were there, Major. How fast do you think it was going?'

'I couldn't say,' replied Jack. 'Obviously it had to be going at a fair old whack.'

Vaughan seemed reassured. 'It must have been, but I couldn't possibly say how fast.'

'So you didn't hear anything, sir?'

Vaughan concentrated on the buttoned arm of his chair once more. 'No, I can't say I did.'

Ashley gave an almost imperceptible shrug in Jack's direction. 'Never mind, sir. However, we have reason to believe that it was your car which was destroyed in the fire last night.'

Vaughan looked stunned. '*My* car? It can't be.'

'Your car was stolen, wasn't it, sir?' Vaughan nodded. 'Well, it's our belief that whoever took the car died in the accident.'

'*Died?*'

'So you see, sir, we're trying to establish who it was.'

Vaughan took a deep breath. 'If it really was my car, it was Durant Craig.'

'Durant Craig?' said Jack sharply. 'I can't credit Durant Craig would steal a car.'

Vaughan swallowed. 'As I said on the telephone, the circumstances were very peculiar.' He put his hands to his mouth and sat without speaking for a few moments. When he looked up, his face was strained. 'Look, before I say anything else, I'd like to be sure of my ground. Are you absolutely certain there was a body in the car?'

'Absolutely certain, sir,' said Ashley. 'It was unrecognizable, but we hope to learn more from the post-mortem. However, you think it was Durant Craig?'

Vaughan took a deep breath. 'It more or less has to be. This is terrible.' He looked at Ashley helplessly. 'What do you want to know?'

'Let's take it in order, sir,' said Ashley. 'When did you discover your car was missing?'

'Just before seven.' Vaughan shook himself as if collecting his thoughts. 'Craig did take my car, but you won't understand why unless I tell you the whole story.'

He stood up and, walking to the desk, picked up the unframed watercolour from the reading-stand. 'About six weeks ago I received this picture and a letter from a Mr Adler Madison, an American art dealer who specializes in antiquities.'

'Have you got the letter, sir?' asked Ashley.

'It's here,' said Vaughan. He opened the desk and, taking out a letter with an American stamp, passed it to Ashley.

'Adler Madison: Fine Art and Antiquities, 1168, Fourteenth Avenue, Manhattan,' he read out.

'As you can see from his letter, Superintendent, Mr Madison stated that he obtained my name and address from the British Museum. They had cited me as an authority on the Nabateans, the ancient inhabitants of Petra. You'll notice that Mr Madison's Christian name is Adler,' he added. 'It's a German name and suggests Mr Madison is of Teutonic origin. I must admit I didn't think anything of it at the time, but it was later to prove important.' He indicated the letter in Ashley's hands. 'You can read it for yourself, Superintendent, but the gist is that Mr Madison stated he was in Arabia in the war, in the region known as the Hejaz.' He indicated the picture of Petra that hung on the wall. 'Petra is the most famous city in the area.' Vaughan smiled fleetingly. 'I'm sorry if this all seems long-winded, but it is important, I assure you. To understand what followed, you must realize that I have long been interested in the archaeology of the Near East.'

He indicated the painting above the fireplace. 'Although Petra is mentioned in ancient chronicles such as Strabo and Herodotus, it was lost for many years until its rediscovery by the Swiss adventurer, Burckhardt, in 1812. It's a wild and remote spot, inhabited, when it's inhabited at all, only by a handful of nomadic Bedouin. I was fortunate enough to be a junior member of the great expedition led by Brunnow and Von Domaszewski just before the turn of the century. I was able to visit Petra again in 1920 but there is still so much more to learn.'

He leaned forward, his face eager. 'Perhaps you can understand how I felt when Mr Madison stated that, whilst in the Hejaz during the war, he and a companion, Simes, stumbled across a ruined city.'

He tapped the watercolour in his hand. 'As I say, he enclosed this picture. It's a painting of the city that they found. Simes had painted it from memory, so Mr Madison couldn't swear to its accuracy, but he thought it was a reasonable representation. To find a ruined city would not be remarkable in itself, for there are many such in the Hejaz, but he included photographs of three pieces he'd found there. I now have the pieces in my possession.' Vaughan leaned forward dramatically. 'Gentlemen, they are Nabatean!'

He went over to the safe and opened it. He took out a small carved alabaster dish, a tiny jug and a delicately carved ivory amulet in the shape of a scorpion, and placed them on the table.

Jack and Ashley gazed at the pieces in admiration. The alabaster dish had handles in the shape of lions, the jug was painted with an antelope and a tree, but it was the ivory scorpion which drew their attention.

'It's beautiful,' said Jack.

Vaughan picked up the scorpion, his fingers lingering over the delicate carving. 'It is,' he murmured.

He passed the ivory scorpion to Jack. As Jack held it in the palm of his hand, he could almost believe that the ivory tail would curl in defiance and the black stone eyes glint with threatening life. There was a hole just below the head for a thong to pass through.

'I believe the purpose of the amulet was to ward off scorpion stings by sympathetic magic,' said Vaughan, 'but whatever its purpose, it is an outstanding piece of work.' He took back the scorpion and replaced it on the table. 'Mr Madison didn't realize the significance of his finds for a long time, but can you imagine it?' His eyes blazed with enthusiasm. 'A Nabatean site totally unknown to archaeology! I'm not overstating the case to say that this could rival Caernarvon's finds in the Valley of the Kings. It was imperative that a preliminary expedition be organized at once. Should the site warrant it, I will return to carry out a full-scale excavation.'

'So what happened then, sir?' asked Ashley. 'With this Mr Madison, I mean.' They seemed to have strayed a long way from a missing Rolls-Royce, but he was interested.

'I wrote to Mr Madison suggesting that he should come

to England at my expense. He cabled to say he would arrive in Southampton on the 26th of this month. I made a reservation in his name at the Savoy.'

'The day before yesterday,' said Ashley.

'Indeed. In the meantime, I had not been idle. There's a great deal of organization involved in even a small expedition and the person I turned to for help was Durant Craig.'

Jack stirred in his chair and Vaughan looked at him apologetically. 'I know Durant Craig can be difficult but he's an absolute fountain of knowledge about Arabia and the Arabs. If he really is dead, he'll be a tremendous loss. He'd been in charge of the practicalities of my expedition in 1920 and he was the first person I thought of to manage this one. He would take charge of the travel arrangements, the hiring of native workmen, the supply of food and all the other hundred and one essential details. Madison would provide the directions and I would finance the whole venture.'

'That must be an expensive undertaking, sir,' said Ashley.

Vaughan shrugged. 'Fortunately, I am well able to afford it. I suggested that all three of us should meet here yesterday afternoon. The meeting, I am sorry to say, went very badly. So badly it resulted in the loss of my car.' Vaughan looked at them. 'I still can't believe it was my car in the fire.'

'We haven't got any definite proof yet, sir,' said Ashley, 'but it does seem likely. Tell me about the meeting. There were three of you, yes?'

'That's correct.'

'There was no one else present, sir?'

Vaughan shook his head. 'No.'

'I see, sir,' said Ashley placidly, with an almost imperceptible glance at Jack. He was, Jack knew, thinking of the woman's footprints. 'How did your visitors arrive, sir? By car or train?'

'By train. Brough, my chauffeur, went to meet them. Mr Madison arrived first, on the 1.46, and Craig arrived an hour later.'

'What went wrong?' asked Jack.

'Durant Craig,' said Vaughan with some bitterness. 'I knew Craig had a violent temper and was subject to blind prejudices, but I hadn't realized how much he hated Germans.'

'Was he still fighting the war, so to speak?' asked Ashley.

'Exactly, Superintendent,' agreed Vaughan heavily. 'Once Craig realized that Mr Madison was of German origin he abused him in a disgraceful way. You know what he was like, Major Haldean.'

Jack shifted uncomfortably. 'I suppose so. I don't really know him.'

'Don't you?' Vaughan looked at him quizzically. 'I thought . . . Never mind. Things went from bad to worse. We had tea about four o'clock. Craig was decent enough to keep quiet while the servants were in the room but as soon as they left, he started again. He said I'd got him here under false pretences and if he'd known there was a German involved – he actually said *bloody Boche* – he wouldn't have wasted his time. Madison, who had kept his temper all afternoon, flared up, and they had a real shouting match. I imagine the servants heard some of that. Anyway, Craig turned on me. He said he'd been to considerable expense over this affair and he expected to be paid for his trouble. I could whistle for the expedition, as he wasn't going to be involved with any damn Germans. I won't repeat what he actually said, as it was highly objectionable. I refused to give him a penny. He slammed out of the house, vowing he'd get his own back.'

'And what time was that, sir?'

'It would have been about half-past five or so. I felt it necessary to make some sort of apology for Craig's outrageous behaviour, so Madison stayed for a little while before I sent for the Rolls to have him driven to the station. I was astounded when the chauffeur informed me that the car was gone.'

'So what do you think happened to it, sir?' asked Ashley

Vaughan looked acutely uncomfortable. 'I thought Craig had taken it. He'd threatened to get his own back and it was the sort of high-handed thing he would do.'

Jack looked puzzled. 'I'd agree he was high-handed, Mr Vaughan, but I don't think Craig would steal your car.'

'I didn't say he stole it,' protested Vaughan. 'I said he took it. There's a difference. Durant Craig wanted me to pay him and I refused. Naturally, I don't imagine that anyone of Mr Craig's standing and reputation would steal a car worth

over three thousand pounds but I can see him keeping it until
I paid him what he thought I owed.'

'Holding it to ransom, you mean?' said Ashley slowly.

'Precisely.'

Ashley looked at Jack. 'What d'you think?'

'He might do that,' agreed Jack. 'Mr Vaughan, did none of
the servants see anything?'

'No. They have their tea about five o'clock or so and were
all indoors. My chauffeur doesn't spend all day in the garage
but works as a general handyman, too. I have –' he stopped
and corrected himself ruefully '– or had, perhaps I should say,
two cars, the Rolls and a two-seater, and the care and main-
tenance of them only take part of Brough's time.'

'Do you know anything of Mr Craig's personal life, sir?'
asked Ashley. 'Did he ever mention a wife or a family?'

'I don't think so, Superintendent. He lived at his club, The
Travellers, when he was in London.' Vaughan laughed
humourlessly. 'I remember thinking how lucky it was that
he was in England.' He hesitated, running a hand through
his hair. 'I can't think of much more to add.'

Ashley rose to his feet. 'You've been very helpful, sir. I'd
like a word with your servants, if I may. Did your butler
serve tea? In that case, I'll start with him. Would it be possible
for me to see him alone?'

'If necessary,' said Vaughan. He rang the bell.

'Thank you, sir. I'd appreciate either you or your chauffeur coming to Hammerholt with me to see if you can
positively identify the car.'

Vaughan's eyebrows rose. 'From what I saw last night it
sounds like an impossible task.'

'Nevertheless, sir, I'd appreciate it.'

'Brough better do it,' said Vaughan after a moment's
thought. 'He's far more qualified than I am to give an opinion.'
He stood up. 'I'll leave you to it.'

'What do you think?' asked Ashley, when he and Jack
were alone. 'It seems odd that Craig should go off the deep
end just because this Madison bloke is German. He's not
even German, not if he's from New York.'

Jack hesitated. 'Craig had a filthy temper. He might act
exactly as Vaughan described.'

'How well did you know him?' asked Ashley curiously.

'Hardly at all. Just enough to know about his temper.'

'I see,' said Ashley dubiously. 'Maybe you'll tell me more later?' There was a question in his words but Jack didn't respond. 'Ah well,' said Ashley, after a pause. 'It could be Durant Craig that Constable Marsh saw in the car.'

'It could be anyone,' said Jack. 'There's definitely some dirty work at the crossroads. That car didn't crash, I'll swear to it. Vaughan didn't take the bait about the noise before the fire, did he?

'No, he didn't. He didn't like the question, though. One thing I must do is get hold of this Mr Madison, to see if his account matches up with Vaughan's.'

'I want to know about this mysterious couple,' said Jack. 'After all, they were here and in the Hammer Valley. That alone tells us we haven't heard the full story.' He broke off as Oxley came into the room.

'Mr Ashley? Mr Vaughan said you wanted to see me, sir.'

FIVE

Ashley smiled at the burly man in front of him. 'Come in, Mr Oxley.' Jack saw Oxley's shoulders relax. Ashley, with instinctive courtesy, had given Oxley the dignity of *Mr*. It was the sort of practical psychology that made Ashley an excellent interviewer. 'I don't want to keep you any longer than I have too, but I'd be grateful for your help.' Ashley indicated an armchair. 'Shall we sit down?' he asked, taking a seat. 'I'm sure Mr Vaughan won't mind.'

'Just as you like, Mr Ashley,' said Oxley, dubiously. He sat gingerly on the edge of the chair. 'What was it you wanted to ask me, sir?'

'It's about yesterday afternoon. You know Mr Vaughan's car was stolen?' Oxley nodded. 'Major Haldean and myself are looking into it and I thought you might be able to cast some light on it all. Because, Mr Oxley, I don't mind telling you that it all seems very odd to me.'

'It was extremely odd, sir,' said Oxley, leaning forward. 'Mr Craig was a rough-spoken man but he was certainly a gentleman and why he should take it into his head to run off with the master's car is more than I can say. At first Mr Vaughan didn't know what to do, but he telephoned the police in the end, which was only right. I mean, gentleman or no gentleman, Mr Craig shouldn't have taken the car, even as a practical joke.'

'It wasn't a joke, particularly,' said Ashley. He glanced at Jack. 'We'd better tell Mr Oxley what Mr Vaughan thinks the reason was.'

Jack cleared his throat, taking up Ashley's obvious invitation to join in. 'Mr Vaughan told us there was some bad feeling between his guests yesterday afternoon.'

'There was, sir,' put in Oxley. 'I've never know anything like it in this house.'

'Apparently Mr Craig felt so aggrieved that he borrowed the car, if I can put it like that, without asking.'

'That makes more sense,' said Oxley, 'but it was a silly thing to do and inconsiderate, too.'

'I agree,' said Ashley, 'Theft is a serious accusation and we need to get the facts straight. So, I thought it would help if we could get some idea of what this argument was about. I know you wouldn't comment on Mr Vaughan's visitors in the usual way, but in this case we really want to hear your opinions. Who was the first guest to arrive?'

'That would be Mr Madison, sir. Mr Vaughan sent Brough to meet the 1.46 from London. It's about quarter of an hour's drive from the station, sir, and it was about two o'clock when Mr Madison arrived.'

'Can you describe Mr Madison?' asked Ashley. 'How old would you say he was?'

Oxley frowned. 'He'd be about forty or so, sir, perhaps a bit less. He was well dressed in a dark grey suit with a dark overcoat and soft grey hat.' Jack stirred but said nothing. 'He looked very smart, sir, but I wouldn't say his clothes were as good a quality as we're used to. His clothes weren't cut in the English way.' Oxley coughed deprecatingly. 'I've seen Americans at the pictures, of course, but I've never met an American gentleman in the flesh, as you might say.'

'What did he look like?' asked Ashley. 'Tall, short?'

Oxley sucked his cheeks in. 'I'd say he was about six foot or thereabouts and slim with grey hair. He had very blue eyes, that I do remember, and a scar on his cheek.'

'Was he pleasant?' asked Jack. 'Americans often are, in my experience.'

Oxley shook his head vigorously. 'No, he wasn't, sir. I didn't care for him at all, though it's not my place to say so. He had a way with him that chilled me through and through. He was hard as flint and as sharp. When he arrived, the master told Brough not to put the car away as he had to fetch Mr Craig from the station. Mr Madison was very put out. 'Craig?' he said. 'Who is Craig?' I could tell Mr Madison wasn't best pleased but the arguments really started when Mr Craig arrived.' He grinned. 'Without a word of a lie, I wondered if Brough had brought the wrong man. He looked like a great garden gnome, with a huge beard that stuck out every which way, a barrel of a chest and big bristling eyebrows. I tell you, sir, when I first saw him, I wanted to laugh.' Oxley's face clouded over. 'Not after he'd spoken to me, though. He marched into the house as if he owned the place, flung his hat and coat at me as if I was dirt and said, 'Here, you! Take these!''

'What were his clothes like?' asked Jack. 'Was he smartly dressed?'

Oxley nodded. 'His clothes were very good quality, sir, but very well-worn. His hat was made by Lock, but old, as I say. It was a deerstalker.'

Jack exchanged a look with Ashley. 'What, a sort of Sherlock Holmes affair?'

'Yes, sir. A lot of older gentlemen prefer them for travelling. It didn't really become him, although perhaps I shouldn't say as much. Anyway, I showed him in here, and that's when the fireworks started.' Oxley coughed and looked suddenly ill-at-ease.

'I don't suppose you happened to hear what was said after you'd shown Mr Craig into the room?' asked Jack. At a guess, Oxley didn't want it to be known he'd listened at the door. 'I mean,' he added, throwing the butler a lifeline, 'if Mr Craig had a carrying voice, you couldn't help but overhear, could you?'

Oxley looked at him gratefully. 'That's it exactly, sir.' He pulled at his ear. 'Having said that, sir, it didn't seem to make any sense. Mr Vaughan said something about the journey and they all talked for a bit, then Mr Craig gave a kind of roar, like a wild beast, and yelled out, 'I'll have nothing to do with any damned Hun and especially you, you filthy Kraut.'

'Good Lord,' said Ashley. 'That's a bit extreme.'

'I know, sir,' agreed Oxley, 'it was. I couldn't understand it. Mr Madison wasn't a Kraut.'

'He was of German origin, apparently,' said Jack.

'Perhaps that explains it, sir, but it did seem strange. I served tea at four o'clock. They weren't shouting, but that's about as much as you can say. You could have cut the air with a knife. Mr Vaughan looked as if he'd had a real turn. Mr Madison was stood by the shelves, and as for Mr Craig, he was sat bolt upright in the armchair, his back to the room, sulking. No one said much and I left the tea things. Oh yes, and Mr Vaughan asked me what Brough was doing. He'd told him to repoint the garden wall that morning, and he wanted to know how it was coming on.'

'And how was it coming on?' asked Jack. 'Repointing is a messy sort of business.'

'All right, sir, although it's a long job.'

'When did you next see Mr Vaughan?' asked Ashley, slightly impatient with Jack's interest in the garden wall.

'I went to clear up at half four or thereabouts, but things hadn't improved. Mr Craig was still sulking in the armchair.'

'Had they all had tea?' asked Jack.

Oxley frowned, remembering. 'Yes, sir. There were definitely three dirty cups and saucers on the tray, and three dirty plates as well, from the sandwiches and cake.'

Ashley looked sharply at Jack, but he said nothing.

'Did you hear any more arguments?' asked Ashley after a pause.

'I did, sir. As I took the tea tray out, they started again but I didn't catch what was said. Then it was time for our tea. We didn't hear anything more until the bell rang about half five.' He looked at them apologetically. 'I suppose I should have answered it, but I was enjoying my tea, and I'd taken my boots off, so I sent Doris, the girl, to see what the master wanted.'

'Could we speak to Doris?' asked Ashley.

'She's in the kitchen garden, sir. Perhaps you wouldn't mind stepping round, gentlemen,' said Oxley doubtfully. 'I wouldn't usually ask but I don't want Doris Tiverton sitting down in the master's study. She has enough ideas as it is, without me encouraging her.'

'Let's go and talk to her, then,' said Ashley, rising to his feet.

Oxley led them through the French windows and around to the back of the house. As he opened the door in the white wall, they could hear a bustle of noise from the kitchen across the yard. A walled kitchen garden, the vegetables in neat rows, stretched down to the woods behind the house. A young girl, holding a basket of rhubarb, was walking up the path.

'Doris!' called Oxley. 'Here's some gentlemen who want

to ask you a few questions about yesterday. This is Major Haldean and Mr Ashley, and he's our Robert's Mr Ashley, so mind your manners.'

Doris, a pretty, fair-haired girl of about sixteen, came forward eagerly. 'Are you from the police?' She turned to Oxley. 'I was right, wasn't I? I said there'd be trouble with that American gangster and that strange man. I knew it as soon as I cast eyes on them. I said as much, didn't I. Mr Oxley?'

Oxley was obviously shaping up to tell the girl off when Jack stepped in. 'Excuse me, Miss Tiverton. Did you say *gangster*?'

She tossed her head back. 'I knew he was a gangster even if he didn't have no tommy gun. Eyes like ice, he had. They went right through you. I've seen gangsters at the pictures *and* he was American. We talked about nothing else all afternoon, and then the master's car got pinched and I'm sure I wasn't surprised, only I'd have thought it would've been the gangster who pinched it, not the other one.'

Ashley, who had also seen Oxley's disapproval, interposed a question. 'You answered the study bell, didn't you, Miss?'

'That's right. We were having our tea, and Mr Oxley had his slippers on, so I said I'd go, because to tell you the truth, sir, although I'd had a peep out and seen both of them as they arrived, I wanted to have a closer look, I'd heard that much about them. I was on my way to the study when I heard the front door give an almighty slam, as if someone had stormed out, and when I got into the study, there's the master and the gangster –'

'Mr Madison,' put in Oxley, unable to restrain himself.

'Mr Madison, then,' she said with another toss of her head. 'Although you said a few things about him yesterday, Mr Oxley, you know you did. I couldn't see the other man, and I wasn't sorry in a way, because he was scary, for all we laughed. I asked the master, I said, 'Has the gentleman gone?' and he said he had. The master had rung the bell for him to be shown out, but he'd gone without waiting. Visitor's coats and things are in the hall, so I don't suppose we have to show guests out, but we always do. He must have been in a terrible rage. Anyway, the master said he wanted a light supper at half seven, which is early for him. That's because he was going to this party, and we knew about that anyway.'

'And how did your master and Mr Madison seem?'

'They were fine, sir,' she said, with a touch of disappointment. 'They seemed very friendly.'

'I can vouch for that,' said Oxley. 'Mr Vaughan rang for me later in the evening to say Mr Madison was going. I saw him to the door, sir, and helped him on with his things, and Mr Vaughan came outside with us, while we waited for Brough to bring the car round.'

Ashley nodded. 'That's useful to know. Can we see the chauffeur?'

'He's in the kitchen,' said Oxley. 'I'll ask him to come outside.' He leaned his head inside the kitchen door and called for Brough. The chauffeur, a moustached man of about thirty with a worried expression, came down the steps into the yard.

'I've been expecting the police,' he said. 'I thought that bloke was a rum 'un.'

Ashley took him through the day, verifying the times of the trains. 'Do you want to ask anything?' he asked, turning to Jack.

'Was there much fuel in the tank, Mr Brough?'

'Yes, sir. I'd filled her up that morning.'

'And was there a rug of any sort in the car?'

'Yes, there was, sir. A big green travelling rug.'

Jack looked at Ashley with raised eyebrows. 'That could have been handy.'

'It sounds as if it was,' said Ashley dryly. 'What time did you get the car out to take Mr Madison to the station?'

'It was ten to seven or so,' said Brough. 'Only the car was gone.'

'Hold on a minute, Mr Brough,' said Jack. 'I just want to get this straight. You put the car away in the garage after picking up Mr Craig from the station at three o'clock, yes? Did you go into the garage during the afternoon?'

Brough shook his head. 'No, sir. You see, I do all the general handyman work.' He gestured to the wall that surrounded the kitchen garden. 'The master asked me to repoint the wall yesterday so I was busy all afternoon. When

I came to get the car, I couldn't believe it'd gone. I opened the garage and I didn't know what to think. I must have stood there for a few minutes, scratching my head, like, and then I thought there was nothing else for it, I'd better tell the master what had happened.'

'I wondered what on earth was wrong, Sam,' put in Oxley. 'We were standing at the front door, me, the master and Mr Madison, when you appeared. You looked bewildered.'

'That's a fact,' said Brough. 'You could have knocked me down with a feather. Anyway, the master couldn't believe it either, and came to see for himself. Mr Madison walked round to the garage with us. He suggested Mr Craig had gone off with the car. I could see the master didn't like the idea, then Mr Madison said he didn't mean Mr Craig had actually stolen the car, only taken it to get his own back.' Brough broke off and looked apologetically at Ashley. 'I didn't really follow what they were talking about, sir, so I might have got that wrong.'

'No, that agrees with what Mr Vaughan told us,' said Ashley.

'Well, the master told me to drive Mr Madison to the station in the two-seater, but Mr Madison said he'd walk as he'd been cooped up all day and wanted to stretch his legs.'

'Would he have time to get to the station?' asked Jack.

'Yes, sir. If he started off there and then, he'd be all right.'

'I felt sorry for the master,' said Oxley. 'He didn't know what to do, but eventually he said there was nothing for it, and he'd have to tell the police. He telephoned them about eight o'clock or so, but didn't say anything about Mr Craig. They wanted to send someone round, but the master said no, as he was going to a party.'

'I drove him there in the two-seater, sir,' said Brough. 'The party was at Hammerholt, about sixteen miles away.'

'We know,' said Ashley. 'If you drove Mr Vaughan there last night, Brough, you'll know there was a fire in the valley.'

'I do indeed, sir. It made us very late home, but it couldn't be helped. A car caught fire, didn't it?'

'I'm afraid,' said Ashley, 'we think that car was Mr Vaughan's Rolls-Royce. And,' he added, looking at Brough's stunned expression, 'I'd like you to come over to Hammerholt to see if you can identify it.'

Brough drove to the Hammer Valley in the two-seater so he could return home under his own steam. This arrangement suited Jack very well as, with Ashley beside him in the Spyker, they could talk freely.

'So,' said Ashley, 'we're supposed to believe that Craig stormed out of the house, took Vaughan's Rolls and . . .' He frowned. 'Do you believe Craig could have taken the car, Haldean?'

'Oh, yes,' agreed Jack. 'Very easily. He was a high-handed sort of beggar.'

'The man PC Marsh saw driving the car sounds like Craig. I think Craig's our victim.'

'Perhaps,' said Jack. 'Although the hat we found in the Hammer Valley was grey. It wasn't Craig but Madison who had a grey hat.'

Ashley whistled. 'This gets more complicated by the minute,' he complained. 'It *has* to be Craig in the Rolls. How on earth could it be anyone else? It can't have been Madison. He was there when Brough reported the car was stolen. The hat might have nothing to do with it. After all, there were enough people in the Hammer Valley last night to have dropped a hundred hats. Incidentally,' he said, looking at Jack, 'I wish you'd tell me what you know about Craig.'

'I came across him in the war,' said Jack tightly. 'We . . . we didn't see eye to eye. That's all.'

'Are you sure that's all?'

Jack took a deep breath. 'Ashley, all I really know is that he had a foul temper. That, and he was the top-notch great-granddaddy expert of experts on Arabia and the Arabs, the "Don't question me, boy, I was doing this when you were wet behind the ears" type.'

Ashley looked at Jack's rigid profile and gave up. 'I wish I knew who this couple in the car were,' he said, after a fairly loaded silence. 'No one knew a thing about them, did they?'

Jack relaxed. 'No, and,' he added with a grin, 'I bet Doris Tiverton would have had something to say if she thought Vaughan was entertaining mystery women.'

'Yes, she was a good witness, wasn't she? It's thanks to her that we know when Craig left.' Ashley flipped open his notebook, checking the times. 'That was at half five.'

'And at quarter to six p.m., as he would say, Constable Marsh stopped a bearded bloke driving what we assume is Vaughan's Rolls-Royce in Lower Haverly. Right?'

'Right. Our next definite time is ten to seven, when Brough realized the car was gone. Almost immediately afterwards he saw both Vaughan and Mr Madison, so they were on the spot for sure. Now I know Mr Madison walked to the station, but Vaughan was definitely around for the rest of the evening, until he went off to the Stuckleys'. And we know there's nothing dodgy about that, because Brough drove him there.' Ashley sighed. 'I know there's been some jiggery-pokery, but it's hard to see what. To be honest, I'm inclined to believe Mr Vaughan is telling the truth as he saw it. It fits in with what I gathered about Craig's character.'

'Yes, it does,' said Jack. 'There was one thing that struck me, though. Brough told us he filled the car up yesterday. Now the fire happened about half ten, and judging from what I saw, the car must have been full of juice. So, granted that Craig nicked the Rolls, what the dickens did he do with it? I'm absolutely certain sure that he didn't do what he was supposed to have done, which is smash it into a tree at half past ten. He can't have driven round aimlessly, otherwise he'd be low on juice.'

'Could he have driven to the Hammer Valley and left the car there? Vaughan could've mentioned the party, which could be why Craig chose the Hammer Valley to hide the car.' He snapped his fingers. 'How about this? Say this mysterious couple are friends of Craig's. What if Craig swiped the car, telephoned them from a public call box and asked them to meet him in the Hammer Valley? Although it obviously went wrong, the idea was that they'd take him back to London or wherever.'

'By jingo, Ashley, that'd work!' exclaimed Jack. 'My word, that'd really work. It doesn't explain the footprints and the car tyres at Vaughan's, but it explains a dickens of a lot.' The speed of the Spyker, which had increased in a direct index to his mood, slowed again. 'Actually, that opens up another possibility, doesn't it? There's a dead body to account for and Craig had a lousy temper. It could be the other man who died.' He shuddered. 'I hope it's not the woman.'

Ashley let his breath out slowly. 'That's something I hadn't thought of. We'll know more tomorrow,' he said, brightening. 'Dr Wilcott will have done the post-mortem by then and we'll know if it's a man or a woman, if nothing else. If it is a woman, Craig's got some questions to answer.'

'There's another possibility,' said Jack, after a pause. 'I know we talked about it earlier, but what if Vaughan drove the car? Again, I'm not sure who on earth this man and woman can be, but he'd have to have some sort of confederate and they're as good as any. If Vaughan was the driver, he'd have to leave the house as soon as he'd spoken to Doris Tiverton at half five and we know the car was in Lower Haverly at quarter to six.' He glanced at Ashley. 'What d'you think? I bet I could get from Vaughan's house to Lower Haverly in quarter of an hour or so.'

'I bet you could,' said Ashley with a grin. 'Whether Vaughan could is a different matter, wouldn't you say? We're back to the idea that Vaughan murdered Craig, aren't we? What about this Madison chap? He'd have to be in on it, too.'

'Maybe Doris Tiverton was right when she called him a gangster. Madison seems to have put the wind up everyone, so let's say he is in on it. Is that an overwhelming objection?'

'Not overwhelming,' said Ashley, after a few moments' thought. 'I'd say it made it unlikely, though. And there's another thing. If this Madison bloke doesn't blink at murder, why bring in this mysterious couple? Why didn't he simply follow Vaughan in the two-seater and bring him back from the Hammer Valley afterwards?'

'Maybe he can't drive,' said Haldean with a shrug.

'Maybe,' agreed Ashley dubiously. 'Yes, that's the obvious answer. At least it explains why they were both in the Hammer Valley *and* at Vaughan's. Vaughan would have to drive like a bat out of hell, though, to be back at his house for ten to seven. I don't know if it's possible.'

'Let's work it out. First of all, I'm assuming that Craig's

tetchiness got too much for everyone and he was bumped off. Now what do you do with a corpse? It's a nasty thing to have cluttering up your study, so Vaughan and Madison decide to dispose of it. Madison can't drive, so Vaughan rings up A. N. Others and asks for a helping hand.'

'He'd have to phrase that phone call pretty carefully.'

'So he would,' agreed Haldean. 'He probably wouldn't Reveal All on the phone. I know I wouldn't, knowing that the exchange were sitting there with ears flapping. He might simply ask for help with a problem. That would cover it. Okey-doke, what now? I noticed that when Oxley served tea at four o'clock, Craig was sitting with his back to the room. He was still sitting with his back to the room when Oxley came back at half four. I wonder if he was dead.'

Ashley choked. 'What! He can't have been. Oxley heard another quarrel break out as he left the room.'

Jack looked at him quickly. 'So?'

'So the quarrel could've been have staged for Oxley's benefit,' said Ashley slowly.

'I'll tell you something else, too. Vaughan told us there'd been an argument and Oxley said they'd been going at it hammer and tongs. Now, does anyone, in those circumstances, break off and calmly have afternoon tea? We know they were all *supposed* to have had tea, because there were three lots of dishes used, but from what we've heard, it seems a lot more likely that Craig would have thrown his cup at Madison, not sat there placidly asking the man to pass him another cucumber sandwich.'

'I'm not so sure,' said Ashley. 'Lots of people like a cup of tea if they've been under a strain.'

Jack grinned. 'There speaks the spirit of England. I still think it's unlikely. The other thing I noticed was that Vaughan made a point of asking if Brough was repointing the wall. You see what I'm getting at? For Vaughan's plan to work, he'd have to be certain that Brough didn't go near the garage.'

'So that's why you were asking about the garden wall! I wondered why you were so interested.'

'You see where this leads, don't you? As soon as Oxley's cleared away the tea things at half four, Vaughan and Madison put the body in the car, knowing the servants are all busy with their tea. It's easy enough to get out of the French windows and the study's on the same side of the house as the garage. Then, come half five, Vaughan rings for Doris Tiverton, staging Craig's supposed departure by slamming a door. As soon as Doris is out of the way, Vaughan, who's been waiting like a greyhound in the slips, grabs his false beard and shoots off to the Hammer Valley, meeting PC Marsh on the way. He places the car artistically against a tree, hops into A.N. Others' car, and is back in the study for ten to seven, prepared to be thunderstruck when Brough tells him the Rolls has been pinched. How about that?'

'Hold on,' said Ashley. 'I want to jot down these times. As I see it,' he said, after a pause, 'Vaughan has from just after half-five until ten to seven, which is,' he said, adding up the times in his notebook, 'an hour and a quarter. I think he'd be pretty lucky to do it,' he said dubiously. 'I don't know if it's possible.'

'An hour and a quarter?' repeated Jack. He made a dissatisfied noise. 'He'd be cutting it fine, I agree. It's about sixteen miles in all. Half of an hour and a quarter is thirty-seven-and-a-half minutes. Thirty-seven minutes isn't much time, and that's leaving no margin to sort things out at the other end.'

'And he was stopped by PC Marsh,' put in Ashley.

'And he stopped to chew the fat with PC Marsh,' agreed Haldean.

'Why didn't Vaughan set off at half four? Granted that Craig was dead by then, that is? After all, he could have summoned Doris Tiverton into the room at any time he liked. He didn't have to call her at half five.'

Jack shrugged. 'Vaughan and Madison would have to have some time to plan what they were going to do. And, if the A.N. Others really were involved, they'd have to get hold of them somehow or other. No, it's not that which bothers me, it's the lack of time. I wonder, granted how desperate the circumstances were, if it's possible. Somebody set fire to that car and that somebody could so easily be Vaughan. If Vaughan drove over and arranged the body, he had to do it between half-past five and quarter to seven. He can't have done it earlier because both he and Craig were seen by Oxley and he can't have done it later because he was seen by Oxley and the other servants, too.'

'It's not impossible, though, is it, Haldean?' said Ashley. 'I quite like the idea. It explains things, you see.' He gestured at the road. 'We're doing much the same journey now and I grant it's going to take longer than thirty-seven minutes, but you're not pushing it, are you?'

'Having to follow Brough is cramping my style somewhat. Besides that, with one of the leading lights of the Sussex Constabulary sitting beside me, it wouldn't be tactful.'

'What if you did push it?'

Jack turned the idea over for a few moments. 'I'll tell you what. This car's as fast as a Rolls-Royce. Would you do the journey with me to see if the shot's on the board? I'd like you there, not only to verify the time but to bail me out if I get nabbed for speeding.'

'All right,' said Ashley. 'It'd be nice to know if it is possible. We should set off at half five, to try and stay as close to Vaughan's supposed times as much as possible. I'll be busy for the rest of the day, but we could do it tomorrow, perhaps.'

'OK,' agreed Haldean. He reached out and patted the dashboard of the Spyker. 'Can you believe it? An excuse to put this old girl through her paces and all in the name of the public good. This is *my* sort of detection.'

SIX

Jack looked up as Ashley came out of Market Breeden police station and down the steps to where the Spyker was drawn up by the side of the road. It was five o'clock on a fine spring evening.

'I very nearly had Isabelle and Arthur along for the ride,' said Jack, opening the passenger door for Ashley. 'Belle's convinced Vaughan's guilty, you know.'

He caught Ashley's look and held up his hands pacifically. 'Don't blame me. I didn't say a dicky-bird. Brough told Doris Tiverton that it was their car, so to speak, that had gone up in smoke and she immediately told her young man, whose mother keeps the fishmongers in Market Breeden, who gave the news free to anyone who brought six penn'orth of cod or a nice piece of haddock. The Stuckleys got the news with an order of hake and Marjorie was on the phone to Isabelle right away. As Isabelle knew I thought there was something dodgy about the crash, it took her about two ticks to decide that as it was Vaughan's car, Vaughan must have bumped someone off and incinerated him, together with the Rolls-Royce. She says she can see it in his eyes, although exactly when she got to stare into Vaughan's eyes is something that beats me. Anyway,' he added, climbing into the car, 'I've asked everyone to keep the gossip under their collective hat for the time being.'

Ashley laughed ruefully. 'It'll take a bit more than a look in someone's eyes to convict them, thank goodness. The fact it was Vaughan's car in the fire will be in the papers tomorrow, in any event. Do they know Craig's involved?'

Jack nodded without speaking. It was odd, this shrinking reluctance he had to say Craig's name. Odd, but Isabelle understood, and so did Aunt Alice.

'It can't be helped, I suppose, but for the time being, we're keeping quiet about Craig. I don't like the idea of Vaughan being talked about as a possible murderer, either. At the moment it's a tragic accident.'

'Don't worry,' said Jack. 'I argued the toss with Isabelle, you know, because although I think it's possible that Vaughan's guilty, that's all I think, and Arthur . . .' He hesitated. 'Arthur thinks Craig's a far more likely murderer than Vaughan. Who he murdered is another question, of course.'

Ashley looked at him sharply. 'What does Captain Stanton know about Craig?'

'He was with me in Claridge's when Craig took exception to my presence.' He smiled reflectively. 'He's a good sort, Arthur. He didn't demand to know what it was about.'

Ashley, who had been about to not demand, but at least ask, what was behind the encounter in Claridge's, took a leaf out of the absent Arthur Stanton's book. 'I've been on to the Travellers' Club, by the way,' he said after a pause. 'The secretary was very helpful. They haven't seen Craig since Saturday morning, but it's not unusual for him to disappear without mentioning it. He told me a few details, most of which we know. Craig's got no family and no close friends, not in this country, at any rate. He can drive, though. Apparently some of the members have heard him mention it, but he doesn't like motor cars much.'

'If he doesn't like cars, he's probably not much of a driver,' said Jack thoughtfully. 'That might or might not be important. By the way, have you got the results of the post-mortem, yet?' he asked, as the car picked up speed.

'Yes, as far as they go. Dr Wilcott apologized for how little information he'd been able to gather, but the body was badly affected by the fire.'

'Is it a man or woman?'

'It was a man, which I must say I was relieved about, but that's more or less all he could say. The body was so badly damaged, he couldn't tell me the age or the height or anything much. The man had all his own teeth, but that was about it. One thing he could verify though, was that the victim was dead before the fire started. There was no smoke or soot in the lungs.'

'Ah,' said Jack in deep satisfaction.

'As you say, Ah. Wilcott thinks he died as a result of that blow to the temple, but what caused it he can't say. He couldn't find anything in the car to account for it, so it looks as if your idea about the body being placed in the car after death is right.'

'Everyone a winner,' murmured Jack. 'It's a bit of a long shot, having seen the fire, to say nothing of the remains, but was there anything left on the body which could identify the bloke?'

'Perhaps,' said Ashley unexpectedly. 'There's a metal card case which might help, together with the remains of a wallet, some loose change, a watch, and a key. The key has a fob and looks as if it belongs to a club or hotel, rather than a private house. The wallet's too charred to be any use but the card case is more hopeful. I got the report and the things from Wilcott just before I came out. Wilcott tried to open it but it was fused shut by the heat. It was in the man's inside jacket pocket and had been sheltered by his arm to some extent. Wilcott had to cut it loose.'

'That sounds pretty gruesome,' said Jack with a shudder. 'I know it's sentimentality, but I'm glad it's not a woman.'

'So am I,' agreed Ashley, as Jack negotiated a corner. 'Anyway, come back to the station with me after we've finished. If all else fails we can have a crack at it with metal cutters. Something else has come up, though, that could kick all our ideas into touch. That Madison chap didn't show up at the Savoy either last night or the night before.'

Jack gave a low whistle of surprise. 'Didn't he, by Jove? Did he leave any message at the hotel?'

'No.'

'But . . .' Jack let his breath out in an apprehensive sigh. 'I don't like the sound of that.'

'Neither do I. I telephoned the Savoy to speak to Mr Madison, and they said they hadn't seen hide nor hair of him since Saturday morning. I'm getting Scotland Yard to look into it. I've already spoken to your pal, Inspector Rackham, and agreed to go up to Town tomorrow. If Mr Madison is there, I need to interview him. If not, Rackham and I are going to take a look at his hotel room.'

'The Savoy, eh? D'you know,' said Jack with a significant glance, 'it's a pleasant place. Particularly good for lunches and afternoon tea and so on. Morning coffee, too. I'd like to have coffee at the Savoy,' he added meaningfully.

'Not at the ratepayers' expense, you don't,' said Ashley. 'However, there's nothing to stop you buying a cup of tea and a currant bun off your own bat.' He caught the question in Jack's eyes and laughed. 'And – I suppose I should have said this in the first place – Inspector Rackham did wonder if you'd be able to give Madison's room the once-over with us.'

'Good old Bill,' said Jack with a delighted smile. 'Thank you, Ashley, invitation accepted with pleasure. I'll be there in my best bib and tucker, posh hotels and haunts of the rich for the use of. But what d'you think could have happened to Madison?'

'I don't know. We worked out that if Vaughan was guilty, Madison was involved, so he could have made a run for it, I suppose. I'll tell you something else, though. After I drew a blank at the Savoy, I spoke to the ticket collector who was on duty at Market Breeden station on Saturday evening. Four people boarded the seven-thirty train to London and the ticket collector recognized them all as locals. So whatever train he did catch, it wasn't the one he said he was going for.'

'If he caught the train at all,' said Jack softly.

Ashley looked at him. 'So that's the way your are thoughts are going, is it? I must say it had crossed my mind too.'

They drove on until they came to the turning for Two Bridges. Jack drew the car into the slanting shadows at the side of the road, turning it round so they were facing up the hill. They were, he realized, in the same spot where the diamond-tyred car had waited. It was a good spot to keep an eye on Vaughan's. They were sheltered from the house by the trees but could easily see anyone coming or going. He looked at his watch. It was twenty-five past five. They had five minutes before they had to go.

Jack switched off the engine and took out his cigarette case, offering it to Ashley. 'I hope we manage to come up with some hard facts soon,' he said after a while. 'We've got too many theories buzzing around at the moment.'

Ashley looked at his watch. 'It's gone half five. Let's start, shall we? At least this'll tell us if one of our ideas is credible.'

'OK.' Jack started the car. 'Hold on to your hat. This is going to be quick.'

Once out on the Chavermere Road, Jack opened up the throttle and the Spyker leapt forward, leaving a comet trail of dust behind. Within minutes they slowed to a crawl to negotiate their way through the vexingly quaint streets of Chavermere and over the narrow packhorse bridge on to the thankfully straight length of the Haverly Road. Jack put his foot down again. The needle flickered and settled to around fifty.

'This is about as fast as I can go,' shouted Jack over the sound of the engine. 'Any more and we'd be in the ditch.'

They gunned up a hill and twisted away to the right, flashing past a solitary cart trudging its way home. They caught a glimpse of the carter's white, startled face as he receded into the distance. Jack geared down as the road turned and Ashley felt the car lift slightly before Jack increased the speed at the sight of a long straight stretch before him. The sun was behind them, throwing long shadows forward as they raced between fields and ditches and lines of oaks and elms.

They were on the road to Lower Haverly when, far in the distance, a cowman stepped into the road and waved them down. Jack braked, skidded, and braked again, running the Spyker to a halt. The cowman stood in the middle of the road, looking placidly at the approaching car. He gave a sign to a boy standing by a field gate, behind which stood a herd of cows. The boy opened the gate, fastened it with a loop of rope to a stone post standing by the side of the grass verge and, stick in hand, slowly ushered the mooing cattle across the road. The cowman leaned against the gate, drew his pipe out of his pocket and lit it with great deliberation. In the evening light, with the banked-up clouds streaked pink against the clear blue of the sky, it was a scene which could have been painted by Constable. It was timeless, rustic and unbelievably irritating.

'Look at the blasted man,' said Jack in mounting exasperation as the cowman, wreathed in blue-grey fumes, watched his charges idle into the opposite field. 'He could be posing for a still life.'

Ashley raised himself up from his seat. 'Hey, you there! Do you always move the herd at this time?'

The cowman looked up, thought for a few moments, and sucked on his pipe before replying. 'Yes, zur. Evening milking.'

'Do you remember stopping a big car, a Rolls-Royce, the night before last?'

The cowman plunged into deep thought. 'Yes, zur,' he said eventually. 'Very impatient, he was. Why, do you know him?'

'If it was a bloke with a beard, yes,' said Jack.

'That's the one.' The cowman smiled slowly. 'It'll learn him to hurry. He had to stop so sharp he broke his lamp, he did, on that post,' he said, pointing. 'He asked me to hurry my cows, but you can't hurry cows.' As if to add point to his words, he turned to watch the dawdling cattle amble through the gate.

Jack, itching to get on, turned to Ashley in exasperation. 'Honestly, if it was Vaughan, I'm surprised he didn't murder this chap while he was about it. This is knocking minutes off our time.'

'And off the Rolls-Royce's,' Ashley reminded him. 'At least we know PC Marsh's Rolls came along here. Get ready, Jack, they're nearly through now.' The cowman slapped a dilatory cow on the behind, closed the gate with painstaking care and sauntered across the road.

With a sigh of relief, Jack let in the clutch, and concentrated on getting the Spyker back up to speed. The long stroke of the engine growled, picked up the pace, and for a few brief, exhilarating minutes, the needle flickered around sixty. Then the road curved round the lee of a valley and started to snake between rolling downs. Jack had no choice but to drop down to forty and, as he crested a hill and saw the lights of Lower Haverly, throttled back to the sedate, if legal, limit of twenty.

They chugged through the narrow streets of the village. Ashley waved a friendly hand as he passed a police constable, toiling out of the village on his bicycle. 'Quarter to six,' he called out, glancing at his watch. 'We're keeping pace with the Rolls.'

For the next few miles the road twisted between a necklace of villages, strung out along the road. To Jack, feverish to get on, it seemed as if he'd scarcely nursed the Spyker into fourth before he had to gear down again. They climbed the gradient to Upper Haverly and coasted down to Hampwood. All the villages, Holt Common, Brabant Marsh, Gifford St Mary, Gifford St Stephen, Gifford St Luke and Shapbridge, had to be negotiated at the legal limit and, in between, there were farms with straying chickens and plodding, patient horses. Even if it were possible, Vaughan couldn't have risked drawing attention to himself by racing through, even though his life depended on it. Which might literally be true, thought Jack, with an odd sensation. It was impossible to do much more than thirty, and that only in short straights. From the crest of a hill they caught a distant glimpse of the river Breeden, gleaming in the last light of the sun, then it was swallowed up as they plunged between high hedges once more.

In Gifford St Luke he turned on the lights and concentrated solely on driving in the gathering dusk on the unfamiliar road. He let her go after Shapbridge, encouraged by the comparative straightness of the road, took a bend too fast, slid, lurched and rolled as they clipped the ditch. Any more like that and they'd burst a tyre. Sobered, he throttled down to around thirty and it was with a real feeling of relief he saw the dark bulk of Hammerholt on top of the next hill. He drew in to the entrance to the Hammer Valley and switched off the engine. 'How long did it take us?' he asked, his voice loud in the sudden silence.

Ashley slowly shook his head, looking at his watch. 'I'm sorry, Haldean. It took forty-one minutes and I can't believe he could have driven any faster than you. You gave that everything you had, didn't you? But if you couldn't do it, Vaughan can't possibly have done it. We have to allow at least ten minutes for him to get the car into the glade and arrange the crash. Even if he had a confederate to rig up the accident, so all he did was drive straight back home, he couldn't have managed it. It just isn't physically possible.'

Jack rested his head on the steering wheel. 'It's one to chalk up to experience, I suppose. So Vaughan's innocent.' He rubbed his face with tired hands and smiled ruefully. 'So much for Isabelle's insights. And my theorizing, come to that,' he added.

'It's well worth knowing,' said Ashley. 'To rule anyone
out is invaluable, especially with this mysterious pair in their
car knocking about and with Mr Madison having disappeared.
We have to clear the wood to see the trees, so to speak.'

'Fair enough,' said Jack. 'Do you want to go back to the
police station?'

'If you don't mind. You're coming to look at the card case,
aren't you? That might tell us something. But,' he added with
a smile, 'stick to the speed limit, there's a good chap.'

Jack grinned and started the car. 'Scout's honour. D'you
know,' he added as he turned out on to the main road once
more, 'I think the solution might lie in London. I wonder if
we'll turn anything up in the Savoy tomorrow?'

'I wonder,' said Ashley, 'what we'll find in that card case.'

The tarnished metal of the card case sat on the table. It had
been a slim, handsome, silver thing with a now illegible
name engraved on the front. 'Here goes,' said Ashley and
picked up the metal cutters. Jack held the case while Ashley
snipped through the end.

Jack turned the case in his hand, picked up a pair of
tweezers and delicately probed inside. With a grunt he drew
out a set of cards. They were browned with the heat but still
perfectly legible: *Adler Z.Y. Madison: Fine Art and Antiquities,
1168, Fourteenth Avenue, Manhattan.*

'Well,' said Jack. 'That puts a different complexion on
things.'

Ashley looked at the cards on the table as if he'd been
thunderstruck. 'Damn me,' he breathed. 'Madison! It was
Madison who was killed, not Craig.' He looked at Jack
sharply. 'You suspected this, didn't you?' Ashley sat down
and rested his chin in his hand. 'I thought it was strange that
Madison should have disappeared. But look, Haldean, if
Madison's dead, then presumably Craig killed him.'

'Well, we know Vaughan can't have done it. I've just taken
about five quids' worth of rubber off my tyres proving he can't
have done it. Besides that, Madison and Vaughan were chattering to Brough after PC Marsh saw the bearded bloke in the
Rolls-Royce.'

'But that means no-one could have done it,' said Ashley

in frustration. 'Madison can't be curled up dead under a rug in the back of the Rolls and be seen alive and well three-quarters of an hour later. It's impossible.'

Jack sat down and lit a cigarette. 'Yes, it is,' he said after a while. 'Put like that it is impossible, therefore we're putting it wrongly. It's like watching someone pull rabbits out of a hat, isn't it? You know they can't be in there but they are. Pick a card, any card . . .' He relapsed into silence once more. 'Let's say Craig swiped the Rolls,' he said, stubbing out his cigarette. 'Let's also say that Vaughan reacted exactly as Brough told us he did. Now we know Vaughan can't have got up to any rannygazoo after seven o'clock. Not only did the servants see him, he was driven to the Stuckleys' by his chauffeur. So that's him out of it.' He looked up at Ashley and grinned. 'You're watching me awfully intently, old thing.'

'I'm waiting for the rabbit,' said Ashley. 'I'm sure you've got one tucked up your sleeve.'

'And jolly uncomfortable it is, too. However, although we know Vaughan's OK, we can't say Madison's OK, because no-one saw him after he left for the station, and he didn't catch the train.'

'If he ended up dead, he's certainly not OK, poor beggar.'

'No . . . Where was I? Durant Craig, in a towering rage, has just pinched a highly expensive Rolls-Royce. So he drives off in the direction of the Hammer Valley, scaring cows and passing the time of day with Constable Marsh on the way. Now, I don't know if it was the sight of PC Marsh or what, but he could have regretted acting so hastily. On the other hand, knowing how filthy his temper is, he might have wanted to continue the quarrel. Either one is possible. So he drives back to Stour Creek and, on the way, sees Madison walking to the station, stops the car and asks Madison to get in. Then things turned nasty.'

'You mean Craig murdered Madison in the car?' asked Ashley.

'That's right. He could have easily hit him with a wrench or something.'

'He could have done,' said Ashley thoughtfully. 'There was probably some sort of tool to hand by the driver's door and if there were bloodstains or marks of violence in the car, that'd give him a pressing reason to get rid of the Rolls. Yes, I quite like that idea. But look, what about the rug or whatever it was PC Marsh saw in the back of the car? It sounded as if it was covering something up.'

Jack shrugged. 'It's hard to know what he saw, isn't it?'

'Perhaps,' said Ashley. 'Leaving that aside, where does this couple fit in?'

'Well, much as we thought, only they're Craig's friends and help-meets, so to speak. He phones them up, arranges to meet them near Vaughan's and together they drive off to the Hammer Valley, with Craig in the Rolls and the help-meets in the diamond-tyred car. Then Craig sets fire to the Rolls and makes himself scarce in the other car.'

Ashley digested this in silence. 'That's fairly convincing, as a matter of fact,' he said eventually. 'It gets rid of the tight timetable and it explains what everyone's doing and why.' He stood up and stretched his shoulders. 'With any luck we should know more when we've had a look round Madison's room. I asked Inspector Rackham to cable New York to see what they could dig up about him.' He glanced at the business cards on the table, their condition bearing mute witness to the fury of the fire. 'I didn't realize I was enquiring about a murder victim, though.'

SEVEN

It was nearly twelve o'clock the following day when Jack and Ashley got to the Savoy, which was, as Jack hopefully pointed out, just in time for lunch.

Ashley, who had entered the hotel in a slightly defensive frame of mind, wasn't thinking of lunch. He didn't eat in places like this. The Savoy: images from some of the more lurid sections of the Sunday newspapers jostled in his mind. Duchesses laden with diamonds, Indian Maharajas, American millionaires, licentious clubmen and Mata Hari-type temptresses, all summed up by that satisfying phrase, The Idle Rich.

He envied Haldean's self-assurance as they walked into the lobby together. Mind you, he thought grumpily, Haldean was the sort of person who would feel at ease here. He was used to this sort of thing. After all, he lived in London and he *looked* the part, damn it, so easily elegant in a dove-grey suit, a violet in his buttonhole and a dark blue tie, with his coat casually unbuttoned. Ashley's mackintosh was both buttoned and belted. His wife had wanted him to buy a new coat last autumn. He wished he hadn't insisted that there was plenty of wear left in it and it would do for another year.

The first person he saw was Inspector William Rackham, deep in conversation with a worried-looking man in pinstripe trousers and a frock coat. Ashley had telephoned Rackham that morning to bring him up to date. He was pleased Rackham was there, but, damn it, even Rackham, although as big, as untidy, and as ginger-haired as Ashley remembered, was perfectly at ease in these luxuriant surroundings.

Rackham turned as they entered the lobby and greeted them both with a broad smile. 'It's good to see you again,' he said in his rich Northern accent. 'Thanks for your call this morning,' he added to Ashley. He indicated his companion. 'This is Mr Bonner, the assistant manager, who's very kindly offered to help us.' He turned to the manager. 'You'll excuse us, sir, if we have a brief word in private.'

Rackham drew Ashley and Jack off to one side, lowering his voice confidentially. 'There's something a bit rum about your Mr Madison. I got a reply to my cable to New York. Mr Madison doesn't exist.'

'*What?*' Ashley and Jack stared at each other. 'But he must exist,' said Ashley. 'You gave them his address, didn't you?'

Rackham nodded. '1168, Fourteenth Avenue, Manhattan. Yes, I gave them that, but it's not an art dealer's, it's a large, cheap hotel called Beletsky's. They've got no record that anyone called Madison ever stayed there.'

'But he must have stayed there,' said Ashley, his voice rising. 'Vaughan wrote to him there. He sent a cable, he was so anxious to meet the man. Damn it, the British Museum recommended Vaughan to Madison. They must have written to Madison too.'

Rackham shrugged. 'If he was under a false name, he could have arranged to collect any post or wires that came in the name of Madison.'

'That's true enough,' said Jack. 'He could have bribed the desk clerk or simply said he was doing a favour for a friend.'

Ashley let out his breath in a long whistle. 'Well, I'll be damned. Look, before I completely go off my head, tell me this hotel knows something about this Madison bloke. He stayed here, didn't he?'

'Oh yes,' said Rackham. 'He stayed here all right.'

'Well, that's something, I suppose.' Ashley glanced to where the assistant manager stood patiently waiting. 'Does he know there's anything fishy about Madison?'

'Not a thing. There's something else, though. You know you were looking for a mysterious couple? Well, a woman came here, first thing on Sunday morning, asking for Mr Madison.' He tapped his breast pocket where he kept his notebook. 'I've got a description of her. She's in her twenties, fair-haired and quite a looker, apparently.'

Jack's brow wrinkled. 'But if she's our woman, so to speak, she must know Madison's bought it. Why's she asking to see him?'

'I think it was a ruse to get into his room. She didn't seem surprised that Madison wasn't here, but immediately asked if she could go up to his room to wait for him. She was so quick off the mark, it put the clerk on his guard. The clerk refused, as they had no instructions from Madison to admit anyone. He asked her if she wanted to wait, but she said she didn't have the time and pushed off. *And* – what d'you think of this? – there was a bearded man waiting for her in the entrance to the lobby. They left the hotel together.'

Jack gave a slow smile of satisfaction. 'Wow. And again, wow. I don't want to leap to conclusions, but that sounds like Craig to me.'

'But if it was Craig,' said Ashley, 'he took a dickens of a risk coming here.'

Rackham shook his head. 'As I said, it was first thing on Sunday morning, and that's only hours after the fire. No one was looking for him then and it was the woman who spoke to the clerk. It was only pure chance that the clerk saw the bearded chap. I think there must be something worth finding in Madison's room, though.'

'I think you're absolutely right,' said Jack. 'Let's go and see, shall we?'

They walked to where Mr Bonner was standing beside the registration desk.

'I believe you're looking for a guest of ours, Superintendent,' said Mr Bonner. His voice had a pleasant Welsh lilt. 'The Inspector tells me Mr Madison may have met with an accident.'

Yes, thought Jack, to Mr Bonner it was an accident. He didn't know if Bonner had read the account of the *Tragic Fatality in East Sussex* that had appeared in that morning's newspapers, but even if he had, the victim was *Durant Craig, the Noted Explorer,* not an obscure American art dealer. The real identity of the dead man wouldn't be published until tomorrow and even then Jack doubted if it would receive more than a few lines. Accidents, unlike murder, weren't news.

'Yes, sir,' said Ashley. 'Can we see the register?'

'Of course.' Bonner opened the book on the desk. 'As you can see,' he said, turning to the relevant page, 'Mr Madison arrived on the twenty-sixth. Last Friday.'

'*Adler Madison, New York*,' read out Ashley. 'That's not very informative. Can you tell me anything about him?'

Bonner shrugged. 'Very little, I'm afraid. I have, of course, gone into the matter since Inspector Rackham telephoned. Mr Madison arrived, I believe, on the *Berengaria* which docked in Southampton at six o'clock on Friday morning. He said as much to the clerk. He arrived at the hotel before midday and took a single room with a bathroom. He told the clerk he was uncertain how long he would be staying. As far as I can ascertain, he had a bath and went out, returning late that evening. He certainly didn't dine here. The next day he left the hotel immediately after breakfast and that, gentlemen, is the last anyone saw of him. His things are still in his room.'

'Did he hand in any valuables for safe-keeping? His passport, for instance?' asked Rackham.

'I'm afraid he didn't,' said Mr Bonner apologetically. 'I've enquired.'

'Did he speak to anyone in the hotel?' asked Ashley. 'Mention where he was going or anything like that?'

Mr Bonner shook his head. 'The only people he spoke to were the desk clerk and the porter who carried his bags to his room. Neither of them can remember anything about him, apart from the fact that he was a man of forty or thereabouts, tall and grey-haired.'

'Was the room booked in advance?' asked Jack.

Bonner nodded. 'Yes. It was arranged in advance by a Mr Vaughan of Chavermere, Sussex.'

The three men exchanged glances. 'Well, that ties up, at any rate,' said Ashley. 'D'you know, Haldean,' he said in an undertone, 'to be fair to him, everything Vaughan told us stacks up.' He cleared his throat. 'Will you show us Mr Madison's room, Mr Bonner?'

'Certainly.' He led the way out of the lobby up the main staircase to the wide first-floor corridor of the hotel. 'This is Mr Madison's room,' said the manager.

Ashley intervened. 'Excuse me, sir, can I try this key?' He opened his briefcase and took out a key with a blackened fob.

It turned in the lock. 'Bingo!' muttered Jack.

Ashley put the key back in his briefcase with quiet satisfaction. 'That's what I expected, but I'm glad it fitted, all
the same.'

Mr Bonner led them into a single room looking out over
the Embankment. It was furnished with a neatly made bed,
a gleaming mahogany chest of drawers, an armchair and a
wardrobe. A desk, containing a blotting pad, a small collection of books and a box of thin black American cigars, stood
under the window. A travel clock, its hands pointing to 3.36,
stood on the table by the bed. The bathroom was at the rear
of the room. Depressingly, from a detective point of view,
both the bedroom and the bathroom had obviously been
thoroughly cleaned.

Jack looked in the bathroom. The only personal belong-
ings were a safety razor, a toothbrush and a plain toiletry
set. He went back into the main room. 'What's in the
wardrobe?'

The wardrobe contained two coats, four suits, five shirts
and a set of evening wear, all bought from Altman and Levy's,
the New York store. 'There's no names on any of these
clothes,' said Jack. 'They're all ready-made.'

'That's an interesting economy,' said Rackham. 'Granted
that he was well-off enough to stay here, I'd have expected
him to have his clothes made by a tailor.'

Mr Bonner smiled deprecatingly. 'You wouldn't credit the
petty economies practised by the wealthy, Inspector, especially if –' he coughed apologetically – 'if they are what is
sometimes termed self-made men.'

'We don't actually know he was well-off,' said Ashley.
'After all, Vaughan paid for him to come over here and for
him to stay in the hotel.'

'Well, never mind his clothes,' said Rackham. He started
to hunt through the chest of drawers. 'I'd like to see his passport, though.' He searched rapidly through the drawers
without result. 'He might have taken it with him.'

Jack started to search in the desk. 'It's not here, Bill, but
look at this. You know you thought he might not be well-
off?' He held out two envelopes he had taken from the desk.
One contained a hundred American dollars and the other a
hundred and fifty pounds in English notes.

Ashley whistled. 'He can't be that hard up, not with that amount of money lying about.'

Jack sat by the desk, looking at the books. There was an anthology of poetry in English, a copy of Nietzsche in German, a couple of American detective stories and a book he recognized as a genuine rarity, Charles Montague Doughty's *Travels in Arabia Deserta*. He picked it up. On the inside cover was written *Adler Zelig Yohann Madison!*

He frowned. Why the exclamation mark? He turned as Ashley gave a little grunt of surprise. He had taken out a large flat cardboard box from the bottom of the bedside drawers and laid it on the bed.

Inside, wrapped in tissue paper, was a leather-covered sketchbook. Ashley opened the book at random. Every page was filled with postcard-sized paintings, three or four or more to a page.

'These are rather nice,' said Jack in appreciation. He turned the pages of the book. 'They're very well drawn.' They were coloured drawings rather than watercolours and they were all scenes of the Near East. Some of the places were well-known; the pyramids, the sphinx, the statues at Abu Simbel. Other places he didn't recognize but they were all desert scenes, some by moonlight, some in brilliant sun. Some showed Bedouin camps or caravans, full of life and movement. There were Turkish and German soldiers and Arabs in white robes and colourful headscarves. Interestingly enough, there were no British troops.

'Who painted the pictures, Jack?' asked Ashley.

'Simes,' said Jack, looking at the neat signature at the bottom of each picture. He turned to the front of the book.

'He's the chap who painted that picture Vaughan showed us, isn't he?' said Ashley. 'The one of the ruined city.'

Jack nodded. 'That's right. I'll explain it all later, Bill, but Vaughan said this bloke Simes was a friend of Madison's.'

He turned to the front of the book. 'Blimey,' he said in surprise. 'His full name's a bit of a mouthful. *Ingulf Eberhard Simes*. He must be another German. A German-American, at least. He's a pretentious sort of beggar,' he added, looking at the front page. In large italics, Simes had written the title of the book; *A Tide In The Affairs Of Men: Pictures From*

The East by I.E. Simes, R.A. and, underneath, a few lines of poetry.

'Listen to this,' he said, and read the poem aloud. '*A hundred thousand dragons lie, Underneath an Arabian sky. The Silent Ones, when asked, will measure, the hidden way to dragons' treasure. With a body once so fair, a princess guards the dragons' lair.*'

There was a pause as Jack, Ashley and Rackham digested the poem. Mr Bonner looked totally blank.

'What's all that about?' asked Rackham. 'Dragons and princesses? What have dragons and princesses got to do with it?'

Jack shrugged. 'Search me. *A hundred thousand dragons lie* . . . Do you know anything about dragons, Mr Bonner?'

The manager, rather surprised to be appealed to, shook his head vigorously. 'Indeed, no. Dragons are the emblem of Wales, of course, but Mr Madison was American, not Welsh.'

'The Chinese have dragons,' said Jack musingly. 'And princesses, too.'

'St George fought a dragon,' put in Rackham.

'I shouldn't think there's much saintliness kicking about,' said Jack. 'Besides that, I don't think, strictly speaking, St George's dragon really is a dragon. It's something to do with the Latin word. Apparently the word for snake is usually translated wrongly as dragon, which means poor old St George is a lot more credible but a lot less fun.'

'Do they have dragons in Arabia?' asked Ashley.

Jack shrugged. 'I haven't a clue. They sound like the sort of thing that'd crop up in the *Arabian Nights*.' He paused, staring blankly at the book. 'The trouble is, it sounds as if it should mean something, but God knows what.' He flicked through the pages of the book once more. 'There aren't any dragons in it. Or princesses either, come to that. I don't know. It's all a bit over the top for a book of watercolour drawings. The pictures are nice enough but they're not great art.'

'What about the title?' asked Ashley. '*A tide in the affairs of men* . . . That's Shakespeare, isn't it?'

'Yes, it is. *Julius Caesar*, I think, although I can't swear to it.'

'Well, between Shakespeare, Julius Caesar, princesses and dragons, we seem to have found a real mare's nest, if you ask me.' Ashley scratched his chin. 'Who the devil is this bloke?'

'Exactly,' said Jack. He tapped the book with his finger. 'I want to know more about Simes. With a name like Ingulf he doesn't sound very British, but the R.A. after his name could mean Royal Academy. There's a chance it's the Royal Artillery, I suppose.'

'He must have been a pretty rum artilleryman,' said Bill Rackham with a smile. 'Quite apart from his blessed princesses and so on, you pointed out there were no British soldiers in his paintings.'

Jack grinned. 'I suppose R.A. could be an American abbreviation of some sort.'

'I don't suppose you've got anything on file about Simes back at the Yard, have you?' asked Ashley.

'I'll certainly check,' said Rackham. 'We might be lucky.'

'We'd better take the book with us,' said Ashley. He rewrapped the book, replaced it in the box and looked round the room in dissatisfaction. 'I must say I'd hoped to find a bit more about Mr Madison, but there's no passport, no notebooks, no diary or letters.'

'There's his full name,' said Jack, picking up the copy of *Travels in Arabia Deserta*. 'Adler Zelig Yohann Madison, with an exclamation mark.' He clicked his tongue. 'Do you think our Mr Madison's having a laugh?'

'It's doesn't appeal to my sense of humour,' said Ashley. 'I don't know what to make of it all, and that's a fact.'

Rackham turned to Mr Bonner. 'Can we take the personal bits and pieces with us – that clock and his toothbrush might have his fingerprints on, for instance – and leave the clothes and so on to be packed up by the hotel? We'll give you a receipt for the various items, and we'll have Mr Madison's cases picked up in due course. That means you'll be able to use the room once more.'

'Certainly, gentlemen,' said Bonner. 'I'll give instructions for Mr Madison's things to be packed up right away.'

Once back at Scotland Yard, Rackham requested the Records Office to see if there was any record of Simes. While they were waiting, Jack opened the watercolours and pulled out his notebook.

Rackham looked over his friend's shoulder. 'What are you doing?'

Jack had jotted down a collection of letters and two names; Adler Zelig Yohann Madison and Ingulf Eberhard Simes. 'I'm trying to see if there's a connection between them,' he said, tapping the pencil on the book.

'Apart from them knowing each other, you mean?'

Jack lit a cigarette. 'They certainly do know each other, but I wondered if the connection ran a bit deeper than that. It could be nothing but coincidence, but both have got English surnames and German Christian names.' He frowned. 'It's the exclamation mark Madison put against his name which is getting to me. It's a bit self-conscious, as if he'd done something clever.'

'How d'you mean?' asked Ashley. 'There's nothing very clever about writing your name in a book.'

Jack raised an interrogative eyebrow. 'Don't you see what I'm getting at? It would be clever if he'd just invented the name. We know there's something dodgy about Madison. I was trying to see if I could turn Simes into Madison and vice-versa.'

'You think they're the same person?' asked Rackham in sudden comprehension. 'By jingo, that's a thought. Do the names have the same letters?' He looked at the paper and shook his head. 'Well, if they do, I can't see it.'

'No, neither can I,' said Jack, regretfully.

The door opened and a uniformed constable came in carrying a buff-coloured folder. 'I believe you wanted see if we had anything on Simes, sir.'

'We've got something?' asked Rackham eagerly.

'Yes sir. It's from the New York Police.' The constable gave the folder to Rackham and left the room.

Rackham opened the folder. 'By God! Simes is wanted for murder.'

'What?' exclaimed Ashley. 'Murder!'

'Yes,' said Rackham, reading the notes rapidly. 'Simes was an inmate of Blackwell's Island Prison. He was a model prisoner until the end of last month. Mind you, he seems to have spent a fair old time as a patient in the hospital. He went down with influenza which left him an invalid for quite a while. He recovered though, which was a bad break for one of the guards, poor devil. On March the twenty-first – that's only a few days ago – Simes killed a guard and escaped. His present whereabouts are unknown. The New York police sent us notification in case he should turn up over here.'

'They weren't expecting him to land up in Britain, were they?' asked Ashley.

Rackham read on and shook his head. 'I don't think so. Look, here's some notes on his background. He's a German-American born in Cincinnati, Ohio, 1883. He served in France in 1918 and the Army of Occupation in Germany in 1919 with the American 15th Light Field Artillery, Second Division. He was discharged in January 1920. In July 1920 he set up as an art and antiques dealer in Manhattan. Madison is an art dealer, isn't he? That's something they've got in common. He's thought to have links to a gang who specialized in the theft of fine art.' He raised his eyebrows. 'Robbery seems a bit more violent in New York than we're used to over here. That was never proved but he's suspected of dealing in stolen artworks. What he was actually had up for was selling forgeries.' He grinned. 'In December 1921 he tried to sell a Mr Abraham P. Fisher, a noted art collector, a Manet that Mr Fisher already owned, and Mr Simes' misdeeds came to light. Well, well.'

'I don't believe that army record,' said Jack. 'Not if Simes painted those watercolours. They're all pictures of the East, not France and Germany. Is there a photo of him, Bill?'

'No,' said Rackham. 'There aren't any fingerprints either. I'll wire New York again. If Simes was in prison, they must have that information. We should be able to lift some prints from his things. Once we get his photograph, we can show it to the Savoy people and Mr Vaughan. If you're right, Jack, and Madison and Simes are the same person, that's one part of the mystery cleared up. With a murder charge hanging over him, he'd want to get out of America in double-quick time.'

'Can I see his photograph, once you get it from New York?' asked Jack.

'I'll send you a copy.' He looked at Ashley. 'I'll send one to you as well, of course.'

'Bill,' asked Jack thoughtfully, 'you know the book of paintings we found? I can't help feeling there's more to it than meets the eye. I wondered if it contained a secret message.'

'A code, you mean? Maybe. It's obscure enough to, that's for sure. I could let an expert take a look at it, I suppose.'

'Good. There might be nothing in it, but I can't help feeling there is. *A hundred thousand dragons . . .*'

'One would be enough to be going on with,' said Rackham with a grin. 'Never mind dragons for the moment.' He looked at Ashley. 'I was thinking about what Oxley, Vaughan's butler, overheard when Craig lost his temper. He said, *I'll have nothing to do with any damned Hun and especially you, you filthy Kraut.* That's right, isn't it?'

Ashley nodded. 'Yes, that's right.'

Rackham leaned forward. 'D'you know, I think that's a very suggestive remark. To my mind that phrase, *Especially you, you filthy Kraut,* suggests that Craig didn't just loath Germans but loathed Madison in particular.'

Jack sat up. 'Bill! That's it! They *knew* each other.'

Ashley smacked his fist into his palm. 'You're right! All the servants thought Madison was an American. For Craig to work out so quickly that Madison was German means he *must* have known him. That accounts for the quarrel. We know there's something not right about Madison. I'll bet those two had some unfinished business. Vaughan knows more than he's telling us, I'll be bound. The question is, where did they know each other from?'

'From Arabia?' suggested Jack. 'After all, Craig's a noted Arabian traveller and Vaughan said Madison had been in the Hejaz during the war . . .'

He broke off suddenly. As he said the words, a possibility so awful came into his mind, his stomach turned over. The nightmare that had whispered to him ever since he had seen Craig that day in Claridge's grew to a scream. It was more than a possibility; he was horribly, sickeningly, absolutely certain. *Eyes like ice, he had. They went right through you.* That's what Doris, the maid had said. *Eyes like ice . . .*

'Oh, my God.' He didn't know he had spoken out loud.

'Jack?' said Rackham. 'Jack, what is it?'

He couldn't find the words. 'Nothing,' he managed eventually. 'Absolutely nothing.' He didn't want them to guess anything was wrong. He tried hard. 'It just reminded me of something, that's all.'

Ashley leaned forward. 'Haldean,' he said, his voice very earnest. 'You know something about Craig. What?'

He couldn't tell them. This was *his* nightmare. If he had to come clean, he would, but he had to be certain. 'I'm sorry, Ashley. I might be wrong.'

Rackham and Ashley exchanged worried glances. Jack was sitting in a posture of rigid isolation, completely unmoving, apart from his right hand which clenched and unclenched on the leg of his grey suit. Rackham moved forward impulsively, then stopped. He saw his friend's shoulders tense and could only guess the effort it took him to straighten up and look him in the eyes.

'The photograph,' said Jack with studied carelessness. 'When you get a photograph from New York of . . .' He stumbled the words. '. . . of Simes, then I'll know. I have to know.'

He tried to smile. It was a miserable failure of a smile, but Bill Rackham suddenly knew he'd seen raw courage.

With Isabelle beside him, Arthur Stanton leaned over the bridge spanning the river that ran through the grounds of Hesperus, watching the bridge make a shivering mirror of itself in the gently lapping waters.

He should have been completely happy. The spring sunshine sparkled off the water, the trees casting broken, shifting shadows over the river. A flock of mallard ducks, the sun catching their glittering spring plumage, circled themselves with sun-flecked hoops amongst the fringes of the weeping willows. He should have been happy, but Isabelle knew he wasn't.

'What's up, Arthur? You're worried. It's nothing to do with the wedding, is it?'

'No.' He hesitated. 'It's Jack.'

'Jack?' asked Isabelle quietly.

'There's something wrong. Something happened in London.

For the last few days he's been as twitchy as a cat on hot bricks and I'm damned if I know why.'

Isabelle bit her lip and said nothing.

'You know what it's about, don't you?' asked Arthur.

She squeezed his hand. 'I don't know what happened in London. He told me he's waiting for a letter from Bill Rackham.'

'You'd think he was waiting for his death warrant, he's so edgy.'

'Don't be mean. It's only because you know him inside out that you've noticed. He was fine with everyone at dinner last night. He talked to the curate for absolutely ages about the Apostolic Succession, and he partnered Mrs Channon-Sywell at bridge without a murmur. I think he deserves a medal.'

'Yes, but he wasn't talking to us, was he?' said Arthur shrewdly. 'It's all very well chatting up the local worthies, but they aren't going to ask what's eating him, are they? This all started in Claridge's, when that ghastly chap, Craig, came and tore a strip off him. I couldn't credit it,' he added moodily, watching a duck up-end itself in the reeds. 'Jack simply took it. He didn't defend himself, he simply stood there. What's more, he said he deserved it, which I can't believe for one minute. I wanted to help but he wouldn't let me. We've been friends for ever, and I can't seem to do a damn thing. I know it's to do with Arabia. I knew he'd been out East but I'd virtually forgotten about it, it was so long ago. Why shouldn't he tell me?'

She looked at him helplessly. 'Something happened to him there. Something he's ashamed of.'

'What?'

She took a deep breath. 'I can't tell you,' she said eventually. She drew an arabesque on the honey-coloured stonework of the bridge with her fingertip, gazing sightlessly at the water. 'Arthur, I wish you'd speak to him. It'd do him good to talk instead of bottling it up.'

'Do you really think it'd be good for him?' asked Arthur.

'Yes, I do.'

'In that case,' said Arthur, 'I'll do just that. The worst that can happen is that he can tell me to mind my own business. '

Leaving Isabelle on the bridge, he walked swiftly back into the house.

Jack was near the front door, looking at the mid-morning post, which had been placed on the hall table. He had a large flat brown envelope in his hand and the expression on his face made Arthur catch his breath.

Arthur had a speech planned, but what he was going to say went out of his head. He looked from the envelope in his friend's hand to his anguished face and reached out impulsively. 'For God's sake, what is it? Let me help.'

Jack swallowed. 'Wait.'

It was one word, yet it brought Arthur up sharp.

Jack picked up the paperknife from the table, his fingers clumsy. He had to concentrate on holding the knife. He slit the envelope open and took out the contents. There were two photographs and a letter.

Arthur honestly thought his friend was going to collapse. Jack gave a juddering breath and clutched at the table for support.

'It's him,' whispered Jack. 'Oh, God, it's him.'

Arthur took an appalled look at Jack's grey face. Catching hold of his arm, he led him out of the hall and into the library. Shutting the door firmly behind them, Arthur helped Jack to a chair and knelt beside him. 'Jack. Please trust me. Please tell me what all this is about.'

EIGHT

Jack sat in the chair and rubbed his face with his hands, his breath coming in little ragged spurts. Arthur looked anxiously round the room. There were decanters, glasses and a soda syphon on the sideboard. He quickly mixed a brandy and soda and put it into Jack's hands. He had to close his fingers round the glass. 'Here, let me help,' he said quietly. 'You're spilling it.'

Jack drank without seeming to know what he was doing, then sat, clutching on to the empty glass. Arthur took it from him and put it on the floor. Jack still sat with cupped hands, his body racked by odd little shudders. Arthur knelt in front of him, trying to get a response, but Jack's eyes were blank and unfocused.

'Jack?' said Arthur. No response. Arthur took one of the cold hands between his own and shook it. 'Jack?' he repeated in a firmer voice.

Jack blinked, then breathed out in a long, juddering sigh. It was like life returning. He tried to speak, but Arthur stopped him.

'Wait a minute. Get your bearings back, old man.' He was rewarded by a grateful look, then Jack shuddered and slumped back in his chair.

'Where's the letter?' he asked at last. 'The letter from Bill?'

Arthur picked it up from the floor and held it out to him doubtfully. 'Are you sure you want to see it again?'

Jack nodded. 'Open it, will you?' He swallowed. 'I don't know if I can.'

Arthur glanced through the letter. 'He's been to the Savoy and shown them the photographs. The clerk on the desk is fairly sure that the man in the photographs – Simes – is their Mr Madison.'

Arthur took the photographs out, holding them away from Jack. They were both of the same man from two different angles, a man in prison uniform. He must have been around forty or so, grey-haired with a high-boned face and thin lips.

There was an old scar on his left cheek. He looked, thought Arthur, an unforgiving, dangerous type.

'Let me see,' said Jack. Arthur turned the pictures towards him. Jack put the back of his hand to his mouth in a defensive gesture. 'OK. That's enough. It's him.'

Arthur put the photographs face down on the floor and Jack leaned forward, elbows on his knees, hand to his forehead and eyes closed. The clock on the mantelpiece ticked the seconds away in sonorous clunks, spacing out the silence. Outside, through the open library window, came the sound of birdsong and, from far away, the distant sound of a lawnmower. Arthur waited.

Eventually Jack raised his head and met his friend's eyes. 'Thanks, Arthur. I'm fine now. Thanks.' He sat back in the chair and tried to get his cigarette case out of his pocket.

'I don't think you're fine at all,' said Arthur in real concern, watching his friend's clumsy efforts. 'Here, have one of mine.' He gave a cigarette to Jack, took one himself, lit them both, then sat back on his heels.

'I've been half-expecting this,' said Jack quietly. 'I had an awful feeling it'd turn out to be him, but it was still a rotten shock.'

'What's it about?' said Arthur. 'There's obviously something badly wrong. You've been living on your nerves the past few days.' Jack shifted uneasily. 'Look, I know what it's like to keep everything bottled up. It doesn't work. Whatever it is, whatever happened, won't you let me help?'

Jack studied his face. 'I don't know if you can.'

'You could try.' Arthur tapped his forefinger on the face-down photographs. 'Who is he?'

Jack smoked his cigarette down to the butt, crushed it out and took a deep breath. 'He's had a few names. Simes, Madison, and, in Arabia during the war, he was known as Ozymandias. He was a sort of Lawrence of Arabia figure. The newspapers made a thing of him at one time. They thought he was glamorous, God help us.'

'Ozymandias?' Arthur repeated the word slowly. 'Hold on, that rings a bell. Is he a Turk?'

'He's German. He was an advisor to the Turks. His real name is Lothar Von Erlangen. He's the most ruthless man

I've ever met. Do you know *Ozymandias*, the poem by Shelley?' Arthur nodded. 'There's a line in it, a chilling line, which sums him up. *Look on my works, ye mighty, and despair.* That's him. He brought despair.'

Arthur moved uneasily. 'Isn't that overstating it?'

Jack shuddered. 'I didn't think so. I don't know if you'll agree when you hear what happened. It was the early summer of 1915. I'd been posted to Ismailia – it was my first squadron. I suppose my first achievement was staying alive. The first few weeks could be lethal for pilots, but after that, anyone was entitled to call themselves a veteran. I'd been there for nearly three months . . .'

The wind sang in the wires of the Farman biplane as Second Lieutenant Jack Haldean, following his flight commander's plane, flew over the tents and huts of Ismailia. He checked the direction of the wind, and brought the craft round for as good a landing as could be managed on the bumpy sandy ground. It had been a quiet patrol, with no sign of any Turkish craft. There had been no sign of anything, apart from dun-coloured sand and scrub, rimmed in the distance by the glittering line of the Mediterranean. The two aircraft taxied to the hangers. Jack switched off the engine, hearing the sounds of the airfield once more as the propeller spun to a standstill.

The heat, as always, once the rush of air from the plane had stopped, seemed to flare up like opening an oven door. Jack unbuttoned his jacket, took off his leather helmet and goggles, stuffed them in the pocket beside his seat and, replacing the helmet with an Australian bush hat, climbed out of the cockpit and jumped lightly to the ground.

The hat had cost him three bottles of beer from a cavalryman in Port Said. The Flying Corps, young and irregular, was indulgent in the matter of uniform, especially in Ismailia, so far away from top brass and spit-and-polish, and Jack's bush hat had set something of a new fashion.

His flight commander, Captain Sykes, was standing by his machine in front of the entrance to the hanger, talking to the chief fitter, McAvoy. He looked round as Jack strolled up. 'Any problems?' he asked.

'Not really, but the left wing's flying a bit low,' he added with a look at McAvoy. 'Can you see to it?'

McAvoy pursed his lips. 'It'll be this afternoon before we can do anything, sir.' He pointed into the green canvas gloom of the hanger. 'I've just been telling Captain Sykes that we've got a bit of a job on with this new plane that's arrived.'

Jack followed Sykes and McAvoy into the hanger, blinking as his eyes adjusted from the blinding sun of the airstrip. Four of the fitters were working on a two-seater aircraft with staggered wings and two machine guns in the forward cockpit. 'My word,' he said, helping himself to a glass of lime juice from the jug on the packing case near the door. 'What is it?' He looked admiringly at the aircraft. 'A B.E.2c?'

Captain Sykes grinned. 'Don't get excited, Jack. It's not for us. McAvoy tells me a delivery pilot flew it in from Cairo this morning. Apparently there's something special on the cards.'

McAvoy nodded and drew a bit closer. 'That's right, sir. There was a passenger with him, a Major Craig.' Sykes glanced over his shoulder to check they couldn't be overheard. 'He's not one of ours. Some sort of army type. He didn't like flying. He was very offhand with the delivery pilot and downright rude to a couple of my lads. Anyway, we've been asked to fit extra fuel tanks. Major Craig's off on a trip somewhere. I don't know where he's planning to go, but it's a long way, that's for sure.'

'I wouldn't mind taking her up,' said Jack wistfully. 'It looks more of a fighting machine than the Farman.'

Sykes pulled a face. 'I'm not crazy about the B.E.s. They're underpowered and sluggish. The pilot sits in the rear cockpit and it's damned awkward. The observer has the guns, but his field of fire is pretty limited. They're not bad for reconnaissance but they're not very nippy. I don't know how this'll perform with the weight of the extra fuel.'

'That's our problem, sir,' said McAvoy. 'With the best will in the world, we can't put all that extra fuel on board without it affecting the climb and speed. At the moment I'm wondering how it's going to get off the ground.' He turned as Corporal Quinn came into the hanger.

'Lieutenant Haldean?' said the Corporal. 'Major Youlton wants to see you immediately, sir.'

'Me?' said Jack in surprise. 'What for?'

Sykes cleared his throat. 'Don't worry, Jack, you haven't done anything wrong. I've got an idea what this is about. Good luck, old man. I'll see you in the Mess later.'

Jack finished his lime juice and followed the corporal across the airfield and into the huts which housed the offices and Mess. He couldn't think why on earth the Major should want to see him. Sykes said he wasn't in trouble, but a summons like this was unsettling.

Quinn knocked at the door of Major Youlton's office. 'Lieutenant Haldean, sir,' he announced, ushering him into the room.

The Major was sitting at his desk. 'Thank you, Quinn,' he said. 'Close the door behind you. I don't want to be disturbed by anyone unless it's absolutely vital.' Quinn saluted and left the room.

'At ease,' said Major Youlton. Jack relaxed and stood, his hands clasped behind him. 'Sit down,' added the Major. 'This will take some time and you might as well be comfortable.'

Feeling rather self-conscious, Jack sat down. He was badly puzzled.

Major Youlton slid the cigarette box across the desk to him. 'Help yourself, Mr Haldean. You do smoke, don't you?'

'Yes, sir,' said Jack, cautiously taking a cigarette. He lit it with some trepidation. It was less than a month since his first cigarette and he hoped he wouldn't start coughing.

'Just landed?' asked Youlton with a smile.

What on earth did he want? 'Yes, sir,' said Jack guardedly. 'We had the sky to ourselves.'

The Major nodded. 'It's too hot for Turks at this time of day.' He steepled his fingers and looked at Jack thoughtfully. 'Before I begin, Lieutenant, I want to emphasize that what I am about to say is highly confidential. I have asked that we should be undisturbed. In addition I have posted two men outside to see that no one approaches the window of this room. Our conversation must not be repeated to anyone. Anyone at all, you understand? Utter secrecy is vital.'

'Very good, sir,' said Jack. This was getting downright mysterious.

Youlton paused once more before speaking and when he

did, what he said was completely unexpected. 'Lieutenant Haldean, your record, since you joined the squadron, has been outstanding. You have shown, on numerous occasions, your intelligence, adaptability and courage. Captain Sykes speaks highly of your abilities. If you carry on as you have begun, you will go very far in the service.'

Jack couldn't speak for pleasure. For Captain Sykes and Major Youlton – *Major Youlton!* – to have such an opinion of him was beyond his wildest dreams. He was seventeen years old and he had tried, with all the devotion, hard work and passion he was capable of, to be a worthwhile member of the squadron. He didn't realize it, but he was aching for recognition. He had never been so grateful to anyone as he was to Major Youlton at that moment. 'Thank you, sir,' he said huskily.

Major Youlton didn't seem as pleased as Jack expected. In fact, he seemed downright uneasy. He pulled at his earlobe before he spoke. 'The fact is, Lieutenant, that there's a difficult job in the offing. Do you know what is meant by a special mission?'

Jack's eyes widened. 'Why, yes, sir.' A special mission! By crikey, if the Major meant to send him on a special mission, that would be really something. Of course he knew what a special mission was. Really top-notch pilots flew special missions. Special missions were glamorous, exciting, dangerous . . . And then, like a shock of icy water, the reality hit him. Dangerous. Scarily dangerous.

A special mission meant flying an agent – a spy – over the lines, landing in enemy territory and taking off again. Sometimes the pilot left the agent to make his own way back and sometimes he waited while the agent completed his job. If the plane was spotted, then all the pilot could do was trust to his lucky stars he'd manage to evade capture somehow. Spying was a job without honour and neither the agent nor the pilot were protected by military laws or conventions. If a pilot were forced down, alone in a two-seater plane, he was deemed to have dropped a spy. There was no defence and the penalty was a firing squad.

It took, perhaps, a fraction of a second, but Jack knew that however long he lived, he would remember that moment in

Major Youlton's office. The Major, with his concerned eyes and worried forehead, the skin showing white creases against the tan of his face. The sun laying hot, dazzling wedges of light on the dark wood of the floor and the metal of the filing cabinet. The open window with the lazily buzzing flies on the window sill, the far-off chunk of a rotary engine and the distant shout of an Arab water-boy. All these things he would remember forever because, in that vivid moment, he left part of his boyhood behind. Spies were fun, terrific fun, to read about, but this was real.

He took a deep breath. 'I'll do it, sir,' he said quietly.

Youlton held his hand up. 'Wait. As I say, this is a difficult mission. I can't order you to do it, only ask you to volunteer. You are perfectly free to refuse. I don't want you to agree yet. O'Leary, who has flown such missions in the past, is on leave and I simply can't spare one of my flight commanders. Of the rest of the officers available, you are the obvious choice, but you must realize what you're taking on.'

I know what I'm taking on, thought Jack. He'd nerved himself to say *yes* like a diver leaving the high board and he wanted to get it over with. Later, he realized just how fair Youlton was being.

'Naturally, the exact nature of the mission is secret,' continued Youlton, 'but its successful outcome could alter the course of the war in the East. Because it is so important, I have agreed to what, to speak frankly, seems a very hazardous enterprise. Did you see a B.E.2c in the hanger?'

Jack nodded. 'Yes, sir. The mechanics were fitting extra fuel tanks.'

'That's right.' Youlton pushed back his chair and stood up, leaning his hands on the desk. 'The reason those fuel tanks are needed, Mr Haldean, is that the plane has to be flown to Petra.'

Jack stared at him. 'Petra, sir?' he repeated in bewilderment. 'The lost city, you mean?'

Major Youlton smiled briefly. 'We know where it is. That's something, anyway. It's about two hundred miles to the southeast, over some of the most forbidding country on earth,' he added quietly. He glanced at Jack. 'Well?'

Jack squared his shoulders. 'If it's possible, sir, if the plane is capable of making the trip, I'll do it.'

Major Youlton's mouth tightened. 'Good man,' he said softly. 'You'll have a passenger with you, a Major Craig. He flew in this morning from Cairo.' Jack nodded. 'Major Craig,' continued Youlton, 'is, perhaps, one of the most important men in the East.' Jack looked suitably impressed. 'He's a well-known explorer and traveller and knows Arabia like the back of his hand. Durant Craig? Does the name mean anything to you?'

'I'm sorry, sir, I've never heard of him.'

For the first time Youlton gave a real smile. 'For heaven's sake, don't tell him. He has a proper appreciation of his talents and, to be fair to him, he's perfectly justified. When the war broke out he was in the Ahkaf Desert and it took him some months to find out what was happening in the outside world. He made his way back up to the coast and offered his services to General Murray. As it happened, he couldn't have arrived at a more opportune moment. We need experts, Haldean, men who know Arabia and can inspire the Arabs, and real experts are few and far between.

'At the beginning of the war we had Captain Shakespeare, who had a real pull with Ibn Sa'ud and the Wahhabis of Central Arabia, but he was killed in action, poor devil. Durant Craig came as the answer to a very pressing problem. He was given the rank of major but if you think of him as a general, you wouldn't be far wrong. He's lived with the Arabs so long he's more of an Arab than an Englishman. He speaks every kind of dialect and knows how their minds work. They call him *Tawr Ta'ir*, which more or less translates as the Angry Bull. It's a good name. He's rather like a bull. He's pretty short-tempered with our lot and can't stand red tape, but he has no end of patience with the Bedouin. Anyway, he's your passenger. Now, I must tell you the details of the trip.'

Major Youlton walked across the room and indicated the route on a large-scale map. 'I'll give you the precise directions to study, Haldean, but this is the route in general. There's a camel convoy, under the command of Captain Hawley, on its way to Esh Shobek. You will intercept the convoy and deliver sealed orders to Captain Hawley. You will then fly to Elji, where the Beni Sakr, pro-British Arabs, are encamped.

Major Craig needs to confer with them. After that, you will take Major Craig on to Petra. Major Craig has, apparently, arranged a fuel dump in Petra, and you'll be able to re-fuel the plane there. Then, leaving Major Craig in Petra, you can return.'

'So I leave Major Craig in Petra, sir?' asked Jack.

Youlton nodded. 'Yes, that's correct. What the Major does afterwards is, of course, none of our concern.' He turned to Jack with a wry smile. 'That's it. It's a difficult journey but vitally important.'

'When do I start, sir?'

'As soon as the fitters have finished with the plane,' said Youlton, coming back to the desk. 'It shouldn't be more than a couple of hours at the most.'

Jack looked at him blankly. 'But that'll mean flying in the full heat of the day, sir.'

Major Youlton clicked his tongue unhappily. 'I know, Lieutenant, but this is urgent. Major Craig needs time and that's what we can give him.' He picked up a small folder and gave it to him. 'That's your flight plan. Keep it with you at all times and don't let anyone see it. I'd better introduce you to Major Craig. After that, get something to eat and drink. With any luck, you'll be back tomorrow. You will, of course, report to me immediately you return.'

'Very good, sir,' said Jack. He stood up and put the flight plan into his pocket.

Youlton nodded, walked to the door and gave instructions to Corporal Quinn to bring Major Craig to the office. Youlton was clearly uneasy. He lit another cigarette and paced edgily round the room, continually looking at the wall map, until the noise of footsteps sounded in the corridor.

'Major Craig, sir,' said Quinn. Quinn saluted and withdrew, shutting the door behind him.

Jack was startled by the Major's appearance. Craig wore the uniform, right enough, but instead of a military moustache, he had a huge brindled beard, piercing eyes and aggressive eyebrows. He looked more like a sailor than a soldier and more like a Yukon miner who had strayed from the Alaska gold rush than either. He was shorter than average but strongly built, with massive shoulders, large hands and skin darkened by the sun. His Arab name suited him, thought Jack. He was a real bull of a man.

Major Craig received Jack's salute unenthusiastically. 'I asked for your best pilot, Youlton,' he said, as if Jack were incapable of hearing him. 'This is just a boy.'

'Lieutenant Haldean is one of our best pilots, Major,' replied Youlton firmly.

'If you say so.' Craig looked Jack up and down. 'He knows damn all about Arabs, though. We're going amongst Arabs, boy, *Arabs*,' he added, addressing Jack directly for the first time. He glared at the hat in Jack's hand in distaste. 'What's that you've got? A bush hat? Ridiculous! Don't you know anything? The Bedouin will shoot you if they see you wearing it. They think hats are immoral. You wouldn't go to Ascot wearing bathing drawers, would you? Then don't insult the Arabs by being improperly dressed. Before you come anywhere with me, get yourself a *keffiyeh*.'

Jack flushed indignantly. A boy? Who was he calling a boy? And what was that Arab thing he wanted him to get? A . . . A . . . 'What was that you said, sir?'

'A *keffiyeh*. An Arab headdress, damn it.'

'I'll see you're properly accoutred, Mr Haldean,' said Major Youlton quietly. 'The last thing we want to do is upset Arab ideas of etiquette. That would never do.'

'It's not mere etiquette, man,' snorted Craig, prickling at the sting of sarcasm in Youlton's words. 'Damn it, we're not going to a vicar's tea party.'

'But why don't they like bush hats, sir?' asked Jack.

Craig sighed dangerously. 'It's not just bush hats, boy, it's any hat. Don't you understand? If a man's wearing a hat, he can't press his forehead to the ground in prayer. It offends Allah and, more to the point, offends the Arabs.' He sighed once more. 'It's no wonder we've had trouble with the Arabs if people can't be bothered to learn a few simple facts.'

'I'm sure Lieutenant Haldean will be guided by you and your superior knowledge,' said Youlton.

Craig grunted ungraciously. 'He'd better be. It'll be the worse for him if he's not.'

Youlton turned to Jack. 'That's all for now, Lieutenant.'

He returned Jack's salute and smiled. 'This mission depends on your skill and courage. I know you'll do a good job.'

And that comment, thought Jack, as he left the office, was more for Craig's benefit than his. Still, he might as well enjoy whatever compliments were on offer. It didn't look as if he was going to get many from Major Craig.

It was just over two hours later that the B.E.2c took off, lumbering into the air with the huge weight of extra fuel. Craig had shed his uniform and was dressed as an Arab. He made a very passable Bedouin, but it would be a firing squad for certain if the Turks or the Germans caught them with Craig in that garb.

Jack's goggles had dark glass in them and he needed it. They were flying directly east into a blinding sun. Below them stretched a yellow and grey wilderness, mile upon mile of the rolling, featureless sand of the Sinai Desert, broken only by the sharp black shadow of rocks or the smudge of camel-thorn. Again and again he raised his hand to his eyes, peering through his fingers past the sun, dreading seeing the crosses of a German or the white-square-on-black of a Turkish plane. On three occasions he saw, far off on the horizon, circling black dots, but he slipped past unnoticed. He was so far over enemy territory they probably assumed he was one of theirs. It wouldn't be so bad if he had some sort of weapon, but both the Vickers and the Lewis machine guns were controlled from the observer's cockpit, in the front of the plane. Craig held no truck with machine guns and had been incredulous at the idea of manning them. He was, Jack was willing to bet, looking at his slumped form, fast asleep.

With the Vickers and the Lewis gun unmanned, he was helpless before the enemy, a sitting duck in the big, ungainly plane. The desert stretched monotonously under him, and then, thank God, the sun was behind him, casting needle-sharp black shadows on the flint-strewn surface of the desert below. He pushed up his goggles, wiping his eyes made watery by the glare.

They had been in the air for well over three hours when he saw the camel convoy spread out below like a picture on a box of Christmas dates. There was the glint of white from upturned faces as he circled overhead and brought the plane down in front of the convoy, flying only feet off the ground at just over stalling speed as he gazed at the sand for obstacles. Then, with a final glance at his fluttering pennon to show him the wind direction, he touched down, bringing the plane to a bumpy, rumbling halt.

Stretching his cramped muscles, he climbed out of the cockpit and, standing in the shade of the wings, took a drink from his canteen. It was warm and brackish but tasted wonderful. He wet his handkerchief and rubbed it over his face, luxuriating in how it felt against his parched skin. Craig hadn't moved so he climbed up to the observer's cockpit. He'd been right. The Major was asleep.

'We've reached the convoy, sir,' he said, shaking him awake.

Major Craig opened his eyes. 'Well, give 'em the orders, man. Don't waste time. We've got to get a move on.' With that he relapsed back into sleep.

Jack dropped back on to the sand. He hadn't expected praise, but Craig could have made some sort of comment. Damn, that had been a monumental journey. The heat haze distorted visibility and the slightest error in his compass readings could have thrown them miles off course. Not only that, but it was hard physical work flying over the desert. Columns of heat rising many thousands of feet made an invisible switchback of the air. Some of the bumps had been so severe that if he hadn't been strapped in he'd had been flung out of the plane and the strain of continually correcting the plane was exhausting. Major Youlton would appreciate it, he thought to himself, as the leaders of the convoy approached. Three hours over virtually uncharted and hostile desert with an observer who wouldn't observe and the guns so much useless weight was the sort of flight that would have got on to the front pages of the newspapers before the war.

With a jingling of harness, grunts from camels and cries from the drivers, the convoy arrived. With a series of shouts the column came to a halt.

'Where on earth did you pop up from?' shouted the leading officer over the noise as he dismounted. He was in Camel Corps uniform with lieutenant's stripes. 'We couldn't believe it when you flew over.'

'Ismailia,' Jack called back cheerfully. 'I've got sealed orders for Captain Hawley.'

Hawley, when he rode up, took the orders, opened them and read them with a frown. He looked at Jack, who was sharing a canteen of water with the young lieutenant. 'Do you know where the information in these orders came from?'

Jack shook his head. 'No, sir. They were given to me by my C.O., Major Youlton.'

'I'd like to know where the information came from, all the same,' muttered Hawley. He looked at the aeroplane. 'Are you in that thing by yourself?'

'No, sir. I've got Major Craig with me, but he's asleep. I did tell him we'd arrived, but he instructed me to hand over the orders and not waste time.' And how he can sleep, thought Jack, in the middle of a herd of grunting camels with all this racket going on, is an absolute miracle.

'Craig? Durant Craig?' asked Hawley sharply. His face cleared. 'That makes a difference.'

'Do you want to speak to him, sir?' asked Jack. He wouldn't have minded an excuse to wake up Craig.

'No, don't do that.' Hawley glanced at his orders. 'If I know anything about it, Major Craig is going to have his work cut out over the next few days. The orders are quite clear. Where are you off to next, Lieutenant?'

Jack hesitated. 'I'm sorry, sir, but I'd better not say. I've been given strict instructions not to tell anyone.'

Hawley smiled grimly. 'Quite right, too. It's about time Cairo started taking security seriously. This front is riddled with spies. All I can say is that if it's anywhere in the region of Qal'at Aneiza or Q'asr Dh'an, watch your step. There's been a lot of activity round there recently. We've heard – I don't know how true this is – that Ozymandias is there.'

'Ozymandias, sir?' Jack repeated the name doubtfully. 'I'm afraid I don't understand.' The only thing Ozymandias meant to him was a poem by Shelley. *I met a traveller from an antique land* . . . Jack's face must have mirrored his feelings, for Hawley laughed humourlessly.

'Ozymandias is the Turks' answer to Durant Craig. To be honest I don't know if he's Turkish, German or Arab, but he's a tough customer, whatever he is. He puts the fear of God into my Arabs. They think he's got the powers of a demon.' Hawley shrugged. 'I don't know about that, but he seems to know everything we do before we do it.' He glanced at the orders in his hand. 'I hope he hasn't cottoned on to this. Anyway, Lieutenant, if Major Craig told you to get a move on, I'd better not keep you any longer. Refill your canteen before you go and good luck.'

The second leg of the journey was a comparatively short hop of less than fifty miles and, now the fuel was low, getting into the air was a far less nerve-racking experience. It was so low that Jack wondered if the problem was shortly going to be not getting into the air, but staying there. Fortunately his directions were good, and less than an hour later he sighted the black Arab tents of the Beni Sakr.

This time there was no need to wake up Craig. Before the engine had juddered to a halt, he had undone his harness and had climbed out of the plane. It was as well he did, for the noise of the aircraft had brought men running into the open. They were armed with long rifles and, although Jack had been in the East for only a few weeks, he knew from experience just how trigger happy a group of excited, nervy and bellicose men could be.

Craig extended his arms in a magnificent gesture and roared out a command in Arabic. There was a medley of shouts in return and a ragged volley of shots, aimed, thank God, not at the plane but into the empty air. Leaving Jack without a word, Craig strolled off like a king visiting his subjects, flanked by the noisy, jostling crowd, in the direction of the largest of the black tents.

Jack, alone and feeling ridiculous in his hastily-donned *keffiyeh,* opened his canteen, took a much-needed drink of water, and lit a cigarette. It must have been over an hour later, an hour spent mainly in fending off swarms of curious wide-eyed children from the precious aeroplane, when Craig came back, this time alone. He clapped his hands and the children scattered.

'They agree to the change of rendezvous,' he said without preamble.

'Change of rendezvous, sir?' asked Jack, puzzled.

'Damn it, boy, are you deaf? You gave the orders to the convoy, didn't you?'

'Why, yes, sir, but I don't know what the orders were.'

'Don't you?' Being amongst Arabs was good for Craig's character, Jack decided. He wasn't exactly charming, but a sort of lordly condescension had replaced his irascibility. 'By George, I'd want to know the reasons why before I went running round at anyone's say-so.'

He indicated the tents in a sweeping gesture. 'We're guests of the Beni Sakr. You know that, don't you?' Jack nodded and Craig continued. 'They're friendly and we want to keep them that way. They're the key to winning the war. I told Archie Murray – that's General Murray – the only hope of success was to inflame an Arab revolt and he agreed. That's what I'm doing here. I'm going to lead the Arabs against the Turks.'

The thing was, thought Jack, that although Craig was a difficult man to like, he was willing to bet that he was perfectly capable of doing exactly what he said.

'My word, sir,' he said enthusiastically, 'that'd turn things around all right.'

'Wouldn't it though,' agreed Craig, looking kindly at Jack for the first time. 'The Turks have ruled the roost for far too long.'

'Have the Beni Sakr agreed to follow you, sir?'

'With conditions,' said Craig with a short laugh. 'I really respect these people, you know. They haven't gone soft, like the so-called men you find in England. They want honour and adventure and are prepared to endure fantastic hardships. I can promise them all that, and gold as well.'

'Gold, sir?' asked Jack, startled.

'Yes, gold,' repeated Craig impatiently. 'You don't expect the Arabs to fight for nothing, do you? I told Murray that grubby banknotes or promises won't do. It has to be gold and lots of it.'

'But how will you get gold, sir?'

'From the convoy of course, boy.' Craig laughed once more. 'Hawley's convoy is my convoy. I organized it. Murray gave me a free hand. The convoy's carrying enough gold to satisfy the Beni Sakr and spread the word across Arabia.'

His face grew grim. 'I made a promise and I never go back on my word. You can't let the Arabs down. They neither forgive nor forget. If I hadn't stepped in, all the gold would have ended up in Turkish hands. I received news an ambush was planned and it's the Arabs – my Arabs – who would come off worse. The convoy's too heavily guarded for the Turks to attack, but as soon as the convoy delivers the gold, they'll strike. The convoy was going to rendezvous at Esh Shobek but the place is swarming with Turks. I'm going to ride up to Petra with the Beni Sakr and meet the convoy there. Those orders you gave the convoy told them of the change of rendezvous.'

'Aren't you flying up to Petra with me, sir? That was the original plan.'

Craig shook his head. 'So it was, but it's not on the cards.'

'That'll be difficult, sir,' said Jack anxiously. 'I need help to take off from Petra. I need someone to swing the propellers to get me off the ground. Without someone to do that, I'm stranded.'

Craig shrugged. 'I don't know anything about that. You'll have to manage somehow. Either that, or you'll have to stay put till the convoy arrives. They should be in Petra in a couple of days and so should I. I don't want you here, that's for sure. These people need careful handling and you're bound to put your foot in it. Besides that, they'll wreck the plane.'

'Wreck the plane, sir?'

'Souvenir hunting. As soon as you drop your guard they'll be all over it.' He glanced over his shoulder at the tents. 'I've got to stay. Not to put too fine a point on it, they suspect a trap, so I'm to be the hostage. Take some food and water with you and let's hope the convoy turns up, eh?'

There really didn't seem anything else to be done. Jack drew a deep breath and accepted the inevitable. 'Can you tell me where the fuel dump is, sir?'

'I'll draw you a map. It's fairly well hidden but you should find it. By the way, keep your gun handy. The Bedouin often camp in the caves in the city and they have a fairly short way with visitors. Show them you mean business and you might be all right.'

This was getting less and less appealing by the second.

Major Youlton certainly hadn't underestimated the dangers of the trip. Jack looked at Craig's inflexible face and swallowed. There was nothing else for it and he might as well do it with as much grace as he could muster. 'Thank you, sir. Is there anywhere to land inside the city?'

'Damned if I know. You'll have to see for yourself. If not, you'll have to land in the desert but you'll have to carry the fuel a hell of a way.' He laughed. 'Rather you than me. I'd sooner have a camel than an aeroplane any day.'

With the plane low on fuel and without the weight of a passenger, the B.E.2c soared into the air. Jack climbed for height and levelled off at a thousand feet over the mountains of Edom. With ridge after ridge of white and red sandstone flinging back the heat from the sun, torturing the air he flew though, he checked his compass and headed for Petra. It was less than ten miles from Elji to Petra and he soon spotted the black lines and dots which was how the ancient, abandoned city appeared from the air. The name Petra meant rock and to anyone who didn't know what the rocks housed, it would be virtually impossible to find. No wonder the city had been lost for so long. It was the shadows that gave it away. Those regular lines had never occurred in nature.

A plateau stretched out under him and then he saw it. A thin black line split the earth beneath him. That must be the entrance to the city. He had heard of it, a thin snaking chasm through towering cliffs which extended for well over a mile. The plane twisted in the overheated air and his tired senses quivered as he searched for a landing ground.

He circled overhead before picking out the only possible landing ground, a paved street with columns. He flew down the street slowly, before turning, climbing, then putting the cumbersome plane down in a steady glide. His wing-tips whispered over the broken colonnades and then he was down, bumping to a halt. With a heartfelt prayer of thanks, he turned off the engine.

The quietness that enveloped him was so intense he thought it would crack his eardrums. The sounds of the engine cooling were like rifle shots. Quietness was the perfect word, he thought uneasily. Living things could choose to be quiet. It was as if the quietness was waiting for him: inhuman, huge and hostile. He had never been in a place that was so utterly silent.

He climbed out of the plane, and, with Major Craig's warning in his mind, grasped his revolver tightly. The chink of his shoe against a pebble echoed round the cliffs. As the noise died away, the silence rushed in once more, like a physical wave.

He couldn't believe there was another living soul for miles. Unconsciously he relaxed. He walked away from the shelter of the aircraft and gazed at the city in awestruck wonder. He seemed to have stepped outside of time. Around him stood what looked like a Roman street, with pillars, temples and palaces, but he didn't seem to have gone back in time but rather forward, forward to the end of the world, when all the works of man stood deserted. As far as he could see, nothing had been built here. Everything had been carved, carved out of the sandstone. The sun was getting low and made the colours in the rock glow as if they were lit from within. White, yellow, orange, pink, crimson, green – more hues and shades than he had ever imagined – swirled in dips and waves in a silent symphony of colour. He could easily have watched the rocks until the sun went down but he forced himself to withdraw from a contemplation of the eternal and back to practicalities.

He lit a cigarette and the scrape of the match was so loud it made him wince. He had to find the fuel dump but from Craig's hastily drawn map it looked as if the cache was some considerable distance away. He glanced at the sun. He reckoned he had an hour of light left at the most. He would find the fuel first thing tomorrow. He didn't want to risk being lost in the ancient city after dark. Besides that, he was bone-weary. Perhaps it was just as well, for it would be easy to let his imagination run riot, faced by the black entrances of caves and temples. Tired as he was, he wanted to explore. A great staircase ran up the side of the rocks and he climbed part of the way up, hoping to get a better view of the city. Here, between two obelisks flanked by altars, he found a large pool of rainwater. He could hardly believe his luck. He drank his fill, then, stripping off his clothes, had the most enjoyable bathe of his life.

He retreated back to the plane. The sun was rapidly setting and the shadows were getting long. Some camel-thorn trees had grown out of the rocks and he gathered up a few armfuls of tinder from under them. With a tiny amount of petrol from what remained in the plane, he soon had a cheerful, crackling fire. A jackal screamed when he was by the open petrol tank and he whirled round, pistol in hand, forgetting that a single spark would send him to glory. When he worked out what it was, he laughed in relief. The sound was caught and echoed by the cliffs.

He didn't like the sound of his laugh. It sounded like an intrusion on the city's brooding presence. He shivered. The place was silent and *aware,* as Browning said somewhere or other. He tore the flight plan into strips and put it on the fire, then opened a can of bully beef and, together with a few flaps of Arab bread and a mug of milkless tea, made as good a supper as he could.

He thought about spending the night in one of the caves, but he preferred the open, next to the comfortingly familiar bulk of the aeroplane. He told himself it was a perfectly rational fear of scorpions and snakes, but he knew it was a more primeval fear that kept him out of those dark places.

The camel thorn on the fire crumbled and perished in a shower of red sparks and Jack, utterly exhausted, wrapped himself up in a blanket and, with the Arab headdress for a pillow, went to sleep.

NINE

Someone was shaking his shoulder. Jack grunted and tried to turn over and go back to sleep, but the shaking increased. He opened bleary eyes and stared down the barrel of a pistol. He tried to sit up but a harsh command and a painful grip on his shoulder stopped him.

The moon had risen. In its hard brilliance he could see a seamed, moustached face inches from his own. The man was a Turkish captain. About twenty Arabs, mounted on horseback, their white robes gleaming in the moonlight, surrounded him. Two more Turkish officers were with them. A horse whinnied and pawed the ground.

'Oh, God,' said Jack very quietly. His mouth was dry, his stomach churned and the raw taste of fear welled up in his throat.

The Arabs started to laugh. The dead city caught the sound and chopped it into staccato, separated bursts, a mocking, inhuman jeer of triumph. The man holding the revolver stepped back and gestured for him to get up. Jack slowly scrambled to his feet, his hands raised in surrender. The officer smiled humourlessly and, with another gesture from the pistol, barked out a command.

Jack, unable to understand, shrugged helplessly. The Turkish officer stepped forward, drew back his hand and slapped him hard across the face.

Jack staggered back and fell to his knees. The blow had hurt, but more than that, he was completely shocked. He knew how prisoners should be treated and this wasn't in the rules. 'You can't do that!' he said indignantly. 'I'm a British officer.'

The Turkish officer stepped forward and picked up Jack's revolver from where it had been lying in its holster beside him on the ground. That was evidently what he wanted. He tossed the blanket to one of the Arabs, who caught it and stowed it in his saddlebag. Another welter of Turkish followed, to which Jack could only shrug in reply.

The two other Turks swung themselves into the cockpits of the B.E.2c. They stripped out the Vickers and the Lewis guns and the belts of ammunition, then rifled through the contents of the plane, tossing them over the side in a careless heap. The Arabs picked them up and packed them away in their saddlebags. Another flood of commands followed. Three Arabs dismounted and, pulling back the bolts, brought their rifles up to bear.

Catching his breath, Jack squared his shoulders, waiting for the shot. It didn't come. They prodded the rifle barrels painfully into his ribs, forcing him to walk towards the horses.

Under the ever-present guns, he mounted the horse. His feet were lashed to the stirrups and his hands were tied at the wrist. He could hold on to the saddle, but that was about all. A rope harness secured his horse to an Arab's. The three Arabs who had threatened him were evidently ordered to stay with the plane. He didn't know what would happen to them and was too miserable to care. His only comfort, and it was a small one, was the thought that if the convoy or Major Craig should turn up, they should be more than a match for three Arabs.

Then, with shouts from the Arabs, a jingle of harness and a muffled thud of hooves on the sand-covered stones, they set off down the valley of Petra. Jack felt as wretched as he had ever done in his life.

Opposite a vast carved building, the column swung and seemed to go into the heart of the mountain. They plunged into a deep, narrow fissure in the cliff that seemed to stretch for miles. Jack, concentrating on staying on the horse, took in little of this part of the journey. He guessed this was the dark line he had flown over but all he was really aware of was that the man leading his horse never seemed to stumble, for which small blessing he was grateful.

The fissure abruptly opened out into desert and the column set off at a gallop across the sands. Jack, flung sideways by the sudden motion, bounced miserably on the saddle. A wayward memory of his interview for the Royal Flying Corps made him grin mirthlessly. 'Do you ride?' the Colonel had asked. He must have known what was in store.

They travelled for over two hours across the desert, the moon laying great silver sheets across the sand, the occasional clump of oleander, tall camel thorn and scrub silhouetted in deepest black. Despite himself, Jack's eyes kept closing and he awoke time after time to find himself slipping. Then, as the moon was riding down towards the western horizon, making all the shadows huge, they came to a high-walled fort. They were challenged from the walls. The Turkish captain shouted back, the gates creaked open, and Jack rode into the garrison of Q'asr Dh'an.

He flinched away as an Arab approached, long knife in hand, but the man only cut the ropes that bound his feet. Muscles stiff, he was unable to move right away and the man pulled him off the horse, where, with hands still tied, he sprawled on the ground. The Arab laughed and kicked him in the ribs. Angry and sore, Jack staggered to his feet and lowered his head, about to charge the man who'd kicked him, but as he did so a lantern shone in his face, blinding him.

From behind the light, a voice, cultivated and accentless, spoke in English. 'A British officer. And a pilot. This is a prize, indeed.'

Jack blinked in the light. 'Who are you?' His voice was cracked by thirst.

'Oberstleutant Von Erlangen.' Oberstleutant. The rank was equivalent to a lieutenant-colonel, and even in his misery, Jack wondered what on earth a German colonel was doing stuck out in this godforsaken spot. The Colonel raised his voice and spoke in Turkish. Jack was seized by the arms and marched forward into the building, where a door was opened and he was flung, face down, into a room. The two men who had frogmarched him in stood to either side.

Absolutely furious, Jack raised his head. 'What the blazes . . .' he began, and then speech failed him. He was in a richly furnished room. Thick Turkish carpets covered the floor and oil lamps shone a warm glow on a fine collection of water-colour paintings. Books lined one wall, the gold print of their leather bindings catching the light. A small fire burnt comfortably on the hearth behind him and at an oak desk sat a girl. She was young, hardly older than himself, with pale skin and fair hair gathered into a long plait. She cried out and leapt to her feet, standing with a hand clasped to her breast in alarm at his sudden entrance. The combination of the room and the girl was so surprising that Jack couldn't speak. He levered himself to his knees and stared at her.

She stared back, then raised her head sharply as Oberstleutant Von Erlangen entered the room. 'Lothar, what's happening?' she asked in German. 'Who's this?'

Although she spoke quickly, Jack was able to catch her meaning. He had studied German at school and, after war was declared, had worked hard at the language. He carefully betrayed nothing of his understanding. He wasn't giving away any more than he had to.

Von Erlangen didn't answer her at first. Instead he turned to the two Turks by the door and barked out a command. They withdrew, closing the door behind them. Then, still without speaking, he strolled across to the desk and selected a thin black cigar from a silver box, lighting it without haste. He leaned against the desk, his gaze resting on Jack for a moment, then he turned to the girl.

'This is a British pilot, Freya. Captain Talaat and a party of Aityeh found him bivouacking in Petra. They saw his aeroplane over Edom and went to investigate. Fortunately, Talaat was able to restrain himself and took our – our guest – prisoner instead. It was just as well that he did. I would have been annoyed if anything had happened to this young man.' He looked up from the tip of his burning cigar and his blue eyes lanced through Jack. He spoke in English. 'Welcome to Q'asr Dh'an. We are going to have a lot to talk about.'

Jack swallowed. 'You're entitled to my name and rank,' he said, trying to keep his voice level. 'That's all.'

'So I am. Let's start with your name, shall we?'

'Haldean. Second-lieutenant Haldean.'

'Good. Christian names?'

'John Carlos,' Jack answered as steadily as he could. He felt the oddest flicker of comfort that, although the answer was true, this terrifying man with his ice-chip eyes and scarred face couldn't know he was always called Jack. It was as if he'd managed to retain a little secret place within himself.

Von Erlangen lifted his eyebrows. 'John Carlos, eh? I didn't think you were pure-bred. Spanish?' Jack didn't answer. He wasn't saying anything he didn't have to. Von Erlangen shrugged. 'It doesn't matter. Well, Second-Lieutenant John Carlos Haldean, what were you doing in Petra?'

Jack met his stare unflinchingly and said nothing.

Von Erlangen sighed. 'I can see you are going to be diffi-cult, John. I thought you might be.' Putting down his cigar he walked to the fireplace and selected a lithe, thin twig from the pile of kindling in the basket. He bent it absently in his fingers as he spoke. 'You will end up telling me everything, Lieutenant. Why not do it now?'

Jack, his mouth dry, awkwardly got to his feet. 'Are – are you going to shoot me?' he asked.

Von Erlangen looked at the girl and laughed. 'He wants to know if I'm going to shoot him.'

The girl didn't share the laughter. She stood with her hand nervously playing with a gold locket on the front of her blue dress. In the gleam of the firelight, Jack noticed the glint of a gold ring. They had called each other by their Christian names. Was she his wife?

'Are you, Lothar?' she asked.

Von Erlangen shook his head. 'Oh no, he's far too useful.' He looked at Jack, standing in the middle of the room with his hands still tied. He spoke in English. 'Shoot you? Certainly not, my dear Lieutenant Haldean. Death at my hands is something to be earned.' He snapped the twig in his fingers, his eyes blazing with sudden fury. 'You will beg to die.'

Jack made a huge effort. 'There are rules protecting pris-oners. You've got to follow the rules.'

Von Erlangen gave an amused laugh. 'Rules?' His lips parted, showing sharp white canines. 'Do you realize who I am? Try hard, Lieutenant.'

Jack's voice cracked. 'Ozymandias?'

Von Erlangen gave Freya a swift, pleased glance. 'Even this boy's heard of me. Ozymandias,' he repeated, drawing out the word. 'I make my own rules.' He took Jack's chin in a firm grip and twisted his face round to the light. 'Are you frightened yet?'

'No,' said Jack uselessly.

Von Erlangen smiled. 'You're a bad liar.' He dropped his hand, walked back to the desk and picked up his cigar. 'Freya, my dear, I think you'd better go. You know this sort of thing upsets you. Send Captain Talaat and his men in here.'

Freya nodded and went to the door. With her hand on the door frame, she paused as if to speak, then, with a glance at Von Erlangen, obviously thought better of it. She closed the door behind her. Without another glance at Jack, Von Erlangen drew a chair up to the desk and picked up some papers.

Jack stared at him. His stomach felt like water, but he forced himself to speak. He had heard rumours of how badly the Turks treated their prisoners, of the neglect and the harsh conditions, and he had also heard stories of what the Arabs could do, but for a German – a civilized, sophisticated German from the land of Beethoven and Goethe – to act like Von Erlangen was outside anything he'd ever imagined. Yes, there'd been stories of brutality, but those, surely, had been carried out by ignorant and frightened troops, not officers. 'I don't care what fancy name you call yourself,' he said in as even a voice as he could manage. 'You're still bound by the rules of war. I'm a British officer.'

Von Erlangen didn't bother to look up.

Captain Talaat and five other Turks entered the room and saluted. 'You sent for us, Herr Oberstleutant?' Talaat asked in German.

Von Erlangen looked up then. 'Yes,' he replied. 'Did you find any papers or maps in the aeroplane?'

'There were maps, Mein Herr, but no papers.'

Von Erlangen frowned. 'Were the maps marked in any way?'

'No, Herr Oberstleutant.'

Von Erlangen nodded, crushed out his cigar and lit another one. 'In that case, Talaat, you'll be pleased to hear, we have to do this the interesting way.' He stood up, flexed his fingers and walked over to Jack. 'You see, John,' he said in English, 'part of what keeps my men happy is providing pleasure. Illegitimate pleasure, but pleasure all the same. Take his shirt off,' he added in German.

Talaat drew out a knife, stepped forward, and taking Jack's shirt by the back of the collar, cut down. Then he grasped the front and ripped, leaving the sleeves hanging where Jack's hands were bound. He ran his hand over Jack's chest as if he were inspecting a horse he was about to buy.

Von Erlangen nodded towards the other four and they came forward. The leader, a thick-set, dark-jowled man, had a thin black leather whip in his hands which he coiled and uncoiled. His mouth worked with excitement.

'Now,' said Von Erlangen, casually flicking the ash off his cigar, 'would you care to tell us what you were doing in Petra?'

Jack shook his head, dumbly. He was roughly turned round and pushed face downwards on to the chair. The whip cracked. A line of fire ran down his back and he shuddered. The Turks laughed and the whip snaked out once more. Despite himself, Jack grunted. The hands holding his shoulders dug into the flesh as fingers of pain etched across his back. After the tenth crack of the whip he screamed. His scream encouraged the Turks and the blows came faster. Jack slumped, lying half over the chair.

'Stop!' Von Erlangen came forward and took the whip. He rolled Jack off the chair to sprawl helplessly on the floor. Von Erlangen knelt beside him and placed the butt of the whip under Jack's chin. 'What were you doing in Petra?'

Jack shook his head once more and Von Erlangen tossed the whip to one of the waiting men. 'Carry on.'

There was a frenzy of pain, of shouts, of laughter and through it all the ribbon of fire kept falling and rising. Von Erlangen retreated to the desk and smoked his cigar, placidly watching while a human being disintegrated before him. When the cigar was smoked down to the tip he ground it out in the ashtray and walked to Jack, kneeling beside him again.

'John,' he said quietly. 'John.' There was a silence, broken only by Jack's laboured breathing. Von Erlangen ran his hand softly over Jack's face and waited for the blurred eyes to focus. 'John, look at me. You were in Petra because of the gold convoy, weren't you?'

A tiny light of defiance flickered in the dark eyes.

'If you say yes, John, I can get them to stop.' His voice was tender. 'Please help me, John. I want them to stop. Was it the gold, John?' Von Erlangen looked up, nodded, and the whip whistled out once more. Jack whimpered and tried to writhe away. 'It was the gold, wasn't it, John?'

'Yes.' His voice was a distant whisper.

'Where are they taking the gold to?'

Von Erlangen was swimming in and out of focus. Jack had a brief moment of clarity and summoned up his strength. 'Go to the devil.'

'I am the devil.' He stood up and dusted off his knees. 'Get on with it, Essad. I know you're waiting.'

He stepped back and watched, a quiet smile on his lips as the cloth was ripped from his victim's body.

There was a roaring in Jack's ears as more blows landed. There was the smell of garlic and filth. He drew his head back and cracked his tormentor's face as hard as he could and then the violence he had been dreading burst upon him. Shame twisted him as unclean hands grasped his body. He tried to roll away but there was nothing but this white wall of agony. As the Turks stood up, panting, something deep inside had fractured and was dying.

Von Erlangen knelt beside him once more. He reached out and stroked Jack's hair gently. 'John, make them stop. Tell me where the gold is going to, John. I don't want them to hurt you, John. Where is the gold going?'

John. John. John could tell them. Jack wasn't a traitor but this was someone called John. A tiny voice in his head whispered 'No!' but that, too, was dying.

'Where is the gold going to, John?' The voice was very tender and John wanted kindness then. 'Where is the gold going to, John? Is it Petra?'

It was so much easier to agree. 'Petra,' he breathed.

Von Erlangen smiled and carried on stroking Jack's hair. John turned his face so his cheek would be stroked too. 'Who was flying with you, John? Who was the passenger in the plane?'

Jack shook his head. 'Not . . . allowed . . . to . . . tell you.'

Von Erlangen sighed and taking a poker from the fireplace, put it in the fire until the tip glowed bright red.

He snapped his fingers and one of the Turks handed him a knife. He turned Jack over, cut the rope that bound his hands, then rolled him on to his back again. 'You see, John, what you are making me do.' He took one of Jack's hands in his, then inspected the glowing end of the poker carefully. 'If I put this on the back of your hands, the nerves will shrivel and you will be left with useless claws. You can't fly then, can you?' Von Erlangen lightly touched Jack's knuckles with the glowing metal, watching his reaction with satisfaction. 'You like flying, don't you?'

'Yes.'

'If you make me put it in your eyes, you'll be blind. Blind pilots can't fly. Now, who was flying with you?'

Jack didn't care about the future; there was only the present and all he wanted was the pain to stop. He watched as the poker came nearer, then threw back his head and screamed as it was pressed under his shoulder-blade. Von Erlangen held the poker close to Jack's face.

'Who was flying with you, John? Who was your passenger?'

The red tip was flickering by his eyes. The heat from it was hurting.

'Who was flying with you, John?'

'Craig. Durant Craig.'

There was an indescribable light in the ice-chip eyes. 'Craig? Where's Craig now?'

'With the Arabs.'

The poker still flickered by his eyes. 'Which Arabs?'

'The Beni Sakr.'

'Are they going to Petra?'

'Yes. Soon, very soon.'

Von Erlangen put the poker back in the fire, smiled broadly and got up. 'That's all I need to know, John. You're a traitor. Traitors aren't fit to live.' He looked at the Turks and gestured to Jack on the floor. 'You can finish him off,' he said in German. 'Finish him off,' he repeated in English, savouring the words.

As the Turks closed in once more, Jack whimpered in terror and grasped Von Erlangen's leg convulsively. 'You said you'd make them stop.'

Von Erlangen kicked Jack away in disgust, and walked to the desk, indifferent to the scene behind him.

A soft, damp cloth washed his face. Jack flickered his eyes open. Freya was kneeling beside him, her face drawn with anxiety. She smiled in relief as he opened his eyes and said something in German which he couldn't catch. Her voice was kind and he felt a surge of gratitude. She had a basin full of water and was wiping the blood away from his wounds. Her hands were cool and gentle. She held a glass to his lips, but his throat was too dry to swallow and the water ran down the side of his mouth. Patiently, she tried again, and this time he was able to drink a little. 'Did I tell them?' he mumbled.

She listened intently, obviously working out what he'd said. '*Ja.*' She put the English words together with difficulty. 'It is over now.'

A great wave of despair washed over him. He was a traitor. He wanted to die.

Von Erlangen was sitting, writing at his desk. Jack rolled himself over on to his elbows and crawled painfully across the room. Von Erlangen laid down his pen and waited for him. 'Yes?'

'You said I could die.' His voice broke. 'Please.'

Von Erlangen picked up a revolver from the desk and toyed with it before aiming it at him. Jack rested his forehead on his hands and waited, empty of all emotion.

'No, Lothar!' Freya Von Erlangen quickly crossed the room and put her hand on his.

Von Erlangen paused with his finger on the trigger. 'No?' He lowered the gun. 'It makes little difference to me.' His eyes flicked back to Jack. 'No. I won't kill you, my dear John. You want it too much. Besides, the carpet you're lying on is a Tekke Bokhara. It's too valuable to soil with your brains. I'll give you to the Turks. They might slit your throat for you.' He picked up his pen and returned to his writing.

'Was it worth it, Lothar?' asked Freya in German.

Von Erlangen clicked his tongue, irritated by the interruption. 'Of course, my dear. Vital.' He half-turned. 'Ask Talaat to take him away, would you?' He yawned, delicately covering his mouth with his hand. 'My God, I'm tired.

Yes, of course it was worth it. When Craig arrives we'll be waiting for him.'

The Turks didn't slit his throat. They didn't do anything much, apart from carry him to a prison cell, and leave him there. The next few days were spent in a daze. All Jack really knew was that Freya Von Erlangen helped him drink, helped him eat, cleaned and bandaged his wounds, and without her he would have died. He fell in love with Freya in those few brief days. Perhaps it was easier to think of Freya than of what he had done, but she filled his world and gave him the strength to live.

Three days had passed before he was able to sit up and take stock of his cell. It was a bare mud-brick room, lit by a small slit of a window high up in the wall. There was no bed, just a blanket on a dried mud ledge against the mud wall and a bucket to use as a lavatory. It was crawling with vermin, which, if he hadn't been so spent, would have revolted him. By the fourth day he was able to stand and was let out under the care of a bored Turkish guard to empty the bucket and to walk briefly round the yard. He was so clearly incapable of any resistance that the guard relaxed, leaning in the shade of the wall while Jack stumbled a few hesitant steps.

One guard was inclined to be friendly. He had been a waiter in London in his uncle's restaurant before the war and wanted to exercise his small stock of English. His name, he told Jack, was Basak. He was a keen supporter of Fulham Football Club and was disgusted to hear that football matches had been suspended for the duration of the war. Their halting conversation about Fulham, Arsenal, Manchester United and Preston North End must be, thought Jack, one of the most unexpected ever conducted in the sun-baked fortress of Q'asr Dh'an.

It was Basak who gave him the news. The convoy had arrived in Petra and, under the eyes of Von Erlangen's men, hidden in the city, had rendezvoused with the Beni Sakr, led by Craig. From what Jack could make out from the guard's hesitant English, the convoy had left the gold and set off, back into the desert. The Beni Sakr celebrated their new wealth with much singing and dancing. At that moment Von

Erlangen and the Aityeh had struck. It was, Jack gathered, a massacre. He didn't want to know any more.

About a fortnight later, Jack was sitting against the wall in the shade of the parade ground, Basak beside him. The gates of the fortress were open, and outside, a party of green-clad Turks toiled in the sun, moving rocks. Jack couldn't think what they were doing, then it struck him he had seen men doing similar work before. More than that, he'd done it himself. He sat up, suddenly interested in the work beyond the wall. They were clearing a landing strip, surely?

He turned to ask Basak if he was right, then decided against it. Basak probably wouldn't know, and he didn't want to betray any interest in the activity outside the fortress.

Basak, indifferent to what was happening outside the gates, was deeply depressed. He wanted to go back to Turkey, to Anatolia. More than that, he wanted to go back to his uncle's restaurant, where he was respected, the owner's nephew, in his beloved London, where, one day, he wanted a restaurant of his own. He hated Q'asr Dh'an, he hated the desert, he hated the dust and most of all, he hated the Arabs.

There was an abandoned city some distance from the fort, a place of gaping tombs and whispering ghosts, where the Arabs had massacred a party of Turkish soldiers. Most of the soldiers had been his friends. It was Beni Sakr work, led by that chief of all devils, Craig. The soldiers were mown down by machine-gun fire and horribly mutilated after death. The way the Beni Sakr treated their fallen victims was unmistakable. Basak pronounced Craig's name *Krig* and it took Jack a few moments to work out who he meant.

'Craig?' he repeated stupidly. 'But Craig's dead.'

Basak shook his head vigorously. 'No. He escapes and kills many, many peoples.'

The next evening, the gates of the fort stood open again. Jack looked yearningly at the outside. Was it a landing strip? With Basak beside him, he got as close to the gates as he could. No one paid him any attention as he stood in the dying light, in the shadow of the wall.

He turned round as Freya approached. She looked worried. She drew him away from Basak who, with a shrug of indifference, leaned against the wall and picked his teeth.

'John, listen to me,' she said in German. 'Oberst Hirsch will be here very shortly. He is being flown in.'

Flown in? So he was right. It was a landing strip the Turks had constructed.

'You are going to be questioned.'

Jack's stomach turned over.

She glanced around to see if they could be overheard. 'What do you know of the Beni Sakr?'

'Nothing. Absolutely nothing.'

Her face twisted. 'They won't believe you. I know you talk to Basak. He told you about the bodies? The bodies of our men?'

Jack nodded.

'Craig did it, Craig and the Beni Sakr. The gold was being taken to the coast. When it didn't arrive we were told. My husband found the bodies. Oberst Hirsch is coming here to investigate.' Her mouth quivered 'My husband believes you will know where Craig and his Arabs have taken the gold.'

'I don't know,' he said desperately. 'I know nothing about it.'

'He will kill you,' she said quietly. 'He is Ozymandias. He will watch you die and . . . and I don't want you to die.'

In the distance came the unmistakable growl of a Mercedes engine. Instinctively he looked up to see the tiny black speck in the sky.

'Oberst Hirsch,' she breathed. She reached out her hands to him. 'I'm sorry, John, so sorry.' She walked away, her head bowed.

Basak came up beside him. 'Time, yes?'

'Let me see the plane,' begged Jack, pointing to the rapidly growing speck. Basak, totally indifferent, shrugged and resumed picking his teeth.

The plane, easily identifiable as a Rumpler Taube Dove, with its distinctive, bird-like wings, circled overhead, flying low above the fort.

The pilot circled once more then came in to land, gliding down before rumbling to a halt on the sand. The pilot climbed out, stretched his shoulders, then hurried round to salute the officer now climbing out of the cockpit.

Jack sank back into the shadows as Von Erlangen came

across the square. There were formalities and a few brief words, then the two senior officers went inside. The pilot relaxed and, catching sight of a Turkish officer, called out something about a drink. The Turk replied and the pilot walked over to him, obviously wanting to know the way to the Mess.

The plane was tantalizingly close and Jack suddenly knew it was now or never. He would have to risk it and it would have to be now, while the plane was still warm, before the propellers needed to be turned to start the engine.

Jack sprinted for the cockpit of the Dove and flung himself aboard. Basak, taken completely by surprise, didn't react until Jack had clambered over the side.

Jack lashed out and caught Basak across the throat, hearing him grunt with a real regret. He fumbled over the unfamiliar controls, then the plane roared into life and he was away, skimming over the level sand. He remembered that the controls were reversed and thrust the joystick forward, utterly exhilarated, as the plane soared into the air.

From beneath him came the crack of rifles but he didn't care. He wouldn't care much if they'd hit him, as long as he didn't have endure another interrogation. Glancing back, he saw the white faces like dots on the parade ground, then settled down to fly back to Petra. With any luck, the fuel dump would still be there and that would get him home.

TEN

I t was incredible, thought Jack, that outside the window, the birds still sang and the lawnmower still clattered over the grass. He was in Hesperus, where he had fled to once before, wounded by Von Erlangen. Sitting in Uncle Phil's homely library, in a sagging armchair, with a friend beside him, was like a second homecoming, an echo of that first. The solid reality of the present – the library, the books, the smell of cigars, the worn leather armchairs and, most of all, Arthur's concerned face – grew, forcing the stomach-churning terror of the past back into yesterday, back into the sealed-up vault of the over-and-done-with.

Only it wasn't over and done with.

Arthur Stanton let out a deep breath. 'Bloody hell, Jack, I had no idea you'd been through anything like that. Why on earth didn't you tell me before?'

Jack didn't answer for some time. 'I was ashamed,' he said at last. 'And then . . . Quite honestly, I forgot. I got posted to France and no one knew. I didn't *want* to remember, of course, and, after a time, it stopped being important. You know what it was like in France. We lived from minute to minute. I didn't have time to go over the past and I certainly didn't want to.'

'Yes,' said Arthur. 'I can see that. What happened after you'd pinched the Dove? Did you get back to Petra?'

Jack nodded and, getting up, lit a cigarette. 'Yes, I got back to Petra. I remembered where Craig marked the petrol dump on his map and filled up the plane. The B.E.2c was still there but it was badly choked with sand, so I set fire to it, rather than let the enemy have it, and stuck with the Dove. I managed to start the engine by putting the throttle to tick over, which is not something I'd do for fun. I stowed as much fuel as I could in the observer's cockpit and managed to get back to Ismailia with only one stop.'

He gave a humourless smile. 'Believe you me, it's no joke flying what's virtually a bomb back over the desert, knowing that any bright lad on our side would take a pop at what seemed to be some demented enemy pilot flying flat, straight and very slowly into British territory. The only thing that got me through was that it was night. Still –' he thrust his hands into his pockets, – 'I made it. I'd been given up for dead, of course, and when the euphoria was over, I had to explain what happened.'

Arthur winced. 'A Board of Inquiry?'

'That's the one.' Jack walked to the window and looked sightlessly on to the terrace. 'What counted in my favour was that I'd made such strenuous efforts to get back. The Dove spoke for itself and so did my previous record. I was pretty young, too. I was only just seventeen. I'd fudged my age to get in.'

He turned and looked at Arthur. 'They liked that. It showed evidence of keenness. They were very keen on being keen. Major Youlton understood what the flight back entailed, too, so that was a good point. However, the Inquiry wasn't fun. It's a capital offence to wilfully supply the enemy with information. I certainly hadn't done it wilfully, but there was a definite feeling amongst some members of the board that I could have held out longer. Anyway, Donahue, the medical officer, gave me a thorough going-over and testified I'd been put through the mill a bit. The fact I'd had Ozymandias to deal with caused a real stir. So, with Major Youlton's support and a certain reluctance in some quarters, I was exonerated. What really put the cat amongst the pigeons was when Craig blew in.'

'Craig?' repeated Arthur. 'But that would have told in your favour, wouldn't it? I mean, he swiped the gold back. As far as the mission was concerned, he'd succeeded.'

'He didn't.'

Arthur stared at him. 'What? But Craig and his Arabs attacked the German convoy. That's why that chap, Oberst Whatisname, flew in to investigate.'

'Not according to Craig,' said Jack. 'That's the story I got from Basak, the Turkish bloke, and from Freya Von Erlangen, but Craig had another story. Craig said he'd got to Petra with the Beni Sakr right enough, and taken charge of the gold from Captain Hawley's convoy. Then, just as Basak had told me, as the Beni Sakr were celebrating, they were attacked. And that, as far as Craig was concerned, was that. He managed to escape with a few men, but there were far too few of them to lead a counter-attack. He was livid that my story had been believed. As he saw it, I was a coward and a traitor who'd blabbed at the first opportunity and cost the lives of his men, to say nothing of the gold. I'd made up this story of a counter-attack to make it seem as if we'd succeeded, which would be better for me.'

'Blimey,' said Arthur after a few moments' thought. 'So the gold just vanished? That's awkward.'

Jack nodded in vigorous agreement. 'It damn well was awkward, Arthur. You see, the Board had given its verdict, so I was officially in the clear. I wondered if the Beni Sakr had taken the gold independently of Craig. He was there when I said it and hit the roof. They were his men, he trusted them implicitly and so on.' He sighed and crushed out his cigarette. 'It was pretty awful, really. Craig blamed me, first, last and foremost. And, to be fair about it, I can see his point of view.'

'You would,' said Arthur.

Jack smiled briefly. 'No, I mean it. You can't get round it, Arthur, he was ambushed because of me.' His face grew grave. 'Craig came off very much worse from the affair. If he'd been a different sort of man, he might have weathered it, but, like a lot of these bluff types, he's deeply sensitive and resented the shadow cast over him and his doings when the real villain, as he saw it – me – got away scot-free. He pushed off into Central Arabia and spent most of the war out there. His pet scheme, that of starting an Arab revolt, was taken up by Colonel Lawrence and Prince Feisal, and so we had T.E. Lawrence, Lawrence of Arabia, not Durant Craig in the starring role. As for me . . .' His voice broke off abruptly.

'Well,' prompted Arthur gently. 'What about you?'

Jack walked to the mantelpiece where he stood, restlessly turning a paperknife over and over in his hands. 'I went through it,' he said quietly. 'Men had been killed because of me.' He rubbed his face with his hand. 'When I went to France I fought like a maniac, trying to . . . well, you know. I don't know why I survived.' His voice shook. 'I actually got given a couple of medals. It didn't *work*.'

With a sudden movement, Jack drove the tip of the paperknife into the wooden mantelpiece. 'It should have *worked,* Arthur. God knows, I didn't want to live. Not then. Every so often it comes back. I read Dante, years later, and that struck deep. In his journey through hell he has a special place for those who betray others. Right at the bottom of the pit. Ice, you know. Coldness. I couldn't touch the book afterwards.'

'You were pushed beyond your limit,' said Arthur firmly. 'You wouldn't blame anyone in those circumstances. I certainly don't blame you.'

Jack looked up. 'Thanks,' he said quietly. He drew a deep breath. 'Anyway, you now know why I've been acting so damned oddly these last few days. I couldn't help it. The very thought of him gave me the jimmies. I'd suspected Simes might turn out to be Von Erlangen and it was shattering to be proved right. Oddly enough, now I do know it's true, it's stopped being quite so scary.' He looked at the discarded envelope on the floor. 'I'd better tell Bill that Madison or Simes wasn't what he appeared to be. And Ashley, come to that.'

'You do realize,' said Arthur, picking up the envelope, 'that this means Von Erlangen's dead?'

Jack looked up, startled. 'My God, yes!' He gave a harsh laugh. 'No wonder Craig fell out with him. I wonder how long it took him to work out exactly who the urbane Mr Madison was?'

'D'you think he did work it out?'

Jack hesitated. 'Well, as far as I know, the two men never met, but I think Craig would have cottoned on to Madison being Ozymandias. That could explain why Craig came back looking for Madison. If Craig suspected Madison's true identity, that would be a real motive. Craig could have taken Vaughan's car and waited around, hoping to see Madison on his own. Then, afterwards, all he has to do is disappear back East.'

The library door opened and Isabelle came in. She looked at the letter in Arthur's hand.

'This is what Jack was waiting for,' said Arthur. 'It's a photograph of the man who called himself Madison.'

Jack took a deep breath. 'And whom I knew as Von Erlangen.'

'Oh, Jack.' It was all she said, but she took his hand and squeezed it.

'He's dead, Isabelle,' said Jack. 'I can hardly believe it, but he's dead.'

'So what now?' she asked, her eyes on his face.

'I think I'd better tell Bill Rackham.' He drew a deep breath, 'I need to see him face to face. I'll have to tell Ashley as well, but I'd rather tell Bill first. He was in the war and Ashley wasn't. I don't know if that makes a difference, but I think Bill will understand.'

'We'll come with you,' said Isabelle swiftly. 'You can't go alone.'

Arthur did most of the talking. Jack was grateful for that. He was able to stay on the sidelines, distance himself from the ghastly memory and – he realized he'd been holding his breath – watch Bill's reaction.

Rackham was shocked, there was no disputing it. Shocked at what he'd done? With an emotional lurch like someone grasping for the edge of a cliff, he knew Bill was on his side.

Arthur replaced the photograph of Von Erlangen in the envelope and put it back on the desk with a gesture of finality. 'So that's who Mr Madison is.'

There were white lines of anger round Rackham's mouth. 'Lothar Von Erlangen. *Ozymandias*. It's a pity he's dead. I'd have liked to have strangled the swine with my own hands.'

Jack cleared his throat. He wanted to get away from the past, to have some action to occupy his thoughts. 'So what now, Bill?'

Rackham hesitated, then dropped his eyes and, picking up his pipe from the desk, concentrated on reaming out the bowl with his penknife. 'The short answer is, I don't know,' he said after a while. 'We've got to find Craig, of course, but he'll have left the country by now.' He looked at Jack understandingly. 'I know you want to be up and doing, but there's nothing much to do.' He stuffed tobacco in his pipe and rammed it down with his thumb. 'It's a matter of waiting until we get a lead on Craig. Until then?' He shrugged. 'Business as usual, I suppose. Have you anything planned for this evening?'

'Nothing much,' said Arthur. 'We thought we'd have dinner before we went back to Hesperus. Do you want to join us?'

Bill pulled a face. 'I wish I could, but I've promised one of the neighbours to make up the numbers at a whist party. I know they'll be stuck if I skip it so I'd better say no, worse luck. However,' he added as Jack scraped his chair back, 'there was something else, before you go. You know that book of water-colours we found? The one with the poem in it? I wouldn't mind your opinion on it. It definitely belonged to our man. We were able to get a good set of fingerprints off it and they matched up with the prints we got from New York.'

'I thought there was something more to that book than met the eye,' put in Jack.

'What sort of something?' asked Isabelle.

'A secret message.' Jack smiled as Isabelle's eyes bright-ened. 'It sounds a bit melodramatic, I know.'

'What sort of secret message?'

'That's just it, Miss Rivers,' said Rackham. 'It looks as if it should mean something, but I'm blessed if I know what. I gave it to our tame expert, Professor Bruce, to see if he could make anything of it, but I'm afraid his considered opinion is that the poem is just a poem and the pictures are just pictures.'

Isabelle looked so crestfallen that Jack laughed. 'It's all very well,' she said, 'but the idea of secret messages is thrilling.'

'Even when they don't exist?'

'They're not the most thrilling sort, I grant you.'

'So what do you want our opinion on, Bill?' asked Jack.

'I'm not satisfied,' he said, getting up from the desk. He went to the filing cabinet and took out the cardboard box containing the book. 'I don't know what we can see that an expert didn't spot, but I wouldn't mind looking through it with you all. You never know, something might click.' He opened the book on the desk.

'*A hundred thousand dragons lie, Underneath an Arabian sky,*' Isabelle read softly. 'That's rather nice, isn't it?' She turned the pages. 'I like the drawings, too. How would you make a secret message out of pictures, though?'

'Count the camels and divide by two?' suggested Arthur with grin. 'I know what you're getting at, though. It feels as if it should mean something, doesn't it?'

'Only it doesn't,' said Jack. 'Not according to the expert.'

A sudden frustrated weariness possessed him. 'Nothing seems to mean much, not even knowing who Madison really is. It doesn't change anything.'

'I don't agree,' said Bill. 'We've found out Craig's motive.'

That was true, but . . . 'It doesn't help us to find out where Craig is now, does it? Mind you, the way I feel, if Craig can get away with it, it'll be fine with me.'

'I'm not surprised,' said Bill. 'By the way, you know you said Von Erlangen was married? Well, it's a bit of a wild guess, but there's a woman in the case. I wonder if that's Freya Von Erlangen by any chance?'

Jack inwardly shied away. It seemed wrong, somehow, to have Bill say her name. Freya Von Erlangen. She'd never been a Von Erlangen in his thoughts. She'd only ever been Freya. *Freya* . . . He didn't even know if she was still alive. 'You mean the woman in the car in the Hammer Valley?' he asked, with a puzzled frown.

Rackham shook his head. 'No, I wasn't thinking of her. This is another woman, a Miss Kirsch, who was clearly involved with Von Erlangen in New York.' Jack looked a question. 'I found out about her from the British Museum. I enquired about the letters which passed between the Museum and Madison, as we knew him then. The curator didn't know what I was talking about at first, because he'd never written to anyone called Madison. However, he had written to a Miss Kirsch in New York, who wanted the names of the leading authorities on the Nabateans. The address is right. 1168, Fourteenth Avenue, Manhattan.'

'So that's this Miss Kirsch in the frame, right enough,' said Jack thoughtfully. 'What's your idea? That she's really Freya . . .' He forced himself to add the surname. 'Von Erlangen?'

'She could be, Jack,' put in Arthur.

'I suppose she could be,' he agreed doubtfully. 'It's possible.'

'It's just a guess,' said Rackham. 'I suppose if she really was Freya Von Erlangen, she'd call herself Mrs Something, not Miss.'

'Couldn't this Miss Kirsch actually be Von Erlangen himself?' asked Isabelle. 'After all, it's easy enough to say you're a Miss Anyone, if all you're going to do is write letters.'

Rackham looked at her with respect. 'That's not a bad point, Miss Rivers. However, the letter to the British Museum was written and replied to while Von Erlangen was in prison.'

Jack glanced up sharply. 'That's why he needed this Miss Kirsch. He wouldn't want to receive a letter in prison. They get checked by the authorities. You might be right, Bill,' he was compelled to add. 'About who she is, I mean. He'd have to trust her and there can't be many people he'd trust.'

'What I can't understand is why Von Erlangen picked Mr Vaughan,' said Arthur. 'It sounds as if they'd never met before. I wondered where he came into the picture.'

Jack looked at him with quick gratitude. He knew Arthur had guessed his reluctance to talk about Freya and he appreciated the tactful change of subject.

'I wondered that too,' said Rackham, 'but it's easy enough to work out. Von Erlangen wanted an expert on the Nabateans and they're fairly few and far between. If we can believe what Vaughan told us, Von Erlangen wanted him to fund an expedition to Arabia, to this lost city he'd found. I asked the bloke at the Museum and apparently it costs a mint to get out there. Vaughan's one of the very few – perhaps the only – chap in Britain who's interested enough in the Nabateans and has the means to consider an expedition.'

'But that still doesn't explain why he asked Mr Vaughan,' said Isabelle with a frown. 'Surely there must be rich collectors in America? Why come to England?'

'Because . . .' Rackham stopped. 'I don't know,' he said slowly.

'Why not go to Germany?' asked Jack with abstracted eyes. 'Why come to England? That was a good point of Isabelle's. After all, he's German.' He clicked his tongue. 'Maybe that's just it. He's probably a great deal more well-known in Germany than anywhere else. He might be afraid of being recognized.'

'That's true, Jack,' said Arthur.

'But why not ask an American?' muttered Jack. 'Bill, when did the British Museum write to Miss Kirsch?'

'I've got a copy of the letter here, together with the rest of the paperwork,' said Rackham. He took a folder from his drawer and laid it on the table.

Jack opened it, read through the letter, frowned and pulled the desk calendar towards him. He picked up a pencil and jotted down a few notes, then looked up. He didn't like what he'd found.

'Here's the answer,' he said, pointing to his notes. 'Look at the sequence of events. Miss Kirsch received a letter from the British Museum, detailing the various experts she could approach. Then there's a gap of about a week or so, in which, I imagine, she made enquiries as to who was both independent and wealthy enough for her purposes. The New York Public Library would have that information, but a copy of *Who's Who* would probably do it. She writes to Vaughan in Madison's name. She might have written to a couple of others, but it's Vaughan who sends the cable yipping excitedly about the Nabateans and inviting Madison to England.'

He put his finger on his notes. 'Look for yourself. Simes or Madison or –' he swallowed – 'to give him his real name, Lothar Von Erlangen, murders the guard, makes his escape, and, the very next day, he's on the *Berengaria* to England. *That's* why he didn't approach an American archaeologist. He knew he was going to commit murder to escape from prison and wanted to get out of America and over to Britain where he'd be safe.'

Rackham looked at the notes. 'My God,' he breathed. 'You're right. He had it all worked out. He had his escape all worked out before he moved a muscle.'

Arthur Stanton whistled. 'That's pretty cold-blooded.'

'It's typical of him,' said Jack, grimly. 'What's more, if he hadn't run into Craig, it would have worked. He would have been safe.'

'That was rotten luck for him, wasn't it?' said Arthur. 'I mean, what were the chances of him meeting Craig?'

Jack sucked his cheeks in. 'Pretty high, I would have thought. After all, although Durant Craig isn't exactly a pal, I can't deny he's the first man you'd turn to if you were planning an expedition to Arabia. Von Erlangen probably underestimated just how eager Vaughan was. It must have been a real shock for him. He thought he'd have a gentlemanly archaeologist to deal with, not a hardbitten type like Craig who knew all about Ozymandias. Craig blamed me for the death of his Arabs, but that wouldn't stop him blaming Ozymandias as well. He'd want to settle with Von Erlangen and no mistake.' It was odd, he thought. The more he said the name the less scary it became.

'I still don't understand it,' said Isabelle. 'It made sense when we thought Von Erlangen was Mr Madison, an innocent art dealer who wanted to find a lost city, but I can't make head or tail of it now. I mean, I follow everything you say about how he contacted Mr Vaughan and murdered the poor guard and so on, and why Craig would have acted the way he did, but why was Von Erlangen so anxious to get to Arabia? You said he was very cultured, but there must be more to it than a thirst for knowledge, surely?'

Bill Rackham looked startled. 'That's a very good question, Miss Rivers.'

'It's a damn good question, Belle,' said Jack. He sat down in a chair and, tilting it back, lit a cigarette thoughtfully. 'No, I can't see that Von Erlangen had a merely academic passion for archaeology.'

'Well, if you ask me,' said Arthur Stanton hesitantly, 'I think it's obvious. The gold from the convoy went missing, didn't it? I think he was after the gold.'

Jack's chair abruptly jerked forward. 'Bloody *hell!*' He glanced at Isabelle apologetically. 'Sorry about that. Arthur, you're a genius. The gold! Of course, it hits you between the eyes, doesn't it?'

'But how could he have known where the gold was?' asked Isabelle. 'The Turks thought the Arabs had taken it, didn't they? Craig's Arabs.'

'Craig denied it,' said Jack. 'If Craig or his men had recovered the gold, he'd have been cock-a-hoop. He'd have told everyone.'

'But didn't you say the gold had been taken by the Beni-whatever-it-is Arabs, Jack? I thought you knew that because of the way the bodies were treated.'

'I *didn't* say it. That's what everyone assumed. Those poor devils of Turks had actually been massacred by machine-gun fire and mutilated afterwards.'

'But Von Erlangen wouldn't attack his own men,' said Isabelle. She stopped and drew her breath in. 'Would he?'

'For a fortune in gold?' said Jack thinly. 'I think he very

well might. He'd know enough to make it look as if the Arabs had done it, as well. He must have got the Turks to hide the gold and then massacred the lot of them. I'll tell you something else, too. I didn't see any machine guns when I was a prisoner in the fort, but Von Erlangen had at least two. Both the Vickers and the Lewis guns and the ammunition were taken from the B.E.2c when I was captured.'

'But could he really do it?' persisted Isabelle. 'Physically, I mean? After all, he would be one man against a whole troop of soldiers.'

'Easily,' said Bill Rackham. 'Especially as they'd be totally unprepared. Did you say a Lewis gun, Jack? That has a rate of fire of about six hundred rounds a minute, as I recall.'

'And a Vickers is even faster,' said Arthur. 'That's about seven hundred rounds a minute. He could do it, Isabelle.'

'All right, I suppose he could, if you're so sure. But why's the gold still there? Why wait all this time before trying to get hold of it?'

'It might not have been safe for him to try and get it,' said Rackham. 'We know he went to America after the war and set up as an art dealer. He was probably trying to get enough money together to get back to Arabia when he went to prison.'

'He'd have a problem actually moving the gold, too,' said Arthur. 'I don't know how much there is, but it's heavy stuff to cart about.'

Jack clicked his fingers. 'Exactly, Arthur. You've got it. That's why he needed Vaughan to pay for an expedition. He'd need help to transport the gold back to civilization from this lost city.'

'If the city exists,' said Rackham sceptically. 'After all, it would be easy enough to paint a picture of an imaginary place and produce a few bits and pieces to convince Vaughan there's really something out there.'

'It exists, all right,' said Jack thoughtfully. 'Basak, my guard, told me the massacre had happened in a deserted city. They're not that uncommon, Bill.' He drummed a tattoo on the table. 'D'you know, it's just as well for Vaughan that he did ask Craig along to the meeting that afternoon. Otherwise, Vaughan, the poor sap, would have forked out for this expedition and, as soon as Von Erlangen got to the city, I bet he'd have been murdered for his pains.' He shook his head reflectively. 'Nothing can make me love Craig, but I don't half feel grateful to him.'

'Yes, I can see that,' said Rackham. 'I'll say this, though. Once we do manage to get our hands on Craig, it'll do wonders for his defence when it becomes known exactly who Madison was. If Craig has a decent lawyer, I wouldn't be surprised if he managed to get away scot-free.' He cocked an eyebrow at Jack. 'How would you feel about appearing for Craig in court?'

'I suppose I will, if I have to,' said Jack unenthusiastically. 'I can't say . . .' He broke off as Isabelle gave an excited squeak.

'Jack! Look!' She was pointing at the poem in the front of the book. 'It's all about treasure! *A hundred thousand dragons lie, Underneath an Arabian sky. The Silent Ones, when asked, will measure, the hidden way to dragons' treasure.* Dragons collect treasure, don't they? In fairy tales the dragon always has a hoard. The treasure must be the gold, the gold from the convoy.'

Jack looked to where she was pointing. 'Good Lord, Belle,' he said softly. 'You're right.'

Isabelle laid the book flat on the desk. They all studied it intently. 'There's another clue,' said Jack. 'Look at the title. *A Tide In The Affairs Of Men.* You remember *Julius Caesar*, don't you, Arthur? We did it at school.'

'A tide in the affairs of men? Hang on a mo. Yes, I've got it. *There's a tide in the affairs of men which, taken at the flood, leads on to fortune*,' said Arthur softly. 'I say, Jack! *Fortune!*'

ELEVEN

All four stared at each other. 'So what we're saying is that somewhere, somehow, hidden in this book are the directions to a fortune?' said Rackham. He sat down, shaking his head slowly. 'How come Professor Bruce missed it?' he demanded.

'He doesn't know what we know,' said Jack. 'After all, we know – or I'm as certain as I can be of anything – that Von Erlangen stole the gold convoy and hid it in the desert.' He ran his hand round his chin thoughtfully. 'Why's he writing a coded message? He must know where the gold is.'

'Perhaps he was afraid of forgetting it?' said Isabelle doubtfully. 'Maybe he painted the pictures to remind himself where it was.'

Arthur clicked his tongue. 'I can't say I'm convinced.'

Isabelle wriggled in dissatisfaction. 'Neither am I, but it's the only reason I can think of.'

'Miss Kirsch,' said Rackham suddenly. 'Miss Kirsch who might be Freya Von Erlangen. I bet he painted the book for her. He was very ill in prison. He was nearly a goner. If he had any feelings at all for her, he'd want to make sure his secret didn't die with him.'

'But you found the book in Von Erlangen's room, didn't you?' objected Arthur.

'He must have taken it back,' said Jack. 'Say Bill's right and he did paint the book in prison. I doubt if he'd give Miss Kirsch or whoever the key to the code, because that doesn't square with what I know of him. He wouldn't want to risk having the gold pinched while he was in stir.'

'He might have intended to give her the key if he was ill again,' suggested Isabelle.

Jack nodded. 'Yes. He probably wouldn't mind her having it if he was dead, but once out of prison, he'd want to keep the book safe and sound.'

'So safe and sound he brought it with him,' said Rackham. 'Yes, that adds up. I wish to goodness we did have the key to the damn thing,' he said in irritation. 'If there really is a convoy of gold lying in the desert, the government will be interested, to say the least.'

'Can't we have a go at cracking it?' asked Isabelle. 'After all, we've got a good idea of what it's about.

Jack looked at Rackham. 'Why not?' He picked up a pencil from the desk. 'Describe the pictures, Isabelle, will you? Something might click.'

'All right. The first picture is of an Arab. The second is of palm trees at sunset and the third picture is of a lot of rocks. Hang on. That's three pictures altogether and the next page has three pictures too, arranged in a triangle. There's a big flock of birds, some camels and a picture of some soldiers.'

'Turkish soldiers,' said Jack, looking over her shoulder.

'Turkish soldiers, then. The next page has . . .' She paused while she counted them up. 'Eleven pictures all together. 'There's one of oil drums, the next one is some odd looking black tents . . .'

'Arab tents,' interposed Jack.

'And a battery of guns.'

'Field-guns,' said Arthur. 'Artillery. Isabelle, how many pictures are on the next page?'

She turned the page. 'There's only three but the page after that has nine.'

Rackham sat up. 'Maybe it's an alphabet code.' He jotted down the alphabet quickly. 'Miss Rivers, how many pictures are on the first page?'

'Three.'

'Equals C. The second?'

'That's three, as well.'

'Oh. C,C.'

'It's not looking good, is it?' said Jack. 'There's eleven on the third page, as you said. That equals L. I think we're barking up the wrong tree but carry on. Page four?'

'That's three.'

'C again. C, C, L, C.'

'And page five is nine.'

'That's I. At least it's a vowel.'

'Page six has five pictures,' said Isabelle.

'And that's E,' said Arthur. 'Another vowel.'

Rackham tapped the pencil on the table. 'This can't be right. It doesn't make sense.'

'They look like Roman numerals, don't they?' said Jack. 'One hundred, one hundred, fifty, one hundred and one. I can't see that gets us very far and the E tears it. Go on, though. I suppose we might as well carry on to the end of the book but I'm not very hopeful.'

After the best part of a quarter of an hour, they looked at the letters on the paper. 'C, C, L, C, I, etcetera' said Rackham moodily. 'If you can make anything of that, you're a better man than I am, Gunga Din.'

'How about if we take every third letter?' asked Isabelle, optimistically. 'Does it give us 'All is known, flee at once,' or something?'

'No,' said Jack. 'It gives us L, E, C, C, C, E, C, H, C and two letters left over at the end. There's not enough vowels to make a readable message if we substitute letters for numbers like that.' He tapped the pencil on his teeth. 'It can't really be a message of the 'All is known, flee at once,' variety, because that implies haste. If you were in a rush you'd hardly sit down and painstakingly paint dozens of pictures. Besides that, we'd worked out it was meant to tell us where the gold was.'

'So what does it imply?' asked Rackham in frustration.

'Give me a few minutes,' said Jack, retreating to the window sill. 'I want to think.' He hitched himself on to the sill, lit a cigarette and fixed his gaze upon a spot on the ceiling. Rackham, Arthur and Isabelle gazed at him with anticipation.

'It's not very exciting, watching Jack think,' said Isabelle after a few minutes.

'Well, you can think as well,' answered her cousin absently. 'I haven't taken out the patent.'

Isabelle shrugged, picked up the pencil and idly started rearranging the letters to pass the time.

Jack finished his cigarette and stood up. 'Look, I'm going to assume that although Von Erlangen was an officer he wasn't a cipher expert. That means he'd probably use one of the common military codes.'

'What, such as the Playfair code, Jack?' asked Arthur.

'I'd say that was the obvious choice, yes.'

Bill Rackham and Isabelle looked at each other blankly. 'You'll have to explain what you mean,' said Rackham. 'I've heard of it but I never did any signalling work.'

'The theory is simple enough,' said Jack. 'You need an alphabet square.' He walked over to the table, picked up the pencil and a piece of paper, and marked six lines down and six lines across. 'You see what I've done. I've divided it into twenty five little squares, one square for each letter of the alphabet.'

'But there're twenty-six letters in the alphabet,' pointed out Isabelle. 'Or there were last time I counted.'

'Ah, but in this system you pretend you're a mediaeval monk or an ancient Roman and count I and J as one.'

'You need a keyword now,' said Arthur. He glanced at Isabelle. 'Choose a word.'

'What, any word?' She looked down at the paper in her hand where she had arranged the letters *I.E. Simes, R.A.* in a neat little pyramid. 'Could this be the key word, Jack?'

He looked at it critically. 'You'd have to be goofy to send the key word and the cipher together. And you've got a repeat of I, S and E in it. Ideally, you don't want any repeated letters.'

'If there are any you simply leave them out,' said Arthur.

'Ter-rue. OK, we fill up the remaining squares with the letters of the alphabet that don't occur in the key word.' He quickly filled in the squares. 'Like this. And, having got our alphabet square, we can read off the code. Let's say the letters we culled from the book are indeed the message.' He tapped the sheet of paper Rackham had written on. 'Now, if you're putting a message into code, you substitute it with the letter on its immediate right.'

Rackham nodded. 'I see. So if you've got a message and want to put it back into plain English, you read off the letter to the left.'

'That's right. Or left, I should say. What have we got? C, which gives us D, and then a repeat of C. DD. Then we've got LC, which becomes ND, and I, which is at the beginning of the row so we substitute it for the letter at the end which is R . . .'

'I thought this was meant to be simple?' complained Isabelle.

'Don't be so impatient, old prune. And the next letter is E, which gives us S, then F, which gives us A and C again which gives us D. Another C – I feel as if I'm all at sea – which is D and E which gives us S once more.' He looked at the letters he had written down and scratched his nose. 'D, D, N, D, R, S, A, D, D, S. I could have a crack at pronouncing that, but it'd sound as if I needed false teeth.'

'It sounds half-baked,' said Isabelle.

Jack scratched the side of his nose. 'Well, it is, really. We don't have the key word and we don't have a coded message to read. I can't believe that C, C, L, C and so on is the code. It's too easy.'

Isabelle threw the pencil at him. 'Do you mean to tell me that we've been fiddling around with bits of paper when we could have been having dinner?'

'It was you who wanted to have a crack at the book,' said Jack, dodging the pencil and returning it to her with a grin.

'It's about time I was off,' said Rackham, standing up and boxing his papers together. 'I'll ask Superintendent Ashley to interview Vaughan again. He might know more than he's let on about the location of this city.' He paused, looking at Jack. 'Do you want to talk to Ashley first? I don't want to say anything that you're not happy with him knowing.'

'Tell him, Bill,' said Jack, reaching for his hat. 'Tell him everything.' He buttoned up his coat, avoiding Rackham's eyes. 'I'd . . . I'd be grateful if you could do that. I think a dickens of a lot of Ashley and I don't know how he's going to react.'

'He'll be fine,' said Rackham reassuringly. 'You just wait and see.'

Jack, Isabelle and Arthur turned the corner into the crowds on the Strand. 'Where shall we eat?' asked Arthur.

'There's always the Savoy,' suggested Isabelle.

'I might have known,' said Arthur with a grin. He turned to Jack. 'That's all right with you, isn't it?'

'Fine,' agreed Jack absently.

'What's the matter?' asked Isabelle.

'It's Freya,' he said slowly. 'If it wasn't for her, I wouldn't have made it, you know? If she is Miss Kirsch, she must know Von Erlangen murdered the prison guard. She'd know an innocent man died.' His face twisted. 'I don't like to think of her mixed up in it.'

'She might not be,' said Isabelle. 'After all, you said he was a secretive type. It would be easy enough to say he was planning to escape without going into details.'

'That's true,' agreed Arthur. 'Not that we're sure she is Miss Kirsch, of course,' he added. They stopped on the corner of the entrance to the Savoy Hotel, waiting for a stream of cars and taxis to go past. 'It beats me why she married a swine like that.'

'She must have been very young,' said Isabelle. 'She's our age, isn't she, Jack? And, after all, he was a Von Something. Poor thing,' she added softly. 'She was frightened of him, wasn't she?'

He nodded. Freya must have felt trapped. If he ever met her again, could he persuade her to trust him? He'd like to have her to trust him, to see her smile, for heaven's sake. She wasn't married any longer. She was free ... *'God Almighty!'* he said, stunned. 'It's her. The woman in black coming out of the Savoy. It's Freya Von Erlangen.'

Jack dived through the traffic and, threading his way through the crowd on the opposite pavement, intercepted the woman in black.

It was Freya. She looked anxious and annoyed as he stood in front of her, effectively barring her way. She obviously didn't recognize him.

'Freya? Mrs Von Erlangen?'

Her face paled and her eyes widened. 'I ... I think you must be mistaken.'

She moved to get past him. Instinctively he reached out and put his hand on her arm. His senses flared. His memory hadn't played him false; she was a lovely woman but her beauty was hidden by her fear.

'Freya! Please. You saved my life. You saved me from

him.' She shrank away, her eyes darting round for an escape. 'Please, Freya, don't go. I don't want to harm you.'

'Who are you?' The words were a frightened whisper.

'I'm Jack, Jack Haldean. I was at Q'asr Dh'an. Don't you remember? You stopped him from shooting me. You looked after me.'

He saw a flash of recognition in her eyes. 'You are the British pilot,' she said wonderingly. She spoke with a soft German accent but her English was fluent. 'I remember. You escaped in the aeroplane.'

'Yes, that's right.' He dropped his arm. 'Look, I know you're in trouble.'

'You can't know anything.' She stepped back from him, looking for a way to escape.

He felt as if he'd caught a wild bird between his hands. At any moment she might dart into the crowds and be gone. Bill Rackham's guess came to his mind. 'I know you're Miss Kirsch,' he said quietly.

He thought she was going to faint. Once more he took her arm, but this time to stop her from falling. 'I'm sorry,' he said. 'I really do mean you no harm.'

Her lips moved soundlessly but she couldn't speak. She leaned against him for support and it was as if a flicker of fire ran through him.

'Come over here,' Jack said, gently ushering her to the side of the building.

'Do I have a choice?' she whispered.

Jack nodded vigorously. 'Of course you have a choice.' He released her arm and stood back. 'If you'd rather, I'll say goodbye now. I'll walk away, but all I want to do is help you.'

Her breathing steadied and her eyes searched his face. 'How?'

'I can try. After all,' he added, 'if you are Miss Kirsch, you're in trouble.'

'Yes.' The word was scarcely audible. She shook her head, like someone coming up from under water. 'How did you know?'

Jack took a deep breath. 'As a matter of fact, I didn't. It was a friend of mine, a police inspector, who guessed.'

'You're in the police?' Her voice was very low.

Jack took her hands, feeling her tremble. His mind was racing. There had been two women, Miss Kirsch and the woman in the Hammer Valley. If Freya was Miss Kirsch, she should be in New York but she *wasn't* in New York. Unlikely as it seemed, she was in England and therefore, unlikely as it seemed . . . 'You were there, weren't you? You were there in the woods in the Hammer Valley, the night the car caught fire?'

She gave a little cry. '*Mein Gott!* Who saw me? Did you?'

He shook his head. 'Not exactly, but I know you were there.' And he did know. Her reaction left him in no doubt.

She clutched his arm. 'And the man who was killed? Madison? The newspaper, it said it was a man called Madison. You know about Madison?'

'I know Madison is your husband.'

There was no mistaking her fear. She gazed at him wordlessly.

'Freya,' he said awkwardly. 'When I say I want to help you, I mean it.'

Her breathing steadied. 'You – yes, you. I remember now. You were grateful to me. You were always grateful to me. Perhaps you can help.' She looked around at the crowds and the traffic. Her hand tightened on his arm. 'We cannot speak here. Will you meet me? Later on, I mean? Come to my hotel in an hour. We can talk there.'

'All right,' said Jack guardedly. It would, he thought, be remarkable if he saw her again, but what choice did he have? There was a policeman on duty a few yards away. As she had admitted to being Miss Kirsch, he could have her arrested as an accessory for the murder of the American prison guard, but his stomach turned over at the thought. 'Which hotel are you staying at?'

'My hotel? It's . . . It's the Stirling on Melbourne Street, off Tottenham Court Road. You know it?'

Jack felt his heart sink. She'd had to think about that answer. If she was staying at the Stirling, he was a Dutchman. The hotel might exist but he was fairly sure she wasn't a guest. 'Who do I ask for?'

'Miss Kirsch,' she said, after a few moments' hesitation. 'Yes. Ask for Miss Kirsch.'

She walked off. Out of the corner of his eye Jack saw Isabelle and Arthur about to cross the road and, with a small gesture of his hand, motioned for them to stay where they were. As she turned to walk on to the Strand, Freya looked at him intently before disappearing into the crowd.

He looked across the road to where Isabelle and Arthur were standing. With a slight inclination of his head towards them, he walked towards the Savoy. They didn't speak until they were in the lobby and out of sight of the street.

'Well?' demanded Isabelle. 'Was she Freya Von Erlangen?'

'She's Freya Von Erlangen, sure enough, and Bill was right. She's Miss Kirsch. Not only that, she's also the woman who was in the Hammer Valley.'

Isabelle stared at him. 'What are you going to do, Jack?'

'I'm supposed to be meeting her in a hour's time at her hotel. She said she was staying at the Stirling on Melbourne Street.'

Isabelle and Arthur exchanged worried glances. 'Are you sure that's a good idea?' asked Arthur.

Jack shrugged. 'What choice do I have? I couldn't detain her by main force and she was as jumpy as a kitten. She was scared to death when I jumped out in front of her and she nearly had a fit when I called her by her proper name. I don't know if she's really staying at the Stirling, but I'll give it a go. Thanks for staying out of sight, by the way. I don't know if she was being watched, but I don't want to draw either of you into it more than necessary.'

'But who could be watching her?' asked Isabelle.

'Craig? Now I know she's the woman from the Hammer Valley, she has to be associated with him in some way. Look, I'm sorry about dinner, but I'm going to have to skip it.' He broke off, thinking. 'Will you go into the lounge and wait for me there? I want to check something with the clerk at the reception desk.'

It was nearly a quarter of an hour later before he joined them. 'I was right,' he said, sitting down. 'I thought Freya must be trying to get hold of Madison's stuff from his room and she was. She told the clerk she was a relative of Madison's and asked if she could have his things. He told her they'd all been given to the police.'

'D'you think she's after the paintings?' asked Isabelle.

Jack nodded. 'I'd say that's certain. I can't see her lusting after the alarm clock. I phoned Bill but his landlady said he'd left for this card party. I left a message and she promised to get it to him.' He picked up his whisky and swirled it round in the glass. 'I wish to God I knew I'd done the right thing. I told Freya I wanted to help.' He looked at them wryly. 'I don't think this is what she had in mind.'

'If she's under Craig's thumb, you are helping her,' said Arthur. 'I thought he was a brute.'

'Yes . . .' He drank his whisky unhappily. 'I know that,' he said eventually. 'She was scared stiff of the police, though. Thanks for the drink, Arthur,' he added absently.

'That's all right,' said Arthur. 'We thought we might as well have something while we were waiting.'

'Waiting?'

'We're coming with you, of course.'

'Don't be idiotic,' said Jack shortly.

Isabelle put down her gin fizz decisively. 'Jack, listen to sense, for heaven's sake. I know you've always thought she's the bee's knees, but we're not elbowing our way into a date, we're trying to keep you out of danger.'

'Danger?'

Arthur leaned forward. 'You must think there's some danger, old man, otherwise you wouldn't have rung Bill Rackham and you wouldn't have been so leery about letting her know we were around. You can't go alone. It's not just her, it's Craig. Having said that, I don't see how you can possibly trust her.'

'I don't know if I do trust her,' he said in irritation.

'Well, act as if you don't trust her, then!' Arthur lowered his voice. 'By her own admission, she's been mixed up with two murders, one in America and one here. I don't know why she was in the Hammer Valley, but it seems damned odd to me.'

'I can't understand that business in the Hammer Valley,' said Isabelle thoughtfully. 'Not unless she bumped off her husband.'

'I don't think she's bumped anyone off,' said Jack seriously. 'I don't think she could. Seeing her again brought it all back, you know?' He intertwined his fingers and looked down at his palms, then shook himself and stood up. 'Come on. If you are coming with me, it's time we were going.'

They took a taxi, instructing the driver to drop them on the Tottenham Court Road at the top of Melbourne Street.

Isabelle got out of the taxi, looked around her and shivered. Melbourne Street was a narrow passage leading off the Oxford Street end of the Tottenham Court Road. It opened out into a small cobbled square, intersected by alleyways.

Two sides of the square housed cheap hotels, their lights glaring in the gathering dusk. The other sides of the square were blank with the blackened brick walls of warehouses. The Stirling was the second hotel on the right-hand side. It had obviously been a private house at one time, and its grimy, stuccoed porch and worn mock marble steps testified to how both house and square had once seen better days. A dog, sitting by the railings of the steps down to the kitchen, eyed them warily as they passed, before subsiding with a low growl. The air was dusty and still and a heavy silence hung over the square. Even the noise of the traffic on the Tottenham Court Road was deadened.

Jack looked at his watch. He had five minutes to go before he'd promised to call for Freya. By common consent, they retreated out of the square and back into the narrow passageway.

'There's not enough cover for a mouse,' said Jack in disgust, standing under an unlit street lamp. 'I hoped you'd be able to come into the hotel and sit in the lounge, but these hotels are more like boarding houses. Anyone who's not a resident would stick out like a sore thumb.'

'I think our best bet is to stay put,' said Arthur. 'We're in the shadows here and I don't think anyone would notice us unless they were particularly looking.' He indicated Isabelle with a sidelong glance. 'I think we're safe enough here. Off you go, Jack. We'll be all right. If necessary, we can be back on the Tottenham Court Road in a couple of ticks.'

As Jack approached the Stirling Hotel, rather to his surprise Freya came down the steps. She had changed out of black and was wearing a blue coat and a blue cloche hat that suited her fair skin. He smiled in involuntary appreciation and Freya smiled back with a shyness that took him unawares.

'I thought you might not come,' she said, taking the arm he offered her.

'You needn't have worried,' he said, feeling her arm on his. 'I wanted to see you again. Shall we have dinner or have you eaten?'

She shook her head. 'No, I haven't eaten.' She gave a mock shudder. 'English food is horrible but there's a nice Italian restaurant in Soho I've been to before.' To his relief she directed them away from the Tottenham Court Road and towards the bottom of the square. 'There's a road which will bring us out on to Oxford Street,' she said. 'It's not very far from there.'

Walking along with Freya by his side, Jack felt a sense of disbelief. This was Freya he was with. Freya Von Erlangen, for heaven's sake, and she was talking about restaurants in Soho.

He tried to force himself to listen to her, but his mind was buzzing. She had been his lifeline in Q'asr Dh'an. In his memory she was all that was good, an icon rather than a human being. But she was *real*. He glanced at her quickly, seeing how a strand of fair hair had escaped from the blue hat, falling over her cheek.

She brushed the hair back and it seemed incredible that she should move so instinctively, that she should actually be here. He had treasured her memory, and now, confronted with the real woman, he wasn't sure how she fitted into the space he had carved out in his mind. His time in Q'asr Dh'an had been a whip-sharp contrast of good and bad, and she had been all the good.

His picture was too stark. He had been a boy who needed kindness. But now? He needed to add colour, life, intelligence – humour, for heaven's sake. He needed to match up his venerated image with reality. He had loved her, missed her, thought about her, and now she was here he wasn't sure if he loved her or the image he had made. Guilt shadowed his thoughts. Freya needed help. If Craig was around she must need help. And he had cared for her, he thought, feeling a sense of pleasure in the certainty of the memory. Her arm nudged his and the little physical touch took his breath away.

She was trying very hard to seem at ease but it was artificial, a mere chatter of words to fill in the gaps. Any minute now and she'd start talking about the weather. He could sense her nervousness, and once again the sensation of holding a fluttering, frightened bird came to mind. He heard a faint footfall behind them and knew that Arthur and Isabelle were following. She gave a little start as if she'd heard it too.

'Why are you calling yourself Miss Kirsch?' he asked quickly, anxious to distract her from the sound. He was anxious, too, to get the conversation away from banalities and on to something he really wanted to know.

Once again she shuddered, but this time it was genuine. 'Lothar said it was necessary. When we went to New York, Lothar sold paintings, yes? He said it was better for business if I was not his wife. He had clients – rich clients – you understand? I had to be nice to them.'

Jack was appalled. 'You mean he used you as a bait?'

Her face twisted, as if she had smelt something rank. 'We had to live.'

'The paintings were forgeries, weren't they?'

Her mouth tightened. 'You know a great deal. It was necessary.' Jack felt a jag of disappointment, but damn it, why *should* she conform to his image? Maybe it had been necessary. 'I would tell the clients a story, how a picture had been stolen or looted in the war or sold for a fraction of its value afterwards, all the things which made these rich, fat Americans think they were getting a bargain.' She shrugged. 'What could I do? I spoke little English then and I was in a strange land. Lothar promised me that eventually we would have enough money to go back to Germany.' Her face softened. 'My home is near Freiburg, in the Black Forest. I wanted to see the mountains once more. My family was respected there. I wanted to go home.'

Home? That was something he could sympathize with, but . . . 'Why didn't you? I know he went to prison. You could have gone home then.'

'Gone home to what?' she demanded bitterly. 'In Germany, without Lothar, I had nothing.' He winced as she said his name. He couldn't help it. 'Lothar had plans, great plans. Germany has suffered but there is a new movement that will change everything. You have heard of the *Sturmabteilung*?' Jack shook his head. 'In English they are called Brownshirts.

Lothar said they are the future. He wanted to be part of it. Besides that, he was ill and needed me.' She paused and spoke very quietly. 'He never needed me before.'

Jack swallowed. It was as if another piece of his icon had flaked away. He'd thought of Von Erlangen and Freya as opposites, and now it seemed as if they had far more in common than he'd ever wanted to believe.

They turned out of the square and on to a high-storied dismal brick canyon of a street, where the dust swirled in the gutters and the gloom was broken only by lights from the occasional shop window. He thought of Isabelle and Arthur behind them. There were very few other people around, but there was, thank goodness, more cover than the square had provided.

Jack shook himself. Yes, he was with Freya, but he was also with the mysterious woman whose footprints he had followed. He had to find out what had happened in the Hammer Valley. 'Talking of need, why did your husband need Vaughan?'

'I don't know,' she said quickly. Too quickly, Jack thought.

'You see,' he said casually, 'I wondered if it had something to do with Q'asr Dh'an.' She drew her breath in and shot him a scared, sidelong glance. That had gone home. Perhaps later he could find out just how right they were in their guess about the gold convoy. 'Have you ever met Vaughan?' She shook her head. 'But you know Craig, though, don't you?'

She gave a little gasp. 'Craig? I don't . . .'

She was scared. That much was obvious. 'Please, Freya, tell me the truth. Tell me about Craig.'

'I . . . I can't,' she said faintly.

'Well, tell me what happened in the Hammer Valley, the night Vaughan's car caught fire,' Jack said, trying another tack. He tried to smile, to lighten everything up. 'What the dickens were you doing there in the first place?' He cut short her denial. 'I know you were there. I don't know why, though.'

It was some time before she spoke. 'Lothar liked to know where I was,' she said eventually. 'He wanted me there. He wanted someone he could trust in case things went wrong. He hired a car so he could take me with him. I waited outside Vaughan's house in the car.'

Von Erlangen had hired a car? 'But Vaughan said Madison had come on the train.'

She gave a short sigh of exasperation. 'That's what he said, yes. He *always* had another plan. Do you not see? It was dangerous for him. Vaughan knew Arabia. If Vaughan had guessed who Lothar was, there might have been difficulties. Lothar knew the English hated him. He thought he was safe with Vaughan, but he didn't *know* he was safe with Vaughan, and he didn't leave anything to chance. He wanted to have a way of escape, so he could get away quickly.'

'But it wasn't Vaughan who was the problem, it was Craig,' Jack said slowly.

She shuddered once more. 'Craig spoilt everything.' She stopped, looking round anxiously. 'I feel as if we're not alone.'

'We're in the middle of London,' Jack said easily.

'No, it is more than that.'

Jack squeezed her arm. 'Come on. Which way is it now? We must be near Oxford Street.'

'We're not far.' She pointed to an ill-lit passage. 'That will take us to Oxford Street, yes?' She swallowed and he knew she was suddenly nervous. 'It is what you call a short cut.'

'Why don't you trust me, Freya?' said Jack, without moving. 'Why don't you tell me what Craig has done?'

'Craig?' Her voice caught on the word.

'I know you're in trouble. If you're Miss Kirsch you're in big trouble. Is that what he's holding over you?' She looked at him without understanding. 'There was the guard, the prison guard,' explained Jack patiently. 'If you know someone's planning a murder and you don't stop them, then you're guilty of murder, too.' She looked frankly puzzled. 'Your husband killed a prison guard, didn't he?'

'You're wrong,' she said faintly. 'You must be wrong. Lothar didn't murder anyone.' She put her hand to her mouth. 'He can't have done. He can't have lied to me.'

He looked into her anxious eyes and felt a surge of fellow feeling. He'd had an image of Freya and Freya had an image of Von Erlangen. Perhaps that was why she'd never left him. If she could delude herself, then she could be content. He was suddenly impatient with how blind she'd been. He sighed and started down the alleyway. 'Freya, he did.'

On the street behind them, Isabelle raised her eyes from the collection of old furniture in the shop window. 'Have they gone?' she asked without looking round.

'They've just set off again,' said Arthur. He narrowed his eyes. 'It's difficult to see in this gloom. They've turned into an alley, I think.'

They walked to the entrance. The alleyway twisted between the blank high walls of the surrounding buildings. The grunt of traffic from Oxford Street sounded faintly, echoing through the narrow passage. Arthur pulled a face, looking at the two retreating backs of Jack and Freya. 'It's going to be fun staying out of sight along there.'

Isabelle put her hand on his arm. 'Arthur! Look!'

Hugging the wall halfway along the alley, a man slipped out of the shadows. Arthur had a brief glance of an overcoated figure with a hat pulled low. The man pulled something that looked like a stumpy stick from his pocket and then, with one voice, both Isabelle and Arthur yelled together. 'Jack! Look out!'

The man in the overcoat struck.

Jack must have sensed something before they yelled, for he turned his head and raised his arm to ward off the blow. They heard the crunch as the cosh went home. Jack crumpled. Isabelle screamed as a long-bladed knife caught the light.

Freya Von Erlangen leapt at the man's arm, sending the knife clattering to the ground. He turned and struck her a vicious blow with the back of his hand, sending her reeling. As Isabelle and Arthur raced up the alley, the man snatched up the knife, hauled Freya forward and, grabbing her arm, ran. Freya shook herself free, turned and saw Isabelle and Arthur.

'Freya! Come back!' yelled Arthur. She shrank away, then turned and ran after the man up the alley.

Jack was lying sprawled with his arms flung wide. Arthur hesitated, seeing the fleeing figures ahead, but a groan from Jack brought him up sharp. He dropped to one knee as Jack groaned once more. He opened Jack's coat, checking anxiously for blood. He breathed a sigh of relief as he saw his friend was unharmed. Freya Von Erlangen had saved him from that at least, thank God.

'Stay with him!' he said to Isabelle shortly and then ran along the alley.

A few yards later and he was on Oxford Street, with its surging crowds and streams of traffic. Freya and the man were nowhere in sight. He walked a few yards up the pavement on either side of the alley, itching with frustration as he realized how hopeless the search was. They could be anywhere in this bright jungle of shops, cars and people. There was a policeman on point duty and, heedless of the squeal of brakes and shouts from outraged motorists, Arthur skirted through the traffic to him.

'Here, what's going on?' demanded the policeman. 'You'll do yourself a mischief, crossing the road like that.'

Arthur explained as rapidly as he could, and the policeman put his whistle to his lips and blew. 'We'll be there as soon as we can, sir,' said the policeman.

Arthur went back down the alleyway. Jack, he was relieved to see, was standing up, leaning against the wall, his head in his hands.

He looked round as feet sounded in the alley. Two policemen loomed at the Oxford Street entrance. A third man in evening dress was behind them. It was Bill Rackham.

'You absolute idiot, Jack,' said Rackham. 'What the devil d'you think you're playing at, gallivanting off with Freya Von Erlangen, of all people? Who hit you?'

'I think it was Craig,' said Jack, nursing his temple. 'All I can really tell you is that the bloke had a beard. By jingo, my head hurts! I half-heard something, then Arthur and Belle yelled a warning and I spun round. I only caught a glimpse before he lammed me with what I assume was a cosh.'

'He pulled out a knife after you went down,' said Arthur. 'Freya Von Erlangen leapt at him and stopped him from stabbing you.'

'Did she?' asked Jack, looking heartened.

Rackham looked at Arthur. 'Did she get away?'

'I'm afraid she did,' said Arthur. 'I shouted to her to stop but the pair of them were off like the clappers when they saw us coming.'

'Freya too?' asked Jack.

Arthur looked at him sympathetically, seeing his friend's

shoulders sag. 'I'm sorry, Jack. She could have escaped from him quite easily but she ran for it.'

Rackham turned to the two policemen. 'Go and see if you can find them. What are they wearing, Stanton?'

'The man's got a dark overcoat and soft hat and has a very full beard. The woman's fair-haired and wearing a blue cloche hat and blue coat.'

Jack nursed his head once more as the policemen set off. 'Just because she ran off with him doesn't mean she's heart and soul on his side, you know. I'd just frightened her silly by talking about being an accessory to murder. It must have scared her witless, seeing Arthur and Belle bear down on her.'

'If you say so,' said Rackham dryly.

'Incidentally, Bill, you guessed right. She's Miss Kirsch and the woman in the Hammer Valley.'

'So I gather,' said Rackham. 'My landlady sent your message round. I set off right away and was hunting round the Tottenham Court Road end of Melbourne Street, when I saw there was a flap on and was told a man had been assaulted in an alley off Oxford Street. I thought you were probably at the bottom of it. Honestly, Jack, you might have known you were walking into trouble.'

'Go easy,' pleaded Jack. 'I've got a dickens of a headache. And really, Bill, what else could I do? I couldn't let her simply walk away, could I? If she really is staying at the Stirling, that's one more lead than we had before.'

'I suppose so,' said Rackham. 'I'd better get on to that right away.' He looked at Jack critically. 'You don't look up to much. How are you getting home tonight?'

'I'm driving,' said Stanton. 'I parked my car in Jack's garage.'

'Well, if you'll take my advice, you'll go back to Hesperus.'

Jack started to protest but Rackham waved him quiet. 'I'm not lumbering myself with a bloke who's just been coshed.' He put his hand on his friend's shoulder. 'Off you go, Jack. You look all in. And don't worry. I'll ring you tomorrow.'

TWELVE

Bill Rackham was as good as his word. The following afternoon he telephoned, but the news was, predictably, negative. 'The Stirling Hotel deny all knowledge of either a Miss Kirsch or Mrs Von Erlangen,' he said.

'I'm not surprised. When I asked her which hotel she was staying at, she had to think. She obviously knew the Stirling though, and was close enough to be on the steps of the place when I went to meet her. What about the other hotels on Melbourne Street? My guess is she's staying at one of those.'

'Well, I checked those, of course, and drew a blank as far as any real information goes. However, I had my suspicious of the owner of the Balmoral, which is next door. He's a foreigner of some sort, a big greasy beggar who I wouldn't trust as far as I could throw an elephant, the type who'd say black's white for a couple of quid. There's no trace of Craig, of course, not that I expected to find any.'

'He seems to have disappeared like an eel into mud,' agreed Jack. 'It's surprising he's still around. I thought he'd be on his way East by now.'

'It might have taken him some time to arrange his exit.'

'True. And he could have hung about for a bit trying to get the watercolours. I don't know if Freya was working under her own steam when she tried to get the watercolours back or if she was prompted by Craig.' His voice sounded doubtful.

'What is it?' asked Rackham.

'Well, I would have said that Craig wasn't a thief. Actually, that could be it, couldn't it? If he finds the gold and comes clean, that'd clear his name of any lingering suspicions he was party to its disappearance.'

'That's going to do him a fat lot of good if we nail him for murder.'

'Yes, but we haven't made a fuss about it being murder, have we? As far as the newspapers are concerned it's a tragic accident.'

'I'm trying to get a toehold on this bloke's character,' complained Rackham. 'You seem to be saying he wouldn't run off with the gold . . .'

'I wouldn't have thought so, but I may be wrong.'

'And yet, at the same time, he wouldn't blink at murder? To say nothing of pulling a knife on you?

'I was in the way. As for killing Von Erlangen, he'd probably see that as a justified execution. I didn't say he was a nice bloke, Bill, just not a thief. Look, to go back to your search for Freya's hotel. Freya said that she and Von Erlangen hired a car to go down to Vaughan's. If you can find the garage they hired it from, it might give you a line on the hotel.'

There was an exasperated noise followed by a pained silence from the other end of the telephone. 'Have you the faintest idea of how many garages there are in London?' Rackham demanded.

'Heaps, I would have said,' replied Jack cheerfully. 'You could ask the Savoy which garage or garages they usually recommend to guests, and if that draws a blank, you can try the garages round Melbourne Street.'

'The same Melbourne Street which is between the Tottenham Court Road and Oxford Street? Why don't you ask me to do something simple, like find a needle in a haystack?'

'Because if you do find the garage,' continued Jack, cutting through Rackham's protests, 'you might find a witness to what actually happened in the Hammer Valley. If Von Erlangen drove the car himself, we're no further forward, but if he hired a driver then you need to speak to the bloke.'

Once more there was silence while this sunk in. 'Blimey, Jack, you're right,' said Rackham enthusiastically. 'OK, I'll do it. It'll take time, but it'll be worth it. What are your plans for the next few days? I want to keep you posted.'

'Thanks, Bill, I'd appreciate it. I'll be back in London on Sunday night for a few days. I've got a stint at the magazine, then I'm coming back for Isabelle's wedding.'

'Right you are,' said Rackham. 'I hope we can dig up something before the wedding, at any rate. Incidentally, I spoke to Ashley this morning.'

Jack felt his stomach knot. 'Did you tell him?'

'Yes, of course I did. He'd guessed something was the matter, you know. You are an idiot, Jack. How did you expect him to react?' Jack didn't answer. 'Don't worry.'

'Thanks, Bill,' said Jack quietly. 'Thanks.'

He put the phone down, but before he left the hall it rang again. It was Ashley.

'Haldean? Is that you?' Ashley sounded ill at ease. 'Look, before I say anything else, Inspector Rackham told me what happened with you and this Von Erlangen character. He said you weren't sure how I'd react.'

'No,' said Jack evenly. 'I'm not proud of it, Ashley.'

Ashley snorted dismissively. 'You young fool. Give me some credit. I knew something was wrong. My word, when we do finally get our hands on Craig, I'm going to shake him by the hand. I've never heard anything like it in my life. I know there were some pretty beastly stories going the rounds in the war, but I thought most of them were propaganda. It took my breath away when Inspector Rackham told me what you'd been through. By jingo, I feel Craig deserves a medal.'

'Thanks, Ashley,' said Jack. He was more moved than he could say and hoped his voice wouldn't betray him.

'If Craig hadn't seen him off, I'd be tempted to do the job myself. Anyway, that's that.'

And knowing Ashley, that was that. Jack felt such a surge of gratitude to the older man, he was glad that Ashley couldn't see his face. 'All I can say is thanks, Ashley.' He paused. 'Is that why you rang?'

'Partly. I wanted to tell you I've just telephoned Vaughan's house to arrange another interview.' Ashley paused.

'And?' prompted Jack.

'And I spoke to Oxley, Vaughan's butler. Vaughan's left the country.'

'He's done what?'

'He's gone. He left yesterday morning. He told Oxley he expected to be away for some time, and although he didn't say exactly where he was going, he's headed East. I suppose he's going to look for this lost city.'

Jack clicked his tongue. 'I suppose he is.' He paused for a moment. 'Look, Ashley, we are right, aren't we? I mean

Vaughan can't be up to anything dodgy, can he? I don't like him chasing off like this.'

'Well, I'm not crazy about it, but I think we've proved as much as it can be proved that Vaughan is in the clear.'

'That's true enough,' said Jack doubtfully. 'Well, good luck to him. I don't know as I'd care to wander about the Hejaz on the off-chance.'

'I was wondering if he was in any danger. I heard what happened to you last night and if Craig turns up, he might not be too happy to see Vaughan.'

'No, he wouldn't. Still, unless Vaughan knows a lot more than he told us, I imagine his chances of finding the city are nil.'

'If he kept information to himself, he's only got himself to blame. Incidentally, would Miss Rivers and Captain Stanton think it a liberty if I sent them a wedding present?'

'I think they'd be very touched. Oddly enough, they're off East as well. They're going to Egypt for their honeymoon. Uncle Phil and Aunt Alice were stationed out there, years ago, and Isabelle's always wanted to see the place.'

'Well, if they run into Vaughan, tell him to send us a postcard.'

A few days later, Sergeant Munson turned into Taylor Street, an obscure cul-de-sac off the Tottenham Court Road. Taylor Street contained a newsagents, a pie-and-mash shop, a cheap drapers, a Unitarian chapel and, at the end of the road, a commercial garage. According to the brightly coloured metal sign it belonged to The Klassy Kab Motor Hire and Conveyance Company (Prop: J.K. Bellweather). This must be, thought Sergeant Munson, about the fifty-first garage he'd been to.

Sergeant Munson called to the boy washing down an Alvis in the yard, and repeated a version of what he had said so many times that week. 'Hello, son. Is the boss about?'

'Mr Bellweather, sir?' asked the youth, putting the cloth in the bucket and wiping his hands on his overalls. 'Did you want to hire a car?'

'No,' said Sergeant Munson, producing his warrant card. 'I'm just making a few enquires. Nothing to get alarmed about.' Or excited by, either, he thought, following the youth into the garage. It was Thursday afternoon and Sergeant Munson was bored to tears. Inspector Rackham himself had checked the garages the Savoy had recommended, and when that proved fruitless, had handed the job to him. However, if Inspector Rackham wanted him to check garages, he'd check garages until he was told to stop, however pointless it was.

'What did you say the gentleman's name was?' asked Mr Bellweather, picking up the ledger, once Sergeant Munson had explained his business. 'Madison?'

'We're not sure what name he used. It might not even be a man.'

Mr Bellweather frowned, running his finger down the page. 'There's no one called Madison, but we did have a booking on the 27th which might be the one you're looking for.' Munson felt a jolt of excitement. 'Look, here we are,' said Mr Bellweather, pointing out the entry. 'It was a Mr Smith, staying at the Balmoral Hotel on Melbourne Street. He hired our Crossley 25-30 h.p. all-weather five-seater for the day at a cost of six pounds, four and sixpence. He took it down to . . . Sussex. That's right. I see the driver's made a note that he arrived back just after ten o'clock. Who was it? Oh yes. Bert – that's Gilbert – Faraday.'

'He was the driver?' asked Sergeant Munson quickly. This is what Inspector Rackham wanted. 'Would it be possible to speak to Mr Faraday?'

''Fraid not. He's left. He went home that evening and sent a message round the next day to say that he'd found a better job.' Mr Bellweather pursed his lips. 'These youngsters have no staying power. Someone offers them three pounds a week and they're off. Now, we pay our drivers two pounds five bob, but the money's safe. These big money places are here today, gone tomorrow.'

'Was Faraday friendly with any of the men here?'

Mr Bellweather thought for a moment. 'Crutchley's your best bet. I think he's in the garage now if you want a word with him.'

Paul Crutchley put down the contact breaker he was cleaning and gave Sergeant Munson a worried smile. 'I'm glad someone's taking an interest in poor old Bert at last.

I can't make it out. I haven't seen hair nor hide of him since last week. No one has.' He shrugged. 'It's probably something and nothing, but I'd like to know who the geezer was that turned up for Bert's wages.'

'His wages?' asked Sergeant Munson.

'Yes. The day after he took the Crossley out, a bearded bloke came in and said that Bert had found a better place and could he have his wages? He'd asked this bloke, the one who turned up, to get them for him. You remember that, don't you, boss?' asked Crutchley, turning to Mr Bellweather.

'I do indeed. I sent him away with a flea in his ear. If Faraday wants his money, he can come and get it himself.'

'What did this bearded man look like?' asked Munson, concealing his excitement.

Mr Bellweather frowned. 'I'm not much of a hand at descriptions. I didn't really pay much attention to him because I was annoyed at having been let down.'

'Yes, I can see that, sir,' said Munson. 'This Crossley which Mr Smith hired. Is it in the garage by any chance?'

'It is, as a matter of fact,' said Mr Bellweather. 'Do you want to see it?'

'If you don't mind, sir.'

Mr Bellweather led the way out on to the forecourt to where a large, dark blue Crossley was standing. 'This is it, officer.' He looked on with interest as Sergeant Munson, taking a piece of paper and a block of graphite from his case, knelt down and took an impression of the tyres. 'Is there something special about the tyres? They're just ordinary Michelins as far as I know.'

'It's just a matter of routine, sir,' said Munson, completing his impression.

A bearded man and diamond-patterned Michelins on the Crossley. Sergeant Munson noted down Gilbert Faraday's address and left, feeling he'd done a really good afternoon's work.

'The driver's disappeared?' asked Jack. After a day at the magazine offices, he had called in to Scotland Yard to see if there was any progress with the long-winded hunt for the garage. 'I don't like the sound of that at all, Bill.'

'No more do I,' agreed Rackham. 'Especially with Craig turning up the next day. It's clever, isn't it? Because the garage owner assumed Faraday had left him in the lurch, he was annoyed but not suspicious. God knows where Faraday is now. The only bright spot is that we haven't had any unidentified bodies turn up, which is something. We're searching for him, of course, and I just hope we have a stroke of luck. Incidentally, I went back to the Balmoral. Lord, I loathe that man who's in charge. I wouldn't trust him an inch. Apparently a Mr Smith stayed with them – he sounds like Craig – but there was no Miss Kirsch that he owned up to. Mr Smith left the hotel the evening you were attacked. And that, Jack,' he said drumming a pencil on the desk, 'is that. I'm damned if I know what to do next.' He looked up hopefully. 'Any ideas?'

'None, I'm afraid,' said Jack, running his hand through his hair. 'I won't have much time to think about it either for the next couple of days. It's Isabelle's wedding this weekend.'

'Well, that's something for you to look forward to, anyway,' said Rackham getting to his feet. 'Give them my best, won't you?'

Mark Stuckley escorted his grandmother to a pew halfway up the church, retrieved his sister's bag and assured his mother that he would be back in plenty of time before what he irreverently termed 'the kick off'. Composing his features into what he hoped was a mixture of sobriety and devotion, he walked to the east door of the church. He had seen Arthur disappear round a handy buttress with Jack at his side. Arthur, thought Mark with a grin, as he saw the two men, hardly looked as if he were about to embark on the happiest day of his life. 'Are you nervous?' he asked.

'What do you think?' said Arthur, pulling at a cigarette as if it were his last one before he was marched before a firing squad.

'At least it's not St George's, Hanover Square,' said Jack.

'No,' said Arthur with a shudder. 'No, thank God.'

Mark Stuckley patted his pocket. 'I've got a hip flask with me if that's any help.'

Arthur ran his tongue over his dry lips but shook his head

regretfully. 'I'd better not.' He finished his cigarette and threw away the butt. 'Hadn't we better get into the church? You're sure you've got the ring, Jack?'

'All safe and sound, old man. Relax, Arthur, it's going to be fine.'

They took their places in the church. Yes, thought Jack, he was glad Isabelle had decided to get married in the village church. The organ played softly and the spring sunshine streamed in through the porch, painting bars of gold on the worn flagstones and striking deep, warm life from the oak pews, rich after centuries of care.

It illuminated the brass tablet commemorating the life of Augusta Rivers, wife of Sir John Rivers, Bart., of Stanmore Parry of the County of Sussex, drowned off the coast of Bombay, July 3rd, 1830. A dutiful and obedient wife and loving mother, whose virtues were, apparently, too many to enumerate. *And her children shall rise up and call her blessed.* Jack wondered. 'Augusta' had a discouraging air about it. Maybe they called her 'Gus' in private.

His eyes wandered on to the next tablet and he swallowed. *Second Lieutenant Frederick Staples, Gunnery Officer, HMS. Tiger, died at the battle of Jutland of wounds received 31st May 1916. And the sea shall give up her dead.* He hadn't thought of Freddy for years. He'd been a stammering, curly-haired boy with a passion for wildlife who had the best collection of birds' eggs in the village. They had once spent a whole night crouched in Hesperus woods, watching a family of badgers. Now all that was left of Freddy was a memory and a brass plate in Sussex. Jack shivered.

'I know,' whispered Arthur, misinterpreting the emotion. 'This waiting's awful.'

'Don't worry.' His gaze drifted round the church once more. Fine collection of hats . . .

The sun glinted through the stained glass window, gift of Sir William Rivers, 1852, jewelling John the Baptist's cloak in deep ruby. Christ being baptized jostled for position with Christ subduing the Sea of Galilee and presiding over the miraculous draught of fishes. Noah, at the bottom of the window, leaning out of an ark that looked exactly like a canoe with a house on top, had released a dove, that, olive twig in mouth, flew away over the waste of waters. The dove reappeared as the Holy Ghost further up the picture.

They were all sea pictures; that was to be expected this close to the coast. The window was a replacement for a medieval one that had attracted the attention of Cromwell's men. Fortunately the rood screen, damaged as it was, had escaped Sir William's zeal for restoration. Some seventeenth century iconoclast had taken a carpenter's chisel and gouged off the faces of the saints that had ornamented the panels. Anonymous now they stood, martyrs of the Civil War, known only unto God, silent witnesses of a time when religion inflamed men's passions and wasn't simply a thing that must never be discussed at dinner parties. It was funny to think of violence in this setting. Yet there was the memorial to Freddy . . .

The organ music swelled and Isabelle, with her father beside her and her two friends – Bubble and Squeak Robiceux, the bridesmaids – following behind, entered the church.

Arthur turned round and gave a little gasp of pleasure. Jack saw the nervousness go out of him. The two men stood up and walked to the steps of the altar.

Mr Simpson, the vicar, who had known Isabelle since her cradle, gravely informed them that marriage was not to be entered lightly or unadvisedly – no one seeing Arthur's face would suspect him of that for a moment – nor that he was wantonly thinking of satisfying his carnal lusts and brute appetites; which was another possibility which had occurred to the authors of the Book of Common Prayer. After checking that there was no impediment – Arthur's four-year-old nephew coughed at this point, causing an outbreak of shushing three-quarters of the way up the church – Arthur Christopher agreed, according to God's holy ordinance, to take Isabelle Alice to be his wedded wife. Isabelle Alice, for her part, agreed to obey, serve, love, honour and keep Arthur Christopher, and Jack, who had been listening with delight to the dignity of the words and looking with enormous affection at Isabelle Alice, suddenly froze.

He had it! All the pieces of the puzzle whirled and settled in his mind. He saw a quick succession of images; the burnt-out Rolls-Royce, the ruby and sapphire of the stained glass window, the rug in the car and Isabelle herself; they all settled into one seamless pattern. But if he was right . . . His stomach felt as if he were going down in a lift.

'The ring, Jack,' hissed Arthur. 'We need the ring.'

With an apologetic smile, Jack pulled the ring from his pocket and forced his mind back to the ceremony.

The photographer, standing in the ballroom at Hesperus, emerged like a Jack-in-the-box from his black shroud and beamed insincerely on Master Alan Rutherford, whose four-year-old charm had done so much to enliven the proceedings. 'Just move in a little closer, young man . . . that's it.' Magnesium flared and Master Rutherford, released from his father's grip of iron, was a free agent once more.

Jack, separated from the bride and groom by a crush of relatives, found a small, hot hand slipped into his.

'You're Uncle Arthur's friend, aren't you? You played lions with me at Christmas. Uncle Arthur's got married now and I've got to call her Aunty Isabelle and be good.'

'Quite right, old son. I'd like to see your Uncle Arthur but there's too many people around.'

'I want to see Aunty Isabelle. She's with Uncle Arthur.' Master Rutherford surged confidently through the sea of legs towering over him, hauling Jack behind him. The crowd magically parted and Alan tapped Isabelle on the hand. 'You're Aunty Isabelle, now. You've got a pretty dress.' Beaching Jack, he disappeared into the crowd once more.

'That child's got a future as a tugboat,' grinned Jack. 'And he's quite right. You have got a pretty dress. You look lovely, Belle.' He kissed her. 'I know you'll be very happy.'

'Thanks, Jack. What happened? With the ring, I mean. You were as white as a sheet.'

'I'm sorry about that. Something suddenly occurred to me.'

'Not your speech?' said Arthur anxiously. 'The speech for the wedding breakfast, I mean? You've got it ready, haven't you? I've been tearing my hair out over mine.'

'Absolutely, I have. Don't worry.'

The speeches, together with the wedding breakfast, came

and went. The bride and groom left for Southampton en route for Egypt amid a flurry of good wishes and, after all the fuss had died down, Jack sought out Mark Stuckley.

'Mark, I've got an idea about the fire at your party but I need your help to prove it. Are you free on Monday?'

'As it happens, yes,' said Mark, looking curious. 'What's it all about?'

'I'll tell you later. I need to get some details worked out, but I'm on to something.'

'Right-oh.'

No one noticed the best man slip away to the telephone, but on the other end of the line, Ashley listened in mounting bewilderment. 'You want to do another speed trial? But what for? We've proved it doesn't work.'

'I don't want to say too much on the telephone, but meet me tomorrow and I'll explain.' Ashley could hear the wry amusement in his voice. 'That is, if I don't get nicked for burglary in the meantime.'

THIRTEEN

Superintendent Ashley, pipe in hand, sat in the shade of an alder tree on the grassy bank of Stour Creek, watching the midges dance over the still water. It was an idyllic spot in the sort of landscape he loved, but despite his outward calm, he was too tense to appreciate his surroundings. He glanced at his watch once more. One hour and four minutes. Their time limit was seventy-five minutes. Eleven more minutes to prove the impossible possible.

He narrowed his eyes, looking down the shaded, sun-dappled waters of the creek beneath the bridge. Surely there was movement on the water? His heart gave a leap of triumph as he saw the rippling light catch the blade of a paddle. Seconds later, a narrow, pointed canoe cut through the water towards him. The man on board, who had been kneeling up in the boat, sat back, and, with a lazy dip of the blade, brought the frail craft to the shore.

Mark Stuckley got out of the canoe and, with a broad smile, pulled it on to the bank. 'My word, that was a trip and a half. I'm going to get one of these little beauties. They go like the clappers. What was the time?'

'Sixty-five minutes,' said Ashley enthusiastically. He looked to where the white wall of Vaughan's garden ran down to the creek. 'Say another minute to get to the boat-house and that's sixty-six in all. That's well within our limit.'

Mark Stuckley stretched his shoulders and lit a cigarette. 'Old Jack'll be pleased.'

'I should damn well think he will.'

He was. It was over a quarter of an hour later when they heard the engine of the Spyker on the road above the bridge. They scrambled up the bank and, as Jack saw Mark Stuckley, he looked an anxious question.

'Sixty-six minutes,' said Stuckley in triumph.

Jack sat back in the seat of the Spyker and breathed a deep sigh of relief. 'Wonderful. Absolutely wonderful. Mark, old son, you're a marvel. Let's get the canoe back into the boathouse, then I'm going to take you both to the pub. I want to celebrate.'

It was still early in the evening and they had the snug of the Fisherman's Rest to themselves. 'Congratulations,' said Jack, raising his pint of bitter. 'I can't help thinking it should be champagne, but congratulations. And especially to you, Mark.'

Stuckley grinned. 'I enjoyed it. But come on, Jack, you were blinking mysterious earlier on. All I really knew was that I had to go like a bat out of hell and that somehow or other that would tell you what had happened at the fancy-dress party.'

'Okey-doke,' said Jack, with a look at Ashley. 'It is all right, isn't it?'

'That's fine, Haldean. I'm sure Mr Stuckley realizes that this is all in confidence.' He smiled. 'Besides that, he must know or have guessed so much already, it seems churlish to hold out on him.' He picked up his bitter. 'And, speaking for myself, I've got the broad outlines of the thing, but I'd like to hear you put it together.'

'Right-oh.' Haldean lit a cigarette and blew out a reflective mouthful of smoke. 'We'll start with what happened at Vaughan's, the day of your party, Mark. Now Vaughan, as you know, is a keen amateur archaeologist, and he'd received a letter from one Adler Madison, a New York dealer in art and antiquities, saying he knew the whereabouts of a lost city, an undiscovered Nabatean site, in the Arabian desert.'

'That'd get him going,' commented Stuckley. 'I've heard old Vaughan carry on about the Nabateans before. No one else has ever heard of them, as far as I can make out.'

'As you say. Vaughan invited Mr Madison over to England, his idea being that he'd fund an expedition to the Hejaz if Madison told him where they were heading for. He also, as he wanted to get the ball rolling as quickly as possible, and without reference to Madison, invited Durant Craig to make a third at the meeting and organize the practical details of the expedition. OK?'

'I'm with you so far. Go on.'

'Now unfortunately, unbeknownst to Vaughan, Craig and Madison – Madison wasn't his real name – were old enemies.'

'Madison's real name was Von Erlangen,' put in Ashley. 'He was an evil brute. A real swine.'

Jack flicked a quick glance of gratitude in his direction. He didn't want to explain about Von Erlangen. 'To put it mildly, the meeting didn't go according to plan. Durant Craig rumbled who Madison was and they had a real set-to. The quarrel ended in murder.'

Stuckley gaped at him. 'I say, Jack! Murder? And this was at Vaughan's house?'

Jack nodded. 'That's right. I don't know who did the actual deed, but Vaughan was in the soup and no mistake. He could have yelled for the police, but that would mean giving up his expedition. He might have been subject to some sort of persuasion, but his subsequent actions shows he was in it up to his neck. At the very least he's guilty of covering up murder.'

'The devil,' breathed Stuckley. 'I never liked him, you know. If he wanted something enough, I don't think anything would stand in his way.'

'Events prove you right, Mark. Anyway, our Mr Vaughan had a body to dispose of. He was due at your party that evening and time was limited. He couldn't afford not to go. That would mean drawing attention to himself by changing his plans. And then, I imagine, the party gave him the idea how he might carry it off. You remember his costume, don't you?'

Stuckley nodded. 'Yes, of course I do. He came as Rasputin with a whacking great beard. It was nearly as good as mine.'

'Exactly,' said Jack with a grin. 'I bet it was the beard which gave him the idea. Ashley and I nearly got the truth of this first crack out of the box. We suspected Vaughan disguised himself with his false beard, drove over to the Hammer Valley early in the evening, smashed the car into a tree and arranged the body in the driver's seat. Then, at your party, we believe he slipped away to the car, laid a trail of petrol, nipped back up to the terrace and struck a match.'

Stuckley stopped with his beer halfway to his mouth. 'So it was *Vaughan* we have to thank for the fire? Damn it, he nearly set the house ablaze!'

'I don't suppose that was his intention, but yes, you can blame Vaughan for that. Anyway, as I said, we thought Vaughan's part in the proceedings was a bit rum, but it seemed impossible he could have been involved. It was totally impossible if the car had crashed when it was supposed to have done, and even granted there were some shenanigans beforehand, it was still impossible. I simply couldn't see how Vaughan had arranged the smash and got back to his house in the time allowed.'

'So when did you click?' asked Mark. 'When did you work it out?'

Jack grinned. 'I don't know if you noticed or not, but I nearly gave poor old Arthur a heart attack at his wedding by being late with the ring.'

'I noticed you seemed to have gone into a trance, yes.'

'What happened was I'd been distracted when Isabelle was taking her vows. I mean, it was all very moving and so on, and it struck me as a shame, in a way, especially as we were standing in a church stuffed full of references to her ancestors, that she had to give up her surname.'

'Rivers,' said Stuckley.

'Precisely,' agreed Jack. 'Rivers. And then, you know how it is when your mind wanders. There was the tablet to Augusta Rivers who'd been drowned and the memorial to poor old Freddy Staples – do you remember him, Mark? – who was killed at Jutland, and the stained glass window with its pictures of the river Jordan and the Sea of Galilee and that ark which looks just like a canoe with a child's building-brick house on top and suddenly everything seemed to be saying 'water' to me. I looked at Noah leaning out of the ark that looked so like a canoe and suddenly realized how Vaughan must have done it.'

'That's excellent work, Haldean,' said Ashley in deep appreciation. 'I wondered what you were talking about, mind, when you telephoned, especially when you mentioned burglary.'

Jack grinned once more. 'I had to get a canoe from somewhere and that's one of the things Uncle Phil hasn't got at Hesperus. So, it struck me, as I was convinced that Vaughan had used a canoe, I might as well pinch his. I broke into his boathouse yesterday and stole it with very little trouble.' He looked at Ashley. 'Mark knows this, of course, but Vaughan's canoe isn't a rigid thing. It's a canvas affair with poles you can take to bits. I knew it more or less had to be and that's one of the reasons I wanted to take it well in advance, as I thought Mark and I would need practice putting it together. There's another thing, too. When it's rolled up on the back seat of a car, and covered with a rug, not only does it cover up any corpses that you might have lying about . . . Well, you see what I'm getting at.'

Ashley stared at him. '. . . It looks like a rug or a tent,' he breathed. 'My God, Haldean, that's *exactly* what PC Marsh said!'

'It's a brilliant little craft,' said Mark reflectively. 'There's no draught to speak of and it goes like greased lighting if you know how to handle it. The water route is very quick because it cuts out that great loop of land round Gifford St Luke and all those villages, but it never occurred to me that you could sail anything bigger than a paper boat on the Hammer.'

'That's right, Mark,' agreed Jack. 'That's why it took me such a long time to tumble to the idea. I can't prove it, of course, but we suspected Vaughan and we've shown it can be done. Vaughan was back home for ten to seven at the latest, as that's when he spoke to his chauffeur, Brough.'

Stuckley frowned. 'Hang on a minute, Jack. I read what was in the papers, of course, and as I understand it, this bloke who called himself Madison was seen with Vaughan after the Rolls-Royce was stolen. He actually spoke to Vaughan's chauffeur, didn't he? He can't have done that if he was dead.'

Jack raised his eyebrows. 'So?' he questioned softly.

'So that means it's impossible or . . . *Good God!*' Stuckley put down his glass and stared at him. 'It was *Craig* who was killed.'

Ashley couldn't help laughing. 'You've got it, Mr Stuckley. My goodness, you should have heard my reaction when Haldean sprang that one on me. We'd been led up the garden path all right, and no mistake.'

'So that means that this other bloke, this German type, is still alive?'

'Yes,' said Jack, in a very controlled voice. 'That means this German type is still alive. I'm sure he was the one who attacked me in London, Ashley. I should have guessed, you know. Freya Von Erlangen was scared rigid when I met her. Von Erlangen would scare anyone.'

'But where is he now?' demanded Stuckley.

Jack shrugged. 'I presume, as Vaughan's left the country, he's with Vaughan somewhere in the East.'

'What? Searching for this lost city, you mean?'

'That's my guess. And quite frankly, Vaughan might as well try and tame a cobra as go anywhere with Von Erlangen. He can't know who he's dealing with.'

Ashley sipped his beer thoughtfully. 'It's his own fault, Haldean. Mind you, if he does get back safely, he'll have some questions to answer. Or I hope he will,' he added. 'I'll have to put these ideas to the Chief, and as you say, Haldean, we can't actually prove it. It's all a case of what could have happened, you see, and unless the Chief believes we can make the charge stick, he won't move on it. I know what he's going to say. It's all very well having theories, but we could do with some physical evidence.'

Jack thought for a moment. 'Why don't you take a dekko in Vaughan's study? Or rather, as it might be awkward for you if it came out you'd been sloping round without a warrant, why don't I?'

'You can't do that, Haldean,' said Ashley, shocked. 'It's one thing borrowing his canoe. Breaking and entering is a very different kettle of fish.'

Jack held up his hand pacifically. 'Leave it with me, old thing. D'you know, I can't help feeling I've missed my way. I bet I could have carved out a really successful career as a burglar.'

Oxley, the butler, showed Jack into the study. 'Do you know where the book is Mr Vaughan offered to lend you, sir?' He surveyed the well-stocked bookcase dubiously. 'It'll take you some while to hunt through all those.'

'I should be able to find it,' said Jack easily. 'I think I remember where Mr Vaughan put it.' He cocked his head to one side as the doorbell rang.

'If you'll excuse me, sir,' said Oxley, leaving the room. 'That was the bell.' Leaving the door ajar, he went into the hall.

Jack picked up the four marble figurines that stood on the bookshelf, one after another. Nothing. He glanced round the room and walked towards the fireplace with its surrounding chairs, visualizing the scene in his mind. Craig there, Vaughan facing him, Von Erlangen sitting to one side? On the mantel-piece was a pair of bronze statues of what were probably Greek goddesses. They were about nine inches tall and looked very solid. He heard voices in the hall. He didn't have long. Whistling softly, he quickly tipped over first the right-hand and then the left-hand statue. The metal of the heavy square base of the second statue was pitted with age and, turning it to the window, he could see a dark substance in the minute holes.

He rapidly replaced it on the mantelpiece and by the time Oxley came back into the room, a few moments later, Jack was standing by the bookcase once more, book in hand. 'Is that the one you were looking for, sir?' asked Oxley. 'I'm glad you found it.' He cleared his throat. 'Mr Stuckley's in the hall. He's been doing a bit of fishing and said he recognized your car parked on the road. He wondered if you were here.'

'Mr Stuckley?' asked Jack, walking to the door. 'I bet he's after a lift. Thanks for the book, by the way. I'll return it in a couple of days. I'm grateful to you.'

'Not at all, sir,' said Oxley, showing him into the hall.

'And that,' said Jack, as he and Mark drove back to the Fisherman's Rest, 'was well worth doing. If there wasn't blood on the base of that statue, I'll eat it.'

The next morning Ashley had an interview with the Chief Constable, Major-General Flint, the results of which were both irritating and unsatisfactory.

'The Chief,' he said to Haldean, after he was shown into the morning room at Hesperus, 'is going to have a word with Vaughan when he returns.'

Jack paused with the coffee-pot in his hand. He was going back to London that day but he had waited to find out what General Flint proposed to do. He looked at Ashley quizzi-cally. 'And that's it?'

'And that's it.' Ashley let his breath out in disgust. 'The trouble is, Haldean, General Flint doesn't really believe it's anything more than an accident. He finds it unlikely that a gentleman such as Vaughan should be party to murder and he can't credit that he should willingly sacrifice his Roll-Royce. A Rolls-Royce, as he said to me, costs over three thousand pounds.'

'It's a point,' agreed Jack, handing him a cup of coffee, 'but I imagine it was insured. Help yourself to milk and sugar. Besides that, the stakes were pretty high.'

'That's more or less what I said.' Ashley lit a cigarette and blew out the smoke in disgust. 'General Flint has got some sterling qualities but he's got no imagination. He wants things to be simple and straightforward and when they aren't, he doesn't like it. What's that thing I was reading about the other day? It came into a detective story. Occam's Razor, that's it.'

'*Entia non sunt multiplicanda*,' murmured Jack. '*Entities are not to be multiplied*. Occam argued that the simplest answer is always the right one.'

Ashley shook his head. 'It sounds all right, especially when you say it in Latin, but in real life things usually aren't straightforward, are they? I mean, take this business. The simplest explanation is that it was an accident, but we know damn well it wasn't. However, it's easier for the Chief to believe that you were mistaken about not hearing a crash rather than Vaughan – who he occasionally goes shooting with by the way – is up to no good.'

'What about Dr Wilcott's findings from the post-mortem? They showed Craig was dead before the fire started.'

'He doesn't think it's remotely surprising that we can't find what actually killed the victim. He thinks it was destroyed in the fire. PC Marsh's sighting of the Rolls driven by a bearded man ties in with what Vaughan told us and as for Vaughan coming back to Stour Creek by canoe – well, he didn't laugh, but I could see he thought it was fairly amusing.'

'And what about the blood on the base of the statue? Did he find that amusing?'

'He found it incredible. He said he'd have a look at it when he goes to see Vaughan, but that's it.'

Jack stood up, and with his hands in his pockets, walked to the window. 'He can't deny that Vaughan entertained a bloke called Madison who we can prove to be also known as Simes and who's wanted for murder. He can't get round that.'

'Oh, can't he though! He doesn't deny it but he can ignore it. It's not a problem for the Sussex Police, it's a problem for Scotland Yard.'

'And what about Von Erlangen's driver, this poor devil, Gilbert Faraday, who's so conveniently and mysteriously disappeared? We know he was in the Hammer Valley. I imagine that Von Erlangen drove there to check Vaughan really had arranged matters.'

'That also is a problem for Scotland Yard. And, incidentally, granted there has been a murder, which he's very dubious about, he'd like me to make up my mind who, exactly, has been murdered. First it was Craig, then it was Madison and now I seem to be saying it's Craig again. He was pretty cutting about that.'

Jack sat down on the window seat. 'I seem to have let you in for some fairly swingeing official criticism,' he said eventually. 'Help yourself to more coffee, by the way.'

'It's not your fault,' said Ashley, pouring out another cup. 'I *know* we're right, Haldean. I'm utterly convinced we've got the truth but I don't see how we can prove it.' He stirred his coffee absently. 'I think the Chief is going to have to wait a long time for his word with Vaughan. Like you, I believe if Vaughan's gone off with Von Erlangen, it's a one-way trip.'

Jack made a frustrated noise. 'I'm stuck. Vaughan's gone, Von Erlangen's gone and Freya's gone as well. We can't actually *do* anything. If we had the faintest idea where Von Erlangen had got to, I suppose we could ask the RAF in Transjordan to find him, but we can't ask them to fly round the desert on the off-chance. Although this lost city more or less has to be in the region of Q'asr Dh'an, once you've said that, you've not said much. And, quite frankly, even if we could tell the RAF exactly where to look, it's not really a matter for the air force, it's a police problem.'

'It's a possibility, though,' said Ashley. 'General Flint has more or less tied my hands, but Rackham might be able to make things happen. Especially if, as you believe, there really is a fortune out there.'

'It all comes down to what I believe again, doesn't it?' Jack smacked his fist into his palm. 'I believe that Von Erlangen is out in the Hejaz but I can't prove it.'

Ashley sat back and drank his coffee. 'How about finding out which ship they left England on?'

Jack raised his hands questioningly. 'What makes you think they went by ship? They could have easily taken the ferry across to Calais or Dieppe, down to Marseilles and across the Med from there.'

'But Vaughan did go by ship,' said Ashley with conviction. 'When I spoke to Oxley he said his master had gone by long sea. That means a proper ship, doesn't it? Not just a ferry, I mean.'

Jack stared at him. 'Yes, it does. Hold on. Vaughan paid for Von Erlangen to come over from New York. I don't know if he paid for Freya or not, but she came anyway. He'd probably pay for Von Erlangen to go East and the chances are they'd travel together.' He clicked his fingers together. 'That explains why Von Erlangen was hanging about in London. Yes, I bet he wanted his things from his room, but if he was travelling with Vaughan, he'd have to wait. There aren't that many sailings. It's not like a bus service. If we can find the name of the ship we can see if Vaughan was on the passenger list.'

'Would he be under his own name?'

'Why not? Vaughan's in the clear. He believes he's got away with murder and, thanks to General Flint, he probably has. Vaughan wants to find his lost city. I bet he hasn't a clue about the gold.'

'I doubt whether Von Erlangen would have told him,' agreed Ashley. 'It doesn't sound his style.'

'You're right. God knows who or what Vaughan believes Von Erlangen to be, but he could have convinced himself that Von Erlangen's really after nothing more than an undiscovered Nabatean city and Craig was nothing more than a ruddy nuisance. Vaughan is looking forward to making a real splash. He mentioned Caernarvon and his discoveries in the Valley of the Kings when we talked to him, remember? He reckoned that this city would be even more important than Tutankhamen. This is shaping up to be the find of a lifetime and he can't get the recognition due to him if he's sloping round under a false name.'

'That's true enough. Let's see if we can find out what ship he sailed on. The newspapers carry notification of sailings, don't they? That'll tell us.'

'And Uncle Phil,' said Jack with a sudden grin, 'keeps all

the old newspapers. They're used for lighting fires and so on. I'm not sure where they are, though. Come on, Ashley, I'll ask Aunt Alice where they're kept.'

They found Lady Rivers in the garden. 'The old newspapers, Jack?' she said, after he'd explained what they wanted. 'They're stacked up by the boiler in the cellar. I'll show you where they are.'

They clattered down the stone steps into the cellars of Hesperus, where, in neatly separated bundles, back issues of *The Morning Post*, *The Daily Telegraph*, *The Times*, *The Daily Express* and *The Daily Messenger* were stacked in old tea chests.

Jack seized an armload of *Daily Telegraphs* and started to hunt through them. 'Vaughan left the country the day I was attacked, didn't he? That's the 31st, Ashley. Got it! Not burnt yet, thank goodness. Shipping news, shipping news . . .'

He flicked over the pages impatiently, squinting in the dim light. 'Here we are – page three. *Shipping Intelligence.* Wrecks and Casualties first – cheerful how they always start with that. Cape Town, Sydney, Valparaiso . . . Port Said! I bet they're heading for Port Said. Here we are. The mail boat *Burma* left London for Karachi at half past eleven on the evening of the 31st, calling at Lisbon, Gibraltar, Malta and Port Said. She calls at Aden, too, but that doesn't concern us.' He looked up in triumph. 'Howsat!'

'Well done, Haldean. When did the *Burma* reach Port Said?'

'Hang on, hang on. I'm not a shipping clerk, you know, and they only give arrivals after they happen. They're worried they may end up as a Wreck or Casualty, I suppose.'

'The journey takes about twelve days,' put in Lady Rivers.

'Thanks, Aunt Alice. That gives us the twelfth of April, so we want the day after . . .' He seized another pile of newspapers. 'Ships, ships, where are you? Why do they keep moving the damn column round? It's inside the back page, now. Bingo! The *Burma* reached Port Said on the twelfth.'

'That's a few days ago,' said Ashley with a click of his tongue. 'Still, I can check if Vaughan and anyone answering to the Von Erlangens' description were on board. Or, at least, Rackham can. At least it tells us where they were.'

'Yes, but I could do with knowing where they *are*.' He

braced his arms on the tea chest. 'Even if they were on board, I can't see it gets us much further.'

'The location's in that precious book of Von Erlangen's,' said Ashley. 'Or so you think.'

'Which is a fat lot of good to anyone.'

'I'd like to see the book,' said Lady Rivers unexpectedly. 'I've heard a lot about it. In fact . . . Jack, you're leaving soon, aren't you? Would you mind if I came with you? I can get the train back this evening. That'd be all right, wouldn't it?'

'Of course,' said Jack, in surprise. He thought for a moment. 'Let me give Bill a ring. I'll ask if he can bring the book round to my rooms. I want to tell him we think Vaughan and his friends sailed on the *Burma* too.' He glanced at his watch. 'Shall we have lunch on the way?'

'I think that would be very nice,' said Lady Rivers. 'You're packed and ready, aren't you? Let me tell your uncle and we'll be off.'

'Go up to Town?' said Sir Philip doubtfully, looking at his wife after she'd run him to earth in the stables. 'Yes, of course, Alice. I'll send the car to the station for you this evening. But why are you going? I've heard about this book and I can't see you're going to get anything out of it. From what Isabelle told us, it's just a lot of pictures. Arthur said they couldn't make anything of it. Nobody could.' He scratched his ear unhappily. 'I can't see it'll do any good.'

'It probably won't, Philip,' agreed Lady Rivers, 'but you never know. At least the book will give Jack something to occupy his mind. Besides that, I hope as there's just the two of us in the car, he might get things off his chest. I'm worried about him.'

'It's this ghastly business with this German feller,' said Sir Philip, shifting uncomfortably. 'He'd be much better off not brooding over it. In my opinion,' he said with sudden insight, 'this girl, Freya, or whatever she's called, is the trouble. She's complicated things.'

'Yes,' said Lady Rivers quietly. 'I rather think she has.'

As the sun set on the mountains of Steamer Point, Aden, Mrs Cynthia Coire sat upright in the button-backed plush chair next to the dressing table. She always sat upright; posture, training and disposition dictated it.

All the homely noises of Aden flooded though the open window. The creak of the waterwheel, the bray of a donkey and the shouts from the parade ground mingled with the musical, carrying voices of Somalis, the higher accents of the Hindustani cook and the occasional guttural note of Arabic. She was glad to be back. Noise in England had a grim, impersonal quality.

Her ayah served tea and Cynthia Coire relaxed, watching as Ayah unlocked her trunk. Her cup of tea was good. Ayah knew just how she liked it. Tea in England, in those new, noisy tea shops with palm trees and orchestras, often left much to be desired, both in quality and presentation. Here, in her own house, things were different.

It was good to be home. Mrs Coire's family usually travelled P&O but the mail boat had been perfectly acceptable.

Ayah opened the cabin trunk on the floor. The smells were richer here than in England. Flowers, hot earth, mustiness. Very musty . . . Cynthia Coire wrinkled her nose and made a mental note to inspect the kitchens. The cook wasn't going to serve second-rate meat disguised as fresh at *her* table.

Ayah rose from beside the trunk holding, not the sensible, well-cut suit of navy blue shantung that Cynthia Coire knew should be at the top, but a wispy creation in red.

Cynthia Coire glared at the excuse for a dress and sat up even straighter in her chair. 'That is not mine,' she declared and looked hard at the cabin trunk. It was hers, no doubt about it. The trunk was new, bought from the Army and Navy Stores, only six weeks before. Her labels were on it, and there was the scratch which had cost the porter his tip at St Pancras. She looked closer. The scratch *wasn't* there.

Cynthia Coire crossed to the trunk and rapidly removed the top layer of clothes. And then, for the first time in her life, she screamed. Underneath three cocktail dresses and wrapped in a blue wool coat, lay the rather awful remains of Freya Von Erlangen.

FOURTEEN

Taking her glasses from her bag, Lady Rivers looked at the book of watercolour paintings Bill Rackham had laid out on the table in Jack's rooms. She was glad Rackham was there. Jack hadn't said much, but she knew the strain he was under and guessed how volatile his mood was. The big, easy-going Rackham was just the sort of person Jack needed and she thoroughly appreciated his common sense. 'Do you think this book contains some sort of message, Mr Rackham?' she asked.

Rackham ran a hand through his ginger hair. 'I *did*,' he said cautiously. 'When you look at the poem and so on, it certainly sounds as if it means more than it apparently all adds up to.'

Lady Rivers read the title page softly. '*A hundred thousand dragons lie, Underneath an Arabian sky. The Silent Ones, when asked, will measure, the hidden way to dragons' treasure. With a body once so fair, a princess guards the dragons' lair.*' She looked up. 'I see what you mean. It has a sort of significant quality, doesn't it?'

'Oddly enough, Aunt Alice,' said Jack, 'it wasn't so much the dragons that got us going, but the quote from *Julius Caesar*.' He put his finger on the page. '*A Tide In The Affairs Of Men*, which, as Arthur pointed out, leads on to fortune. We worked out that the fortune in question was the gold from Craig's convoy.'

'And so these dragons and so on don't really matter then?' asked Lady Rivers in disappointment.

'That's what my expert concluded,' said Rackham. 'Apparently those words mean exactly what they say. Which isn't very much,' he added in an undertone.

'I don't agree,' said Jack. 'You see, I had a bright thought about those dragons.' Lady Rivers breathed a little sigh of relief. She'd been right; he needed to get his teeth into something.

He cocked his head as the telephone in the hall rang. His

eyes gleamed with suppressed excitement. 'And if I'm lucky, that's my answer. I'll be back in a tick.' Lady Rivers and Bill Rackham looked blankly at each other as Jack left the room.

When he came back, he had a broad smile. 'Got it!'

'What?' asked Lady Rivers.

Jack grinned. 'That was Bingo Romer-Stuart on the phone from the War Office. I asked him how much gold was in this convoy of Craig's.' He took a flat brown leather box from his pocket. 'I'd like you to look at this. It's the present Arthur gave me for being his Best Man.'

'It's a watch and chain,' said Lady Rivers, puzzled, opening the leather box. 'I know.'

'And Arthur had it inscribed with my name and the date.'

'Well, so he did . . .'

'And he also attached a newly minted sovereign to the watch chain. It looks good, doesn't it?'

Lady Rivers held the watch in her hand. 'I don't see what you're getting at, Jack.'

'Look at the sovereign, Aunt Alice. Look at the picture on the coin.'

'It's the King.'

'And on the reverse?'

Lady Rivers turned the coin over and stared. 'It's a *dragon.* St George and the dragon.'

'Exactly!' said Jack in delight. 'And the convoy consisted of gold. Gold sovereigns.'

Bill Rackham gasped. 'Blimey! How much was there, Jack?'

'A hundred thousand pounds in gold sovereigns. Or, to put it another way, a hundred thousand dragons. Bill, this book *has* to contain a message.'

'But how, Jack?' demanded Rackham. 'I agree. Don't get me wrong, I agree. This dragon thing ties in so neatly it has to mean the convoy. It's too great a coincidence for it not to. But our expert analysed that poem every which way it *could* be analysed and found nothing.'

'So therefore the answer isn't in the poem, it's in the pictures.'

'But he looked at those, too,' said Rackham in frustration.

'Yes, you can make a code out of pictures, but he knows that.' He flicked through the pages of the book and sighed. 'It doesn't add up.'

A piece of paper fluttered out of the book to the floor. 'What's this?' asked Lady Rivers, picking it up and putting in on the table.

Jack twisted his head to see. It was a drawing of a pyramid with the letters *I.E. Simes, R.A.* arranged around it. R at the top, A underneath it, M at the side and so on, round the pyramid. 'Isabelle drew it.' He smiled affectionately. 'Pyramids! She was thinking of her honeymoon, I'll bet.'

'I imagine she was,' said Lady Rivers. 'I enjoyed planning the Egyptian trip with her. They're visiting Tutankhamen's tomb in the Valley of the Kings and going up the Nile to the Second Cataract. Abu Simbel really is magnificent. There's an enormous temple built of sandstone with four vast statues at the entrance . . .'

Jack knew his aunt was still speaking, but her voice seemed to be coming from far away. He stared at the paper on the table. He gave a low exclamation. Pyramids meant Egypt, meant the sphinx, meant the Valley of the Kings, meant Abu Simbel, meant four vast statues carved out of sandstone . . .

'Did you say Abu Simbel, Aunt Alice?'

'Yes, that's right,' said Lady Rivers, taken aback. 'Abu Simbel. The temples of Rameses the Second and . . .' She frowned. 'Now who's the other temple dedicated to? One of his wives, I think. He seemed to have dozens but she was the important one. His temple is the biggest, of course. The entrance is stunning. As I said, there are four absolutely enormous statues, all of him . . .'

'Rameses the Second,' interrupted Jack in an odd voice. His mind was racing. Rameses the Second, the greatest pharaoh of all, worshipped as a god, demanding immortality by nailing down the land with temples and statutes. 'There are four huge statues of Rameses the Second at Abu Simbel.'

'All right, Jack, so there are four whacking great statues of Rameses the Second at Abu Simbel,' repeated Bill Rackham. 'We've got the point. So what?'

Jack seized a pencil and, taking Isabelle's drawing, scribbled a word down rapidly, and passed it across to Rackham.

With a puzzled frown Rackham glanced down at the piece of paper, and gasped.

The letters *I.E. Simes, R.A.* had magically transformed themselves into Rameses II.

Lady Rivers took the paper from his hands. 'The names are the same,' she said in sudden apprehension. 'The same letters, I mean. Did Simes – Von Erlangen, I mean – think of himself as Rameses?'

'He had a pretty good opinion of himself, that's obvious,' said Rackham. 'I say, Jack, do you remember when we tried to crack the code before? You said we needed a keyword. Is this it?'

'What's a keyword?' asked Lady Rivers.

'Well, to put it briefly,' said Jack, 'a keyword gives you the key to understanding any coded message in the Playfair system. Playfair invented a well-known military code. It's easy enough to understand. We thought that Von Erlangen, who was an officer, after all, would have used it.'

'That's what Professor Bruce, my expert, thought as well,' said Rackham. 'What d'you think, Jack? Is Rameses the Second the key we've been looking for?'

Jack got to his feet and walked to the mantelpiece, where he stood for a few moments, deep in thought. 'I can't see it,' he said eventually. 'I.E. Simes, R.A. might be Rameses the Second but the word's scattered throughout the book. I remember saying to Belle you'd have to be goofy to send the keyword and the cipher in the same document. It's too simple.'

Rackham laughed derisively. 'You really think so?'

Jack nodded vigorously. 'Simple for him, I mean. Say we did find out what the code was and used *I.E. Simes, R.A.* as the keyword. The letters are the same as Rameses the Second, and although there'd be parts of the code that wouldn't make sense, it's wouldn't take anyone who'd done basic signalling, or even had a natural aptitude, long to figure out that other parts of the code *did* fall into place and what order the actual letters of the keyword should be in.'

'Could the keyword be *Madison*?' asked Rackham. 'I remember you scratching your head about that.' He turned to Lady Rivers. 'He'd written it on one of the other books we found in his room, a thing about desert travel. You thought it was odd, didn't you, Jack?'

'That's right,' agreed Jack. 'The name was a bit of a mouthful. *Adler Zelig Yohann Madison*, but what puzzled me was the exclamation mark after the name. It was as if he'd done something smart. I suppose Madison could be the keyword, but once again, it seems a bit simple for a tricky devil like him.'

'I don't suppose you can turn *Adler Zelig Yohann Madison* into anything clever?' asked Lady Rivers hopefully.

Jack shook his head. 'I can't. I tried.'

She frowned at him over the top of her glasses. 'All right. The name Simes has to be more than a coincidence, though. Did he ever call himself Rameses the Second or use the name in any way?'

Jack shook his head. 'No, not that I . . .' He broke off and stared at her.

'Here we go again,' muttered Rackham. 'What is it this time, Jack?'

Jack ignored him. 'Aunt Alice, do you remember when I was a kid, you used to read stories and poems and so on to me when I came to stay?'

'Well, yes, of course I do,' she said in surprise. 'You loved being read to.'

Jack crossed the room to the bookcase by the window. 'I've still got some of the books you and Uncle Phil gave me.' He knelt down, running his finger along the spines of the books. 'There's some real old favourites here. *Treasure Island,* Marryat and *Robin Hood* and so on....' He paused in his search. 'But it's this I'm after.' He held up a green-covered book triumphantly. On the front cover, blocked in gold, was the title: *A Child's Garden of Verse.*

'Go on,' said Rackham with a laugh. 'Tell us what a child's book of poetry has to do with anything.'

Jack grinned and, bringing the book back to the table, started to flick through the pages. 'It's a Victorian thing,' he explained. 'There's some good stuff in here and it's all very educational and improving. The hard words are explained, there's historical and factual notes and some lovely illustrations. Like this one. It's the illustration to *Ozymandias* by Shelley.'

The picture was of a gigantic, shattered statue of an Egyptian king, lying in ruins on the desert sands. In the distance were the pyramids and the Sphinx. At the top of the page was a note in italics.

Ozymandias is a sonnet, a fourteen line poem in iambic pentameter. The poet Shelley reflects how wealth, fame, pride and power are vanquished by the relentless march of time. The ruined statue in the sonnet is a colossal depiction of Rameses II, also known as Rameses the Great, the 'Mighty Pharaoh' of the book of Exodus in the Bible, who vainly attempted to keep Moses and the Israelites enslaved. The Greek traveller, Diodorus, refers to Rameses II as Ozymandias.

'Ozymandias!' breathed Rackham. 'Jack, it's what Von Erlangen called himself. *Ozymandias.*'

'Exactly,' said Jack in deep satisfaction. Rackham saw his eyes narrow thoughtfully. 'Hang on a mo.' He picked up the pencil once more, pulled the piece of paper towards him and jotted down the name. After a few moments he glanced up. 'Look at this. We've got Ozymandias *and* Adler Zelig Yohann Madison. Now, if we simply put Madison's initials in, so his name reads A.Z.Y. Madison and switch the letters round a bit, what have we got?'

He had written the letters of both names in two circles. Rackham whistled in appreciation. '*Ozymandias!* Damn me – sorry, Lady Rivers – the letters are the same! Ozymandias is A.Z.Y. Madison and vice versa.'

'And that's his keyword,' said Jack. 'I'll swear to it.' He looked at them both and grinned. 'You can applaud now, if you like.'

Lady Rivers clapped her hands together softly. 'You deserve it. Well done, Jack.'

'I think that calls for a drink, don't you?' asked Jack. Walking over to the sideboard, he took out three glasses. 'Is sherry all right for everyone? I know it's a favourite of yours, Aunt Alice.'

Bill Rackham accepted the glass Jack gave him with a frown. 'Look, Jack, I don't want to spoil the party, but are you sure Ozymandias can be the keyword? Wouldn't he go for something more obscure?'

Jack sat back in his chair. 'I don't think so,' he said after a few moments. 'The name Ozymandias obviously means a great deal to him. It's a powerful name, but it's concealed power, a secret power. That fits his character, you know? This is all a guess, but I bet he wanted to keep a memory of the name when he got to New York. As Ozymandias he had been known and feared and keeping the name, even if it was concealed as Simes or Madison, must have been a sort of promise to himself that he wasn't finished yet.'

Rackham lit a cigarette disconsolately. 'You're probably right, you know. Ozymandias is as good a guess as any. But it's not much good having a keyword and no code to go with it.'

Lady Rivers picked up the book from the table and opened it on her knee, turning to the first page. 'What lovely pictures,' she said thoughtfully. She looked at the first page, with its pictures of an Arab in bright sunlight, four palm trees and rocks silhouetted against the evening sun. 'Three pictures,' she murmured. She turned the page. 'And the next page has three, as well, but the page after that has . . . goodness me, eleven,' she said, rapidly counting them. She frowned. 'Jack, isn't there a Sherlock Holmes story that uses pictures as a code?'

'There is. It's called *The Dancing Men*, but there the pictures stood for clearly defined letters and, not to be too dismissive, once you know it's a code, it's a bit of a sitter. Do you remember that one, Bill?'

'I do,' agreed Rackham. 'If it were as simple as that, I can't see it puzzling Professor Bruce for very long.'

Lady Rivers clicked her tongue. 'The number of pictures don't stand for letters of the alphabet, do they? Three pictures equals the letter C, for instance?'

Jack shook his head. ''Fraid not. We've tried that.'

Lady Rivers stared at the book and sighed. 'The clarity and the precision of the drawing is outstanding. I can't help thinking that with such a talent at his fingertips, it's worse than ever that he should be so *wicked*. I learnt how to paint and draw, of course, when I was a girl, as it was the sort of thing which girls did, but artists were always suspect. Even the fashionable ones had to be treated with caution, what with life classes and drinking extraordinary things and everybody living in each other's pockets and wanting to run off with everyone else's wives, but that's not wickedness but just ordinary immorality and the sort of thing one would expect, really.'

Jack exchanged glances with Rackham and laughed. 'You seem to expect some rum things, Aunt Alice.'

'I mean for people in those circumstances,' said Lady Rivers, laughing too. She broke off as she saw Jack's frown. 'Have I said something wrong?'

'Not wrong, exactly,' he said slowly, 'but you've done something I haven't. You've looked at the pictures as works of art. I got so caught up with the idea of the book being a code that the paintings *as* paintings got obscured.' He knelt down beside her chair and looked intently at the pictures. 'Can you turn the pages for me?' he asked after a little while.

Lady Rivers did so.

'We noticed, of course, how the pictures are grouped in a very odd way,' he said thoughtfully, 'but I didn't see what you pointed out, Aunt Alice, that the drawing is outstanding. It's very, very sharp.' He rocked back on his heels.

'So what, Jack?' asked Rackham after a pause.

Jack stood up. 'I was wondering *why* the drawing was so razor sharp. After all, these are watercolours. You'd expect fades and washes. It's part of the technique of watercolour painting.' He leaned forward and tapped the book. 'The painting I saw in Vaughan's study, the one supposed to be painted by Simes, was an ordinary watercolour. These are more like coloured drawings. The objects in the pictures are startlingly vivid. Unnaturally so, I'd say.' He pulled at his earlobe thoughtfully. 'What if it's not the number of pictures on each page but the number of objects in each picture?'

'Let's have a look,' said Rackham. Lady Rivers obligingly turned the book round for him. 'I see what you mean,' he said after a little while. 'They're coloured drawings, aren't they? Let's give your idea a go, Jack. The number of objects in each picture?' He shrugged. 'At the very least, it's something we've not tried before.' He went back to the table, and pulling the notepad towards him, picked up the pencil. 'How many objects are in the first picture?'

'One. An Arab.'

'So if this an alphabet substitution code, that gives us the letter A.'

'Yes. Don't forget I and J count as the same letter. We want twenty-five letters, not twenty-six in this alphabet.'

'Fair enough,' said Rackham. 'What's the second picture?'

'That's four palm trees and the third picture is of . . . crikey, hang on, there's lots of rocks. There are twenty-four in all.'

'What about the second page?'

'That's three pictures again, and the first picture is of about a million birds. How many would you say there are, Aunt Alice?'

They counted up the birds quickly. 'Twenty-five, Bill.'

'Which gives us Z.'

'The next picture has four camels.'

'Which gives us D.'

'And the next picture is of . . . fourteen Turkish soldiers.'

'Giving us O.'

'The next page has eleven pictures and the first one has . . . Wait a moment . . . eighteen oil drums in it.'

'Which is S.'

'The second has eight tents.'

'Which is H.'

'And the third is another big one. Twenty-three field guns.'

'Which is X.'

Lady Rivers looked at what Bill Rackham had written. 'A, D, Y, Z, D, O, S, H, X. It doesn't make any sense, Jack.'

'Give the boy a chance,' he pleaded. 'At least we've got some letters. I've got a feeling in my bones about this. And don't you think the pictures on each page correspond to the length of each word? I bet they do. So that's two three letter words and the beginnings of this eleven-letter monstrosity.'

By the time they had got to page six, Rackham had written out a string of letters that Lady Rivers looked at in frank perplexity. 'It might make sense to you two,' she said, 'but I can't make head or tail of it.'

'Again, wait,' said Jack. 'Or perpend, if you'd rather. I think it's time we got our code square going, don't you, Bill? That'll tell us if we're on the right lines.'

'The keyword's Ozymandias?' asked Rackham.

'Ker-rect. Drop the second A.'

Rackham, watched by the fascinated Lady Rivers, drew out the squares for the code.

'What do we do now, Jack?' she asked.

'Now, I hope, everything starts to fall into place,' he said, rubbing his hands together. 'Bill, the first letter we've got to read is A. That's at the top right-hand corner of the square, so it transposes with the letter at the bottom of the column.'

'Which is X.'

Jack's face fell. 'Is it? That's not very promising. The next letter is D. That gets replaced by the letter to the immediate left.'

'And that gives us N.'

'XN? Strewth, I hope this picks up soon. Next is Y which gives us . . .'

'Z.'

'God in heaven, does it? XNZ? What's the beggar playing at?'

Frowning, Rackham carried on for a while. 'This is no good, Jack,' he said eventually, putting down the pencil with a sharp click. 'I've got X, N, Z, U, N, T, I or J, C and T. It just doesn't make sense.'

'No, it doesn't,' said Jack regretfully, looking at the paper. 'And yet I was sure we were on to something, you know. Damn!'

'Let's have another sherry,' Lady Rivers suggested. 'Maybe something will occur to you.' She looked at the code and sighed. 'I feel it should mean something.'

'I wish I knew what,' said Jack. He refilled their glasses and flung himself into an armchair. With his hands behind his head, he stared at the ceiling. 'Objects,' he muttered. 'Objects in the pictures. It all seemed to be falling into place. I was sure that's what it was.'

Lady Rivers sipped her sherry. 'Maybe it is. Jack, I know you know about codes . . .'

'I know a bit,' Jack put in. 'Anyone who worked with signals had to.'

'I'm sure they did. But although Von Erlangen was a German officer, you don't know he's got any knowledge of codes, do you?'

'That's true enough,' agreed Rackham. 'After all, I was in the Cheshires and I haven't got a clue about codes or ciphers. I left that to the experts.'

Lady Rivers nodded. 'Of course you did, but you had got experts to turn to. Von Erlangen would have to rely on what he knew. I was thinking about the Sherlock Holmes story, *The Dancing Men*. I don't know anything about codes either, but I understood the story. How did Holmes crack the code?'

Jack got up, and walking to the bookcase once more, crouched down and pulled out a couple of books. 'Here we are,' he announced after a brief search. 'Dancing men . . . No dancing ladies. It sounds like a bit of a grim night out, doesn't it? The Ritz would have to shut down if a lot of blokes turned up without girls.'

'Get on with it,' said Rackham with a laugh. 'How does the Great Detective crack the code?'

'I imagine, knowing Holmes, he smokes like a chimney,' said Jack, flicking through the pages. 'D'you know, it's remarkable that although he never does any exercise, doses himself with cocaine and smokes tobacco that smells like old socks, he's always fighting fit? I don't know how he does it. Hello, here we are. He whistles and sings according to this – I'd whistle if I thought it'd do us any good – and he sits with *furrowed brow and vacant eye*. He says he's familiar with all forms of secret writing, which is a dickens of a claim, and the author of a trifling monograph – I love how he never writes a serious monograph but only trifling ones – in which he analyses a hundred and sixty separate ciphers. Wow. Now that's what I call an expert. It's a straightforward alphabet substitution code, as a matter of fact. He sees which one of the little dancing men appears most often, assumes that's the letter E, and, with a nod to the fact that it's not all plain sailing after that, assigns other letters to various figures. T, A and O are the next most common letters – he goes through the alphabet – and says that to analyse the code he needed a fair old bit of material to work with.'

'Can't we do that?' asked Lady Rivers. 'After all, if we had the whole message to work with, we might be able to see which letter occurred most often.'

'We could,' said Jack, putting the book back. 'We might as well get all the letters we can. You're quite right, Aunt Alice, it's not a bad idea. We might be lucky.'

After about a quarter of an hour's work, Rackham looked at the collection of letters they had culled. 'I'd say D occurs most often, wouldn't you?'

'Which means that D equals E, or it should do,' said Jack.

'After that . . . Well, there's not a lot in it.' He glanced across the table to where their coded square lay discarded and sighed. 'I was sure the word *Ozymandias* had something to do with it. It seemed to fit so perfectly.'

'It does!' said Lady Rivers excitedly, stabbing her finger at the paper. 'It does fit! Not the way you read the letters at first, but see. In the squares you've written *Ozymandis* without the extra A and the rest of the alphabet and see – the D comes above the E.'

Jack and Rackham looked to where she was pointing. 'By jingo, so it does,' said Rackham slowly.

'I wonder if that's it,' breathed Jack. 'Perhaps we've all been right, so to speak. Von Erlangen *wasn't* an expert in codes but knew enough to compose a square and a keyword. What he didn't know or couldn't remember was how to read off the letters.'

'So he made up his own method,' said Lady Rivers. She picked up the pencil again. 'Let's try it. We're reading the letter above the coded letter, yes? So the first letter is A which gives us . . . I've run out of letters. It's off the square.'

'Try the letter below it, Aunt Alice,' suggested Jack. 'That gives us B.'

'All right. And the next is D which gives us E.'

'And Y which gives us I or J.'

'B, E, J?' said Rackham. 'Or I. That's not a word.'

'Maybe not,' said Jack. 'Let's carry on, though.'

Rackham looked at him sharply. He could hear the excitement in his friend's voice but couldn't see any reason to justify it. 'All right. The next letter is Z.'

'Which gives us D.'

'And D.'

'Which gives us E again.'

'O'

'Oh for the wings of a dove . . . Which is N.'

'And now we're on to the next page. The first letter is S.'

'Which is G.'

'H.'

'Turns into R.'

'X.'

'Which is off the square so I'll try A.'

'Then A.'

'Which is B,' said Jack, again with that odd note of suppressed excitement. 'To be or not to be . . . Sorry Bill.'

Rackham looked at him critically. 'I don't know what's eating you, because so far we've got *bej* or *bei den grab* which doesn't make any sense.'

'I think,' said Haldean, his eyes dancing with black fire, 'it would make a great deal more sense if we spelt *grab* with a capital letter. All nouns in German start with a capital.'

'*What!*' Rackham stared at the paper. 'You mean it's German? But damn it, none of the rest of it's German. Why's he suddenly changed language?'

'We worked out he painted the book for Freya,' said Jack, hesitating slightly over the name. 'The top part, the public part of the book, is in English. It's as if he's inviting anyone to look at it. But the secret part, the part underneath, is in German. I can't imagine he talked to Freya in English.'

'No, he wouldn't,' agreed Rackham. 'So what does it mean?'

Jack leaned back, lit a cigarette and grinned. 'I'm willing to bet that this word of eleven letters is *Grabstätten* or *tombs*. *Bei den Grabstätten. By the tombs* . . . Dear God, it works,' he added in a different voice. 'It really does work.'

Rackham shook Jack's hand vigorously. 'Congratulations, old man. I'd virtually given up on it but you've done it. By jingo, even the expert, Professor Bruce, couldn't read it but you've done it.'

'Your Professor Bruce didn't have my advantages. I knew the significance of the name Ozymandias and he didn't have Aunt Alice to point out that although it might be set out as a Playfair code it wasn't written by Playfair's rules. Well spotted, Aunt Alice.'

'I just happened to see it,' she said, blushing, 'as we were thinking about Sherlock Holmes and the letter E. I do *like* Sherlock Holmes,' she added. 'Even if he is rather crushing to poor Dr Watson. I suppose, if this was written with Freya Von Erlangen in mind, they must have used this code before. Perhaps not with pictures, which seems very complicated, but just with ordinary words. He'd have to know she could read it.'

'Perhaps,' agreed Jack dubiously. 'As I say, he's a secretive blighter.'

'There's something else I thought, too,' said Lady Rivers. The two men looked up sharply. 'It's the paintings themselves. They're silent, aren't they? I wonder if that ties in with the poem.'

Jack snapped his fingers. 'The Silent Ones! *The Silent Ones, when asked, will measure, the hidden way to dragons' treasure.* I wonder if that's it?'

'You see, these pictures have shown us the way, haven't they?

'Let's get the rest of the code worked out,' suggested Rackham. 'Then we can see what these Silent Ones really are telling us.'

With the help of *Cassell's German Dictionary* they threw themselves into the work and within half an hour Von Erlangen's renderings of scenes as various as Turkish carpets, lizards, oil drums and the pyramids by moonlight (amongst others) had turned into German prose. *Bei den Grabstätten die wispernden Toten stehen Sie vor Petra. Treten Sie in den Löwen hinein. Kämpfen Sie mit den Skorpion. Drüden Sie den Adler. Suchen Sie die Jungfrau. 33* (this had been a picture of thirty-three birds in flight and had caused them some hesitation) *KM SSO Q' asr Dh' an. 48* (these had been squares on a mosaic floor) *KMS Petra. Pferdkopfstein.*

'And now let's get it into English,' said Jack. 'Heave the dictionary over. My German's a bit rusty. Here goes. *By or at the tombs of the whispering dead . . .* Crikey. It sounds a cheerful sort of place. *Stand you in front of Petra.* I suppose that means face towards Petra. *Step or go you in the lion inside.* Go into the lion we'd say, I imagine. *Fight you with the scorpion. Crush or squeeze or vex you the eagle.* Would it do to simply irritate it, I wonder? *Search you or look for the virgin or maiden. 33 kilometres SSE* (*ost* is the German for east) *Q' asr Dh' an. 48 kilometres S. Petra. Horsehead rock.*'

'And what,' said Rackham with great feeling, 'does all that rigmarole mean? The directions are clear enough, but what's all this about vexing eagles, fighting scorpions and looking for maidens?'

'Search me,' said Jack. 'It sounds as if he's going to start a barney in a zoo. And who's the maiden, I wonder?'

'It all sounds perfectly thrilling,' said Lady Rivers, her eyes alight. 'What are you going to do now, Jack?'

Jack looked at Rackham. 'It's really up to you, Bill. If we're right – and I bet we are – there's rather more than a king's ransom waiting to be picked up, to say nothing of our pal, Von Erlangen.'

'I'm going to see the Assistant Commissioner,' said Rackham. 'He'll know what to do.' He glanced at the clock. 'He might be at the Yard. If not, I'm going to his house. This is important enough to warrant it.' He picked up the decoded message. 'Can I take this?'

'Half a mo. Let me copy it out first,' said Jack. 'I want to keep it amongst my souvenirs. Aunt Alice and I are going out for dinner, Bill. Do you want to join us?'

'I'd rather get on to the Chief,' said Rackham. 'Thanks, though.'

They parted at the door, Rackham to Scotland Yard and Jack and Lady Rivers to dine on the balcony at Romano's on the Strand. After dinner, he escorted her to Waterloo Station and saw her on to the train home.

As her train pulled out of the station, his good mood evaporated. He'd known how fragile it had been. Nothing, he thought, as he let himself back into his rooms, seemed to add up to anything very much. Yes, they knew how Vaughan had done it. Yes, they'd cracked Von Erlangen's code.

So now what? he asked himself as he mixed a whisky and soda. Perhaps the Assistant Commissioner would be able to pull the right strings. Maybe Von Erlangen would be arrested. It was far more likely, thought Jack bleakly as he lit a cigarette, that Von Erlangen would escape. And Freya? His stomach twisted at the thought.

He put down his glass as he heard footsteps on the stairs and stood up to answer the caller's knock. He wasn't expecting anyone.

Bill Rackham came into the room. 'I'm sorry to have to tell you this,' he said, taking off his hat and cutting Jack's greeting short. 'A cable's arrived at the Yard. I'm sorry, Jack. Freya Von Erlangen is dead.'

FIFTEEN

'**D**ead?' Jack echoed the word blankly.

Rackham nodded. 'She was found in a trunk in Aden. There was another body, too, the body of a man. At a guess, he's Gilbert Faraday, the missing driver we've been looking for. I'll swear the manager at the Balmoral knew something was wrong, even if he didn't know it was murder. I'm looking forward to asking him a few questions.' As succinctly as he could, Rackham related Cynthia Coire's gruesome discovery. 'What I think happened is that Von Erlangen killed her, put her in his trunk and, once he was on board ship, got down into the hold and swapped the labels on his trunk with the labels on Mrs Coire's. It was a new trunk and she didn't notice anything wrong until it was unpacked.'

Jack sat down slowly, numbed by the sick taste of grief. 'She was killed because of me,' he said, more to himself than Bill. 'That night he attacked me, Freya saved me from being knifed. He'd never forgive her for that.' Sudden anger flared. 'If only I'd worked out the truth sooner! I talked about Craig, for God's sake! If I'd had the truth, the real truth, if I'd had the sense to realize Von Erlangen was alive, she'd have trusted me. I told her I could help and yet, with every word I said, it was obvious I couldn't.'

'Easy does it, Jack,' said Rackham uncomfortably. 'If she had told you the truth, you would have helped her.'

'Oh yes?' Jack's voice was savage. 'I talked about her being an accessory to *murder*. It's not reassuring, is it? She didn't even know her precious husband murdered the American guard. That's the bitter irony of it.'

'She must have known Craig had been murdered though.' Rackham's voice was measured. 'And there's this poor young devil, Gilbert Faraday. She must have known about him. And if she'd told us, we could have stopped Von Erlangen there and then.'

Jack started to speak, then stopped, covering his hand with his mouth. 'You're right, damn it,' he said dully. 'Of course you are. Yes, she could have turned to us. To me. I wish she had, but she wasn't a free agent. Can you imagine her state of mind? She must have felt like a rabbit trapped by a stoat.'

'She had a choice, Jack.'

'Technically, yes. Really? I don't know.' He got up and walked to the window, staring sightlessly at the plane tree in the yard. 'What's the Assistant Commissioner going to do?' he asked after a time.

'He's contacting the Transjordanian Police. We discussed what Von Erlangen was likely to do but I hadn't realized the distances involved. I knew Petra was off the beaten track, but I hadn't realized just how far it is from anywhere else. What'll probably happen is that the police will try and nab Von Erlangen on his way back. He's got to return to civilization and there are only so many places he can go. That way, as the Chief pointed out, the local police will recover the gold – if it's there – and get him as well.'

'He'll escape,' said Jack flatly. Rackham said nothing but shifted awkwardly. Jack swung round to face him. 'You agree, don't you? You know who we're up against. It's not dawned on anyone else yet. He knows Arabia, Bill. There'll be a hundred and one ways he can vanish and we won't be any the wiser.' He took a deep breath. 'There's only one thing for it. I'm going to get him.'

'*What?*' Rackham looked thunderstruck.

'I'm a reserve officer in the RAF,' said Jack coolly. 'I've a perfect right to arrest him. You agree, don't you?'

'Of course I do, you idiot, but you can't charge off into the back of beyond. Apart from anything else, how will you get there? It takes twelve days or something like it to get to Port Said and that's only the start. It's over a week's journey after that, as far as I can make out, and I don't suppose there's a fleet of buses waiting. It'll take you forever to arrange transport and God knows how much it'll cost. That's why Von Erlangen needed Vaughan in the first place. He knew you couldn't stroll out there. It's a crazy idea, Jack.'

'There are quicker ways to Port Said than sailing round the Bay of Biscay.'

Rackham made an impatient gesture. 'So what? You've still got to get across the Med and into the desert. By the time you turn up, he'll have long gone.'

'I'm not so sure. It'll take him time, Bill, lots of time. He'll have to organize a boat to Aquaba and transport from there, or some sort of convoy across the desert. With any luck, I'll get there before him.'

'But *how*?' demanded Rackham.

'Fly, of course. How else?'

Rackham gaped at him. 'For God's sake, there aren't any flights to Petra.'

'I'll buy a plane.'

Rackham looked at him incredulously.

'Why not?' asked Jack. 'There's plenty of second-hand machines around. Only the other day one of the men at the club asked if I knew anyone who wants an old air-taxi. He's asking eight hundred quid for it but I should be able to beat him down. That should do the job.' His face was grim. 'I've got to do this, Bill. You see that, don't you? Don't worry. I'm not going off the deep end. I'll get all the correct documents and carnets and the rest of the paperwork I need.'

'Never mind the ruddy paperwork. That's the least of your problems. Say you do fly out there. What then?'

'That,' said Jack quietly, 'is something I'll decide when I arrive.' His mouth curved into a humourless smile. 'He won't be expecting me, that's for sure. And don't worry, I won't be working alone. I can call on RAF Kantara if need be, but I'm going and I'm going just as fast as I can. He shouldn't have harmed Freya.'

Arthur Stanton leaned contentedly over the balcony of his cabin, watching the last streaks of the setting sun dip into the Mediterranean. The deep blue of the sea looped round the dazzling white stonework of Valletta harbour made a stunning view. He turned his head and called into the cabin. 'Come and look at the sunset, Isabelle. It's marvellous.'

'I'll be with you in a minute,' said a muffled voice from behind the bathroom door.

Arthur grinned and felt in his pocket for his pipe and matches. He had never been so happy. They had docked in the Grand Harbour, Malta, that morning and spent the day exploring the wide, steep streets and the cool cathedral of the old city. The nightmares that had plagued him since the war had been completely routed and now there was a trip ashore with dinner under the velvet-blue Mediterranean night to look forward to. And Isabelle . . . A deep contentment washed over him. Life was good, all good.

Isabelle, dressed in crisp green and white linen, came out of the bathroom. A knock sounded on the cabin door. 'It'll be the steward,' she said knowledgeably and went to open it. Arthur swung round as he heard her astonished gasp. 'Jack!'

Jack? And there, incredibly, was Jack. Arthur swallowed a mouthful of tobacco smoke the wrong way and nearly choked.

'I'm sorry to butt in like this, but I saw the ships in the harbour as I flew over,' said Jack bewilderingly, strolling into the cabin as if it were the most natural thing in the world. 'I wondered if one was yours, and it was, so here I am.'

'You'll have to tell us a bit more than that,' said Isabelle. She had her hand on his arm, as if reassuring herself he was real. 'What on earth are you doing here?'

They sat down, listening intently as Jack told them. 'Bill Rackham thought I was nuts,' he concluded, 'but I have to try. You see that, don't you? I bought Skip Roscoe's – you remember Skip, Isabelle? – old D.H.9. He used it as an air-taxi for a time. It's not terribly fast but it's sturdy enough.' He gave a small smile. 'He wanted eight hundred for it but I beat him down a bit.'

'Eight hundred?' repeated Isabelle in disbelief. 'Jack, that must be all the money you've got.'

He shrugged. 'More or less. So what? If I manage to recover even some of the gold, the government ought to be grateful enough to cough up some of it.'

'Never mind the government,' said Arthur. 'What about you? What do you plan to do next?'

'I thought I'd spend the night here and push on to RAF Kantara in the morning. With any luck I'll be in this lost city by tomorrow evening.'

'What about the police, Jack?' asked Arthur. 'The local police, I mean. Do they know what you're doing?'

'They know,' replied Jack. 'They know because Bill told them. To be honest, I'd hoped they'd offer some assistance. That's certainly what Bill wanted, but they weren't pleased about me sticking my nose in. They can't stop me, of course, as I've a perfect right to go wherever I please, but they'd rather handle the matter themselves. The gold's the sticking point. If it really is there, they don't want me collaring it.' He laughed. 'I don't think they realize how much we're talking about. It weighs a ton.'

'A ton?' asked Isabelle. 'A ton of *gold*?'

'Well, not a ton exactly, but a dickens of a lot. I worked out that one hundred thousand sovereigns weighs in at just over at one thousand, six hundred and five pounds. That's over half a ton. I can't stick that in my pocket.'

Arthur chewed on his pipe stem for a little while. 'You could stick some of it, though. I can see why they're leery. It's awkward. What about the RAF? Presumably, as you're headed for Kantara, they're involved.'

'To some extent, yes,' agreed Jack. 'The CO is a bloke called Masterson. I don't know him, but he's a friend of Canning, whom I knew in France. Masterson's offered refuelling, fitting and rigging facilities, but that's as far as he can commit himself. He said he'd help as much as he can, so I'll have to be content with that.'

'I see,' said Arthur. 'So, not to put too fine a point on it, you could be tackling Von Erlangen on your own?' There was a dead silence. Arthur waited for a few moments, apparently intent on the glowing tobacco in the bowl of his pipe. 'What were you intending to do if you do find him?'

'Arrest him, of course,' said Jack quickly. Arthur raised his eyebrows quizzically. That answer had been too glib.

Jack sensed his disbelief and hurried into speech. 'What did you expect me to say? If the RAF are there, well and good. If not, I'll hold him prisoner until they arrive. I was going to talk to Masterson about it tomorrow.'

'And if it comes to shooting? I mean, you are armed, aren't you?'

'Oh course I am,' said Jack impatiently. 'You don't think I'd tackle a swine like that without a weapon, do you? I'm not setting out to murder him, Arthur. I'm going to give him the chance to come quietly. It won't be my fault if he doesn't.'

'I thought that was the size of it,' said Arthur quietly.

Jack slumped. He looked, thought Isabelle with a sudden twist of fear, beaten already.

'What the devil *can* I do? He's bound to be carrying a gun and he won't be squeamish about using it.'

Arthur looked at him acutely. He'd seen that defeated look as well. 'Which you will be. He's a killer. You're not. He'll have you for toast, Jack.'

Jack dropped his gaze. 'I have to try.'

Isabelle looked at her husband. 'Arthur?' she asked quietly.

Arthur nodded in understanding. 'Yes. Yes, I think we better had.'

Isabelle turned to face her cousin. 'We're coming with you.'

Jack's chin came up. 'Oh no, you're not. That's a stupid idea.'

'There's room in the aircraft for us, isn't there? I mean, if it was an air-taxi, there must be.'

'Yes, it's got a cabin,' he said absently. 'That's not a problem.'

'Then why?'

'It's *dangerous*, Belle.' He looked to Arthur for support. 'Von Erlangen's bad enough, but Vaughan could be there as well and there'll be workmen, too.'

'The workmen probably won't want to get mixed up in violence,' said Arthur. 'After all, the authorities know where you're going, so they'll have to account for themselves if you don't come back. And if, by any chance, it's Von Erlangen who doesn't come back . . . Well, you've still got a problem.'

Jack shrugged.

'It's no use trying to dismiss it,' said Arthur, leaning forward to add weight to his words. 'Von Erlangen will get you unless you get him first. If there are three of us, it shortens the odds, wouldn't you say? Say he does – I'm looking on the bright side here – come off worst. What then? The local police aren't happy about you getting involved and they'll probably take a fairly dim view if they've got a corpse on their hands. If we're there, we can testify that you didn't shoot him on sight. I don't know, granted Von Erlangen's record, if it would come to trial but you might find it difficult without our say-so to convince the police you acted in self-defence.'

Isabelle laid her hand on Jack's arm. 'I don't want you to go alone,' she said quietly. 'You're right. It is dangerous.'

Jack rested his chin on his hand. He should have anticipated Isabelle and Arthur's reaction, but he hadn't. He knew why he'd been so pleased when he'd spotted their ship in the harbour. In his heart of hearts he thought it was his last chance to say goodbye.

Von Erlangen; his stomach twisted at the thought. It was more than an intelligent apprehension of danger – he was familiar with that – but a disabling, courage-sapping fear. He had to face the man or, deep down inside, be a coward forever. That had fuelled his flight to the East. Freya's death was the spark that lit the fuse.

He'd steeled himself to go it alone, but the presence of his friends would make it all so much easier. It was a seductive offer and he desperately wanted to say yes.

'Let's go and have dinner,' he said eventually. 'I want to think this one through.'

The aircraft circled over the jumble of savagely sharp rocks. Twisting into the sun, their colours varying from nearly pure white to deep, angry red, the mountains were as uninviting as the surface of the moon.

When Jack had gone to sleep the previous night, he had been certain he was going alone. He hadn't reckoned on Arthur and Belle standing by the plane when he arrived at the airfield. He hadn't reckoned, either, on how his spirits soared at their insistence. The ship would leave Malta without them and they would rejoin the tour in Egypt; everyone had been informed. All the practical details, which didn't matter a tuppenny damn, had been taken care of.

So they were on board and now, with those savage rocks beneath him, Jack wished he had had the resolve to send them away. He couldn't even promise himself that the RAF would help. Masterson, the Commanding Officer, had taken note of their destination and promised what aid he could.

It should, he said, be all right. Should and Could. Not Can and Will. It was all far too conditional for comfort.

He fought with the controls to keep the D.H.9 steady in the heat-drenched air, as, nearly at stalling speed, he droned over the alien landscape. According to his compass readings they should be more or less over the city. There was about an hour of daylight left. If they couldn't find the city in that time, he'd have to land in the desert and resume the search in the morning.

A series of regular shadows set into the rocks caught his eye. Surely they were too uniform to be natural? He saw a perfect semicircle of steps cut out of the walls of the wadi below and a deep line of black snaking through the mountains to the desert beyond. The way in. As at Petra, the ancient masons had used the sheer slopes as their castle and a cleft in the rocks as their gateway. Compared to Petra, the site was tiny. There was nowhere to land inside the circle of rocks, so he banked and flew down the black line, the plane lurching as they flew into the barrier of colder air beyond the cliffs.

Flying as low as he dared, he picked out a landing ground, rose, banked and coasted in. Unconsciously, he held his breath. The surface of shale and sand *looked* all right, but if it was soft, then the wheels would sink on landing, ripping off the undercarriage. Even if they got down safely, without the wheels, they would never take off again. Down . . . bump . . . slide . . . hard ground! Thank God. He taxied the aircraft to the shade of the cliffs and switched off the engine.

As the propeller rumbled to a halt, Jack thankfully took off his flying helmet and rubbed his eyes, which were sore from the glare, took the cap off his canteen and had a much-needed drink. The heat, which had been tempered by the rush of air, struck him like a hammer blow. It must be about a hundred degrees out here and he knew it could get a great deal hotter. Stretching his weary shoulders, he swung himself out of the cockpit as the cabin door opened.

'Did you see anything?' he asked as Isabelle and Arthur jumped down on to the sand. 'There's a gorge that runs through the cliffs leading to the city.'

Isabelle shook her head, feeling the skin on her face tighten.

Automatically, she went to wipe her forehead, then realized
there was nothing to wipe. The dry heat of the desert sucked
up any moisture immediately. She gazed up at the towering
cliffs looming over them. 'Not a thing, Jack. It just looked
like a range of mountains to me.'

'I'm not surprised. It takes a bit of experience to spot
things from the air.'

'What now?' asked Arthur.

Jack glanced at the sky. 'We haven't got a lot of daylight
left so we'd better make the most of it. The first thing to do
is find the entrance to the gorge. If Von Erlangen's arrived,
I want to know about it.'

Taking their rifles, they walked to where the gorge split
the rocks. If they hadn't flown over it, it would have been
incredible to suppose it was anything more than a narrow
fissure that would peter out within a few feet. 'No one's been
here for a very long time,' said Jack in satisfaction, examining the ground.

'It's too late to explore tonight, I suppose?' asked Isabelle.

'Far too late,' said Jack. 'I don't want to be stranded in
the gorge in the dark. Besides that, we've got work to do.
The plane's all right at the moment but if we have to leave
her in the full sun tomorrow, it'll play havoc with the fabric.
I can rig up a shelter with a tarpaulin but let's scout round
and see if we can find some natural shade.'

Clinging to the shade, they set off round the base of the
cliffs. Isabelle was silenced by the gaunt, wild beauty of
the landscape. The desert, quivering in the heat, stretched
away to the horizon in an endless expanse of reds, browns
and yellows. Out there were more rocks and crags, their
shapes made uncertain by the shifting air grilling in the sun.
It seemed incredible that back home there were April showers
and blustery winds and it was possible to feel cold.

They walked for about ten minutes or so before they came
to a cavernous overhang in the rock. 'This is perfect,' said
Jack approvingly, stepping into the echoing space. 'There's
plenty of room for the plane.' He stopped sharply, then
relaxed.

'What is it?' asked Arthur.

Jack turned to him with a grin. 'For a moment I thought

there was a wild animal in here, a lynx or something.' He pointed to the back of the cave where the rocks were streaked with faintly glowing yellowish-white bands. 'It looked like a cat's eyes, but it's only light from the rocks. There must be an outcrop of natural phosphorus. It's fairly common in the desert.'

'I can see why you thought it was an animal,' said Isabelle, coming cautiously into the cave. 'I hadn't thought of lynxes. What's bothering me is the thought of scorpions. I hate big beetles and cockroaches and huge rustly things with too many legs, but scorpions are really loathsome.'

'You've certainly got to watch out for them,' said Jack. 'However, if you're careful to knock your shoes out before you put them on and don't stick your hand into holes, it should be all right. It's not only scorpions you've got to be wary of though, there are poisonous snakes and spiders, too. Don't touch the rocks, Belle!'

She turned with her hand outstretched. 'Why not?'

'It's probably all right, but phosphorus can give a nasty burn. There's no point taking unnecessary risks.'

She dropped her hand with a rueful grin. 'I'm going to have the jumps if this keeps up. What with lynxes, scorpions, poisonous things and burning rocks, I'll be a nervous wreck. Why don't you taxi the plane here and we can make camp? We can get a fire going and have something to eat. I'm hungry.'

'All right,' said Jack with a yawn. 'Before we make ourselves comfortable, though, I want to make sure we've got a runway prepared in case we need to take off in a hurry.' He looked out of the mouth of the overhang. 'This'll be all right, as long as I avoid the obvious boulders and crags. With any luck, most of the rocks are loose. I've got a crowbar in the cabin. We'll be able to shift them without much trouble.'

It was well over an hour later before they finally settled down to a meal of tinned stew, washed down with hot tea laced with tinned sweetened milk. 'That was good,' said Jack with a yawn, wiping round his plate with a piece of bread. He was desperately tired. It had been a long flight and clearing the runway had been exhausting. 'I suppose we'd better keep a lookout.'

'You take the last watch,' said Arthur, who could see his friend's eyes drooping. 'That's the easiest one,' he explained to Isabelle.

'I'll take the first one,' she offered. 'I don't feel very sleepy yet.'

The two men settled down in the cabin of the aeroplane. Isabelle, who had worked hard clearing the rocks, scrubbed the plates clean by scouring them with sand, put some more camel-thorn on the fire and made herself another cup of tea. Nursing the hot liquid between her hands, she was surprised how grateful she was for the warmth. Jack had warned them how cold the desert could be at night and he was right. There was no moon but the stars were brilliant enough to see far across the sands. Very far...

She sat up with a guilty jerk, the empty cup falling from her hands. She had been hovering on the edge of sleep and had fallen into a waking dream. For some reason she had been thinking of the seaside and boats. Not big ocean liners or cruise ships, but trips from the pier at Brighton. Had she heard something? A Brighton boat? That was crazy.

The wind shifted and, although she listened intently, she couldn't catch any other noise than the wind sighing through the rocks and the occasional flat, staccato bark of a desert fox far in the distance. She couldn't understand it.

'Boats?' said Jack when, considerably before dawn, they were breakfasting on hot coffee, tinned ham and bread. 'You were dreaming.'

'I don't think I was asleep exactly,' she said doubtfully.

'Of course you were,' said Jack with a laugh. 'Let's leave a cache of food and water buried at the back of the cave. It'll be a lot cooler there than left in the plane all day.'

'It's hard to believe how hot it'll get,' said Isabelle, shivering with cold.

The temperature had plummeted in the night and the air was chilly, which, in view of the loads they had to carry, was just as well. They all had packs slung over their shoulders with enough supplies to see them through the day, plus rifles and ammunition.

As they came to the entrance of the gorge, the sun was colouring the eastern sky. Jack smiled in relief as he knelt down, looking at the undisturbed shale, sand and rock. Von Erlangen should be along soon, but it was good to know they'd beaten him to it.

It was cold in the gorge, cold enough to make a brisk walk a pleasure. Above them the sky had turned to a pillar-box slit of blinding, impossible blue. Here, hundreds of feet below, it was nearly dark. It was a real shock when, a quarter of an hour or so later, the gorge bellied out to form a space about twenty feet across. Sunlight caught the walls obliquely, splashing the ground, catching and reflecting light from a carpet of quartz. It was like looking at a field of diamonds.

'It's beautiful,' breathed Isabelle. The rocks caught her voice and echoed it back in hundreds of tiny fragments.

'I bet this was a whirlpool thousands of years ago,' said Jack softly. It seemed wrong to speak loudly. 'Look how smooth the rocks are, twisting round and up. It still might be a whirlpool. It rains in the winter and this would trap the water into a flood.'

'It's as if we're at the bottom of an enormous well,' said Arthur.

Isabelle caught hold of his hand. 'Don't, Arthur. That's rather frightening, somehow.'

They walked forward, their footsteps crunching over the quartz, but on the other side of the sunlit space they faced a problem. The trail divided into two, separated by a tall, narrow boss of rock. Jack shrugged. 'One way's as good as another, I suppose. We can always come back.'

'That's true . . .' Arthur began, when Isabelle gave a cry of excitement.

'The horse's head rock! Can't you see it? It's the horse's head rock from the code! It's the rock dividing the two paths. If you look at it from here it's just like a horse's head.'

Arthur glanced up and was immediately struck by the resemblance. 'So it is, if you think of a horse as being about a hundred and fifty feet high. Well done, Isabelle. The nose sort of points the way, doesn't it?'

They walked for another ten minutes before they came out of the gorge.

Before them, the valley of the Nabateans lay open to the sun. The site, as Jack had seen from the air, was small, a natural arena in a roughly circular bowl in the surrounding rocks.

Across an ancient pavement stood a temple carved from white rock so bright it hurt their eyes to look at it. Four pillars supported a pediment that rioted with figures petrified in a moment of time. A man with a lion's head stood in the middle, surrounded by a crowd of worshippers. A sunburst shone round him and he had his arms raised to catch the solar disc. On either side of the temple entrance were a series of open doorways carved into the rock, their mouths black in the brilliant sun. The tombs?

Feeling as if they were intruders, they walked forward towards the temple and stood in the middle of the arena.

There was a white stone altar standing alone in the middle of the pavement and behind them, cut from crimson stone on either side of the gorge, rose the banks of seats Jack had seen from the air. The scale was small; fewer than three hundred people could have filled those seats. It was obviously only for the use of the select. Silence wrapped round them like a silk blanket. Isabelle felt she had never been in such an utterly private place. She had never really believed in ghosts, but here, surrounded by the sunlit, crumbling temple and tombs, it was easy to feel the brooding presence of another world.

'My God,' said Arthur, awestruck.

The ancient builders had understood the science of sound. His words were caught by the stones, echoing round in rolling, whispered waves. Isabelle jumped and clutched at his arm.

'The whispering dead,' said Jack. The stones picked up his words. 'We're in the Tombs of the Whispering Dead.'

They crossed the pavement and entered the white temple cautiously, their voices low. Not only did it seem wrong to speak in an ordinary voice, but anything louder than a whisper reverberated round the open space.

From an opening far above them the sun jagged down into darkness, full on to an immense white throne. Despite its size, it seemed to be floating on empty air. Arthur walked forward and crouched down beside the white seat. 'I see how it's done,' he said practically. 'The supports are made of black rock so all you see are the white bits.' He looked round. 'There's a throne but surely this was never a palace. It's not a tomb, either. At least, I can't see where anyone's buried. I wonder what it was used for?'

'Don't you see?' said Isabelle with a catch in her voice. 'This is where the new kings were crowned or proclaimed or whatever they did. The king would be sanctified by the sun.'

Jack's eyes were growing accustomed to the light. In front of them was a black stone block about the size of a bed. It was completely smooth. 'I think I get the idea,' he said softly. 'If you buried a king in one of the tombs, his body would be brought through the gorge. You'd come out of the gloom into the light of the square, then into the darkness of this place. Can you imagine the effect of music or chanting with those echoes outside?'

'Spooky,' said Isabelle with a shudder. 'Downright scary, actually.'

'Impressive, certainly. What d'you think? Maybe the king's son walked with his father's body. The body would be placed on this stone table, while the new king would walk on to be crowned, drenched in the sun. The symbolism must have been breathtaking.'

'Death into life,' murmured Arthur.

'It's the classic Eastern contrast, isn't it? Ormuzd and Mazda; darkness and light. Vaughan'll go doolally when he sees all this. If he's still alive, that is.'

'Talking of which,' said Arthur, going back to the entrance, 'hadn't we better be getting a move on? We don't know when they're going to show up.'

'I suppose so,' said Jack. They had decided last night it was impossible to be too rigid in their plans but, broadly speaking, they would try and find the hidden gold, then lay in wait for Von Erlangen to arrive. Surprise was the one advantage they had and they didn't want to squander it.

Once out of the temple and on the pavement again, Jack pulled his copy of the coded message from his breast pocket. '*At the tombs of the whispering dead, stand you in front of Petra*. I presume that means we see where Petra is and go in that direction.' He consulted his compass. 'Now, Petra's north-west of here, so we've got to go . . . there.' He pointed towards a group of open doorways. '*Step you or go you in the lion inside,* is our next direction, whatever that means.'

They walked together, talking little, making as little sound as possible on the smooth, venerable pavement. The soft thud of their footsteps on the stones made it sound as if they were being followed by something not quite human. Isabelle couldn't rid herself of the feeling they were being watched from the black, gaping doorways that lined the street. She wished she could stop thinking of ghosts.

Here and there, a breath of wind whirled sand into a dust devil before passing on, leaving all as before. A green lizard looked at them with indifferent, glittering eyes from the basin of a sand-choked fountain. It was the only life they had seen.

Isabelle looked at the carvings above the doorways. Some were too weathered to make out, but she could see an eagle, a scorpion and what looked like a gazelle. 'The carvings above the tombs could be like coats of arms. Maybe these are family tombs. If we find one with a lion over the entrance it could be what we're looking for.'

'There it is!' said Arthur, his voice vibrant with excitement. He pointed to a mountain lion carved over a doorway. 'Well done, Isabelle. What does the code say next, Jack?'

Jack consulted the paper again. 'It says *Fight you with the scorpion,* whatever that means.'

Many years ago there had been double doors guarding the entrance to the Lion Tomb, but they had since long rotted away, leaving their outline in the dust where they had fallen. Light streamed through the entrance, touching the bottom of the far wall of this shallow, empty space. Jack, who had taken out his torch, re-clipped it on his belt and stood in wonder in the empty, ancient, shadowy room.

The floor was paved with smooth stones and the red walls were full of pictures of people, carved into the rock and picked out with paint. Most of the paint had fallen away but enough remained to show them that when new, the chamber must have been a blaze of colour.

Jack whistled. 'My word, this is interesting. There isn't a trace of paint anywhere in Petra. If this is a Nabatean site, they must have reserved the art for their most honoured dead.

Actually . . .' He turned to Isabelle, his eyes alight. 'You know I said your mother helped to work out the code? She talked about the Silent Ones, from the poem in the book. Do you remember it? *The Silent Ones, when asked, will measure, the hidden way to dragons' treasure.* She guessed the people and the things in the book – the painted objects – although silent, were showing us the way to the treasure. Now there are more paintings, more Silent Ones, if I can put it like that. I think we're getting very warm, don't you?'

'The Silent Ones,' said Arthur softly. He gently touched the gold face of the man in the relief beside him. The paint flaked on his fingertips and drifted downwards to mix with the heap of dust beside the walls. Feeling like a vandal, he regretfully brushed his fingers and stood back from the wall. 'There's something wrong, though, isn't there?' he said, looking round. 'If this is a tomb, then where's the coffin or sarcophagus or whatever? There have to be tombs somewhere. I mean, the whole city is called the Tombs of the Whispering Dead, but this is just a room.'

'Maybe this is an antechamber,' said Jack. 'Perhaps the actual bodies are in a crypt somewhere underneath.'

The sun only caught the bottom of the far wall. Isabelle switched on her torch and immediately gave a cry of triumph. 'It's a door! And look, there's the scorpion!'

It was a door, but a door without a handle. It stood proud of the wall, a single slab of stone. The central panel consisted of a large scorpion with fragments of gold paint still clinging to it.

Arthur put his shoulder to the slab and pushed hard. 'It's no use,' he said, panting. 'It felt as if it should move but I can't shift it. What does the code say? Fight the scorpion? How the blazes do we do that?'

'I dunno. Maybe we have to pull it, not push it,' suggested Jack. He rested his rifle against the wall, gripped his hands round the stone, and heaved. 'It's moving,' he said, his voice thin with effort. '*Bloody hell!*'

He jumped away from the slab as a scorpion scuttled out from under the door.

Isabelle screamed. The scorpion, eight inches long at least, was by her foot, stiff-legged with tail raised, ready to strike.

Arthur hefted his rifle, stepped forward and brought the butt down with a crunch on the creature. He stamped on the remains for good measure, then opened his arms to Isabelle. She leaned against him shakily. 'It's all right, now,' he said gently. 'It's dead.'

'I'm . . . I'm sorry I screamed. I really don't like them. It startled me.'

'It startled me, too,' said Jack. 'I've never seen such a brute.'

'Do you think there are any more about?' said Isabelle, trying to keep her voice steady.

'I don't know,' said Jack. 'I don't know if they come in ones, twos or lots.'

'In that case I'm going to wait outside,' said Isabelle. She looked at the scorpion and shuddered. 'Let me know if you find anything.' She went outside, crossed the street to the shade and, after examining a fallen column closely for anything lurking there, sat down and lit a cigarette.

'That really was a brute of a thing,' said Jack, turning his attention back to the door. He kicked what was left of the creature out of the way, and, for the second time, gave a startled exclamation and jumped away.

'What is it?' asked Arthur quickly. 'It's not another one, is it?'

'No, it's not that. The ground moved. I felt it sway.' He looked at the stone floor closely. 'Arthur! There's a picture of an eagle on this stone slab, beneath the picture of the scorpion.'

'An eagle? That's in the code. *Fight the scorpion, crush the eagle.*'

'The slab and the door must be connected. We probably weakened the door by heaving at it. Crush the eagle . . . How do you crush something?'

Arthur looked puzzled. 'Well, you sort of squash it. Grind it down, I suppose.'

'Crush it,' muttered Jack. 'Squash it. What do you do when you crush or squash something? Damn it, you stamp on it! Stamp on the eagle and fight the scorpion . . .'

'We must have to hit the blasted thing,' said Arthur excitedly. 'Stand on it, Jack, and I'll press down on the scorpion. Go on.'

Jack ground his heel hard into the eagle's head and felt it give slightly. Arthur put his shoulder to the carving.

Although they had worked out what should happen, it was a real shock when the door swung open.

'We've done it,' breathed Jack. 'We've actually done it.' He shone his torch through the doorway. There was a short passage with steps leading down. He turned and raised his voice. 'Isabelle! Come and look at this!'

Isabelle, still pale, came back into the room. She looked dubiously at the steps in the torchlight. She couldn't see any scorpions but there were certainly cobwebs. Lots of cobwebs. She swallowed before she spoke. 'Look, do you mind if I don't come with you? I'm not crazy about cramped spaces at the best of times, especially in the dark. I'd really rather wait outside.'

'What about Von Erlangen?' asked Arthur. 'Don't forget we're expecting him. Shall I wait with you?'

She could see he was itching to explore the passage. 'No, don't do that. I'll be fine. If Von Erlangen turns up, I'll hear the echoes a mile off. You could probably do with someone on guard anyway.'

'All right,' said Arthur, after a moment. 'If you hear anything, come and get us right away.'

Jack cleared away some of the cobwebs with the muzzle of his rifle. 'Come on. We have to *Seek the maiden* next.'

The stairs were as gorgeously decorated as the ante-room had been but here, preserved from the sun, sand and wind, the paint was as fresh as the day it was finished. The stairs led down for about ten feet and gave on to a narrow passage which, in turn, opened on to a long, narrow L-shaped room.

The torchlight picked out vibrant colour. The figure of a lion was repeated but there were also people, camels, palm trees, flying birds, blue water with reeds and a boat with white sails.

'It's beautiful,' said Arthur softly.

'Maybe it's their idea of heaven. And look, there are the coffins.'

Set into niches at regular intervals down the walls lay a row of sarcophagi. They had been covered with white plaster and a life-size and lifelike picture of the person within painted on it, a top view on the lid, a side view along the length.

Arthur shivered. 'That's a rum sort of notion. It makes the coffins look transparent.'

Running the torch along the line of tombs, Jack wished his friend had kept that idea to himself. 'I've seen this sort of thing before,' he said thoughtfully, in an attempt to distance himself from the thought of transparent coffins. 'There are some Roman coffins in the British Museum which are painted like this. The Romans knew Petra. That's obvious from the architecture, apart from anything else. Maybe this isn't a Nabatean site but a Roman one. That amphitheatre, or whatever it was, looked a bit Roman.'

'Perhaps it's both,' suggested Arthur. 'After all, the Romans adopted local customs and gods and so on, didn't they? I suppose the locals could have learnt from them, too.' He played the torch over the sarcophagi. 'These are all men, Jack. We're looking for a maiden.'

'Maybe her tomb is round the corner.' They stepped into the adjoining room. Jack shone the torchlight in front of him, then leapt back with a startled yell. Arthur, nerves on edge, jumped and swore.

There was only one sarcophagus in the chamber. On its lid sat a skull, glowing whitish-yellow in the light of the torch.

'My God,' said Jack, breathing rapidly. 'I'm sorry, Arthur, but it's enough to give anyone the creeps. I'm sorry I shouted. I wasn't expecting anything like that.'

'What's making it shine?' asked Arthur when he had recovered himself. 'Phosphorus?'

'At a guess, yes.' He gave a rueful laugh. 'By jingo, it's a ghastly-looking thing. I think this is the tomb we're looking for, though.'

Arthur shone his torch along the side of the sarcophagus. The painting on the side showed a girl of about twenty, with long, dark hair, a blue and red dress gathered softly round her and her eyes shut as though in sleep. The plasterwork on top of the coffin, though, had shattered. Someone had evidently wrenched the coffin open, breaking the delicate work.

'The maiden,' said Jack. 'It's the maiden. *With a body once so fair, a princess guards the dragons' lair,*' he quoted softly. 'We've done it, Arthur. We've found the princess.'

'Have we found the treasure, though?' Arthur stepped towards the sarcophagus and put his foot on something that cracked. He drew back sharply. 'What the devil's that?' He shone the torchlight on to the floor and blenched.

Parts of a skeleton lay scattered over the floor. A length of cloth, in faded blue and red, was twisted round a rib-case.

'It must be the princess,' said Jack, stooping to pick up a fragment of bone. 'Poor little devil. *With a body once so fair . . .*' He looked at the picture of the girl. 'She was beautiful,' he said. 'It seems wrong to throw her remains on the floor. I suppose the treasure's in the sarcophagus.'

'You're quite right,' said a voice from the doorway. 'Let me congratulate you, gentlemen.'

Jack and Arthur whirled. A fierce, blinding light shone into Jack's eyes, but, with his flesh crawling, he recognized the voice. It was Lothar Von Erlangen.

SIXTEEN

The light stabbed the darkness in a wavering line as Von Erlangen walked into the chamber. Jack blinked and squinted away as the beam shone full in his face. 'Now this,' said Von Erlangen, 'is familiar. I was holding a torch the first time we met, Mr Haldean.'

Jack felt his stomach churn, but he forced himself to look impassively towards that hated voice. He wouldn't – he *mustn't* – give any sign of fear. Their very lives might depend on it. He's only human. Remember. Only human. And he killed Freya. Anger licked like flame along the edges of his fear. Hold on to that. He killed Freya.

There was an ominous click behind the light.

'Please don't move. I do have a gun and that sound was the hammer being drawn back. I remember our first encounter with very great pleasure, Mr Haldean. You provided considerable entertainment on that occasion. Maybe you will again. My Turkish confederates are, alas, no more, but I believe my Arab associates share their tastes in these matters. Leave your rifles on the floor. That includes you, Captain Stanton,' he added sharply, as Arthur made a slight move. Arthur stopped and they could hear the satisfaction in Von Erlangen's voice. 'Very wise.'

'Where's Isabelle?' demanded Arthur, his voice sharp with worry.

'She's being taken care of by my men.' They could hear the satisfaction in Von Erlangen's voice. 'I trust they'll resist their natural inclinations.'

Arthur started forward but Von Erlangen's voice brought him up sharp. 'Don't move, Captain! I cannot credit you left a mere girl on guard. We found your aeroplane in the cave and your tracks were plain to see. We left the lorry at the entrance to the gorge and came on foot. The girl never heard a thing. Shall we go upstairs?'

Even in his misery and anxiety for Isabelle, Jack's mind

was working. Von Erlangen said they had left their lorry at the entrance to the gorge. The lorry! Isabelle must have heard the chug of the lorry's engine last night. Mentally he kicked himself. He should have realized.

'Do keep your hands raised,' said Von Erlangen silkily. 'To be forced to shoot in an enclosed space would be a pity. It brings on temporary deafness, you know. I would find it inconvenient.'

Utterly wretched, Jack and Arthur walked along the passage, up the stairs, into the ante-room and through the open doorway into the bone-white sunlight of the arena.

Across the pavement, in the shade of the cliff, stood Isabelle. She had been gagged with a chequered cloth and her hands were tied but she was, thank God, unharmed.

There were three men with her. Vaughan, looking very impatient, stood with his arms folded, his rifle propped up beside him. The other two men were Arabs. They both wore keffiyehs and ordinary, if dirty, shirts and trousers. They lounged against the rocks with machine guns slung negligently in front of them and belts of ammunition across their chests.

As they emerged from the tomb, Vaughan looked at them in bewilderment. 'What the devil are you doing here?'

His words were caught by the cliffs and chopped up into whispering echoes. The two Arabs shifted uneasily and Von Erlangen's eyes flicked towards them.

It was enough. Hurling himself forward, Jack jabbed one fist into Von Erlangen's stomach and smashed the other on the point of his jaw. The revolver skittered out of Von Erlangen's hand and, as Jack grasped for it, the ground exploded around him in a spray of machine-gun bullets. The cliffs thundered the echoes in an ear-splitting, earthquake of noise.

'Stop!' yelled Vaughan. 'You'll damage the site! Stop!'

Jack, flat on his face, waited for the echoes to die away.

The two Arabs stopped shooting and grinned nervously at each other. 'Jeez,' said one in pure Brooklyn, against the dying rumbles of sound. 'That's really something, boss.'

Von Erlangen rose to his knees in the dust. 'Pick him up,' he bit out, pointing to Jack. The two Arabs hauled Jack to his feet.

Von Erlangen dusted off his knees, picked up the revolver, drew back his hand and, with a crack that reverberated round the arena, struck Jack across the face. He stood back, breathing quickly. 'Mr Haldean, don't do that again.' He indicated the two Arabs. 'Amir and Kazim will be happy to teach you a lesson.'

'Can someone tell me what's going on?' demanded Vaughan. 'Preferably without all this melodramatic posturing.'

Arthur looked at Jack, then at Isabelle. His glance flicked back to Vaughan. 'Release my wife,' he said icily. 'Vaughan, how can you ill-treat a woman? I thought you were a gentleman.'

Vaughan's shoulders went back, but he stepped forward and pulled the cloth away from Isabelle's mouth.

She fell against Arthur with a little cry. 'I'm sorry. I tried to fight, but it was no use.'

'Quite right, my dear,' said Von Erlangen in satisfaction. 'I trust Amir and Kazim have looked after you?'

The two Arabs sullenly looked up. 'We wanted to, boss,' said one. 'But this dude –' he indicated Vaughan with the barrel of his machine gun – 'sez nothing doing.'

'Bad luck,' said Von Erlangen smoothly. 'Maybe you'll have your chance later.'

'No, they damn well won't,' said Vaughan. He looked at Arthur. 'Captain Stanton, you have my apologies, sir. I will not permit any of you to come to harm.'

Von Erlangen's eyebrows rose sardonically, but he said nothing.

'Why are you here?' asked Vaughan. He glared at Von Erlangen. 'I could ask you the same question, Madison. You said this was an archaeological expedition but insisted on bringing these slum-sweepings with us . . .'

'Watch it,' said Amir dangerously, hefting his tommy gun. 'We ain't from no slum. We've been to America. Show respect, right?'

'I'd have a bit more respect if you didn't behave like a couple of gangsters,' said Vaughan tightly. 'Have you any idea of the damage you could cause with those guns of yours?'

Amir and Kazim laughed. 'Is this guy for real, boss?' asked Kazim.

'I,' said Vaughan stiffly, 'am paying for this expedition. That includes your wages. It's about time you remembered that.'

The two Arabs swapped glances and laughed again. 'We work for the boss,' said Amir. 'We worked for the boss in New York.' He patted his machine gun. 'The boss wanted us special.'

Vaughan gave them a withering look and turned away. 'Well, Madison?' he demanded.

Jack wiped the blood from his mouth. 'Why don't you tell him, Von Erlangen?' He cocked an eyebrow at Vaughan. 'I don't know why you're calling him Madison, by the way. His name's Von Erlangen. Mind you, I can see why anyone would be confused. He's had a few names. Ozymandias, for instance, as I imagine Durant Craig would've mentioned. He's Simes, too. You know that, don't you?'

Vaughan looked confused. 'Simes? I don't understand.'

'You've been used, Mr Vaughan,' said Jack. 'Used from beginning to end. Incidentally, you should reconsider returning to England. The police know about the murder of Durant Craig.'

'I never . . .' began Vaughan hotly.

Jack glanced at Von Erlangen. 'So it was your German friend who actually did the deed, was it? Never mind. You disposed of the body. You're an accessory.' He held up his hand to cut short Vaughan's angry protests. 'They know all about it.'

Vaughan fell silent, struggling for words. 'You don't understand about Craig,' he said eventually. 'I really believe he was insane. I tried to reason with him but he was past hearing. It wasn't murder, it was self-defence.' He looked at Jack, hungry for understanding. 'I'm not a murderer. Don't you see? It was the chance of a lifetime but Craig would've ruined everything. He struck the first blow. He attacked Madison.' His mouth compressed to a straight line. 'It really was self-defence. I wouldn't have gone along with murder. You mustn't think that. But Craig was past help. Madison and I worked out the plan between us. It was better that way. I didn't do anything wrong, not really wrong. It was necessary.'

'Necessary?' repeated Jack. 'How? If it was self-defence, why couldn't you report it?'

'That was my first idea, but to explain everything would mean publicizing this site. While we were held up in endless delays, someone else would have got here first. I wasn't going to let some casual tripper grab the glory and ruin the site, not when I could investigate it properly. Madison said as much and I agreed.' Vaughan glanced at Von Erlangen. 'He's an American. He didn't want to get involved with the police. There was some minor technical difficulty about his passport. He'd have been held up indefinitely.'

'Minor technical difficulty?' repeated Jack with an incredulous laugh. 'The minor technical difficulty is that Madison, as you call him, is wanted for murder in New York.' He swung round on Von Erlangen. 'Deny it.'

Von Erlangen smiled urbanely. 'So you say, Mr Haldean.'

Vaughan looked at Von Erlangen doubtfully. 'I don't believe it,' he said, but his voice lacked conviction.

'You're unhappy about Madison, aren't you, Mr Vaughan?' continued Jack. 'I bet you've become more and more suspicious as the journey's continued.' Vaughan's face told him he had hit home. 'It's true, isn't it?

Vaughan didn't answer for a few moments, then he squared his shoulders and drew himself up with sudden decision. 'Yes, damn it, it is,' He turned on Von Erlangen. 'You've always managed to persuade me that we were doing the right thing. I wanted to hire proper native workmen but you insisted on bringing these toughs.' He looked at Amir and Kazim with distaste. 'When I wanted to inform the authorities of our intentions, you dissuaded me. We can't just rip up the site, Madison, or whatever your name is. It has to be properly organized. We're not looters or grave-robbers.'

Jack laughed once more. 'All of which would be very re-assuring if Von Erlangen had archaeology in mind. This isn't, and was never intended to be, an archaeological expedition.'

'What other reason is there for coming here?' asked Vaughan. 'If you mean I intend to strip the site for my own gain, you're wrong, Major Haldean, and I won't permit anyone else to do it, either. Madison, you promised me this site was untouched. I hope you were telling the truth about that, at least.'

Von Erlangen's lips thinned. 'You think I am guilty of

mere treasure hunting, Mr Vaughan?' He took a thin black cigar from the case in his pocket and lit it. There was a little white line round his nostrils. 'A grave robber, eh? Can I suggest you actually go and look at the tomb that was occupying Mr Haldean and his friend? You will find my actions have been *tout au contraire* as the French say.'

Jack made to speak again but Von Erlangen whirled on him in sudden fury. 'Enough! You have said enough, Mr Haldean. Kazim, if he talks again, kill the girl.'

Kazim brought his gun up, ready to fire.

Vaughan looked at the machine-gun levelled at Isabelle and swallowed. 'I'll have something to say about this later, Madison,' he said curtly and strode off.

Von Erlangen flicked the ash from his cigar and waited. 'Now, Mr Haldean,' he said, once Vaughan had gone. 'I want a few answers. Let's start with the obvious one. How did you find this place?'

Jack glanced at Kazim. At a nod from Von Erlangen, Kazim relaxed his grip on the gun. 'We read the code, the code you left in the book.'

Von Erlangen's eyebrows rose. 'I congratulate you,' he said softly. 'Did Freya tell you how to interpret it?'

Jack shook his head. 'We worked it out all by ourselves. Incidentally, you did paint the book for her, didn't you?'

Von Erlangen inclined his head. 'As you say, Mr Haldean.'

'And yet you killed her. Why?'

Von Erlangen's eyes glowed dangerously, then he suddenly gave a wolfish smile. 'Haven't you guessed? It was because of you. You told her what happened in New York. You made her doubt me. Freya was *my wife*, Mr Haldean. She obeyed me absolutely, but you wanted to change that, didn't you? You offered her help and she very nearly accepted it. I wanted to kill you. She stopped me. Nobody – nobody at all – stops me.'

'You arrogant bastard,' breathed Jack.

Von Erlangen laughed. 'I know what I want and I get it. If I had let her live, she would have come to you. I could not allow that.'

'One of these days,' said Jack soberly, 'you'll get what you deserve. You might have fooled Vaughan, but you can't fool me. I know why you're here. You're after the gold.'

Amir and Kazim looked up alertly. 'Gold, boss? Did he say gold?'

Von Erlangen bit his lip. 'You'll get your share. Mr Haldean, you know far too much.'

'Yes, I do, don't I?' said Jack with a smile. He'd seen the reaction of the two Arabs. A bit of dissension in the camp wouldn't hurt. 'Gold,' he said, making his voice carry. 'The gold you stole from the convoy. There's about a hundred thousand pounds in that tomb, yes?'

Amir and Kazim started forward. 'That's a lot of dough.'

'You'll get your share,' said Von Erlangen thinly.

Jack made his stance and his voice as casual as possible. He had an idea in mind, a desperate idea, but the one hope he could think of. 'The thing is, Von Erlangen, old bean, this isn't a lost city anymore. Quite a few people know about it, such as the London police, the Transjordan police and the RAF. I had to call at Kantara to refuel and Masterson, the Commanding Officer, promised to send a flight over to see how I was getting on.'

'You're lying.'

Jack shook his head. 'No, I'm not.' He studied his fingernails. 'You've left quite a trail of corpses behind you, Von Erlangen. It's been noticed.'

Von Erlangen's face twisted in sudden fury. Raising his hand, he was about to strike when the two Arabs gave a yell of terror.

'Look, boss!' shouted Kazim. 'Look!'

Vaughan came out of the ante-room. He was swaying and his feet made a shuffling, dragging echo on the stones. Clasped to his chest was the skull. Even in the harsh sunlight, the skull glowed a faint yellow. Vaughan's face was deathly white as he stumbled to the altar. He collapsed, the skull rolling away from him. His hand grasped feebly at the air, then he shuddered and lay still, his eyes wide open to the glare of the sun.

Isabelle gave a little cry of dismay and buried her face in Arthur's chest.

Jack looked at Vaughan's open hands. They were burnt and chapped as if rubbed by something corrosive. The skull, which had been so impressive in the darkened tomb, looked like a cheap stage prop. 'You set it up, didn't you? You put that skull on the coffin. What was on it? Phosphorus?'

'Exactly, Mr Haldean. I thought a phosphorescent skull would deter any wandering Arab.'

Jack knelt beside Vaughan. The sight of the dead man stretched out beside the sickly yellow skull filled him with unexpected anger. There was no dignity in Vaughan's death. He had died by an underhand trick. 'He's been poisoned,' he said flatly.

'Sometimes,' said Von Erlangen, drawing on his cigar in satisfaction, 'appearances, however dramatic, are not enough. A little nicotine – a very useful substance and quite deadly in its effect when properly prepared – mixed with the phosphorus gets the poison into the blood with gratifying results.'

'And you deliberately sent Vaughan down there.'

'Of course I did!' Von Erlangen's temper flared again. He turned on Amir and Kazim, who had shrunk back, talking in a stream of Arabic. 'Silence, you fools!'

'It's ghosts, boss, ghosts!'

'It's no such thing. I killed him, d'you hear? You knew I was going to. I said I'd take care of it.' The two men continued to talk, darting quick, frightened glances at Vaughan. 'Silence!' roared Von Erlangen, real fury in his voice. Amir and Kazim reluctantly subsided, looking uneasily at the skull.

Von Erlangen turned back to Jack. 'Now, Mr Haldean, I have shown considerable patience. You were telling me that the RAF are on their way, I believe?'

'They are.' Jack forced himself to smile. 'You can't escape, you know. Even if you get away, they'll pick you up in the desert.' He gestured to the sky. 'You can see for miles up there.'

Von Erlangen looked up and Jack could see him become thoughtful. 'How much weight can that plane of yours carry?'

Jack remained silent.

'Amir,' said Von Erlangen without heat. 'Hit the girl. Make sure you hurt her.'

'No, wait!' said Jack quickly. 'Don't do that.' He spoke reluctantly. 'The plane can carry about four thousand pounds.' He knew he was overestimating wildly.

'Four thousand, eh?'

'That's about two thousand kilograms.'

'I know, Mr Haldean, I know. It should be enough.'

'Just a minute,' said Jack. 'If you're thinking of collaring my plane, I'd like to point out aircraft don't fly themselves. Unless those two boneheads of yours are pilots, you're stuck.'

'Amir,' called Von Erlangen, without taking his gaze from Jack, 'we have some leather straps with us, haven't we?'

'Yes, Boss.'

Von Erlangen turned to Jack, his teeth showing in a humourless smile. 'I remember you being open to persuasion, Mr Haldean. As I mentioned before, these gentlemen can be very enthusiastic. They have worked for me before.'

'Shall we beat him up, boss?' called Kazim, grinning. 'We've got a camel-whip on the truck.'

Von Erlangen's smile grew wider. 'A camel-whip? Just the thing. Camels are obdurate animals, and require a yard-long cane to urge them into action. Used on human flesh, the results are fascinating. And should that not prove enough . . . Well, surely you haven't forgotten how I managed to influence your decision last time.'

Jack folded his arms and laughed. Von Erlangen's words had shaken him but he was damned if he was going to show how the sick taste of fear filled his mouth. 'Come off it. What sort of state would I be in to fly anything after you'd finished with me? It took me months to recover last time. You'll have to do better than that.'

'There are other ways,' said Von Erlangen, softly. His gaze slid towards Isabelle. 'You would not, I believe, care to see the girl treated as you were. Such a disagreeable way to die.'

Arthur jerked his head up. 'You wouldn't do that!'

'Captain Stanton, I would.'

Arthur said nothing, but held Isabelle closer.

Von Erlangen watched them for a moment, shrugged and turned to Jack. 'Mr Haldean? The ball, as you say, is in your court.'

Jack reached for his breast pocket, smiling as Von Erlangen started forward. 'You don't mind if I smoke, do you? Thank you.' He took a cigarette and held it thoughtfully for a while before striking the match. 'You see, you've given me a bit of a problem. I don't like you. I don't like what you did to me, I don't like what you did to Vaughan and for what you did to Freya you deserve to die.' For a moment his eyes were like black fire. He gave a short laugh. 'However, she's gone and I'm no martyr. I don't want to be hurt and I don't want to see my friends hurt either. Having said that, I didn't ask them to come. They insisted.'

'In that case ...'

'In that case, Von Erlangen, old fruit, why don't you talk sense? The trouble is, you keep on gloating away about doing nasty things to people, which is, I s'pose, the first thing that occurs to you, but you won't actually offer me what I want.'

'Which is?'

'Money.' He stood up straight and put his hands wide. 'For God's sake man, what the blazes d'you think I want?'

For the first time Von Erlangen looked discomfited. 'Revenge?'

'As if! Do me a favour. I'd sooner see you dead than alive but I'm damned if I'd fly halfway round the world for the privilege. I came for the money. There's a hundred thousand in gold salted away here and, by God, I wanted it.'

'And yet you informed the RAF?'

'I didn't tell them about the gold. Good God, no. What d'you take me for? I told them in case I met you. If things had gone to plan, I'd have been out of here with the money before you were any the wiser.' He jerked his thumb at Arthur and Isabelle. 'They've got an expensive way of life. They like money as well.'

Arthur shifted uneasily. Isabelle put her hand on his arm and squeezed it. She didn't know what Jack had in mind, but she didn't want to spoil it.

Jack flicked the ash off his cigarette. 'You want my plane. The least you can do is offer me a decent slice of the cake and I'll fly you wherever you want to go.'

Von Erlangen walked over to Jack and, taking his chin between very firm fingers, searched his face. Then he stepped back and nodded. 'You have changed, I think, from the young man I met in Q'asr Dh'an.'

Jack laughed. 'Absolutely. I'm older. Much older. I aged after meeting you. Do you know what happened to me after my heroic last stand? I was severely censured, stripped of my privileges and, as a huge favour, allowed to sweat my guts out in the service of my beloved country. With enough money I can start to get my own back. I've got some scores to settle and, by God, I'm looking forward to doing it.'

'Your friends cannot come with us,' said Von Erlangen with a sudden change of tone.

Jack shrugged indifferently. 'All right.'

'Jack!' said Isabelle, appalled. She couldn't help herself.

He turned to her apologetically. 'I'm sorry, Isabelle. You'll be all right.' He drew Von Erlangen a little distance away. 'We'll have to be careful,' he said in a low voice. 'The woman isn't just anyone, you know. Her father is Sir Philip Rivers. If she comes off worse, I'm for it. There are very few places British justice can't reach. Bloody uncomfortable places for the most part and I don't want to live in them.'

'I shall bear it in mind, Mr Haldean. What shall we do with them now? I cannot spare a man to guard them.'

'I'd tie 'em up,' said Jack with another shrug. 'But you're the boss.'

On instructions from Von Erlangen, Isabelle and Arthur were securely tied up. After Amir and Kazim had finished, Jack leant over to check the rope. Von Erlangen was very close at hand.

'Jack,' hissed Arthur. 'What the hell are you playing at?'

'I'm not playing, I'm afraid. You'll be all right. You'll be a bit uncomfortable until the RAF arrive, but I can't help that. Keep quiet and when you get back to England, we'll share the money.'

A few yards away, Von Erlangen nodded in satisfaction. He despatched Kazim to fetch the lorry and, sitting with a machine-gun across his knees, ordered Jack and Amir to bring the gold up from the tomb. There were eighty canvas bags, each weighing about twenty pounds. In the relentless sun it was back-breaking work and it was over an hour before the gold was out of the tomb and loaded on to the back of the lorry. During that time Jack had not looked at Isabelle and Arthur.

When the last bag was on the truck, Jack opened his water bottle, took a long drink and, wetting his handkerchief, mopped his face in relief.

'Thank God that's over. Now we've got to get it loaded on the plane.' He caught a pleading glance from Isabelle that would have melted a heart of ice and, taking his water bottle, uncapped it and walked over to them. 'Drink?' he asked, kneeling beside them.

Isabelle nodded. Her throat was nearly completely dry and she couldn't speak until Jack held the leather-covered bottle to her lips. 'Jack,' she said unhappily, as he helped Arthur to drink, supporting his shoulders with his hand. 'Please don't do this.'

His face softened and for a moment it looked as if he were about to speak, then he turned as Von Erlangen approached. 'I'm leaving them some water. It'll be a bit awkward for them with their hands tied, but they should be able to manage. I don't want them to die of thirst before they're rescued.'

Von Erlangen seemed highly amused. 'I can promise you they won't die of thirst, Mr Haldean.' He leaned forward and caressed Isabelle's face. 'That would be most unpleasant.'

Arthur stirred menacingly but said nothing.

'Shall we go?' asked Jack abruptly.

He sat on the back of the lorry beside Amir while Von Erlangen and Kazim sat in the cab. The engine started, the lorry pulled away and the echoes of the engine gradually rumbled away into silence.

'I wish I knew what Jack was up to,' said Isabelle, her voice flat with despair.

'I do,' said Arthur. 'Have those bruisers gone?' He wriggled himself into a different position. 'When Jack gave me a drink, he put his arm down beside me. He had a knife hidden up his shirt sleeve. I'm sitting on it now. As he knelt down he whispered, "As soon as we've gone, cut the ropes and follow us, but for God's sake don't be seen." He eased himself up. 'Why, Isabelle, you're crying.'

'I know,' she choked. 'I thought we were going to die.'

'If we don't look sharpish, we might. We're not out of danger yet, not by a long chalk.' He wriggled the knife into position. 'I want a long and happy life with you and that swine isn't going to stop me.' With a feeling of relief, he felt the rope go. Rising stiffly, he cut Isabelle free. Clumsily, they got to their feet, feeling the circulation return slowly to their arms and legs. 'Let's go,' said Arthur, slipping the knife into his boot.

They were only a short way up the gorge when Isabelle stopped. 'I can hear someone coming,' she said quietly, her mouth close to Arthur's ear.

'Back to the Tombs,' whispered Arthur. 'Quickly.' He'd thought the chances of Von Erlangen letting them live were slight. He cursed inwardly. All the rifles were gone and the Arabs had machine guns. One knife wasn't much use against a tommy gun. Perhaps he could lie in wait? Perhaps.

Kazim came into the arena, his machine gun cradled in his arms. He hated this place with its brooding temple and the black open mouths of the doorways. He hated how his soft footfalls echoed like a march of bandaged feet and how his breathing whispered back at him in ghostly mockery. Kazim knew there were ghosts here.

He swallowed hard and felt the knife in its sheath at his belt, reassured by the familiar feel of the corded handle. The boss wanted him to use the knife and not bullets. He'd rather use bullets. The most intense pleasure Kazim had ever known came from playing a raking burst of fire over human flesh, seeing how the body lifted, twitched, danced and splattered. That was real power. That was modern, that was progress, that was American, that was good. Maybe the boss would let him kill the pilot. He wanted to kill the pilot. But as for now . . . He had to use the knife.

He grinned in anticipation. The knife was nearly as good as a gun, if the victims were tied. Not as intense but a more thoughtful, inventive pleasure. The moment could be made to last. The man first. He could be carved up, then left to watch as the woman writhed in helpless submission. Kazim licked his dry lips. He wanted the woman with her soft white skin. He wanted to feel her shrink under his hands. And, afterwards, he'd kill her. The thought of that pleasure made his blood pound. She would live a long time, dying bit by delicious bit.

He rounded the spur of cliff where his victims should have been trussed up like chickens. He swore as he saw the cut ropes lying on the ground. The cliffs took his words and gave them back to him in fragments. He froze. Mixed in with the obscenities was another sound, a harsh rumbling laugh. It was as if the rocks themselves were laughing.

He gripped the tommy gun and turned very slowly. In the middle of the arena was the altar. The dead man, Vaughan, whom Kazim despised, should have been lying beside it. But he wasn't lying down, he was standing up. He leaned over the altar, his eyes wide open, staring into Kazim's soul. Between his hands was the skull.

Kazim gave a little moan of fright. With a rasping noise as the bone scraped on stone, the dead man moved the skull. Kazim cried out, a jerky whimper of terror.

Then the skull spoke. 'Go. Go. Go.'

It was the one word, first whispered and then rising to a shout and echoed, echoed in a terrifying wave of sound.

Kazim whimpered once more and that ghastly noise, the bone scraping on the stone, rasped out again as the dead man moved the skull.

Kazim brought up the tommy-gun. His fingers, slippery with sweat, closed over the trigger, sending bullet after bullet thudding and ricocheting into the stones, the dust, the altar, in a jerky arc of destruction. The dust billowed up in a blinding sandstorm and through the clouds of grit and sand, his eardrums punched with sound, Kazim saw the dead man fling his arms outwards and fall, the skull rising high in the air, shattering to a million flying chips of bone. Kazim kept the trigger pulled hard back until every bullet had gone. The gun clicked uselessly. Then he heard the scream.

It started as on a high pitch and got higher. The cliffs screamed back. Kazim felt himself scream, heard his own voice, thin against the scream of the violated skull and malevolent cliffs.

Through the billowing clouds of dust, a man loomed towards him.

For a few hundredths of a second, Kazim saw the jerky movements, the outstretched hands, the shambling walk, then, with a scream louder than even the scream of the skull, he ran.

Jack leaned on the cabin door of the aeroplane and unscrewed the cap of his water bottle. He had taxied the D.H.9 out of the cave, close to the lorry. He and the Arab had heaved nearly fifty of the heavy canvas bags into the cabin. Von

Erlangen, sitting in the shade, his back to the cliff, watched them, his rifle beside him and his revolver in his hand. Jack didn't know where Kazim was but all he could hope was that Arthur and Isabelle had managed to get free and somehow get to safety. He paused with the cap of the canteen in his hand. Faintly, like a distant rumble of thunder, came a booming, repeated noise.

Von Erlangen jerked his head up, listening intently. His lips thinned as the noise rolled on. 'Fool,' he snarled. He looked to where Jack and Amir had stopped, listening. 'Get on with it,' he said, in icy anger.

Jack, his stomach leaden, picked up another bag. That had been machine-gun fire. He hefted the bag in his hands, feeling fury course through him. He could hurl the bag at Amir, try and get to Von Erlangen . . . The revolver was aimed steadily at him and, stupefied with despair, he put it in the cabin with the rest.

They heard Kazim before they saw him, his feet thudding on the ground. Amir jumped down from the lorry, yelling out a string of Arabic. Kazim ran towards him, his face a ghastly pallor. He stumbled against Amir, tried to speak and managed a few jumbled words. Amir shrank back from the terrified man, then, with a sudden movement, they both leapt into the cab of the lorry.

'Stop!' yelled Von Erlangen. He shouted a volley of orders but his words were lost in the growl of the engine. The lorry accelerated away, bumping wildly over the uneven ground, sending up vast clouds of dust. Von Erlangen brought the rifle up to his shoulder and fired. The bullet pinged off the cab of the lorry. Von Erlangen fired three more bullets, but the wild progress of the lorry and the billowing dust made it impossible to aim.

He whirled as Jack approached. 'Keep your distance!'

Jack tried to keep the joy out of his voice. He didn't know what Arthur and Isabelle had done, but they had done *something*. They were alive! Or, at least, he thought, sobering, they had been before that burst of machine-gun fire. 'I just wondered what all the fuss was about.'

'Stupidity,' said Von Erlangen between clenched teeth.

Out of the corner of his eye, Jack saw a little movement

where a camel-thorn bush clung to an outcrop of rock by the base of the cliff. He walked away from the bush, keeping Von Erlangen's attention away from that flicker of movement. 'Well, there goes the rest of the gold,' he said, watching the cloud of dust.

'Thank you for stating the obvious, Mr Haldean,' Von Erlangen said sharply. He flexed his fingers. 'I shall look forward to meeting those two again. In the meantime, we might as well go. Is the aeroplane ready?'

'As ready as she can be,' said Jack. 'Where are we flying to, by the way?'

'Turkey. Scutari. I have useful friends there.'

Jack nodded. 'The Black Sea, eh? I'll have to plot a course. We don't want to fly over Cyprus if we can help it.' Taking maps and compasses from the cockpit, he sauntered back to the cliff, and settled down, apparently working out distances.

A whisper sounded from the rocks behind him. 'Jack, we're here.' It was Isabelle.

Jack took out a cigarette and lit it with what he hoped was idle unconcern. With the hand holding the match shielding his mouth, he risked a whisper back.

'How did you scare off Kazim?'

'Arthur propped up Vaughan's body against the altar and put the skull in his hands. He picked it up with his jacket. He didn't touch it. We had some rope underneath it. We hid behind the altar, pulled on the rope and made the skull move. Kazim was frightened rigid.'

'He blasted away on his tommy gun. He used all his ammo,' whispered Arthur. 'Then Isabelle screamed and he thought it was the skull.'

'There was no end of dust and Arthur lurched towards him, walking like something that had risen from the tomb.'

Jack smothered a grin behind his hand. 'Good work. They've run off, so that's two down.' He glanced up at Von Erlangen and risked another whisper. 'You'll be safe. If I've got to go the distance, best of luck. Thanks for being here.'

After a few more minutes, he gathered together his papers and strolled back to the aeroplane. 'You'll have to swing the propeller,' he said to the waiting Von Erlangen. 'I'll start the ignition and when I shout *Contact*, give it a good heave.'

Von Erlangen climbed into the plane and stood inside the open door of the cabin. The gun hadn't left Jack once. 'Mr Haldean, I do not intend to be left outside the aeroplane. You can swing the propeller. I have seen it done many times.'

'Just as you like,' said Jack, getting in to the cockpit and setting the switches.

It had been worth a try but he wasn't surprised it hadn't worked. Von Erlangen evidently thought he might fly off and leave him stranded. With the heavily laden plane, there wasn't a hope. Unfortunately, although Von Erlangen didn't know that, he evidently knew enough about aircraft to avoid the deadly arc of the propeller.

With the switches trembling on contact, he swung the engine into life and made a jump for the cockpit.

'You'd better sit down and strap yourself in,' he shouted back to Von Erlangen in the cabin, raising his voice to carry over the noise of the engine. 'We're going to run into bumps.'

'Bumps?' yelled Von Erlangen.

'Bumps,' shouted Jack, bringing the engine up to full power. 'Irregular variations in the air. Makes you go up and down. Bumps!' The plane lurched forwards. 'Suit yourself,' he called over the steady thrum of the engines. 'I don't mind if you fall out.' He didn't know if Von Erlangen had strapped himself in but a glance behind showed him that he'd stepped back from the cabin door.

As the plane taxied away, Arthur and Isabelle came out from their hiding-place. The wheels of the D.H.9 juddered across the sand, faster and faster. 'I don't understand it,' Arthur said, a line creasing his forehead. 'That's not the runway we marked out.' He voice strained in sudden anxiety. 'What the devil's he doing? He'll hit those rocks if he's not careful.'

Isabelle held her breath as the plane lifted, bumped and lifted again with daylight under the wheels, inches from a long outcrop of rock. She gasped in horror as the D.H.9 brushed its wingtip against the boulders.

They could see Jack struggling to get out of the cockpit. The plane slewed to one side, catherine-wheeled round, then, with a ghastly, lazy motion turned over and over, spinning across the desert on its wings like a rolling cross, before plunging its nose into the sand, engine screaming. There was a sharp, intense noise as if the sky had ripped apart, then flames and black smoke leapt high into the air. Jack was flung out and lay motionless on the sand. With a shattering roar, the aeroplane exploded.

'Come on!' shouted Arthur, sprinting faster than he had ever run before. Under a deluge of burning wood, twisted shards of metal and floating scraps of fabric, they got to Jack and taking an arm each, dragged him away. A second explosion blasted them off their feet and hurled them against the cliff. Bruised and shaken, they lay blind, deaf and helpless in a blizzard of whirling shale, sand and debris.

After a long time, Arthur lifted his head. 'Isabelle, are you all right?'

'I . . . I think so,' she said shakily. 'How about you?'

'OK.' He got to his knees, bending down anxiously to Jack.

Jack's eye's flickered open. 'Is he dead?'

Arthur looked at the blazing skeleton of the aeroplane, a black and red outline in the clouds of burning oil. 'He's dead, all right.' The wind shifted, bringing a gust of black smoke that set him coughing. 'Can you walk?'

'My leg hurts. I'm sorry. I don't think I can.'

Isabelle winced as she saw how Jack's leg had twisted. It was broken for sure. 'How do you feel, Jack?' she asked anxiously.

'Feel?' With her help, he sat up, looking at the fiery cross that was the remains of the aeroplane. 'I feel . . . I feel free. At last.' A faint smile twitched his mouth. 'And sore.' He reached for Isabelle's hand. 'I'm sorry. It was the only way.'

There was water and food in the cave, left from their stockpile of the night before, but as the day lengthened, Jack's condition worsened. They bandaged his leg as best they could and used part of their precious water supply to keep him cool but, despite their efforts, his temperature rose and he moved restlessly on his makeshift bed, muttering in delirium.

The sun sank to the west and a thin purple line showed the horizon. The purple line vanished and, under a thick blanket of stars, night fell on the tombs of the Nabateans.

After the heat of the day came the bitter cold, kept only

partly at bay by the flames of a camel-thorn fire. Jack, semi
conscious, tossed and groaned. As the night wore on, hi.
temperature subsided, and Isabelle thankfully realized he wa
drifting in and out of sleep.

Much, much later, when the stars had disappeared beneath
the horizon, far above, in the immense black velvet bowl o
sky, came a shooting star, and another. Jack, restless and
senses on edge, clutched Isabelle's arm. Jerked back to ful
wakefulness, she bent her head to listen to him.

'The stars, Belle, the stars! Can you see them?'

Blearily she looked up at the stars. 'They're beautiful
Jack.' She stroked his forehead, trying to comfort him. 'Go
back to sleep.'

He laughed. 'Don't you see? It's the sun. We're safe, Belle
We can't see the sun, but they're high enough.' His voice
broke. 'The sun. *It's catching the wings of an aeroplane.* It's
the RAF. We're safe.'

And he rested against her arm.